Whitechapel

Autumn of Error

Whitechapel

Autumn of Error

Ian Porter

Matador
Unit E2 Airfield Business Park,
Harrison Road, Market Harborough,
Leicestershire. LE16 7UL
Tel: 0116 2792299
Email: books@troubador.co.uk
Web: www.troubador.co.uk/matador
Twitter: @matadorbooks

ISBN 978 1805143 987

British Library Cataloguing in Publication Data.
A catalogue record for this book is available from the British Library.

Printed and bound by CPI Group (UK) Ltd, Croydon, CR0 4YY
Typeset in 11pt Bembo by Troubador Publishing Ltd, Leicester, UK

Matador is an imprint of Troubador Publishing Ltd

To my great grandmothers and grandmothers,
born London 1838-1876

"Dank roofs, dark entries, closely cluttered walls,
Murder-inviting nooks, death-reeking gutters,
A boding voice from your foul chaos calls,
When will men heed the warning that it utters?

...

Red-handed, ruthless, furtive, un-erect,
'Tis murderous Crime – the Nemesis of Neglect"

Punch, September 29, 1888

Prologue

Many of the women employed in the world's oldest profession were part-timers, spending much of their lives earning a pittance for long hours of tortuous work in other industries. Some attempted to live a double life of apparent respectability, keeping their night work a secret.

Maud Nash was such a woman. She kept her ex-stevedore husband, unable to work after a fall into a ship's hold, and their six children out of the workhouse by spending ten hours a day in a sweat shop, before dragging her aching body onto the streets at night to pleasure rough trade. She walked an exhausting mile to Whitechapel each evening to ensure she did not come across anyone she knew, before donning her brightly coloured posy and rouge, her 'for hire' sign. Nobody knew of her double life, least of all her husband. Such women did not use a ponce to protect them, and years before the grim reaper appeared in the guise of the Whitechapel Murderer, disappearing down a dark alley with some filthy specimen was fraught with potential danger.

Maud had just serviced such a man, who gave her a gratuity of a punch in the face after an argument over payment. She staggered into the light and was soon the subject of unwelcome attention from the local policeman on his beat. In her highly upset state, she made the mistake of telling him her identity, and it was obvious to the bobby what had happened and why. Wheels were set in motion and before she knew where she was, her husband had been informed of everything.

He might not have been fit to work in a back-breaking job in the docks, but he was certainly able enough to beat his wife to within an inch of her life. Or he would have been, but for the intervention of his oldest child, the thirteen-year-old Alexander. He was a big boy for his age, already a gang-member with a score of crimes under his belt, and he was not scared of anyone or anything.

His father had already rained several blows on his mother. Young Nash had heard the gist of the story and along with the other children had made himself scarce, out in the yard. Father regularly hit mother, so it was nothing new. There were the usual shouts and abuse, screams of panic and pain, the noise of fist on face, scuffling boots on floorboards, furniture flung to all parts. But then there was a sudden eerie silence. This was not right. Nash crooked his head round the door to see his father strangling his mother, two thumbs pushing into her throat as she gurgled, tongue lolling out, staring bug-eyed back at her attacker.

The boy's weight hit his father at speed; his right shoulder thundering into the man's back, knocking the breath out of him. The three of them fell to the floor. The woman rolled away heaving as she tried to get her breath, while father and son fought on the floor. The older man was putting up quite a fight until young Nash caught him with a straight-fingered jab to the throat. It was now his turn to gasp for breath. The boy got quickly to his feet and waded in with his boots, aiming at the head. He could have killed his father that day but for his mother flinging herself on the prone body of her husband, screaming hoarsely at her son.

Nash left and never saw his parents again. He joined a kidsman's pickpocket gang. He planned to go back and see his mother sometime, but it was not long before he heard that his family had entered Poplar workhouse. Like all families entering the institution, they were separated; the parents sent to their respective men's and women's sections; Nash's siblings to the children's ward, where they were checked for infections, before the older ones were dispatched to a pauper school miles away. The two parents never saw each other or any of their children again, the debilitating inhumanity relentlessly draining away the mental health of one, the physical wellbeing of the other.

One of young Nash's fellow boy pickpockets told him from first-hand experience what happened when his own father had presented himself to the workhouse, in the forlorn hope of receiving outdoor relief. He had faced the Guardians in a meeting that resembled a criminal trial, standing in the dock of a board room, a large horseshoe table of men surrounding him on all sides.

"The house!" was the lofty decry of the chairman, before the man had even stated his case.

"They don't listen Nashey," complained the little urchin.

"They will one day, boy."

***

The workhouse staff tried their hardest to instil it, but Mary Kemp felt no shame. Consequently, she would be allocated the worst job. Picking oakum. Old ship's rope, caked in oil, tar and salt, hard as steel, to be unpicked until fingers bled. Perversely, she preferred this to easier duties. The pain and misery fed the anger. It helped.

Her fellow inmates were mostly the sick, infirm, idiots or imbeciles. They sat down on benches in the middle of the day room. She would find an old, calm mannered woman with whom to sit back-to-back, the two of them supporting each other. There was nothing to do to exercise the mind. She just watched the imbeciles march up and down talking to themselves or rocking back and forth. And then it was back to the dormitory for the next ten hours, to try to sleep while listening to women relieving themselves into the drain that ran down the centre of the room.

Twice a day the staff ushered the women into the yard for half an hour's exercise. The one advantage of being amongst imbeciles was that everyone was allowed to run around like whirling dervishes if they so desired. And she did. She ran till her empty stomach told her chest and limbs to stop such foolishness. Then she walked over to the wall. All fourteen feet in height of it. And listened. She could hear children's voices on the other side. One of those voices was her girl's. On one occasion she had tried to call out to her.

"Mary Kemp, stop that right this minute!" had shouted the Mistress. "Any more of that and you will not be allowed into the yard again!"

It was made plain that far better behaviour was expected of a well brought up young lady like her.

Mary's daughter Jane had been forcibly taken from her arms on the little one's second birthday and whisked off to the children's ward. That was the rule. Under twos with mother. Over twos in a separate ward until they were old enough to be despatched off to a pauper school.

The plan had been for Mary to wait till Jane's third birthday and then check herself out of the workhouse.

Any woman choosing to leave would have her children returned to her immediately. The authorities thought this would ensure women did not abandon their offspring in the workhouse. It showed the level of ignorance of their charges. What mother would abandon her children? Had they allowed a woman to leave on her own, she could have found herself a place to stay, a job and got herself straight, and then been able to retrieve her family. But having children at her apron strings as she left the workhouse meant she was simply back in the same situation that had caused her to enter the much feared and hated institution in the first place.

Mary was going to check herself out and spend the day in the park with Jane. She had just enough money to buy her an ice cream and a slice of cake. And then she would return the two of them to the 'house' in time for readmission, delousing, tea, and to have her daughter taken away again.

She would repeat the process six months later, but this time they would not return from the park. At three-and-a-half-years, it was thought Jane could be left with a toy in the safety of a locked rented room for an hour or two, while her mother sold on the streets whatever was necessary to ensure they never had to worry about being interned again.

But the plan never came to fruition. Just shy of Jane's third birthday Mary was summoned before the Mistress.

She wondered what she had done wrong. She was told her child, no name bestowed, had died. After Mary's tears subsided, which had been hastened by being shouted at to pull herself together, she asked the obvious question and was informed that the girl had always been sickly.

Mary asked when the funeral would be. Her naivety knew no bounds. The burial had already taken place. Mary did not bother to ask. She knew. In an unmarked pauper's grave. Even the hardest of work could not stop the darkness descending thereafter.

Things changed when all the able-bodied and able-minded (Mary was one of the few inmates who could claim both honours) were sent before their Master. He informed them that the Metropolitan Railway were opening a new station at nearby Pinner. The line had been extended from Harrow, and Pinner was the new end of the line terminus. There was to be an opening ceremony, with the local Member of Parliament in attendance to listen to speeches from the railway's managing director as well as the mayor. Among other things, a refreshments tent, music, a tombola, and maypole dancing would be provided for the public's entertainment. It was to be quite the event. And their workhouse, the Hendon Union, was to supply representatives. They were to stand in line, in brand new uniforms that were to be provided specially for the day. And they would be inspected by the lady mayoress herself!

The details of the day were explained, before the inmates were sent on their way back to the day room. Mary was just turning to leave with the others when she was summoned.

"Not you Mary," said the Mistress. "The Master would like a word with you."

No surprise registered. The days of reacting to anything had gone. She simply changed direction and walked over to stand meekly in front of the Master.

"Well now, Mary," he began in a strangely friendly manner. "It is plain to me and the Mistress that you are clearly from a better upbringing than the rest of the wretcheds who have found their way between our walls. So, we think it would be appropriate for you to represent our inmates at the railway station. You will stand next in the line after myself and the Mistress and should the lady mayoress wish to be introduced to an inmate, I will introduce her to you."

Mary thought this an odd tack. Would not someone with her middling accent being in a workhouse be more shocking to a lady's sensibilities? Was she not more undeserving as she had obviously wasted her advantages? But her torpor was such that this did not weigh heavily on her mind. More details of the day were explained to her, and she simply nodded and said 'yes sir' in all the expected places.

The big day dawned with the Mistress bringing in people from outside to tend to the women's appearance. Mary got talking to the girl assigned to her. She was Irish but had spent her formative years in Wales. She enthused about the beauty of the Valleys, but there was no work there for a girl except skivvying as a servant, so she had got on a train to London. It transpired that she still ended up in service, but thanks to the hairdressing skills her mother had bestowed on her, supported by both a glowing reference and letter of introduction, both forged, she had managed to secure a position as a lady's maid. Her employer was no lady, but at least such work was better than being on her knees scrubbing. The 'lady' was married to one of the workhouse's governors, so that was how her personal servant had been given the job of making Mary and some of her fellow inmates look presentable for the big day.

The girl worked wonders; hems pinned, stitches sewn, starched apron creases removed. And then it was the hair. Mary had both scalp and hair brushed with great alacrity, not only to make her long red locks appear good and healthy but to get rid of any scurf or dandruff.

Not a drop of water had been used, but it was as if Mary had been bent over a font. She felt something stir inside. But it was not having her hair dinned out. Rather, it was simply having a pleasant conversation with another young, energetic, clear minded woman who treated her as an equal. She asked if she could see her reflection.

The young hairdresser looked around, and when the coast was clear smuggled a small mirror out from inside her pinafore. Just for a moment Mary saw her old self. Seventeen years old without a care in the world. Then she saw the grey of her skin and frowned. She glared at her adult self. A surge of anger coursed through her.

What is the matter with you?! This must stop! Fight back for God's sake!

When getting out of the workhouse and seeing the gaiety of the crowded railway station scene, the powerful surge of emotion transformed into equally strong but more positive, constructive feelings. The fog was lifting.

Mary and her fellow paupers found themselves standing on the wooden planks of a railway platform, beneath a sign which ordered 'wait here for third class'. There was similar signage for holders of more expensive tickets further down the platform, but the people who might otherwise have stood there, had gathered on the station forecourt to hear the speeches. A sea of dignitaries in full top hats as well as the more compact Muller cut downs, accompanied by their ladies giving last season's Royal Ascot ensembles another airing, stood, champagne glasses in hand, sipping and chatting merrily.

The local mayoress fulfilled her duties to the letter. Just as she did when speaking to her lowly maid servants once a year when they all lined up to receive their Christmas present from her. It would always be something useful, such as cloth from which to make new aprons. And she used the same hectoring, uncaring tone she would use at Christmas, towards the pauper who had just been presented to her.

"Tell me girl, what brought you into the fine care of the Master and Mistress here?"

The Mistress had prepped Mary beforehand as to what she should say, but her new hairstyle had clearly gone to her head in more ways than one. She did not stick to the script.

"I was ravaged and made with child at seventeen by a gentleman and cast out," she said with deliberate bluntness. "I had a girl I could not afford to feed. She is dead now though, so I should leave this bloody awful place."

This was not what the mayoress wanted to hear. She did not answer, simply turning to glare at an open-mouthed Master. A moment later the Mistress had hold of Mary by the wrist dragging her away from the scene of the crime. She left her by the new station's bar with instructions.

"Wait there. Do not move. I will deal with you presently!" she said through gritted teeth before hurrying back to her distraught husband and his dishonoured guest.

Mary was pleased with herself, she had to admit. She could feel the old Mary, the seventeen-year-old, funny, intelligent girl returning for the first time in years. She looked about at the busy scene on the platform. The bar attendant, cleaning the inside of a beer glass, smiled at her. A guard waved a flag as a porter took a whistle from his waistcoat. A young man in Metropolitan Railway livery appeared from behind her. He started to doff his funny little uniformed hat, which would not have looked out of place on an organ grinder's monkey and began speaking before he had got a good look at her.

"Good day to you, miss," he said smiling. "The Metropolitan Railway would like you to accept these complimentary second-class tick..." it was at this point that he spotted the workhouse uniform. His face dropped as he hesitated.

Mary was still enjoying the glow of her success in dealing with the mayoress. She looked the railwayman straight in the eye. It was obvious to her that he liked what he was seeing. Why wouldn't he? This once attractive young lady was clearly so again. She thought it amazing what decent hair and a clear eye could do. She offered him the briefest of winks and a coquettish smile.

"Please do not let the uniform fool you," she said in a cultured voice, before deciding to clip the accent further. "I am an actress. Just here to play a part, do you see. Quite relieved I wasn't asked to play a sweep. Cannot abide sooty make up!"

The young railwayman chuckled and smiled back.

"Oh, that's all right then, miss," he said, an outstretched hand now proffering the complimentary railway tickets.

Apparently, one could travel free from this station to anywhere in London today, and return of course, or if that was inconvenient the tickets could be exchanged at a future date. Mary thanked the man, took the tickets and looked up the platform at the mistress, master and mayoress, who appeared to be in deep conversation, before she glanced at the porter and his whistle. He was bringing it up to his lips when their eyes met, which stopped him.

"Are you getting on, miss?" he said, motioning a nod towards his train. "It is just leaving. Stopping service to Bishop's Road. Change there for Baker Street, Marlborough Road, Farringdon Street and all further stations to Whitechapel Mile End."

Mary looked at him blankly. This man seemed to think that she had the same obvious enthusiasm for trains as he. And why did he think that a load of London place names meant anything to her?

The man's left hand gripped a carriage door handle. He looked her way expectantly. It reminded her of when polite young men used to open doors as she approached them.

She found herself saying, "Yes."

The carriage door opened, and she stepped on to the train, the porter slamming shut the door behind her. A whistle blew. She removed her apron and took a window seat. Seconds later she passed the Mistress and the others. They had their backs to her, which was disappointing.

She sat down and looked towards the three people sitting opposite. There was no face within view, rather the front and back pages of three newspapers. A wave of anti-climax swept over her. The surge of power that she had felt over the mayoress passed as suddenly as it had appeared. She felt alone and scared.

Where was she going? Where did that porter say? Baker Street. She had heard of that. Isn't that where that detective chap is supposed to live? It's only in a story of course, but the real place must be respectable enough. Should she alight there? But what then?

She peered out of the window and in the far distance could see her workhouse. She watched it recede and continued looking long after it had ceased to be visible, to reassure herself that it would not return like some evil villain following a heroine in a gothic novel she might have read in a previous life.

That was it. A previous life. That life had ended. Mary Kemp ceased to be. She would not return. She would rather die first.

Chapter 1

Whoredom was the only trade in which the optimum income tended to be paid to the newest apprentice. A young girl could earn more in one night than a week in a sweatshop. But her high earning potential was for a limited period before the evils of disease took their hold.

Kitty Johnson was just shy of her sixteenth birthday. After almost a year on the game she was still very pretty, her outstanding features being her long dark hair and unusually faultless skin. It was Saturday night, and she was excited about going to the penny gaff that had just been set up in an empty greengrocer's shop in Court Street. Her excitement was attributable to the fact that she was going to see a mermaid.

A man with no arms, who could shave and play the violin with his toes, was top of the bill, but experience told her to doubt his credentials. Her last job before falling into prostitution was in Whitechapel Road, as the smiling young girl who turned the handle of an organ to keep the audiences amused before the Elephant Man appeared. She felt privileged to be involved with the only occasion, before or since, that a penny gaff had been able to get away

1

with charging twopence as the entrance charge, such was the demand to see the beast. During her short time there she had seen the gaff get up to all sorts of trickery to first attract, and then fool, their clientele. In the dim light of a barely lit gaff, a pig had once been passed off as a half-man half-beast from darkest Borneo. The wretched creature had been drugged, roped in to sit upright and kicked from a hidden spot below the stage when a response was required. A dog with lion's claws was a poor mutt which had had its forefeet split. The medicine man's cure-all wizard oil was black treacle, formaldehyde, charcoal water and condensed skimmed milk; the first three ingredients to make it dark and disgusting like all good medicine was, and the last was a nod to the working man's sweet tooth.

No, Kitty thought, the violin-playing cripple sounded right rum, but the mermaid were worth a copper of anyone's money, right enough.

Kitty's Saturday night ritual on the rare occasions she was not forced to work the streets by her procurer, was to ding her hair out. After the awfulness of the working week, it made her feel like a human, a woman; an attractive woman, not to men as such, rather the mirror. She would plait her hair, coiling it around the side of her head, before adding coconut oil to make it glossy.

But at the moment she should have been staring a child's wide-eyed amazement at seeing a mermaid, she was sitting on her usual bench in Backchurch Lane waiting for trade. Her ponce had turned up unexpectedly, having previously said he had a little business to attend to over in Hackney. He was in a foul temper because his caper had fallen though and on finding her about to leave for the penny gaff with her mate Vi, had given her a beating (vicious body blows so as not to mess up her face) for not working on a Saturday night when trade was at its busiest.

This individual was also her beau. She was clinging to the false hope of dignity through marriage and wifedom to even this most debased of men. He had sent her out into the night.

Kitty's hair now hung down, wild and disordered, her beauty tarnished by a scratched and bloodied left cheek. The ponce had not reckoned on his target hitting her head on the packing case they used for a table, as she collapsed from his punches.

Being young, she could at least be choosey. She sat and waited to service young wealthy popinjays who would pay much more than the filthy drunks the older members of her trade had to pleasure. Her customers were to marry late when they had reached a position well paid enough to allow them to ask a nice middle-class lady to marry them. Until that time arrived, they found their sexual release amongst the prettiest of the desperate.

Tonight, she would try to get away with only offering uprights and kneetremblers, rather than penetrative sex. The former was allowing herself to be fingered, while the man pleasured himself; the latter was giving hand relief to the man's member. But she had her pessary in place just in case a client demanded more expensive sexual favours. With her ponce possibly looking on from a dark corner somewhere, she could not afford to turn down business.

The recent rain shower had eased at least. This enabled Kitty to indulge in a bit of bubble-blowing. This pastime was all the rage since Millais had painted his famous picture.

Earlier soaps had not provided the right surface tension, but the new stuff provided a girl with lots of innocent fun.

Despite enjoying her bubbles, she was uncomfortable. She did not usually work when she had her monthly 'on the rags`, and it was due, which was why she had planned to have a rare Saturday night off. She was now wearing a menstrual towel of clean rag made from bed linen. The trouble was that it was rubbing against her pessary, an unpleasant feeling home-made compound of lard and flour. She had once paid two shillings for a manufactured one – a small piece of oiled sponge on a string soaked in quinine, which was more comfortable, but the tapes must have detached because she had fallen pregnant. She had tried everything to free herself from the condition – massive doses of Pennyroyal syrup; gin, slippery elm, hot very soapy water; aloes concoctions, vigorous use of turps and even a fall down the stairs; all to no avail. She had been about to go to a woman who used crochet needles, when an abortifacient used by vets did the trick.

A likely customer turned the corner, so Kitty forgot about her troubles below and quickly hid the bubble blower away under the bench. Out of her eyes shot bolts of wrath, contempt and hatred for the man approaching.

Kitty was wearing a dirty linen dress, torn open to reveal her still child-like breasts. As she approached, she realised the man was no young whelp, rather a fellow in his thirties and not particularly well dressed. But time was getting on, and she did not want another beating from her ponce due to lack of income, so she continued up to the would-be client. Her large eyes now sparkled with apparent desire as she pressed herself against him.

4

She pulled him to her and pushed herself back against the wall of a warehouse stuffed with riches from all over the Great British Empire. She expected to feel the man's randy member start to grow but repelled by her youth the man pulled himself away, turned and quickly disappeared into the night. Not a word had been uttered by either party. She returned to her bench, slumped down and buried her face in her hands.

***

'Long' Liz Stride had put the money she had earned from selling her body to filthy sailors down at Limehouse docks into buying some flowers from the Colombia Road flower market. Having walked the streets all night, she was the first customer at the stalls, so had the pick of the best stock. The plan had been to invest the income from hawking the flowers, into gin to drink herself into oblivion; to escape.

She stood on a street corner for hours, selling all but one pathetic bunch which the costermonger had passed off on her with a bit of sleight of hand she had been too tired to notice while he engaged her in cheery banter. Nobody was going to buy them, and her profit margin, as puny as the remaining bunch, had all but gone.

She was about to call it a day when one of the women from Toynbee Hall came along. Liz had never met her before, but she had been pointed out on more than one occasion. She had caused quite a stir in the local community. Tongues had wagged. The woman stopped and smiled. She had the best teeth Liz had ever seen.

The memory of the worst moment of Liz's life thrust itself into her mind, deep from the mire where she had tried to bury it. Born and brought up in Sweden, Liz's greatest physical teenage attribute had been her fine row of gleaming white teeth. But her father had decided that a weak looking 'streak of piss' like her would struggle to find herself a husband unless she could offer something tangible to a prospective young man. She was good for nothing except taking food off the table and keeping the family in poverty as far as he was concerned. He decided low maintenance was to be her great matrimonial asset. The common occurrence of tooth problems due to the poor's preference for all things sweet in their diet, not to mention a lack of calcium-bearing food, and the exorbitant cost of dentistry meant that a young woman who could guarantee not to be a dental burden on her husband had a certain attraction, even if said attraction was not physical. On her seventeenth birthday, without being warned of what was about to happen to her, Liz was taken to the local dentist. An hour later the dentist was sweating from the effort of having removed every tooth in Liz's head. It was her birthday treat from her parents.

If her father had wanted rid of her, she thought, so be it. She escaped to the bright lights of Gothenburg before moving on to London in search of a better life. She proved to be quite a linguist, quickly learning English as well as conversational Yiddish. This was useful in getting work on the Saturday Sabbath, cleaning and sewing for Jewish people. But the shock of her earlier treatment had not left her. And the terrible living conditions she endured in the East End, which included abusive relationships with several men over the years, was not something such a damaged person could handle without the crutch of alcohol.

Liz, her lower cheeks caved in by the lack of support, gave the 'slummer' a toothless smile and bent close enough for the woman to smell a pungent mix of gin, tobacco and sick. Liz thrust the flowers under her nose.

"Smell them. Fourpence to you lady," she said in a cockney accent that gave no hint of her Swedish roots. "Always keep the best of the bunch till last, they keep longer see."

She was trying to sell flowers she was about to throw away for double what she usually charged for the best bunch. She had 'seen this woman coming'.

Sookey Parsons had stopped to offer to take this poor wretch to the coffee room around the corner in Toynbee Hall. The woman looked in dire need of a warming beverage and a rest. But the offer of the flowers made Sookey hesitate. She was desperately trying to be accepted in this new slum world she had recently chosen to live in, and this was awkward. Did she refuse the woman? She had no need of flowers, especially such an ill-looking bunch, because she bought flowers herself regularly direct from the market. Refuse her and then offer her a free cup of coffee instead? Would that be the typically unwanted behaviour of a slummer? Did she try to buy the flowers for less than the price offered, as appeared to be the norm when marketing locally? Fourpence did seem a little excessive. The apparently wealthy charity worker, knocking down the price on a woman who needed every penny to keep out of the clutches of the dreaded workhouse. How could she?

"They do indeed have a fine bouquet," she lied. "Fourpence, you say?"

Sookey had lived in Hong Kong as an army doctor's wife, and had seen slum life there, even if it was through the protective gaze of imperialism, enabling her to deal with the sights and smells of Whitechapel better than most. She had not flinched at Liz's breath. Nonetheless she was relieved to extricate herself from the near-embrace of the saleswoman and proffered a fingerless mittened palm with a sixpence on it.

She had taken a knife to her best pair of gloves and cut the fingers off. She had seen local people start to wear such things as autumn arrived so thought she would too.

Liz handed over the flowers and started to delve in her skirts for the twopence change she needed to give to her client.

"Oh, I can't abide pennies, big dirty smelly things," said Sookey.

She had picked up on how local people would offer drinks as a sort of currency.

"Keep them. Perhaps you could buy me a cuppa some time."

Liz considered the proposition.

I take hands outs from the Church of Sweden when I can get them, because that's as it should be. And seeing someone coming selling the flowers is one thing, that's business, but I don't take charity, and scarce from no slummer.

While these thoughts swirled, Sookey simply looked back at Liz pleasantly, raising her eyebrows ever so slightly in requesting an answer. Liz decided the woman was playing straight with her.

"Yes, a cuppa sometime, it is lady."

A young woman joined them. She had white powder on her face, big lips covered in the brightest red lip rouge, well-tended long carrot-coloured hair and a tight bodice that did more than hint at the ample bosom beneath. She was no more than moderately pretty in the understood fashion, but she radiated sex. She was a head-turner. Men crooked their necks in lust; women in disdain, envy, jealousy, or often all three.

The confident young woman made the opening gambit.

"I didn't know the two of you knew each other."

"Good day Mary. We have just met," replied a smiling Sookey. "This lady here was good enough to sell me these lovely flowers at a reasonable price."

She turned her body as she spoke, so she was square on to her friend with her back to Liz. She glared at Mary, hoping to transmit to her without a word, 'please do not say anything!' Mary caught the stare and made no comment on the pathetic excuse for a bunch of flowers.

She knew Liz from their days when they used the same common lodging house; both of them bent over the fire in the living room, sharing it with the dregs of humanity and some body lice. Haggard old Liz was still living in such places, whilst Mary was able to afford her very own hovel thanks to her greater physical attributes; youth, breasts and last-but-not-least, a luscious mouth rather than one that crumpled. Like Liz, she was a prostitute. Just a slightly better paid one.

The three women exchanged gossip and discussed the horrors of the murders which dominated most conversations in Whitechapel these days. Sookey practised using the odd glottal stop as she voiced a version of estuary Londoner in her attempt to become more accepted.

When the women went their separate ways, Sookey headed for her improvised art gallery, in a building down a narrow alley close to Toynbee Hall. Her dream was to make it a proper gallery one day. The other two women headed for work. It was a Saturday, their best day of the week for clients.

Apart from servicing one local regular whenever he had money in his pocket, usually at the weekend, Mary had given up working late at night after the last murder.

The late September nights were drawing in, and although the first green pea-souper smog of the winter was still in the future, the chocolate-coloured pall of autumnal fog had already arrived on one occasion. The earlier darkness brought men the cover they needed, and many seemed as petrified of the Whitechapel Murderer as the prostitutes, so Mary started at dusk these days and finished before midnight, both for her own safety and that of her customers. It was not the murderer per se, of whom her clients were afraid, rather the fear of being arrested by the police. The place was swarming with them nowadays. And it was full of newspaper reporters too. Any respectable man merely looking for sexual release was only a bit of bad luck away from having their name in the notebook of a police officer, or worse still, in the notepad of a reporter. Consequently, there was not the money around any longer. Gents and other respectable types now headed for other parts of the capital, so even the cream of East End whores, such as Mary, had to make do with servicing rough trade at a paltry fourpence a time. Enough for a double tot of gin, and no more. With twelve hundred women forced by economic hardship to prostitute themselves in the Whitechapel area alone, it was a buyers' market.

Much later than her planned finish, Mary tramped home to her twelve by ten feet single roomed slum. It had once been larger, but a thin petition wall had been put in so the landlord was able to double his income. There was just room for a small double bed, a chair, some firewood and a little table on which Mary kept a box of matches, her rouge and a solitary candle wedged into the top of a broken wine bottle. On warm summer nights she would throw her clothes into the grate. If it was cold enough for the grate to be in use, as it had been recently for the first time this autumn, her clothes stayed on twenty-four hours a day. Whether or not there was space for anything else was academic. She had little else to her name.

Mary slumped onto her bed, soaked to the skin by a sudden downpour, exhausted and aching from the fumbling, groping and thrusting of a series of eager customers. She had grazed knuckles from the delivery of a right cross to one man's jaw, which had been the high point of her evening. She grabbed a gin bottle and found it almost empty. An abbreviated swig later she was cursing herself for having forgotten to stock a replacement. Too weary to head back out to buy one, on this occasion sheer fatigue, rather than alcohol, would transport her into a night's oblivion.

Liz's income was less certain. The streets where she usually plied her trade had been quiet at night since the last murder. Even some of her roughest trade, who raised the money for her services by various illegal nocturnal means, dare not commit street crimes for fear that their next victim might be an undercover policeman. She had heard in one of her many locals that a lot of street thieves had become snakesmen because burglary had become safer since the murders, with so many of the police just looking for the killer. And the law of supply and demand had forced down the price streetwalkers could charge, so Liz's clientele could now afford a younger, more attractive whore. Only the lowest of low-life sought out poor old Liz.

The gangs of vigilantes roaming the streets looking for the killer did not help. Woe-betide any Jewish man caught out on the streets at night, an assumption having been made by newspapers, police and local populace alike, that no Englishman could have perpetrated such crimes. Thus, the latest immigrants to the East End were under curfew if they knew what was good for them, which they did. So, she had not even been able to get a few coppers for a fumble from an old blind moneylender regular.

But she was playing her role in the Whitechapel Murders tableaux. A few weeks ago, she had joined the throng of hundreds who paid a penny to view the backyard of the house in Hanbury Street, where the body of the last victim, 'Dark' Annie Chapman had been found.

And when a famous slummer, Dr Barnardo, had visited her common lodging house, he had asked Liz if she had known Annie.

"I did that; silly as a box o' lights she were, but none the worse for that, and she were always good to me. She'd see you all right. They calls me 'Long' because my name's Stride, long stride see, and they called her 'Dark' because she were very pale skinned. That's our cockney humour down here in the East End."

It was all lies. She had never met Annie Chapman. What a ridiculous question it had been. Why on God's earth would she know her?

People seemed to think that prostitutes were members of some sort of whores' social club. They did not want to know any different. It was lonely work. She drank with other whores, in rough pubs sure enough, and there was laughter along the journey, but all they were doing was sharing the same route out of London; the quickest, the only route. They were fellow travellers. Not friends. She had to work alone to optimise her chances of reeling in a client. Other women were competition. You worked alone. Got cut to pieces alone.

After leaving Mary and the woman who had bought the last of her flowers, Liz thought she would try her luck on the other side of the High Road, in a part of Whitechapel where there had been no murders. Perhaps there would be more chance of finding some business there.

But by the time she had crossed the road she was flagging. She slumped down with sleep-starved exhaustion and the weakness of starvation and fell asleep in a doorway for several hours. It was the rain and cold that revived her. She dragged herself to her feet and raced to the shelter offered by a shop's awning.

She did not know the time but judging by how deserted the streets were, she guessed it was at least midnight, maybe later. She would wait a while to see if the rain stopped. If it did, she would head over to Petticoat Lane. She might be able to get a bit of trade from one of the costermongers.

They would be setting up their stalls for the early Sunday morning market. But if the rain continued, she would head for a night's doss in a common lodging house.

She carefully took out from her pocket a shard of glass wrapped in a piece of leather that did double duty as compact mirror and weapon against any clients who got too rough. She slid the glass from its sheath and gave herself the once over. She removed her black crepe bonnet and flicked off street grime it had picked up while she had been sleeping. She ran her fingers through her curly dark brown hair and then replaced her bonnet. Her light grey eyes were bloodshot, but a client would not be looking at them. She ran her hands down her black jacket and skirt. She was pleased to see her posy of red rose in a spray of fern was still in place. All in all, she thought she looked damn good.

She had been cowering for a few minutes when a man hove into view. He stopped and gave her a cheeky smile. She returned the grin thinking anyone walking around in this weather must be keen. He was, but after a brief negotiation it became apparent that he wished to sample her wares without paying the requisite sum. He threw Liz to the ground, then dragged her back to her feet and was pushing her towards an alley when he spotted another man appear out of the shadows, which was sufficient to send him running off into the darkness. The other man, who went by the name of Charles Lechmere, was quick to go to Liz's assistance. He said all the right things to reassure her, and when she had recovered from the attack, made a financial offer. Lechmere led her into Duffield's Yard, where he throttled her with her own scarf.

Lechmere was about to attack the dead woman's sexual areas with her own knife, which too late she had managed to retrieve from her pocket, her clenched fist dropping it as she expired. But Louis Diemshutz, a seller of cheap jewellery, then attempted to enter the yard on his pony and cart. At the yard's entrance the pony stopped and veered to the left to avoid an obstruction in its path. Lechmere lurked in the darkness at the back of the yard while Diemshutz prodded at the obstruction with his horse whip.

It was too dark to see what it was, so Diemshutz got down from his cart to take a closer look. A woman was lying in the gutter, no doubt just drunk. But he thought he better go off and get a candle so he could get a better look. He wedged his horse's reins into a gap between the yard entrance and the working men's educational society building next door, which would have a candle.

With the man out of the way, Lechmere gingerly crept past the pony so as not to overly disturb the beast and peered out from the yard. The horse owner was heading north towards the bustling well-lit Commercial Road so Lechmere turned right and headed towards the quiet, dark warehouse area of Backchurch Lane.

He almost bumped into a huge man coming out of a tenement on Fairclough Street, but otherwise had no problem making his escape. He soon heard Met Police whistles in the distance, but he quickly headed into an area patrolled by the City Police, who were oblivious of any wrongdoing nearby. He needed to get home, which was back in the Met Police area, so a circuitous route through the City beckoned.

15

He was relieved to be away and clear but frustrated the horse and cart man had stopped him from attacking the woman further. His sexual desire had not been satisfied, but it would have to wait for another night before it could be sated. He would not be seeing any prostitutes in the City, and once back in the East End it would be too risky to try anything.

As he made his escape through Backchurch Lane he was approached by a young whore. She would not do at all. But while heading through the City, only twenty minutes after he had killed, he walked into Mitre Square and could not believe his luck. A haggard woman strolled up to speak to him.

***

Catherine Eddowes had started the night with a trip to Jones' pawnshop. It had become a filthy evening. The rain was now coming down like stair-rods and it had turned cold too. She had to queue as, being a Saturday night, the pawnbroker was busy handing back the pathetic best possessions of the poor for their weekly outing. A threadbare old 'weasel and stoat', a shiny pair of trousers and a ragged waistcoat were being redeemed, less the cost of the pawnbroker's commission, for a Saturday night out at the boozer or penny gaff. They might even get an airing on a Sunday too. A walk or church was free at least. The items would be back in the shop first thing Monday morning to pay for the owners' rent or next meal.

But Kate, as she was known, was trading in the opposite direction to the crowd. As the pawnbroker handed her a redemption ticket and a few pennies for receipt of the better of the two pairs of battered old boots she owned, he asked where she was off to.

"Going to get myself a nice cup of tea. Warm me old cockles."

She had no intention of drinking tea. It was just the expected response. The part she played. Good old Kate, salt of the earth. Respected for her intelligence, well liked for her cheery persona, and known for her sense of humour and tendency to sing at the drop of a hat. But behind the heavily painted cheeks, toothless grin and cheery banter was a woman at rock bottom. Years of abusive relationships had left their mark.

She and her latest common law husband John had just returned from an abortive trip to the hop gardens of Kent. It had been the worst summer on record, there had even been sleet, ruining the hop harvest. Thus, it had been no working holiday full of golden days and fun alcohol-fuelled nights. They had returned to the East End, cold, hungry, penniless.

John had pawned his boots to pay for their first meal in days. And had then set off, barefoot to look for work. The plan had been for Kate to walk over the river to Bermondsey to see if she could track down, and cadge some money off, her married daughter Annie. John and Kate were to meet up in Cooney's common lodging house in the Flower & Dean Street rookery that night.

In her exhausted state, the idea of the four-mile round trip to and from Bermondsey, filled Kate with dread. As she set off through the slums of Spitalfields, her imagination was allowed free reign to escape her reality for a few seconds. She remembered fondly skipping down the streets with her fellow young girls when their twelve-hour shift at the Bryant & May factory had just finished. The only thing she missed about such a terrible job was that sense of freedom and joy when a shift ended; the excitement as she and her mates pushed through the crowds to get outside those factory gates as fast as their legs could carry them. She would skip down the street, singing the latest shocking, dirty ditty, belittling and flirting with lads; ruining a crossing sweeper's work and returning his swearing with interest; stealing something she didn't want from a market stall just for the devilment of it.

A strand of heavy wet hair fell into an eye, the pain reminding her where she was with a jolt. Kate took it as a sign.

"I'm getting bleeding saturated!" she shouted, loud and angry for the world to hear. She was not going to walk to Bermondsey in this.

She was wearing an old alpaca skirt which would become soaking wet and then weigh a ton, with a filthy ragged deep-pocketed blue skirt underneath, a white vest and a pair of tatty lace-up boots. She was not wearing any drawers or stays. They were a luxury she could not afford. Her clothes were starting to stick to her like glue.

There was only one way out of the East End for her right now, and it was not via London Bridge. It was through the end of a glass.

Kate rummaged in the deep pockets of her underskirt. She took out her knife, which she had recently taken to carrying for her protection; a small tin box containing tea, another with sugar in it, a small fine-toothed comb, a piece

18

of old white apron, some menstrual rags, a mustard tin in which lay her pawn tickets for safe keeping, and a tin matchbox in which she kept her cash. Until the trip to the pawnbroker, it had been empty.

She was not going to get far on that little lot. There was one good thing about starving. Drinking on an empty stomach would get her drunk quickly. A pub beckoned.

She would spend all her money in the one pub, so that with a bit of luck she might be able to cadge a few more drinks 'on the mace' from a friendly landlord. She might also see some drinking acquaintances who would stand her a gin. She was freehearted when she had money, so there were plenty of people who owed her a tot. If she could drink till closing time, she should be three sheets to the wind. She would have escaped for a while.

The plan worked. Kate was more than a little tipsy well before closing time and was staggering along the street when she heard bells ringing. They were cow bells; a herd being taken through the empty streets from Liverpool Street station, where they had just arrived on a train from Essex, on their way to the Aldgate slaughterhouses.

"Blimey, a fire engine!" Kate started whirling around with arms stretched wide, shouting at the top of her voice. "Clang, clang, clang, where's the bleeding fire then?! I'll piss on it and put it out for you!"

PC Robinson hove into view. He did not enjoy his job at present, spending as he did, eight hours a night looking into the darkest courts and alleys looking for a knife wielding maniac.

Robinson could have hugged the woman. The easiest of collars, and if he played his cards right, he could spin the arrest out till it was time for his midnight smoke break. She collapsed in a heap just as he got to her. He had the devil's own job half dragging her to his police station. Normally he would have been furious, giving her a quick tap with his tightly rolled up raincoat, which served as a soft truncheon for clipping children and drunks around the head when they were guilty of minor misdemeanours. But he was wearing his raincoat and was patience personified on this occasion. The longer it took the better as far as he was concerned, and she was making such a din that no self-respecting madman would come near or far.

Kate was released from a Bishopsgate police station cell after midnight, when she would not be able to get a drink anywhere. She had sobered up a little but appeared to still be in a cheeky mood as she bade farewell to the release constable.

"Good night, old cock."

It was all bluster. She was dreading having to face John. Whenever that would be. She had no money left, so there was no possibility of her getting a bed in Cooney's doss house to meet him as planned.

With all her money having gone on drink and the pawnshops closed for the night, so that source of income had ceased, she could head for a casual ward but 'the spike,' as it was known, insisted on a two-night stay with a day's work in between, picking oakum. If she did this, she would not be able to track down John for thirty-six hours. She could sleep rough. The police harassed dossers who attempted to sleep openly on the streets but left them alone so long as they hid themselves away; the poor were best out of sight out of mind as far as the authorities were concerned. There was a shed in Dorset Street in which she had slept before on such occasions in company with other members of the homeless fraternity. The problem was that it was likely to be full given the wet weather. But there was an alternative. She only needed a penny to 'sleep on the string'. Many common lodging houses pulled a thick ship's rope hard across the room, and for a penny, dossers could lean over it all night. She would be off the street and it was a roof over her head at least.

Kate made her way into the City. With a bit of luck, she might be able to cadge a penny off a Good Samaritan. She would give them a bit of old flannel about losing the key to her gaff and being locked out for the night. A penny wasn't much after all. And if that didn't work, she would make her way to Petticoat Lane and try to flog something to a coster for a penny. There must be something she had on her that was of value, though she was not sure what.

Ten minutes later she was at the entrance to a covered alley which led into Mitre Square. A man was making his way along its cobbles.

In the past Charles Lechmere had often used prostitutes for sex. So he knew how to approach them, and given their fears these days, knew how to put them at their ease. When approached by Kate, he chatted readily to her, appearing to enjoy a laugh and a joke before ushering her into a dark spot and asking if she wanted some business.

"I ain't no whore, cheeky sod!" she said lightly before placing a hand playfully on the man's chest and adding coquettishly. "But if you got money for whores, you can spare a poor woman who's done up for cash, a penny for a night's doss, can't you?"

Lechmere understood that she was no whore, just a beggar, but no matter, she was a middle-aged woman. She was perfect. He grabbed Kate, strangled the life from her and with frenzied but controlled fury, mutilated her sexual areas, removing part of her uterus.

He hated his mother. He hated the womb from which he had been born.

Chapter 2

Being tall and broad-shouldered with a countenance which transmitted menace was extremely useful in Alexander Nash's world. And he optimised his potential. He looked after himself; did not drink alcohol to excess, other than when he needed to down a few 'tighteners' in a pub to glean some information from someone. He even trained his body like he had heard those public-school boxers did when they were about to take on an East End boy in front of a baying crowd of drunken costermongers down the Radcliffe Highway on a Saturday night. Plenty of meat; push-ups; even some running. As a boy he remembered his father telling him the story of how Tom Cribb, the unbeatable back in the old days, once almost lost to some American fellow half his size because he hadn't looked after himself. He had trained properly after that scare and won the rematch comfortably.

But in Nash's world you could not afford to make one mistake. There were no second chances.

The menace had come naturally. He had always been able to impose his will on people with a glower and a slight lowering, deepening or raising of his voice according to the situation. Even when he was simply chewing the fat with drinking mates (he had no real friends), just a slight enthusiasm for the subject about which he was speaking could have tough, mean men cowering in submission. You did not argue with or show disrespect to Nashey. He was a nasty bit of work.

But this had its drawbacks. Menace drew fear, demanded attention. People kept their eye on him. They averted their gaze, but they were watching, nonetheless, which was a problem when one of his main pieces of business was following people with a view to relieving them of their valuables when an opportune moment occurred.

Nash always ensured that any crime committed went unseen. He could not simply give someone a 'facer in the chops' on a busy street and make off with their Hunter pocket watch. There must not be any witnesses.

Nobody who knew him would say anything to the police; the poverty stricken had no liking or respect for authority, and besides, who would dare say anything against Nashey. But there were all sorts on the streets these days, thanks to the Whitechapel Murders. People who lived part-time in the East End, but who were not of the East End. There were plain-clothes, as well as uniformed police, and middle-class charity workers all over the East End in general, and Whitechapel in particular. It would only take a bit of bad luck; a soup kitchen helper or worst still a plain-clothes copper looking his way at just the wrong minute, and he could be having his collar felt.

From a professional point of view, Nash did not like the increase of policing in his neighbourhood, and he thought many of the philanthropists such as the Salvation Army did more harm than good, but on balance he approved of what was happening in the East End at the moment. The success of the Bryant & May Match Girls'

Strike, the first ever victory of a women's trade union, just two months before the murders began, had shown him the importance of publicity. One little story highlighting the appalling working conditions of the women in an obscure little ha'penny newspaper, and public support for their grievances grew apace. And that was as nothing compared to the fuss being stirred up by the press about these murders. The newspapers were sensationalising everything, but that was no bad thing as far as Nash was concerned. Every gory detail of the murders and the conditions in the area in which they were being perpetrated, 'Darkest Whitechapel', was forcing the ruling classes to sit up and take notice. Nash did not care whether it was middling class guilt, or fear of uprising that was causing the East End to be the focus of national attention; he simply knew that people were no longer looking the other way.

Nash was thus content to overcome his more difficult working conditions. He followed potential targets for as long as it took, till they disappeared down an alley, and nowadays he only worked at night or when the foggy miasma came down. But that had inherent problems too. Noise travelled at night. It was even worse in the fog when there were few horse hooves and wheels rattling over the cobbles to drown the sound of footsteps. And people were more aware, their every sense heightened by the need to find their way whilst fearful of the unseen; of what might be lurking in the shadows. The sound of a single pair of footsteps following them into an alley sounded every bit as sinister as indeed it was in his case.

So, he wore made-to-order shoes of soft kid-like leather that did not make any noise when he walked. The footwear gave him no support and felt paper-thin. He could feel every crack in the cobbles. He would curse, 'my dogs are barking' by the time he got home after a night walking the streets.

Nash lived in a model dwelling on Fairclough Street, next to the Lord Nelson pub. Such tenements had been built for the poor but the charitable trusts who owned them were profit-making, and as land prices rose, rents were raised to ensure profits, which made the housing unaffordable for most of the very people for whom they were built. And even those who could afford to pay were not prepared to put up with the long list of regulations. No homework was allowed in case it was an offensive trade such as fur-pulling or gluing. There could be no hanging up of washing outside or pictures inside. Other restrictions included bans on wall papering, sharing, sub-letting and children playing in corridors or stairwells. And there was a curfew, with the main door locked and gas supply turned off at 11pm.

The Four Percent Industrial Dwellings Company, who owned this property, barred those with earnings of over thirty shillings a week (they should not need charity) or under twelve shillings a week (they could not afford the rent) and tenants had to pay in advance and provide an employer's reference. Middle class female charity workers were used to collect the rent. They were nicknamed, the 'petticoat government'. Nash was not eligible for such a place, but he was on friendly nodding terms with the local vicar at St Jude's, Samuel Barnett, who put a word in, and as they could not fill the places anyway and he could be relied upon to pay the rent…

Perversely the curfew was ideal for a nocturnal animal like Nash. He paid the superintendent to look the other way, and had a key made so he could come and go as he pleased. And his neighbours were safely tucked away for the evening by the time he crept home from a night's work. He never saw anyone from one day to the next, and more importantly nobody saw him.

Nash was slipping quietly out of his abode and on to the street, when a man in a hurry, wearing a shabby suit and deerstalker hat, almost bumped into him. The man glared at Nash for a moment with a strange look on his face before heading off down Fairclough Street.

Nash could not place the man's wide-eyed expression. Was it panic? Fear? Guilt? Lust? He was certainly a big so-and-so for these parts. Not as big as Nash himself, but big enough. Could he be one of those plain-clothes coppers he had heard were deployed locally, in the hunt for the Whitechapel Murderer?

As if on cue, a police whistle rang out from around the corner in Berner Street. But the man ignored it and continued walking. Strange, thought Nash. It was human nature to look in the direction of a police whistle. In fact, it looked as if the man increased his speed on hearing the shrill noise pierce the air. It would seem the fellow was no policeman after all. Indeed, Nash wondered if he might be up to something illegal. And if he was, maybe there might be something to be gained from the situation. Curiosity aroused; Nash set off after him. The man headed into the unlit netherworld of warehouses along Backchurch Lane. Nash knew he would soon lose his man in such a dark area if he did not stay close, so he increased his speed to shorten the gap between them.

The man approached a prostitute. Nash smirked with contempt. The strange look on the man's face had been merely lust. He was not worth bothering with. Nash was about to turn on his heel when he saw the man suddenly move away from the woman as if horrified.

Poor little cow not good enough for his lordship, eh?

The woman sat down on a bench and buried her head in her hands for a few seconds, before taking a breath and bending to pick something up off the ground. A moment later she was blowing bubbles. Nash got a better look at her face.

She was young and very pretty. Why would the fellow turn up his nose at her? Perhaps in the darkness he thought she was a boy at first? He could be a brown hatter looking for a like-minded man to have sex with it. But unlikely. There were certain places for that sort of thing and here in Backchurch Lane was not one of them.

Curiosity duly rekindled; Nash followed the man through a warren of alleys which took them out of the East End into the City.

This was puzzling. If the man was looking for a whore, everyone knew that the City Police were under strict orders not to allow such affronts to decency onto their patch. Any prostitute entering the City would be arrested, and the women knew the score, they kept well away. If this fellow was hoping for a fourpenny kneetrembler or more, the City was the last place to find one. So, what was this man up to?

But a couple of streets later, Nash had to admit he had been proved wrong. A haggard middle-aged woman came into view as the man under surveillance entered Mitre

Square. She looked too roughly dressed to be a prostitute. Even the most desperate of whores would wear a pretty bonnet and some bright coloured clothes to advertise their wares. But she was quick to engage the man in conversation, appearing to flirt and enjoy a joke with him.

Nash decided that she must be a whore after all and was clearly far more to the man's liking than the young girl had been. Odd. But no matter, it was clear that the only way he was going to make this excursion into the City worth his while was to rob this strange cove. Easy pickings. This fellow would spend a little time kissing the cobbles.

Nash had robbed men with their trousers metaphorically down on many occasions; literally down once or twice. The victim would eventually stagger home to his wife to relay how he had been set upon by ruffians. He would shout the odds, promising to write to some eugenics mouthpiece about the growing problem of the underclass; an inferior race of the undeserving poor; the residuum that should be gradually eradicated by sterilisation so that respectable people could walk the streets at night. Such a man would not see the hypocrisy.

Nash had to be careful with this crime. He did not want the woman seeing his face. Most men, when robbed in such a situation, would scuttle away into the night with their tail, amongst other things, tucked between their legs. But occasionally one of them might accuse the woman of being an accomplice to the crime and start knocking her about. Voices become raised and before you know it, a policeman's Bullseye lantern is lighting up the sorry scene. The only chance the woman has to extricate herself from the situation without seeing the magistrate the next morning is to tell the copper who perpetrated the crime. Nash was a well-known face in these quarters; either the woman may recognise him, or the policeman might from her description. If the former, he could not rely on the normal East End rule of not telling the police anything. The woman would have to do what she had to do. That was why she was walking the streets in the first place.

Nash was quickly on the corner looking on, with just his head peeking out from the side of a warehouse in the square, well hidden in the gloom. After what appeared to be a short negotiation, the man guided the woman out of sight into a dark spot. They had no doubt moved to avoid standing beneath the square's solitary streetlamp, a little more privacy being required. This was awkward. If Nash moved towards them, they would see him under the streetlight before he saw them. And the square was overlooked by warehouses and a two-storey house. Somebody gawping out of an upstairs window would see him commit the robbery.

He decided on a different tactic. He would wait for the man to finish his business, after which he would be in a hurry to get away and would leave the woman to attend to herself. She might need to take out her sponge in the privacy of the square as soon as the client had gone. Or if it had been just a kneetrembler, she would want to wash her hands and apron. Either way, she would be looking for a puddle. There would be time for Nash to cosh and rob his prey just after the man had passed by the gas lamp. By the time the woman appeared he would be gone. If she was of a mind to, there would be time for her to give the man a kick in the ribs as she stepped over him. Nash liked to think she would.

The time dragged frustratingly.

Blimey, thought Nash, he's taking his bleeding time. I'm standing here like two of eels!

Nash's mind wandered, thinking of the most recent occasion he had himself been attacked. It was an occupational hazard for anyone in his line of business. There were always others out there looking to wreak violence for the same reason as him. The hunter became the hunted. There had been two of them. He had left them both lying in pain on the cobbles. It would have been worse for them, but he saw how young and poverty-stricken they looked; just lads with their arses hanging out their trousers, trying to earn a crust.

There was movement. The man had re-entered the lit part of the square and was coming towards him. Nash's fingers curled around the cosh inside his right pocket. While his mind had been wandering, he had not been his usual alert self, but instinct now told him to have a quick look about him before making his move.

It was just as well he did. A uniformed policeman was walking towards him. He was not taking any particular interest in Nash and would soon pass by and be gone, so the attack was only postponed for a moment or two. Turning towards the officer, Nash felt in his left pocket for a dog-end and a Lucifer match, both of which he kept there for precisely moments like this, struck the match on the brickwork of the wall at his side, curled both hands around it and lit the cigarette now in his mouth. He then walked towards the policeman, looked straight ahead till almost in front of him before glancing his way casually, momentarily as he passed. It was exactly what an innocent man just going about his business would do. The uniformed man returned the glance but no more than that and continued making his way down the street. Nash feigned the cigarette going out, clicking his tongue with irritation as he stopped to relight it, turning his body slightly as he cupped his hands again, and glanced back.

The constable stopped suddenly. Nash cursed to himself, but then let out his breath in relief when he saw why the uniformed man had stopped. He was unfurling his raincoat. Another shower had started. Suitably attired against the elements, the policeman turned the next corner and disappeared out of sight. Nash saw no sign of his quarry. He surmised the man had obviously spotted the policeman too and retreated into the darkest part of the square waiting for the coast to clear.

Nash knew he would have to move quickly now to catch his man in the square. He started to retrace his steps but within a second his prey appeared, looking about him in all directions, eyes wide open, staring wildly. Taken by surprise, Nash averted his gaze, put his head down and carried on walking past. He felt the man's stare boring in to the back of his neck, before hearing footsteps moving off in the opposite direction.

Nash crossed the street at once, so he had an angle to look in the direction of the footsteps without turning around. The man was scuttling away, head down just as Nash would have expected. But suddenly he slowed to a stroll and straightened, stretching his neck out like a clerk in a collar a size too small. He was making a conscious effort to appear at ease with the world and his place in it. Nash looked on with a grim expression. He thought it amazing what a quick bit of 'how's your father' could do.

The immediate moment to strike had gone, but Nash would follow him till the moment was again right to pounce. He ducked into the dark part of the square where the man had just had his pleasure, to wait a few seconds before following him again. There was no sign of the woman. She should have been out by now.

Nash wondered if her client had hurt the poor old cow.

He stepped quickly along to check on her. He would still have time to return to his slow-moving prey. It was pitch-dark but he could just about make out the dim outline of what appeared to be a pile of scattered old clothes. He took another few steps closer and saw it was the body of a woman. She was dead.

Nash struck a match. The woman's sexual area had been attacked with a knife, her throat cut and face slashed. A replacement match enabled Nash to note that whilst there was blood, given the horrendous damage done to the body, remarkably little of it.

He had seen many terrible things, instigated some of them, but this was not right. This was pure evil. He lurched back into the alley, then back to the street and stopped to look along it in both directions. No coppers. Nobody else either, except at the far end of the street, a man in a deerstalker was folding away a large slaughterman's knife in on itself before slipping it into a coat pocket.

Nash started to run after the figure, but he could not get his breath. It was like he normally felt at the end of a run round the marshes. He could not make any sense of it. Then his lungs began to fill. But accompanying the oxygen coursing through him was anger and unease in equal measure.

People notice runners, he thought, especially at night. If you're running, you've been up to something. Dogs bark; chase after you. Coppers get interested. Seen running away from a murder, his neck would be stretched for sure and not like a clerks' in a tight collar.

Nash slowed to a walk. The killer, little more than twenty yards away, set off again. Nash took a deep lungful of putrid air through his nostrils and followed. Fearful of losing his target in the darkness, he closed the gap. He was now within the man's earshot so needed to sprint forward and overpower him before he had time to reach for his knife. Nash was about to strike when he hesitated and stopped in his tracks. A thought had struck him like a lightning bolt. He allowed the man to go on his way, unmolested.

Nash had made a profound decision. He had chosen not to attack the man the moment it dawned on him that he was following the Whitechapel Murderer.

The pursuit continued, the two men heading along Middlesex Street, otherwise known as Petticoat Lane. Nash could see market stalls along the length of the street, full of prone costermongers asleep, with their wares scattered around them, though even at this early hour there were already signs of life, with men starting to set up. The killer appeared to be making his way through the market towards Liverpool Street station.

Nash's thoughts turned away from his prey for a moment. The station. One minute you could be tripping over the body of a woman who had been hacked to death and the next you could be strolling through the City of London, heart of Empire. But there would be none of the well-heeled, top-hatted nine-to-five brigade on the streets at this hour. The area around the station would be deserted save for the human flotsam and jetsam East End overspill who lived, worked and slept in and around it.

The deerstalker-hatted figure was making his way down the middle of the street so as not to have to pick his way through the stalls. Nash was close behind, drawn to the figure like a moth to a flame. Too close. He stopped and waited in the darkness for a few seconds before setting off again, sticking to the pavement for cover, hopping over and around various stalls, stock and appendages. He had to be careful not to knock anything over. He did not want the killer turning round to see why a costermonger had started cursing. The man looked about him, and appeared to hesitate as to which direction he should head. He looked east and frowned before turning on his heel and heading west towards the station. Nash continued in his wake and pondered what to do.

His mind raced. He could have the fellow by the throat and that would be that. Top him right there, where he stood. Cosh him, strangle him and then scarper. That would end the reign of terror over East End women who had long been degraded and abandoned by the respectable classes, the men of whose ranks did not want to know about prostitutes, though when it suited knew very well where to find them. A dead body covered in blood with a blood-stained knife in its pocket, found yards from a gutted woman. Even Inspector Abberline's bobbies on the beat and his detectives running round after their own tails should be able to work that one out! And who killed the killer? What a mystery that would be if you please! Or perhaps he should just give the man a tap to subdue him and then shout out for a copper? But who was this killer? Supposing he turned out to be a doctor like some of the newspapers reckoned he could be. Perhaps he's only wearing shabby clothes to blend in so as not to be noticed. The word of a doctor against the word of a known villain, the former accusing the latter of attacking him before planting the knife. He could feel the rope tighten round his neck. No coppers.

He thought about the information he now possessed. It was gold dust. He could keep it to himself and use it when needed. If he gets his collar felt, he gives up the killer. No, that wouldn't be right. There's only one reason not to kill the bastard this second. This maniac's thrusting the faces of the ruling classes into the mire. Forcing them to take notice of poor women for the first time.

These thoughts were interrupted by Nash trying to concentrate on keeping close to the killer as the two of them neared the station. The man headed for the Metropolitan underground railway entrance on the main thoroughfare, Bishopsgate. Just outside the entrance a rag seller was collecting up the stock of scarves she sold to people as a barrier against the trapped train emissions they were about to encounter below. And a porter had just drawn the wooden doors of the station across the entrance and was in the process of locking them. The last train of the night had obviously just departed.

Nash thought that if the man's tatty appearance was a disguise he could have been heading into the City. Or if he was simply a shabby local, he could have planned to change trains at Mark Lane down at the Tower to get onto the District Railway and head back into the East End.

The killer headed north towards Shoreditch. There was a train station there, but Nash knew the London & North Western trains would have stopped running too, so if that was the planned escape route, this fellow was going to be disappointed.

But it was when his prey turned to head out of the district of the City Police, moving east along Sclater Street into the Met Police's East End that Nash realised what he was up to. The earlier glance eastwards had no doubt been towards home, but the killer had obviously decided a roundabout route to get there, using public transport, would be preferable given the woman's body would have been found by now so local streets were likely to be full of City policemen looking for him. But with the subterranean railway closed, he had headed away from the City. Kill in the City, disappear into the East End.

Nash thought of the location of the previous murders. Both had occurred just within the East End but a stone's throw from the City. On those occasions had the maniac killed in the East End and quickly disappeared into the City? A copper's whistle blasts out in one police district while the killer strolls undetected in the other. Nash thought it possible. He concluded the killer might be mad, but he was not stupid.

The pursuit continued down Brick Lane before heading east along Hanbury Street and eventually past the back of Whitechapel Mile End station, then crossing Cambridge Heath Road and into a squalid little array of alleys and courts. Half an hour after the fiend had slaughtered a woman in the City, he disappeared behind the door of a little slum in Doveton Street, Stepney.

There was no number on the door, but Nash noted that there was a coloured rag on a stick above the entrance. This was effectively the address for the postman and, from now on, Nash's 'noses' too. Nash did not want to risk the killer spotting and recognising him from their previous near encounters, so would pay a few men to keep watch on the place and keep him informed of the comings and goings. In no time he would have a name, place of work and all sorts of useful information on the killer.

The dullest of light, probably a single candle, escaped through a gap in the newspaper-curtained window, but the glass was so caked in filth, there was nothing to see. And even if there had been, Nash would not have noticed it. He had crossed to the other side of the street, eyes averted. He had just let the Whitechapel Murderer escape, and felt the conflicting emotions of contentment, guilt and disgust about it.

Chapter 3

Nash needed to get off the streets, without any fuss or anyone seeing him. He headed home from the killer's lair through a network of slums and filthy crime filled courts which he knew were off limits to the police. As he slipped into his tenement, he was so deep in thought that he didn't notice the flow of sightseers making their way towards the next street.

Once safely inside his door, he remembered the fuss when the body of the last victim, Annie Chapman, was found three weeks ago. Just after the discovery, he had been pulled by a couple of the Met's coppers, when he had been making his way home in the early hours from a night's ratting. He had been lucky he had not been up to anything illegal so had nothing incriminating on him, least of all blood from assaulting someone, otherwise he would no doubt have been arrested and taken to answer questions in Leman Street police station.

And there were twice the uniformed coppers on the streets these days, and God knew how many plain-clothes. And this time he did have something to hide. Any nose-ache could have seen him leaving that square where the dead woman lay.

There was also the thought that the killer was not just some madman, probably escaped from an asylum somewhere, but a clever, calculating man. It was a chilling one. And Nash had just let this man go. Not liking the direction his thoughts were taking him, he decided to address the matter at hand.

The killer's gaff needed watching with immediate effect, so Nash needed to knock on someone's door to get this arranged. Who did he know who lived over Doveton Street way, who would still be up and about at this time of night and do the job no questions asked? He began to run through some names, but then changed his mind about the idea.

Under normal circumstances anyone who was known to do a bit of ducking and diving could, on having their palms crossed with an appropriate amount of silver, be relied upon to do the job and keep their mouth shut about it. But these were not normal times. As news of the Whitechapel Murderer's latest escapade began to spread, even the most trustworthy might get a little loose with their tongue. Not necessarily even to get a reward or get the police off their backs for some misdemeanour. Nash had noticed how people were gaining some sort of reflected glory from association by living in the vicinity of the murders. They loved talking about it to strangers from outside the area, implying they knew something, passing on the latest snippet of rumour as if it was absolute truth.

People like his drinking mate Will Roud were actually making a nice little living out of such tale-telling for a few bob, especially to newspaper reporters and apparently nosey bystanders who were probably undercover policemen. No wonder the completely innocent Leather Apron, a local butcher, was at one time wanted for questioning by the police and for stringing up by vigilantes, purely on the say so of rumourmongers.

Newspapers were spreading the rumours. Nash was delighted with the interest shown by the press. It was the reason he had, for now at least, let the killer evade justice. But he could not afford to have any journalist sniffing around because they'd heard a rumour that a man was put under surveillance within an hour of the last murder. He needed tight security around his interest in the man, so needed to use professional noses, who could be relied upon to keep their mouths shut.

His thoughts then turned to the mutilated body he had seen an hour ago. It was strange that there was not much blood given the cuts, gouges and slashes inflicted. And come to think of it, a couple of weeks ago when he was last in the Ten Bells, Will had told him the story of how he had bribed a couple of young constables, who were guarding the murder scene while Annie Chapman's body still lay under a sheet waiting to be taken away by the morgue wagon. Having paid them to let him 'have a quick butcher's' Will had been surprised, not to say had his gruesome interest disappointed, by the lack of blood.

"There were so much mayhem going on in the street outside, with most of the coppers being used to push the crowds back, I was able to slip in the yard where it happened quiet, see. I could have been the murderer back to swipe something back, but these two young coppers were so green they let me in for a couple of bob. I'd have paid more. Got my money back and some, charging the world and his wife twopence each for all the gruesome details. Had to make a lot of it up right enough; there weren't nothing much to see truth be told. Scarce any blood. I couldn't help but take the rise out of the coppers. Said to them after, two bob for that!? I've seen worse down the Highway on a Saturday night! I did laugh."

This memory left Nash pondering. So, there's been no blood at two murders. Whores don't bleed much? Syphilis? Perhaps if you got syphilis your blood don't run as quick? Old Rev Barnett's an educated man. He might know about blood. But what a subject to put to the vicar!

Nash had a better idea. He had heard of a middling slummer woman who now lived in Whitechapel. She had fallen on hard times by all accounts. She helped out at Toynbee Hall for nothing, and earned a living as a scribe, copying documents, signwriting and so on.

Sid Beamish, a pickpocket Nash had worked with on occasion, had once told him that she was also being paid well below the going rate as a 'screever' by assorted villains to forge credentials and certificates; write letters of recommendation, hard-luck petitions and the like, without her knowing she was involved in any kind of chicanery. She amused Sid no end.

"Does doctoring for free if you please and speaks with the queerest voice you've ever heard in all your life. She's trying to put on some sort of East End talk half the time and forgetting herself and talking like lady muck the other half. Has a rum name an' all. Sookey. What sort of name's that eh?!"

The crucial piece of information about her as far as Nash was concerned was that she did doctoring. If she had medical knowledge, she should know about blood, and from what he had heard, it should be easy enough to wangle information out of this gullible woman on the telling of a tall tale she would swallow hook, line, and sinker. He would try the pubs later. Someone in one of them should know where he might find her.

Noise from outside brought a stop to these thoughts. Voices. Excited, and a fair number of them. Curiosity got the better of him. He opened his front door and stuck his head out.

"Oi!" he shouted to an urchin running along the passage of the tenement. He did not have to ask what was going on. The boy ran over to volunteer the information.

"The Whitechapel Murderer's only gone and done two of them this time mister!" shouted the boy excitedly. "One just round the corner in Berner Street!"

Nash cuffed the boy round the ear. He waited for the urchin to ask him what he had done that for, but the boy simply looked sheepishly at him. Did he understand? Nash doubted it. The boy continued up the stairs, no doubt to spread the word. Nash resisted the temptation to call him back to explain the news.

Two? One round the corner? What's the soppy little sod on about?

Within minutes the stairwells and balconies of the tenement were abuzz with hysteria, fear, horror, disgust, anger. Nash was the only person registering bemusement.

Nash wandered outside and followed people making their way around the corner into Berner Street. The police were holding back a crowd that had gathered outside the closed wooden doors of Arthur Duffield's Yard, inside of which the murder had taken place. Outside the Working Men's Educational Society next door, people he knew stopped Nash, eager to discuss the latest horrors. They were quick to fill him in on all the gory details. The boy had been right. Two murders, the first clearly just seconds before he had first set eyes on the killer. The slaughtered body he had seen was the second killing of the night. And now everybody in the area would be asking each other if they had seen anything. Woe-betide him if they had.

Chapter 4

Juvenile prostitution was not just for the benefit of sexual deviants. The younger in age girls were, the less likely they were to be diseased, so immaturity was highly prized by men looking for sex on the street. This preference was so widespread amongst the higher-paying clientele that in a trade where once child prostitutes aped the appearance of adults, now young women made themselves look like children as best they could. The most lucrative form of procuring was to supply a virgin to a heavy-spending debauchee. A virginally intact condition could be faked, and a bogus virgin would be passed off as a 'fresh Irish country girl`.

Kitty Johnson looked mature for her age. She could pass for close to twenty. But this was no good thing from a business point of view. According to the law she was too young to have sex. According to certain middle-class sexual desires, she was on the way to being too old. She was already finding the better paying, more refined, cleaner customers more difficult to come by. She feared that she was not so far away from becoming like the poor haggard wretches she saw selling themselves to the roughest of trade for the price of a bed for the night.

Worse still as far as her immediate health was concerned, her fancy man, Harold Saville, was of the same opinion.

He had witnessed her latest failure, when the fellow in the deerstalker cap had rejected her without so much as a second glance. The ponce had been furious. He had heard about the lucrative trade in procuring virgins and had plans for Kitty in that direction, but he was getting increasingly frustrated by her lack of enthusiasm for the job. And having been horrified to find Kitty was planning a trip to a penny gaff on a Saturday night, he was then singularly unimpressed by her inability to tempt a man to hand over at least a small sum for a quick kneetrembler on a dark and lonely night. His fury had further increased when, instead of chasing after the man, she had the bare-faced cheek to just sit back down on her bench and start feeling sorry for herself. When she had started blowing bubbles, it was the final straw. It was now clear to him that he was never going to be able to pass her off as some virginal young Kate O' something from the bogs.

Behaving like a child had been bad for the child's job prospects as a child prostitute. But the irony was lost on the ponce.

Saville went back home after the debacle and waited for Kitty. The original idea had been that he might as well have sex with her one last time before beating her up and throwing her out on the street. But as the minutes ticked by, he worked himself up into more and more of a temper. By the time she got home he did not even wait for her to close the front door. He flew at her as she stepped in.

"I'll give you bleeding bubbles!"

No longer worried about her looks for customers, he attempted to punch her in the mouth as hard as he could, but his right fist came from such a long way back that Kitty had a fraction of a second to react. Flinching, her eyes closed, she brought her head down and threw up an arm, deflecting the punch a fraction onto the top of her head. It stunned her and she staggered backwards before losing her balance on the front step, causing her to fall flat onto the pavement outside. She had not passed out and although in some pain, had her wits about her. She opened her eyes and expected to see Saville's boot heading for her, but he was leaning against the door arch, with his right hand stuck under his left arm.

"Steaming shit!" he screamed through clenched teeth.

His knuckles had made solid contact with the hardest part of Kitty's head. Kitty had got to her feet by the time Saville's attention had shifted from his physical to his mental pain.

"Come here you!" he blared, starting towards her.

Kitty did not react. She stood still, staring back at the snarling ponce as he closed the gap between them. He stopped inches from her, untied his belt, ripping the leather from around his hips in an aggressive flourish.

"You got this coming you little…"

Saville was cut off in mid-justification when a brass heel stamped down on his stockinged left foot. He closed his eyes and screamed in pain, hopping away.

"You've been brassed by a brass!" shouted a young woman's high-pitched voice.

She had arrived from the side of Saville. In his blind rage he had not seen her coming.

The pathetic hopping, groaning man was now an easy target, and a small fist, complete with a ring on one of the fingers, there for precisely this purpose rather than as jewellery, landed on the corner of Saville's mouth, skidding along his teeth, sending him reeling to the ground. The ring had ripped into the gums in the desired fashion, blood seeping from his mouth.

"That's how you punch, ponce!"

She had been taught to punch by her friend Nashey, the technique ensuring she hurt the victim without injuring her own knuckles; a mistake made by a lot of men who liked to think they were handy with their fists. She had told him on more than one occasion since of instances, usually involving clients who had tried to impose roughhouse tactics on her, when she had put his teachings to good use. And now it had come in handy again.

The owner of the fist grabbed Kitty by the elbow as Saville got up on one knee, spitting blood on to the cobbles.

"Come on girl, we've got to leg it! He'll be up on his pins soon enough."

Mary Kelly had been walking home from her long, horrible Saturday night at work, when she happened to glance over from the other side of the street at the pretty young girl at her front door. She had often seen her out and about but never had cause to speak to her. Mary lived in the next court. She was impressed by her neighbour's youthful beauty.

That was me ten years ago, she thought wistfully. Mind you, she's fairer looking than I ever was.

It was admiration rather than jealousy. And she thought any girl deserved better than the bastard of a bully this one had, sucking the life out of her like a leech. When she had seen the girl stagger back onto the street, she instinctively ran to her aid, and arrived with perfect timing to deliver her strike.

Kitty looked dumbfounded at the Good Samaritan.

"Do you hear me, girl? Come on! Let's scarper," implored Mary.

Kitty smiled at her saviour, hitched up her skirt and the two of them ran off down the street together.

***

Nash appreciated that the night's proceedings required further thought. If someone had seen him on the street an hour ago, the police would be paying him a visit. He needed to have a plausible story ready.

And there were the noses to arrange. He had two men in mind, who needed to start on the job straight away, and if that meant getting them out of bed, so be it.

Nash eased his way out of the throng on Berner Street and headed towards the only well-lit thoroughfare in the area, Commercial Road, until he spotted a couple of uniformed policemen stopping people to ask questions. And given that he was leaving the area of the murder site, he was just the sort of character the police might take a particular interest in. So, he turned on his heel and headed in the opposite direction, slipping through numerous dark narrow streets the police had not had time to infiltrate, before eventually knocking on the doors of a couple of accomplices. And having given these men their orders, he stopped off at Will's to tell him that if anyone from the law asked, he was with him all night, playing cards. Will could be relied upon; he and Nash went back years.

Nash eventually returned to his pit and tried to catch up with some sleep while he laid low waiting for the dust to settle. He didn't light a candle, lest some light escape under the door, telling the outside world someone was home. There were several knocks on his door, one of which was by the police, but he did not stir from the darkness. When not in a fitful sleep, he spent the time mapping out in his mind his course of action.

At noon he drifted quietly out on to the street and made his way to The Chimney Sweep, a faded relic of an old gin palace of the lowest order, just off Brick Lane. There were always faces of his acquaintance in there at any given time, and he wanted to sound them out about the rum middling woman. But he had to be artful about it. If he were to show an obvious interest, people would ask themselves why? And if they thought you needed information, they were in a position of power over you.

'What's it worth?' 'Why do you want to know?' 'Let me in on it'.

Glances exchanged; mutterings made. Need was weakness. You never showed need. The information he wanted had to come out as a natural consequence of conversation.

There were a couple of shellfish stalls outside the pub, as well as several Salvation Army people selling the War Cry newspaper and doing their best to intimidate those who looked like entering. A couple of faces were tucking into some winkles. Nash was not particularly hungry but saw it as a good opportunity to get talking to the men. He motioned to the stallholder.

"Give us half pint of whelks, I'm bleeding starving."

Men in Nash's world tended not to use words of greeting. There was no version of 'how are you?' Not even a curt nod. They simply started speaking when they wished to start conversing and would appear to ignore each other until they did. Nash paid for his whelks and turned to look at the Salvation Army people.

"Look at them amen faces," he said with disdain.

He spat on the ground and then raised his voice so said amen faces could hear him.

"What does it matter if a man dies in the workhouse, if his soul is saved!" he called sarcastically, putting on a middle-class accent.

"Amen to that brother," came the naïve agreement.

Nash looked at his fellow shellfish eaters with contempt on his face.

"I'll give them a-bleeding-men."

Nash was impressed by the work done by some philanthropists, but he was bitterly opposed to the Salvation Army due to its acceptance of society as it was, and its indifference to the causes of poverty.

"You tell them Nashey," chuckled one of the men enjoying his winkles. In an attempt to further ingratiate himself, he continued. "Mad sods the lot of them, they ought to put them all in the loony bin!"

Nash glowered at the man.

"Nobody should be put in places like that!"

"No, no, course not Nashey, just er…"

Though not anywhere near as annoyed as he appeared, Nash gave the man his most withering stare. He could now move the conversation whatever way he wished, and the men would be pleased to go along with it to ease the tension. Nash held the stare for a second, before moving his gaze to a small child playing by the door of the pub. The little lad was filling a Woodbines packet with a mix of dirt and sawdust that had been trodden out of the pub door.

Nash tossed the child a farthing.

"Go and get yourself some pop, boy."

Nash turned to the men with a grim smile.

"Got a keep in with them ain't we? Little bleeder will be part of the Adelphi Street gang one day just as I'll be getting weak and feeble!"

The men silently exhaled their pent-up breath in relief at the thawing of the atmosphere.

"Yes, you can say that again Nashey, they breed them tough round here all right," said the second, hitherto silent, man.

His mate, who had passed the remark about lunatic asylums, simply nodded in agreement and uttered a safe, "Yes."

Nash looked up at the advertising signs pasted across almost every square inch of the pub yard wall. One read:

Wine Spirits Vaults Fine Cordials Gin

Nash grunted with contempt before further articulating his feelings.

"Them sign writing wallahs go on till the cows come home. Never give us two words when they can throw six at us."

Given that both men were illiterate, the verbosity of advertising hoardings was not a subject which interested either of them, but they saw Nashey was offering an olive branch; a way of starting a new, friendlier conversation.

"Yes, you're right there Nashey, loads of old flannel ain't much use to the likes of us, is it?" said one of them. He had not been sure whether to say it with a slight chuckle or with

52

grim contempt but given Nashey's mood chose the latter. Nash now made the move he had been angling towards since he first spotted the men enjoying their seafood.

"They should learn how to write better from that hoity-toity piece I've heard about. Some funny slummer woman living round here does a bit of writing, so they say."

"Oh yes, I knows her," said one of the men. "She's a queer fish all right. To look at her you'd think she were a gyppo straight off a fairground. Long glossy black hair, loads of rouge, talks well proper except some words she tries to speak like us. Queerest thing you've ever heard. She does anything like writing, reading, doctoring. She never turns no cove away, does letters, all sorts, mostly for nothing if she gets a sob story, which she always does of course."

"And you say she does doctoring an' all?" queried Nash.

"Yeah, when old granny Betts died, the area where she lived, Chequers Yard and round there, were without nobody who could help out when people were taken ill, so this Soppy Sookey, as they calls her, starts rolling her sleeves up. Her old fellow were an army surgeon by all accounts. Dead a while back since. The doctoring's helped her belong. A bit anyhow. She ain't never going to be one of us, is she? But she'll do anything to help with that, see."

"Soppy Sookey?" chuckled Nash.

The face was enjoying himself now. He continued with enthusiasm.

"Yes, you ought to see her try and do things all women can do, washing and the like. Ain't got a bleeding clue she ain't. Sookey's her name if you please. Somebody calls her Soppy Sookey and it sticks like cobbler's wax."

"Blimey, I'll have to give her a knock myself," said Nash in a cheerful throwaway manner. "I got some gip from this finger since I stiff-fingered some toff in the throat last week. Serves me right for trying to be too easy on him. Used my monkey's fist when I should have used my cosh. I must be getting bleeding soft. He didn't go down and rounded on me. It were over in Frying Pan Alley and you know how bleeding narrow that is. Gave him the straight fingers. Caught some poxy tie pin or something he were wearing. Thought it were just going to be a black blood pinch but it's going to go septic by the looks of it if I ain't careful."

Nash showed them his right ring finger, which was black and swollen with the nail soon to come off. The story had been true. But it was an occupational hazard. He was always carrying some injury or another. He never bothered with medical treatment.

"Looks nasty that do Nashey. Why don't you go round and see her. Lives next door to big Rose in Widegate Street."

Most people in the neighbourhood knew, or at least knew of, Rose Dale. It was difficult not to. She was six feet tall, nineteen stone and had arms like sides of mutton. Her husband once made the mistake of complaining to her about the inferior quality of the sandwich she had made him for his lunch. The next day, in full view of his fellow workers, he unwrapped his lunch to find the rent book between two slices of bread.

Nash had caught the tail-end of what had happened when Rose's husband arrived home after an afternoon being the butt of all his work mates' jokes. The Dales had a full, no holds barred fight which spilled out on to the street. Slum women did not scratch and pull hair in a fight; they fought with their fists like men. And Mr D had a black eye from a right cross to prove it.

Nash had been one of those who had gathered to watch the entertainment. A row of excited ragged boys had gallery seats looking down on the skirmish, their legs and bare feet dangling down from the top of a wall. The wags amongst them had a field-day making fun of the man who could not control his wife.

But he was fitter than her and after a while started to get the upper hand. When a left hook landed on Rose's chin, Nash decided it was time to step in, much to the chagrin of the crowd. But Rose did not appreciate his help and gave him a verbal volley that no man would dare have done. Nash was mightily impressed by the woman but feigned offence.

"Here! Any more of that and you'll get my boot, now bugger off indoors before I throw you in that horse-trough there!"

Rose's husband wanted to round on Nash. No man talked to his old lady like that. But he knew that would be most unwise, so simply put his arm round his beloved.

"Come on old girl let's get indoors away from this lot."

With the common enemy of Nash to glare at, the spouses had reconciled their differences.

That had been months ago, but although Nash had seen Rose about here and there on the street since, he had not had occasion to speak to her. He wondered what his reception would be. This woman was one of the few people whose approval he would appreciate. He suspected the feelings were far from mutual. He gave her door a rap and the woman of the house was quick to appear, filling the entire door space.

"Rose," said Nash, with a nod.

"It's Mrs Dale to you."

"Very well Mrs Dale," he said formally, keeping the amusement he felt out of his face and voice. "I hear you're mates with a woman who does a bit of doctoring. Goes by the name of Sookey or some such?"

"I ain't no mates with her. I puts up with her more than most, that's all," corrected Rose. "After a bit a doctoring are you? Dear o' lore, don't tell me someone's given you a good hiding, I'd hate to hear that. Or is it a nasty disease?" came the mock concern.

"Don't worry yourself missus, I'll breathe," he retorted, this time allowing a smirk to escape as he held up his black finger.

She made it clear from her expression that she was less than impressed.

"Don't look much to me. Want me to pull that nail off for you? I got some pliers out the back. I'd do it with pleasure."

"I'm sure you would, you old cow," said Nash knowingly.

He decided it was time to end the banter and get on with the job at hand. He changed his tone to one he would use when speaking to men.

"She about girl?"

Rose spotted the change and knew it was time to tell this man what he wanted to know.

"She lives there," nodded Rose, at the little terraced

place next door. "But she ain't home. Said she were going up Toynbee to see Henrietta as she calls her."

Rose had made pains to over pronounce the aitch in Henrietta, mocking her next-door neighbour, both for her accent and her relationship with Reverend Barnett's wife. Everyone else in the neighbourhood referred to Henrietta Barnett as 'the reverend's wife' or Mrs Barnett. It was not just respect but distance that brought such formality.

"Mrs Parsons is helping her chum give a lecture on Sir Walter Scott," she explained, using a sarcastically high-pitched well-mannered voice before returning to her usual speech. "Whoever the bleeding hell he is. I'm sure it'll help the young servants they're telling, no end when they're black-leading tomorrow."

Nash understood very well Rose's sarcasm, as Toynbee Hall could be condescending at times, and some of what they did certainly lacked common sense. What was the point of lectures on aesthetics, orchestral recitals or debating societies for the poverty-stricken? But in general terms he greatly approved of the place. It provided useful classes in shorthand, arithmetic and book-keeping, gave legal advice, ran a housing company which provided much needed basic but decent homes for working people, and he thought its events, clubs and library were worthwhile. But most crucial of all, it focused middle class attention on East End poverty. Though Nash believed the nocturnal habits of a knife-wielding maniac were now eclipsing it in this respect.

Not that he made any of this thinking public. He snorted what Rose might assume to be agreement, turned on his heel and headed towards the object of her sarcasm.

Chapter 5

The lecture had already finished when Nash arrived at Toynbee Hall. One of the helpers told him that Mrs Parsons had just left for her art gallery around the corner, so he strolled along to take a look. It was quite a shock. He had never been in an art gallery before. In the filthiest part of London, was what must have been the cleanest, brightest interior in the East End. He immediately felt ill at ease. The place was empty save for pictures on the walls. So much space; so much silence; he was unused to this. His footsteps echoed on the shiny, spotlessly clean, polished hardwood floor. He thought he would certainly never be able to creep up on anyone here.

The gallery was empty, but he could hear someone rummaging around in a back room. It must be the woman he sought. He decided to look around at the pictures and wait for her to appear.

He thought it very clever what the artists had painted. Some of the likenesses were near as good as the camera pictures he had seen in shops, but these paintings were better because they were coloured. And much better than the pictures on advertising boards. Except for the Pear's bubbles picture of course. Nothing could beat that.

One picture made him stop in his tracks. It was so different from the rest. It was not good at all as far as he was concerned. He thought it not a proper likeness. He could see it was a picture of a London music hall, but it was all false looking. The people didn't look real and were all blurred and gesturing in a stupid way. Why would you want to paint something like that? The real thing is only just down the road at Wilton's, and if you're going to waste your time painting it you might as well do it right.

He looked at the caption by its side: Walter Sickert, on loan from the New English Art Club.

On loan? Blimey, he thought, glad to get rid of it more like. He went public with the remainder of his review.

"Reckon I could paint a better picture of a music hall than that."

"Could you indeed sir? I look forward to seeing your work."

Nash spun round to see a woman of indeterminate years, in her thirties or thereabouts, smiling warmly at him. She had white powder on her face, as well as perfectly round discs of rouge on each cheek. Her hair, complete with mid-forehead parting, pinned up at the lowest possible point allowing the loose bundled, long thickly glossed hair as much licence as custom allowed.

Gawd help us if she don't look like some doll, he thought. No. Mrs Punch? No, this woman's too fair looking by half. She's got the shiniest hair I ever did see. It'll be down over her shoulders if she ain't careful, mind. Them pins don't look none too clever, and then she'll look like some little girl. And gawd knows what potions she's got on it. What a queer stamp of a woman. But fair looking, I'll say that for her.

Lost for words, Nash blurted out something just to end the silence.

"This Sickert fellow. Queer sort of name. Lot of Germans round here these days, working in the sugar game. One of their lot, is he?"

Sookey was becoming used to people in Whitechapel simply starting conversations without the usual greetings or introductions in place. She smiled and answered confidently.

"He is a friend of an acquaintance of mine. That is how I was able to secure the loan of such an important piece. Presently he resides part of the time in London, though not Whitechapel, and part of the time in Northern France. He certainly has the rarest of names does he not? I think it is indeed of German origin, but he is a young rake of the middling sort, so I doubt he has any connection with the refining business."

Nash thought she had a wealthy woman's voice all right, but it was unusually attractive and friendly. In his limited experience of the middling type, they had two modes of address to the poor. One was a kindly, condescending tone, each word kept to one syllable if possible, pronounced with definite clarity; the second was a loud, self-assured hectoring note. Doctors, magistrates, officials and clergy were experts at such social intimidation. This voice was neither.

Nash tried to be on his best behaviour.

"I didn't mean to take the er... to be rude about the lad. It's just that all the other paintings seem so much better to my eye," he said, in a defensive, unconfident tone he was unused to affecting.

"There, you have it sir. To your eye. Beauty is in the eye of the beholder is it not?"

Nash had vaguely heard of this phrase before. He was thinking about a reply when she carried on.

"But some art appreciation can only be determined by education. And the raison d'etre of Toynbee Hall is education," she beamed.

Nash did not understand the last sentence. Raisons? Debt? Eh? Blimey, he thought, perhaps it were better when middling types spoke in their usual manner after all! At least he could understand what they were going on about then.

Thankfully, she carried on again, so Nash didn't have to summon a reply.

"You see, Sickert is an impressionist," she said with great enthusiasm. "It is a new form of painting. Yer paints yer own impression of something, not an actual likeness of it. So, it can appear amateurish at first, but given time people come to appreciate it for its artistic thought as well as its painterly skill."

Yer? Nash now realised what coves meant when they said her accent was all over the place. Art was a mystery to him, so he was impressed by the woman not using a condescending tone when trying to explain something that was clearly beyond his understanding. He was not sure he would be so considerate if he tried to explain to her the subtleties of the thieving, dishonesty and general skulduggery of his world. Or God forbid, if he attempted to explain why the Whitechapel Murderer was still at large, courtesy of him. He wasn't sure he could explain that fully to himself, come to think of it.

He felt that he should reply but was not sure what to say. He thought it safest to stick to a subject he knew.

"I take it these here pictures are worth a bob or two, being on show so to speak?" he said, in his usual gruff tone. "You should be careful not to leave them unguarded. They might walk."

"Walk?" queried Sookey.

Her eyes flickered a little as her right hand moved up to touch the top of her blouse for reassurance. Her breezy confidence had evaporated. She was aware she was alone in an enclosed space with this huge, aggressive, dangerous-looking man.

Nash realised that she was not going to understand him if he spoke in his usual manner. The two of them were from different worlds. He spotted that he had now frightened her. He would need to speak in a less aggressive manner, as he sometimes did to little perishers, and try to use proper words and phrases.

"My apologies madam. I did not mean to offend. It's just that there is a lot of crime in this here neighbourhood and I would hate to see your fine pictures stolen. Alexander Nash…"

He hesitated.

Do I say 'at your service' or 'by your leave' or something like that? He tried to remember what he had heard greasy clerks say. He decided to keep it simple, offering his hand.

"How do you do?"

My, she thought, relaxing a little, this man has a fine smile. He seems quite personable.

She gazed at the huge, surprisingly clean hand proffered to her. It had taken her aback, but she did not want to insult him by not responding appropriately. She had spotted immediately (you could not very well miss it), his badly injured ring finger.

"Hello Mr Nash. I would shake your hand, but I fear you would not thank me for doing so," she smiled, nodding down at the blackened finger. "My name is Sookey Parsons, I am the curator here at the gallery, and Henrietta Barnett's assistant at Toynbee Hall." Her hand briefly held his two healthy middle fingers. "It would appear my tiny hand is just able to make acquaintance with two of your fine fingers at a time sir," she said in a self-deprecating voice, leaning her head slightly to one side as she smiled.

The very few people who owned a telephone, had started using the old hunting cry of 'helloo' as a term of greeting when starting a conversation on the new device, though the second 'o' had been dropped. And it was quickly becoming adopted into middle class speech elsewhere too. But Nash had not heard the term before. It had him pondering.

Ain't heard that before. Ice cream sellers use words like that ending in 'o' all the time. Were it Italian for 'how do you do?' But why were this woman speaking to him in eyetie? Perhaps that black glossy hair's Italian? No matter, I better tell her about this finger of mine.

He held up the digit for inspection.

"Did it at work," he explained.

"Indeed sir, and what is your position?"

Christ, he thought, he should have seen that coming a mile off. Talk about walking straight into one.

He chose to ignore the question. Usually, if asked a question he did not like, he would ignore it, stare at the questioner for a second, an unspoken agreement then made between them to move the conversation on in a different direction. He replaced the usual stare with an even broader smile than the one he had been using.

He wondered if he was overdoing it but certainly had the idea this woman liked the look of him. The unfunny joke about the little fingers and the coy sideways look she gave, told him so. This was useful. It could be to his advantage.

He answered her question, with a question.

"You ever had anything half-inched er…stolen from here?"

"Oh no, it is very safe here in the gallery," Sookey explained earnestly. "Nobody would steal from us. Everyone has too much respect for the reverend and what he is trying to achieve here." Her eyes suddenly narrowed with suspicion. "Are you a policeman sir?"

Nash burst out laughing. He had never heard two good jokes in such quick succession. He was not sure which was funniest; people having too much respect for slummers to steal from them, or him being a copper. He thought she was every bit as wet-behind-the-ears as those faces claimed.

He forgot his soft tone and attempt at speaking correctly for a moment.

"Gawd help us, no!" He heard his deep voice echo around the, all but empty gallery. He recovered his composure. "Beg pardon my lady, I meant no disrespect to you. It's just that the police are not well received round here. It's the last position you would seek to hold."

Gawd, I just called her 'my lady'. Is that something you only say to your fancy piece or is it all right? The police are not 'well received`. It's the 'last position'. Blimey, I ain't got a clue how to speak to this woman.

64

Sookey was not sure how to react. Was this man making sport of her? If so, she quite liked it.

She enjoyed being the butt of a joke. It was a means by which she felt transported from the excepted to the accepted. She never felt better than when her friend Mary was being sarcastic at her expense. But as far as she was concerned, it was not an expense, rather a benefit.

She felt that her medical work was crucial in gaining respect within the neighbourhood, but she had noticed that doctors throughout the slums, though respected, were not accepted or even liked. It was through humour that she felt truly part of local society. It was clear to her that humour was an intrinsic part of life in the slums. It was the only thing that kept people going at times, the one possession which could not be taken from them. How often had she heard expressions such as, 'got to laugh ain't you girl? Otherwise, you'd bleeding cry'.

The big handsome man in front of her looked a little uncomfortable. She threw him a smile to reassure; no offence taken.

Nash thought she was probably about to ask again what he did for a living. He quickly got a question in first.

"As you can tell, I ain't someone who visits art places normal. I were looking for you. The people down the Hall told me where to find you. I hear tell as how you do some doctoring and I were wondering if you could have a look at this here finger for me. Well, you've already looked at it so to speak," he laughed, hoping for a similar response.

A reciprocal chuckle came forth. Nash thought it seemed genuine enough.

"Certainly, sir, though I have nothing here with me.

Can you come to my lodgings? Perhaps in one hour?"

There she goes with that 'sir' again, he thought. Cur more like.

If any other woman he knew asked him to come to her lodgings, he would immediately reply with a double entendre and a wink. Not that he particularly enjoyed music hall humour, but like it or not, it was an expected part of life in the East End.

"That'll be good, right enough," he said seriously.

She started to give him directions, but he interrupted her.

"That's all right, you live next door to Big Rose don't you."

He knew that there was every chance that sometime in the next hour, Rose would tell her neighbour that he had been there looking for her. He thought it would sound better if he told her first of his visit.

"I were there earlier see, looking for you. As soon as I did my finger the other day, people kept saying you ought to go and see that Sookey. You're well known round here."

Sookey glowed. Not only was she going to see this interesting man again, but she was, 'well known round here`.

Chapter 6

Immigrants were easy prey for conmen. As soon as Naseer Khan had stepped off the train at Cannon Street station he was accosted by a couple of friendly men claiming to be porters. He had an address in Aldgate, which unbeknown to him was no more than a mile away, but the conmen took him on a roundabout route in an accomplice's growler, and the cabman was very pleased to relieve him of the entire pound he had to his name for what should have been a one shilling ride.

The tall, thin ebony-skinned man had journeyed from Delhi to look for his daughter. She had been a sixteen-year-old servant who accompanied her British employer back to England with the promise of a return fare on arrival. The one subsequent letter he received from her, written in English, told him that her employer had not made good on their end of the bargain, and she was cast adrift without a penny as soon as they arrived in England. Her employers now had plenty of English servants at their disposal. As a result, she was marooned in London until she could find a position with a homebound employer. Having been told that nannies were always popular, she was hopeful of getting home soon via such a position. She was temporarily living in a place called Aldgate. Khan's daughter was illiterate in her own language, let alone English, and the letter so well written that it was obvious that someone had written it for her.

Khan had nursed his ailing wife whilst waiting for his only surviving child to walk back through the door. He was initially unconcerned by the time it was taking for his daughter to find her way home. She had probably got a position with a British family and would no doubt be indentured to the job for some time to recompense the employers for the cost of her passage. And even when she was able to leave, she would be penniless and could be as far off as Calcutta or Madras, for he was realistic enough to appreciate she may not have had much choice as to where in India she could get passage. It would be a long journey home. But the years had passed with no further word, his wife had died, and he was now at a low ebb. He needed to find his daughter. She could, of course, find her way back to the village while he was away in England, but he left behind a large family network who would take her in, awaiting his return.

The address given in England was the Ayahs Home in Aldgate, a stone's throw from Whitechapel. The problem of marooned Indian women had become so acute that philanthropists had established this shelter for Ayahs, the collective term for Indian servants and nannies.

Having had his life savings conned out of him on arrival, he had eked out a living doing whatever was necessary. Slum life was the same whether you were in Whitechapel or Delhi. In fact, the two places were remarkably alike in many ways. You did whatever kept you fed and, if possible, dry. You existed. He had seen how the British in India treated Indians, so the level of xenophobia and racism he had to endure was no great surprise to him, and his lesson about trusting strangers had been quickly, painfully learned.

He had made all the obvious enquiries, including a trip to the India Office but the search for his daughter had come to nothing. And he had no idea if he would ever save enough money for his passage home.

Khan settled into his new life quickly. His first job had been assisting a glazier. This skilled man padded the streets clutching glass in a wooden frame, shouting "winders!" On one cold winter's day, cramp had locked his arm rigid to the glass after hours of walking the streets without a customer. The glazier was too old and weak to do this any longer; the workhouse beckoned. But he remembered what his father always used to say.

"There's always some poor bugger worse off than you, boy."

And sure enough, there was. He was approached for a job by a fellow who appeared to be an old lascar.

"Ain't seen you about here before." he said. "You just off the boat, are you?"

"Yes sir. I am strong as ox. Need work. Place to sleep."

The old glazier had a room to himself in a nearby slum. He only really needed a corner to sleep in but had to pay for a whole room so he could store his glass and tools in safety. There was room for another straw paillasse next to him. He could not afford to pay anything, but the man looked desperate enough to work for nothing.

"Can't pay you nothing, but I got a bed for you, and you can eat what I eat. I'll see you all right on that score. What's your name?"

"Khan."

"Just Khan?"

"Yes sir."

"All right by me boy. Some of you coves have got some right queer names. Can't get me laughing gear round them."

Khan had passed his first job interview with flying colours, and he kept the old glazier out of the workhouse by carrying the glass for him. As the old man's health faded and his own English accent improved, Khan started to do the shouting as well. One morning the old glazier did not wake up and Khan needed to look for another job. Various ones had come his way. He had been a sand-bone man, selling sand for floor covering; hawked brownstone for cleaning and colour-stoning the doorsteps and pavements outside houses; a general dealer of old boots and clothes; egg vendor – eggs came over from Ireland uncleaned, in crates packed with straw, and sold sixteen for a shilling. But some were broken and bad, and these, plus cracked eggs, were sold to the poor at a cheap price by the old lascar egg-man.

Khan came to appreciate that his appearance could, in the right circumstances, be a help rather than a hindrance. He had been to a fair and spotted that many of the people making a living as fortune tellers, mystics, potion sellers and anything considered the least bit exotic or occult, had a similar complexion to his own. Slum life in England had also taught him the popularity of gambling.

He had an idea which was against his religious beliefs, but after much soul searching, not to mention a grumbling stomach, he put his idea in to practice. He grew a full beard and moustache, used kohl around his eyes to make them appear wider and brighter, and swopped various bits of stock he retained from previous jobs for a filthy but striking red outfit in Petticoat Lane market. It was an old army sergeant's overcoat plus a hat not unlike a policeman's helmet. The ensemble was likely to be a relic of the Crimea. And he changed his name to Khano, The All-Seeing. Decked in this garb, he went to all the horse race meetings at Alexandra Palace, Hurst Park, Epsom and any other courses within easy, cheap travelling distance of London. He sold tips; the exotic, mystical man with the big bulging eyes and the sixth sense, who knew the winners. He knew nothing about horse racing but enlisted the assistance of a man he once helped in the street to escape the police.

The man had obviously just committed a crime and had been surprised by an unseen policeman. He was making a run for it with the police officer in hot pursuit when Khan casually walked straight into the pursuer, knocking him down. Khan then quickly dropped on the uniform apologising most profusely whilst actually hindering the officer from getting up.

He didn't know the man he had just helped at the time, but he knew that any action against the loathed police was viewed with appreciation from those around him in the slums, and it was important to gain their acceptance if he was to live among them in peace. And he had no liking for the police in any case. They harassed him at every turn. He called them bobbies, because he once called them peelers, but his accent made it sound like "pillars."

"They ain't pillars of this community," growled the big brooding man he had once helped escape them.

"Very well Nashey, I call them bobbies now."

"Bobbies, crushers, coppers, they're all the same whatever you calls them," came the curt reply.

Nashey was not a friend. Nobody was friends with Nashey, but Khan liked him. Unlike most people, he treated Khan the same as he did everyone else. Khan once relayed this thought to him. Nash grunted.

"Every fellow's the same in my book. You're all some mother's son ain't you? Till you cross me of course. But until then I just treats all men with the same contempt."

Khan saw the merest hint of a twinkle in the man's eye but knew not to show Nashey that he understood he was joking.

"Except bobbies Nashey eh?"

"Yes, except bobbies, and wrong uns."

The two men met up regularly so that Nash could give him tips he could use at the racecourse. Khan always bought his adviser a drink, though he insisted he give Nash the money to buy the drink himself, but other than that the big man seemed content to help him just as a continuing thank you for his one-time assistance. Like any gambler, Nash could only speculate on the best bets, but at least he followed 'the form' and could make educated choices. He left the exotic reasoning as to why a horse was sure to win to Khano. The All Seeing gave his clients knowing reasons for each tip.

"This horse look me in eye. Oh, and what a look. I win today. I run like wind."

And then he would add something more concrete gleaned from Nash.

"The horse tells me, this my course. I win last time I run here. I no like that left hand course last time. And it too

72

wet and boggy. I like sun on back and rattle of hooves on hard ground, like today."

Without exception, the punters accepted the idea that horses understood about racing in different conditions and spoke broken English. One huge slice of luck came when one of the first tips Nash had given him, won at long odds – 100 to 8. Since then, like most tipsters, he lost his customers a little more than they won overall, but he won enough to keep the faith of some clients at least, and there were always new ones impressed enough by this striking looking fellow to hand over some cash.

When he wasn't at the racecourse, Khan was a look out and general information gatherer – a 'nose'. His very incongruity as a black man in a sea of whiteness made him strangely effective at blending into the background, the most important of all a nose's talents. Everyone saw him yet did not see him. They did not want to see him. They saw an old lascar but paid no heed; he was no doubt just selling something they didn't want and would not buy off him even if they did.

And if you told Khan to do something, he did it to the letter, without query, without complaint, and would carry on doing it until you told him otherwise. He was ideal for the job that Nash needed someone to perform.

Nash had rapped on Khan's door in the early hours of Sunday morning. Khan was to stand across the street from the door shown him in Doveton Street. Nash would get another man to alternate with him, doing shifts. It was suggested they sell matches as a cover. Khan was given some coins with which to buy them. He was told to rig up a tray from a box-side with strings attached that he could hang round his neck. Good wages would be paid and he could keep whatever was made on the matches. This was on the understanding that he did not tell a soul who he was working for; that he was working for anyone in fact. He was just selling matches because the racecourse work didn't pay much at this time of year. It was always the same with racing come October – 'the flat' was finishing and 'over the sticks' hadn't got started properly yet. As soon as a man left the house, Khan was to follow him to wherever he was going. He would be a fair size of a feller. Shabbily clothed, likely to be wearing a deerstalker cap.

Suitably decked out in the garb of a match-seller, Khan now stood across the street from where, unbeknown to him, the Whitechapel Murderer was ensconced.

***

Nash had popped back to his gaff to make himself more respectable before meeting Sookey again. He had been home for less than a minute when there was a knock on the door. Whoever it was, had obviously been waiting outside for him. Why didn't they simply make themselves known at the tenement entrance? That was the only trouble in living in a tenement; he didn't have front windows to peer out of. It could be anybody out there.

About to have a wash, Nash was bare to the waist, with his large belt several inches below the top of his corduroy trousers. He slipped it off and held it by its thin end, the big metal buckle dangling just above the floor. And a moment later his cap, complete with small shards of jagged glass protruding from its peak, was resting on his head.

"Who is it?"

"Me, Nashey, Khan."

"Christ!" exclaimed Nash, grabbing the top of his cap to avoid the peak, before tossing it down with a mix of relief and exasperation.

As Nash opened the door, he was about to ask Khan why the bleeding hell he had waited till he was indoors to make himself known, when he remembered that he had told him to keep his work for him as secret as possible. Khan had simply been following orders to the letter. Nash was impressed with his man, though gave no hint of it. No words of welcome were offered, as Nash opened the door, his body simply moving sideways to allow Khan the space to pass by. Khan hesitated, so Nash jerked his head towards the room and his employee scurried in.

"I were just about to have a sloosh out the yard. Sit down."

Khan hesitated and then motioned to sit on the floor.

"On the chair, soppy sod!" barked Nash with obvious exasperation.

There was only one chair in the room, a decaying rickety little wooden affair. Khan had thought he had better not sit on Nashey's only chair.

"It's on its last legs but it'll probably hold your weight, if you're lucky," said Nash with that slightest of glints in his eye that Khan had come to spot.

Nash disappeared out the back with a bucket, leaving the back door open which let in daylight as well as a harsh, biting westerly wind. Khan sat down and looked about the room. The chair was at a table, fashioned from fruit crates. On it was a selection of strange looking implements; the flat cap with its vicious looking peak; a metal spike, a thick rope, a leather cosh, a large ring and a small knife which rested on a thick book. A walking cane rested against a crate. In one corner of the room was an empty coal sack. In another was a single iron bedstead with a horse-hair mattress, hair protruding. Along the wall opposite was a shelf, on which was a lit gas lamp. Beneath the shelf, on the floor, were a pile of newspapers and a tin of paraffin. On the opposite wall was a fireplace, complete with grate surrounded by a fender, on which lay a cat asleep, with its head using one of Nash's boots as a pillow. By the boots was a pair of thin-soled shoes, a chipped enamel teapot and a bag filled with tea leaves. A single heap of clothes piled haphazardly on the floor closest the fender. A vest, a muffler, two shirts, two waistcoats of differing sizes, a spare pair of trousers, a billy pot bowler hat and a huge black overcoat. Nash would wear the whole lot, bar the second pair of trousers, in all but the hottest months, a psychological defence against the world. These scraps of human habitation sat on a hard splinter encrusted wooden floor, with brown crumbling walls rising from it.

Khan picked up the book to see if it had any pictures in it.

Nash walked in, his head and huge muscled torso dripping wet. Khan started to get up.

"Stay where you are," ordered Nash.

He then picked up his bed mattress, took it outside, gave it a good shake and beat it with his walking stick.

"That should 've got rid of the little bleeders. I had to paraffin my head to get rid of them last week."

He rolled the mattress up into a bolster and threw it down next to Khan, then started to rub himself dry, hands rubbed up and down trousers, then chest and stomach slapped with palms.

"Didn't know you read Khan. What you think of Old Moore's Almanac then?"

"Good pictures Nashey."

"Yes, course." Nash sat down on the bolster and changed the subject. "What you got for me boy?"

"I wait Doveton Street like you say Nashey."

"Good boy, and?"

"I sell matches. Good eh Nashey?"

"Yeah, bleeding wonderful," came the sarcastic, increasingly impatient reply.

"I wait long time. But man come out house. He wear cap like you say. I follow to place Broad Street near station."

"What place?"

"Don't know Nashey. Big workplace but no factory, no sweatshop. Lots men, carts, stuff."

"What's it called?"

"Don't know Nashey."

"You PC Thick or something?" asked Nashey with disgust at his man's dense behaviour.

Sergeant (Nash had got his rank wrong) Thick was a policeman who had found fame for his stupidity during the Lipski murder case a year earlier. When the same officer happened to be the man to arrest 'Leather Apron,' the first high profile Whitechapel Murder suspect, despite there being no evidence whatsoever against him other

77

than vigilante-spread rumour, the sergeant's unfortunate surname was just too perfect.

"Thick Nashey?"

"Never mind."

Nash had to make a spur-of-the-moment decision, to take over from Khan and forget about the slummer woman or to still make his appointment with her. He decided, against his better judgement, on the latter course.

"All right, now get yourself back down there sharp and start asking about the place. Find out about it. Tell who wants to know you've heard there might be a job going there. Look for our man and see if you can get talking to him. Ask him his name. On the sly. Crafty like. If anyone asks why you're being so bleeding nosey just tell them it's what you Indian fellows do. You're just trying to be friendly. You got me?"

"Yes, Nashey."

"Stay outside where the cove works till a fellow name of Shanks turns up to take over from you. I got to go off and see someone now so don't come back here. If I don't get hold of you beforehand, I'll see you in the Ten Bells opening time tomorrow. And if I ain't there you wait." Lightening his tone, he went on with a wink. "I'll give you a few winners an' all, I shouldn't wonder."

With this, he got up and pulled on a once white vest now tinged with the colour of Rickett's Blue washing powder as might be expected of old clothing, but there were also pink streaks. Nash caught Khan looking at it.

"Yeah, I know. Bleeding washer woman boiled some old whore's red smalls in with it by mistake. Poor cow ain't all there if truth be told, but I give her the work anyhow. If she don't take in washing from the likes of me, she'd be in the `house for sure."

He then donned just the one shirt, half the waistcoat stock, and ignored the overcoat and muffler, so that he would appear less bulky and intimidating than usual.

Khan started to get up to leave. He nodded at the incumbent asleep in the grate.

"A cat Nashey. No dog?"

"Dogs don't catch mice and rats, do they? They're all right in the pit, but they ain't so clever indoors. And I likes cats because they don't give a tinker's cuss about no cove."

Nash completed his ensemble by treading down into his uncomfortable, thin stalking shoes. Something he would never usually do when not working, but they looked more respectable than his boots.

Irritated with himself, he wondered why he was chasing after some soppy woman who might know something about why whores don't bleed. And what if she does? It's more important to know who the Whitechapel Murderer is. He was having a wash for some woman when he should have been in Broad Street, finding things out for himself. But he couldn't help but think about the blood of prostitutes.

Like somebody else I know, he thought sardonically.

Chapter 7

On the short stroll to Sookey's place, Nash had bought a newspaper carrying the latest on the double-murder story. He held the newspaper at arm's length and skimmed through the gist of the headlined report as he walked. He thought that they might only be doing it for their own benefit, to sell papers, but the role reporters and their likeness wallahs, the photographists, were playing in highlighting the plight of the poor, made them worthy of protection. He had heard one or two of them had been given a thick ear for their snooping so he would look out for them from now on. He would put the word about that they were not to be touched or have any trouble.

On arrival at his destination, Nash was relieved to see Rose was not about. He was in no mood for a verbal joust with her. He knocked on Sookey's door, looking down at the front step beneath his feet. It was dirty. He tutted to himself and shook his head ruefully. Even if you had lived in the area all your life, let alone arrived as an outsider, the first law of being respected by your fellow neighbourhood women was keeping a clean front step.

"She'll learn," he muttered to himself.

The door was almost immediately opened by the woman with the glistening hair.

"Hello again Alexander. Please come in," she said smiling.

Nash had spent the five minutes he had spare after Khan had been despatched, picking the shards of glass out of the peak of his cap. It now looked an even more ragged affair than usual, though it was still in better condition than his billy pot hat, hence it had been his headwear of choice for this visit. Having taken it off as he knocked politely at the door, he realised that not wearing his overcoat he had nowhere to thrust it, so screwed it up in his right hand.

"You should not really be using that hand at all you know. Let me take your cap," said Sookey.

Just as in their first meeting an hour ago, Nash was taken by the complete lack of condescension or scolding in her voice. There was none of the usual doctors' 'I know best' attitude.

"Please take a seat," she said motioning to one. "You will take tea with me Alexander?"

"Nashey, everyone calls me Nashey. Yes, tea will slip down well."

Nash never drank other people's tea. They always made it too weak. But he wanted to have a look around before he had to engage in any further conversation and hoped the woman would be too busy making the tea to talk for a while. He was expecting her to reply with something along the lines of 'but Alexander is such a fine name,' but she surprised him.

"Very well, Nashey it is. Please take a seat Nashey. I will not be but a moment."

A large teapot hung over the fireplace like a witch's cauldron, the infusion inside having stewed awaiting his arrival. As his host busied herself with the tea, Nash scanned the room. He sat on a good solid wooden chair, one of two in the room, the other being on the opposite side of the fine wooden table. The first thing to catch his eye was a brightly coloured songbird in a cage on the table, flitting about and chirruping. Above it on the wall was a framed motto 'East West Home's Best'. On a shelf along the entire length of the wall opposite was a collection of wallflowers in a series of glass jam jars. Beneath the shelf on the floor was a roll of fresh wallpaper, a bag of flour and several tins of condensed milk. Across the room next to the fireplace was a coal scuttle, and three boxes, neatly piled on top of one another, which had once held respectively oranges, soap and wet fish. These were ready for breaking into firewood. A pair of button-up boots and a steel button hook lay next to them. The wallpaper on the front wall behind him was peeling off. The front windows had newspapers over the panes, to keep draughts out.

To the right of this was an archway through to a scullery, off which was the back door to the yard. He could not see fully into the scullery but could hear someone rustling about in there.

"Someone in your scullery?" he asked.

"Oh, tis Rose. She tidies up after me and keeps things in order. It is well she does, as I am rather ill at that sort of thing. She pretends to do so with bad grace, but I think she enjoys keeping an eye on me. I hope you understand but I could not receive a gentleman alone, so asked Rose if she could come in to sort some things out. She was delighted to when I told her who was coming. I think she looks forward to meeting you again. I believe you know each other."

Nash resisted the temptation to make the obvious joke about him being no gentleman.

"Yes, me and Rose's paths have crossed once or twice."
He raised his voice. "Ain't that right Rose?"

The third party did not answer and stayed in the scullery out of sight.

But she's earwigging every word, I'll wager, mused Nash silently.

Sookey put a cup of tea in front of him. She knew not to bother to ask about lemon.

"Do you care for milk or sugar?"

"No…er thank you," he added as an afterthought.

He noticed she didn't have any milk or sugar in her tea either. He nodded over at the tins of condensed milk.

"Looking at the amount of condensed you have in the place I thought sure you'd like it sweet and white."

She giggled and coyly put her tiny left hand over her mouth.

"Oh, forgive me Nashey. Please don't think I make sport of you. It is just that I have the tins of condensed milk purely to make wallpaper paste. I would indeed have to be the most determined drinker of sweet white tea to have so many tins in my possession, would I not!?"

Soppy cow thought Nash.

"Who told you to use condensed?"

"Why, Stan, Rose's husband. He tells me that flour and condensed milk make the best wallpaper paste."

No wonder all his nippers is lousy, thought Nash.

He rehearsed the next sentence in his head. Sound your t's boy.

"Condensed does stick better than water but don't mind me telling you, it attracts bugs an' all. You know the worse time for bugs in wallpaper? It ain't the summer like you'd think. It's bleed…blimming Christmas time. Father and the little uns use condensed to put the coloured paper loops up when mother ain't watching, see."

Gawd, when's the last time I said 'blimming', he pondered. He remembered his mother blowing medicine down a newspaper funnel into his throat on one occasion when he was taken ill as a small boy. He had just started his first job, as a 'nipper'; a boy who held a horse for his master and sat guard over goods at the tail end of the cart. His mother was desperate for him to go to work, knowing he would lose his job, and an important source of family income, if he did not.

"Blimming hell mother," he had said, at the disgusting taste of the powder.

She responded by cuffing him round the ear on almost every distinctly uttered word of her reply.

"Don't (cuff) you (cuff) come it (cuff) with (cuff) me (cuff) boy (cuff) and don't (cuff) you (cuff) dare (cuff) say (cuff) that (cuff) word (cuff)."

Thank Christ the old woman didn't have a better way with words, thought Nash, I could have lost my ear! He smiled at the memory. He had heard sentences with more words in them in his life, but none that had been so long in duration. He never did know whether 'that word' had been 'blimming' or 'hell'.

"You smile sir? You make sport of me, I wager."

"No, no what I says is true about condensed, you mark my words. You going to strip the old wallpaper off?

She ignored his question.

"Then why do you smile, sir?" she said knowingly, still suspecting him.

There's that bleeding 'sir' again, he thought.

He widened his eyes in mock horror.

"May I never move! I'm being straight with you. I were smiling because I were just thinking…" He lowered his voice and leaned forward conspiratorially, nodding towards the scullery with a wink. "I wouldn't want to be round Rose and Stan's for Christmas day. I'd be picking up a few presents what I didn't want, see."

They chuckled at this in unison. He was surprised that she had understood his joke, but he knew an honest laugh when he heard it. He had never met a woman who was so full of surprises. That was for sure. He repeated his question about stripping the wallpaper.

"No, I believe not," came the answer.

Gawd she's hopeless, thought Nash.

"You should strip it so as to get rid of all the bugs as might be in the old paper – fleas, bed bugs, cockroaches and the like. Here, I'll do the stripping for you. Payment for you doing my finger. But I ain't doing the pasting an' all. That's for you to do. Fair?"

"That would be very satisfactory," replied Sookey with mock seriousness.

"And you do it with water," said Nash with a mild glare pointing his black finger at her, also in mock seriousness.

"Yes, indeed sir. Now, let me have a look at that finger before you lose the power to point."

The finger received attention. Following on from the warning that it would hurt, there were repeated apologies for the pain being inflicted. But Nash simply shrugged and replied with a different succinct answer each time.

"It's got to be done, ain't it."

"It don't hurt."

"I've had worse done to me."

"Get on with it, woman." This time accompanied by a wink.

He showed no outward signs of the pain he must have been feeling. Sookey had never had such a brave patient. He was indeed a very tough man.

"I want you to take a sip of this whenever the pain gets particularly irksome," she said, proffering him a small dark bottle without a label on it.

"I told you, it ain't that bad. What is it anyhow?" asked Nash.

"It is opium."

"Opium! How the bleeding hell did you get hold of that?!" spouted Nash, before realising what he had said. "Pardon me. It's just surprising a lady such as yourself would have such a thing."

"It is not that which one may find in a Limehouse den, Nashey," she said with a knowing snigger. "It is merely tincture of opium. Laudanum. Perfectly respectable of course. And if good enough for Miss Nightingale, it is good enough for me. And you."

Nash nodded appreciatively.

The conversation continued easily between them over a range of subjects. Nash learned that the songbird was a goldfinch bought from the Club Row & Sclater Street bird market. He replied that there was some home-breeding, but a lot of birds were trapped in Essex. Talking about animals led him to relay he had a cat, thinking that Sookey, unlike Khan, would like the idea of him keeping a cat rather than a dog. He made it clear that it was not a pet. It was kept purely to keep the rats and mice down, and if it didn't eat vermin, it starved as far as he was concerned. He was not wasting good money buying off the cat's-meat man. And when Sookey asked about its name, she was amazed to be told the animal had not been given one.

"It's just a cat, ain't it," said Nash, with a shrug.

Having ascertained its gender, Sookey named the cat Doris, and Nash promised he would call it Doris from now on, while thinking to himself "there's two chances of that happening, none and sod all."

He asked why she had so many flowers indoors.

"For the same reason I have the bird and the bright wallpaper, to give the place colour, to cheer up the gloom. Along with good coffee, that which I miss most about my previous life is colour. The photographs of the newspapers' black and white world do not omit much in Whitechapel I fancy. I never go more than a week without purchasing a bunch or two at the Columbia Road flower market."

When the inevitably awkward question as to his line of work raised its head, Nash suddenly appeared to notice some cream-coloured balls in amongst the coal in the scuttle.

"Eh? Sorry girl, I were miles away, having a butcher's at them funny ball things of yours. Like cricket balls with holes in. Never seen anything like them before."

"Oh, they are ceramic Nashey. They keep the heat in the fire. A clever invention is it not? I will be using them soon no doubt with the weather so inclement an' all."

Nash smirked inwardly at the failed attempt to sound like a local.

'Inclement an' all`. Gawd help us!

He was also far from convinced of the validity of the ceramic balls.

They saw you coming girl. You've been fed some old Codd's wallop down the market by a coster keen to unload some old Christmas stock.

But he kept his thoughts to himself, to keep the conversation where he wanted it.

"Oh yes, I seen them. Down the frog and toad at the Sunday market. Here, I've finished my River Lea, where shall I put the cup?"

Sookey, bemused, smiled uncertainly.

"Frog and toad? River Lea?"

She had not picked up on his use of the word 'butcher's' but Nash's forced, artificial sentence had done the trick.

"It's the rhyming slang of the costers. Frog and toad, road; River Lea, cup of tea."

It had the desired effect. Sookey was fascinated. The fact that she dropped the odd d and g and turned a th into an f on occasion when she remembered to, in what was obviously a ruse to sound more like the people she lived among, made Nash think that she would be interested in the new rhyming slang. She would be keen to start using it herself.

And he was right. He taught her all the ones he knew. 'Ta'ers' meaning cold was her favourite because Nash teased her about her pronunciation, laughing with her that you had to say "ta'ers," dropping the t, whereas she could not help but say "taters." She liked being teased; and strangely seemed to share a sense of humour with this dark, brooding, menacing man from a very different walk of life. From Nash's point of view, this had the desired effect of getting the subject off his line of employment, and the conversation flowed along very nicely thank you thereafter.

The Whitechapel Murderer was never far from anyone's lips, but Nash was not sure how to broach such an unpleasant subject with a true lady. He bided his time and eventually manoeuvred the conversation adroitly to crime and personal safety.

"You shouldn't leave yourself alone in that gallery of yours you know. I could have been anyone. You came out that back room bold as brass when you heard me talking to myself about that funny painter. I saw you were frightened of me first up. And you were right to be an' all. There's bad men about. Cut your throat as soon as look at you, some of them." He leaned forward and deepened his voice to add gravity. "Especially these days."

There was the bait. Now, would she bite?

"Indeed sir, these horrible murders are truly the work of the devil incarnate."

Nash was pleased with both himself and the odd new woman in his life.

Chapter 8

Nash had first come across Shanks when they were young lads. Nash was enjoying a snowball fight with his mates when he received a painful blow to the side of the head. He looked down to find at his feet the remains of a snowball with a stone inside it. He glanced up to see a lad only a couple of feet away laughing. The boy had wrapped the stone in a bit of snow and thrown it at Nash at point blank range when his target wasn't looking. Nash made eye contact with his assailant for a split second, smiling grimly. He would remember that. He then grabbed some snow, turned his back and continued playing with the rest of the gang. Nash later heard that the stone thrower had Scottish ancestry, so from that moment on started calling him Longshanks, and then simply Shanks. And when Nash gave someone a nickname, it stuck.

A few years later, Shanks had been second in the pecking order of the Dorset Street teenage gang, and when its leader Freddie Boy Langton, had been sent down for robbery, Shanks had assumed he would take up the mantle. But young Nash had other ideas, and his first impression of Shanks remained the same.

He ain't worth the skin off my nose. All piss and wind, he is. The sort of cove who thought wearing nothing except a vest out on the street on the coldest day showed how tough he were. And he picked on those he knew he could beat easy, like the meek little Chinese lads down at the docks. He might even pick on them he weren't so sure he could beat so long as he had his mates behind him. And it were always him what would put that last boot in, when the gang had given some cove a good hiding and were scarpering off. And he'd tap lads on the ankle bone when the gang kicked a stone about. But only them who would not kick back. And he always had to say something and throw pretend punches when he met up with the gang. 'Oi dog turds!' or some such. He's nothing an ounce. A wrong 'un.

Nash was a year younger and therefore a year later joining the gang (there was a lower age limit), but this was the only reason he was below Shanks in the pecking order. Nash had planned to move against Freddie shortly in any case. Pick a fight with him, knock him down, shake hands and that would be the end of it. Now he did not have to. But Freddie had been a nasty bit of work, even by the standards of Whitechapel, and there was no telling what he and his gang were capable of, so the rival Adelphi Street gang would not dare set foot in the Dorset Street neighbourhood. But word had spread round the slums like wildfire about Freddie being carted off to Pentonville by the authorities. It was not long before Adelphi Street gang members were seeing how far they could go in his old territory. Two of them had ventured onto Dorset Street in broad daylight and waylaid a little tot who was delivering clean linen to a customer of her mother, a wretchedly poor woman who took in washing. Kinchin Lays (those who stole from small children) were the lowest of the low at the best of times, and for a rival gang to commit such a crime in Dorset Street was really taking a liberty.

When word got back to Shanks, he started rounding up what he considered his gang now, but Nashey was nowhere to be found. He was supposed to be working the railway station but was not there. Shanks was shouting the odds, mostly swear words and blasphemies, as his gang made their way to the corner of Adelphi Street.

"We're bleeding kill them," was Shanks' call to arms.

And armed he certainly was with every small, easily concealed weapon he could get his hands on. By the time they arrived at the corner of Adelphi Street, Shanks was alarmed Nashey was still not with them. He felt sure the rival gang would be waiting for them around the corner, and he knew very well that Nashey would make early inroads into their boys and he himself could stick close to Nashey's shirt tails, thus keeping himself safe while appearing to be in the thick of the battle.

"Where's that bastard Nashey when you need him?!" he bellowed, with a tell-tale crack in his voice.

They turned the corner to find no rival gang. The street was empty of boys save for one blood splattered individual marching towards them head down below a glinting cap. It was Nashey. As he approached, the boys could see there did not appear to be any cuts or abrasions on him. The blood was not his. He did not look up or slow his stride as he mumbled to the gang.

"There won't be no more trouble with the Adelphi."

He passed by them, his face a mix of grim determination and incandescent rage.

"Where you off to?" asked Shanks.

"I got some gelt for old Mrs Turner," replied Nash.

"Who?" asked Shanks.

"She's the old woman whose washing got swiped off the little nipper by the Adelphi," said one of the gang, quietly.

The level of violence perpetrated on the leader of the Adelphi gang, who had not been one of the two who had robbed the little girl, assured there would not be any further trouble from that quarter.

Nothing needed saying. Nash was the leader of the Dorset Street gang from that moment on, Will Roud moving up to second in command and Shanks relegated down to the lowest rank.

Years went by with Nash and Shanks living in proximity, following the same career path of crime. They even worked together on occasion, and there was never any apparent animosity between them, but though not apparent, and certainly unspoken, it was there, nonetheless.

But Nash thought that if there was one thing Shanks had been put on this earth for, it was using his artfulness to follow people and gather information about them. He was ideal for Nash's present requirements.

Consequently, Nash had passed on to him the limited information he had on his quarry. It was assumed, correctly, that Shanks would be able to find the fellow Nash had described as 'black as a widow' easily enough in Broad Street and replace him on watch.

Shanks now waited outside what had turned out to be a Pickford & Co Removals depot. Standing in the cold, he did not like the idea of being his old adversary's servant. But he was being well paid so had to listen when given orders concerning a big fellow in a deerstalker.

"When he comes out follow him. If he makes his way home, follow him. If he heads for a boozer, follow him. Stay with him till he disappears indoors in Doveton Street. And before you ask, never mind what it's about. That's why I'm paying you good money, to just do as you're told, no questions asked."

Shanks wondered why he had been employed rather than one of Nashey's usual confederates such as Roud or one of the Carter brothers. And why was Nashey in such a hurry to get away? Shanks had never seen him so jumpy. He surmised that something was afoot, and he wanted in on it. He decided he would start asking around about Nashey's movements. He could even pay for information, if need be, thanks to what he had been paid on account for the big job he had coming up. But he preferred to think of the wages paid to him being the money he was in turn giving to noses to inform him about his employer. He chuckled slyly to himself at the thought.

Chapter 9

The first letter and postcard signed 'Jack the Ripper', claiming to be from the Whitechapel Murderer, became public knowledge through the newspapers. A legend was born. The crimes themselves had created a huge public outcry, but they were as nothing compared to the effect of the missives and the new nickname they imparted on the killer.

Nash walked into the Ten Bells looking for Khan. The pub was full of newspaper readers and their audiences. The few semi-literate incumbents were stuttering out loud to the open-mouthed, ragged majority every gruesome word of what purported to be the killer's writings, as well as relaying murder scene interviews and police quotes, and any rumour the newspapers had chosen to print. But there were well groomed whiskers and clothes in the pub too. It transpired these belonged to reporters, dispatched post-haste by their employers to get everything and anything they could from deepest, darkest Whitechapel.

A surge of adrenaline coursed through Nash. This was what he had been hoping. This publicity proved him right, that the killings were an acceptable evil. A sense of well-being grappled with an underlying sense of guilt and foreboding, just as it had when he had allowed the killer, Jack the Ripper as he was now known, to escape.

Khan relayed to Nash that he had not got very far before he had handed over to Shanks. The men he had attempted to speak to had been more interested in belittling and abusing a black feller than giving out information to him. Khan had dropped Nashey's name in order to get a civil response from them. He thought one of the men might know Nashey, and so warn the rest to tell him what he wanted to know.

This was the last thing Nash wanted. He needed to keep his interest in the man a secret. But just as he was about to lay into Khan with his tongue for ignoring his orders, the Indian mentioned an incident that gave Nash pause for thought.

"But they stop swearing me when Leppy come. 'Go on, give us fit Leppy!' they shout him. I keep away till Shanks come."

"Good to hear little Leppy's out," said Nash with a nod of appreciation. "Last I heard he were in the Whitechapel workhouse. Poor little sod. He's got head on his shoulders mind, when he ain't having one of them fits."

Khan had seen from Nashey's glaring eyes that he had not been pleased with him, so was relieved thoughts had moved to Leppy. To keep them there he replied with speedy enthusiasm.

"Yes, Nashey, I walk with him. He tell me he did well as mortuary attendant. He get job at funeral parlour. He work there now."

Nash could not help but show bemusement.

"Mortuary attendant?"

"When first woman killed, Polly Nichols, no mortuary to take her. They cut body to find how she die, in shed against workhouse. They need mortuary attendant, clean, lay out body for doctor. Leppy do it."

"Did he now?" said Nashey with a faraway look in his eyes.

Khan was not sure whether this was a question or not. The words appeared so, but the tone and eyes suggested otherwise. He played it safe.

"Yes Nashey."

But he need not have bothered. His answer went unheard.

***

Now he had time to think through his course of action a little more, Nash came to realise that he had a responsibility to ensure no more women came to be attacked. The killer was only allowed to keep his freedom so long as the publicity surrounding the unsolved murders warranted it. The maniac's killing days were over.

Nash's noses were informed that if the man they were watching encountered any prostitute, or any other woman for that matter if there were no other people about, they should make themselves known to the couple. Blunder in on any negotiation or conversation. The man was not to take a woman into any dark courts. They should ensure the man was never left alone with a woman.

Khan would follow these orders without question, but such instructions would certainly have Shanks' devious mind whirring.

Nash realised that it had been a mistake to get Shanks involved. He did not trust the man any further than he could throw him. It had been a calculated risk to use him instead of one of his usual men. He was playing with extremely high stakes, and not wanting anyone he had any respect for to be at risk, he had kept Khan's involvement to a minimum, and given the main leg work to Shanks. If anyone was going to end up in police custody alongside him, it was going to be the wrong un.

But from now on only trusted men were to be used, and if things went wrong and he ended up having his collar felt, he would take full responsibility. Everyone involved would be warned that the following of the target had an illegal element to it, and that should things go wrong they must turn queen's evidence against him. The usual East End law of keeping your mouth shut was not to be adhered to. If the police picked them up and charged them with anything, they were to inform on him to save themselves.

Consequently, Nash tracked down Shanks for what was to be both his first and last debrief. Shanks relayed that when the target had left work, he had followed him. It turned out he was a carman working for Pickfords, carrying people's possessions on and off carts when they moved home. Shanks followed him a few times doing jobs, before he finally left work. The man then stopped off for a drink in the Commercial Tavern. He seemed a bit of a loner; didn't talk to anyone other than having the odd word with a whore or two.

"What's all this in aid of?" queried Shanks. "When I followed the cove back to Doveton Street, one of them Carter brothers tells me he's taking over from me at watching the gaff. Having three noses work a Pickfords man living in a slum. Where's the return in that?"

"I've told you before, it ain't none of your bleeding business."

It was at this point that Nash told Shanks in no uncertain terms that his employment had been terminated.

***

Mary had found Kitty a new place to stay. Mary had no space in her own little hovel, but the lateness of the hour when they escaped from the ponce meant that it was inadvisable to knock up her landlord looking for help. So, she found his rent collector, Fred, who had a second job as a night superintendent in a local tenement block. Fred did not do anything for nothing. Mary had to pay him the last of her gin money as an incentive to get off his backside. He duly put Kitty in a room sharing a bed with a prostitute her own age, who was pleased to have her rent reduced.

Kitty was relieved to have escaped her abuser, but the surge of adrenaline-fuelled excitement she had enjoyed when making a run for it, had soon been replaced by a terrible sense of anti-climax and dread. Her newfound independence had come at a price. She stared with forlorn hopelessness at her new slum abode. It was a sloping roofed garret with peeling walls, crates for furniture save for an old woodworm-ridden chair, a small fire grate and not much else.

She had made a run for it once before. Her orphanage had provided her with scullery maid training from the age of eleven. She knew how to wash plates, light fires, sweep floors, heat hot water and clean a range. The only job she had enjoyed was attending to the hastener. This was a plate warming piece of furniture that also functioned as a room divider protecting the rest of the kitchen and its staff from the heat of the oven. She had sweated like a pig doing the duty but was happy to do so. It was better than the cold damp of her orphanage dormitory. The house which she would visit to learn these skills was however full of servants who would not even speak to her unless it was to verbally abuse the latest recruit to their ranks. On her fourteenth birthday, when the time had come to leave the orphanage for good and become a full-time domestic servant, she had run off with a young man she used to meet on the street corner on the pretext of posting a letter. But the apparent romance of stealing the odd five minutes of chat and canoodling was soon replaced by the reality of life as a ponce's source of income. He had enticed her away with the promise of the job attracting crowds to see the Elephant Man, but soon enough it became clear that she was expected to become a prostitute.

When Fred had dropped her at this new gaff, she had pondered that there must be something she could do for a living other than being a whore or a servant. She would ask Mary for advice.

But when Mary had bid her farewell, she had considered her job as a Good Samaritan finished. She would no doubt see the girl around sometime. The girl owed her a drink.

So, she had been surprised to find the pathetic waif at her door the next day. And it was fortunate that Mary's donation to Fred's coffers meant that not nursing a hangover for once, she was in the right frame of mind to be helpful to the young girl.

It was clear that the first thing they needed to do was

to retrieve Kitty's things from her abandoned room. Fearful Kitty's pimp would be lying in wait for her, Mary enlisted the help of her old friend, Nashey.

He had seemed rather preoccupied when the two women had tracked him down. But when Kitty's plight had been explained to him, he had begrudgingly agreed to give them a few minutes of his time.

When the three of them reached the little slum, she had shared with her ponce, Kitty gave Nash her key and cowered behind him nervously, looking away down the street as if she were contemplating running away. Mary stood confidently with hands on hips next to the door and scolded her young charge.

"You're in no danger here, you daft ha'p'orth."

Nash used Kitty's key and walked in with Mary right behind him. Kitty heard a bellow from a voice she recognised, a few thunderous running steps from heavy boots on floorboards, some other brief noises she didn't recognise and then silence.

Mary stuck her head back round the doorframe and motioned to Kitty with an irritated sideways nod of the head.

"Come on, we haven't got all day. Get your backside in here and tell us what you want to take with you."

Kitty peered in and gasped. Her ex-ponce Harold lay flat out on the floor, eyes closed, motionless; dead or unconscious, she could not tell which. Nash stood over the prone figure, reaching down and rummaging through his pockets to see if he had anything on him worth stealing. He did not.

"He went down a bit quicker than when I hit him," said Mary with a knowing nod towards Nash.

In his usual gruff manner with strangers, Nash had barely acknowledged Kitty when Mary had introduced them to each other. But now, as she thanked him for dealing with the ponce, he thought her face rang a bell with him.

"Ain't I seen you somewhere before, girl?" he enquired.

Kitty did not think so, but for all she knew he could have been a customer of hers. She had a way of approaching men for business while not focussing on them. They were just a piece of faceless meat as far she was concerned, just as she was to them. She could walk past a client in the street moments after he had been inside her, and she would not recognise him.

"Don't know, Mr Nash," came the non-committal, vague reply.

Mary smirked.

"I know what you're thinking Kit and the answer is no. Mr Nash here, does not go in for that sort of thing. And even if he did, he would not use a whore. Beneath her dignity as well as his own, do you see?"

Nash glared at her before letting go a volley of abuse that made it clear that there was a limit to the cheekiness she could get away with, and she had just exceeded it. Mary knew it was time to apologise and shut up. The argument was immediately forgotten, as was usual between these two feisty characters. And given he was so preoccupied; Nash did not think any further about when or where he had seen Kitty in the past.

Chapter 10

Sookey lived in dark, narrow little Widegate Street. Just fifty yards from the busy, prosperous thoroughfare of Bishopsgate, it was the closest she could live to the City of London, yet still be in what had recently started to be known as 'slums`. The term was an improvement; she had never cared for 'rookeries' and what that implied.

She had money; not a great deal after her recent financial debacle, but she certainly did not need to live in such surroundings. But she desired the anonymity of the poverty stricken and wanted to be of the slums, not merely a visitor to them, as she had in the past. She wished to be accepted by the local populace as one of their own, and in so doing, cease to be what she had always been.

Though she chose to live amongst the poor, she also felt the need to be able to escape quickly to her old world, albeit just for the odd hour or two, when life got unbearable. She allowed herself one great luxury when life got on top of her. The thing she missed most of her old life was drinking best quality coffee. She could not abide the pond water which passed for coffee in Whitechapel. So, on occasion she ventured out of the slums, in her one clean dress, to a fine coffee house on the Strand. She would meet an old acquaintance, Nora. This lady was not a friend per se, but all Sookey's so-called friends had deserted her, or she had chosen to drop them because she would have felt awkward in their company. Sookey felt more comfortable with Nora, partly due to the two of them not being particularly close, but also because the woman had never judged her. They would pass a pleasant hour making the small talk in which middle class ladies were so well versed, without ever venturing on to the sort of topics discussed by real friends. This suited Sookey very well. And there was never any question of visiting each other's homes.

Nora knew her friend had been financially ruined, but she also knew Sookey had an army officer's widow's pension and had not needed to seek a position, so assumed she must still be at least comfortable.

Sookey lied about her circumstances and lifestyle, but it was important to her to bend the truth, embroider or exaggerate rather than tell outright falsehoods whenever possible. And when lies did need telling, she kept them little and white.

Her story went that she lived in the City close to Liverpool Street station (the second part was true); she spent a lot of her time in the slums helping people (true); she was a close friend of Reverend Barnett and his wife Henrietta (more just friendly work colleagues really); and lectured at the reverend's centre for the help and improvement of the poor, Toynbee Hall (she handed out soup and coffee, had set up an impromptu art gallery, and gave some arithmetic, literacy and art classes rather than lectured as such).

And she managed to keep up sartorial appearances too. Even though she kept her home relatively spotless, it was impossible to keep anything completely clean and fresh in the grime of slum life, so she had a reciprocal arrangement with an illiterate tailor who kept a dress for her in immaculate condition at the back of his workshop, and in return she wrote anything he needed. Advertising-related mostly, though she would also write the odd private letter, and read him any answers received.

The first time she took the dress from the tailor she changed into it in the public washhouse in Goulston Street. There was a little drying room there that she could pop in and out of very quickly, and it was the cleanest place in Whitechapel. And it had the added benefit of being next to a tram stop from where she travelled west. She did not want to risk getting the dress dirty from the foul air and filthy streets close to her home.

Sookey used the facilities at the washhouse regularly. It had soap, hot water, towels and a laundry with washing troughs, boilers, irons, drying horses and mangles. Although provided by a philanthropist, it was not free, so the poorest women were unable to use it, but it was nonetheless an important social, as well as work centre. Many women in the neighbourhood did their laundry and socialised there. Sookey had hoped it would be a place in which she could interact with some of these women. To build, if not friendships, for she appreciated she had little in common with them and completely failed to understand their ribald humour, at least an acceptance, a fellowship.

She had found this difficult at first. The women were friendly enough amongst themselves, the endless gossip and double entendre, none of which Sookey understood, helping pass away the hours of backbreaking steamy drudgery. But Sookey remained just as big an outsider as she had always been. Worse in fact. When she had been a lady charity worker, a slummer, women of the slums had at least been respectful to her, if not particularly communicative.

But lady slummers did not do their own washing in the public washhouse. The group's initial reaction was to be taciturn with her, and she noticed the atmosphere of the place change dramatically as soon as she walked in. Banter replaced by exchanged glances; words mouthed silently. If she asked a question about how things worked or enquired if anyone was using a piece of equipment, it was answered by a curt reply.

"Everyone's finished with it so you can have it but you're too late for hot."

But her inability to work much of the equipment, and her obvious general ineptitude, gradually changed the suspicion to amazement and savage sarcasm, and over the weeks eventually to a warmer amusement.

Her next-door neighbour Rose started helping her with a mix of exasperation and camaraderie. When Sookey failed to grasp how to work a simple mangle, tangling the clothes, she was castigated for jamming the contraption.

"You're an awkward sod and make no mistake! I've never seen anything like it in all my life. Soppy as a box o' lights you are girl!"

It was soon after this that she had acquired her nickname. She occasionally had someone shout across the street to her.

"Soppy-ey!" with the end 'ey' higher pitched and louder than the first, bone man shout-style, which was a common form of friendly greeting from afar.

She had never been addressed in such a way, but a moment of shock and effrontery was immediately replaced by a feeling of well-being. The acquisition of a nickname, albeit derogatory, was a badge of honour. Better known as soppy than as the things she had been called in the witness box at the trial. Better the butt of good-natured humour than the barbs of a barrister, playing to the crowd up in the gallery.

But some of the women were still suspicious of her.

"She's more ar than eff that one," was said knowingly.

They were convinced nobody could be that stupid. She was putting it on, and for what purpose?

And when she appeared from the drying room wearing a 'hoity-toity' frock, and quickly disappeared without so much as a by-your-leave, even the friendliest of the women started to doubt her.

Sookey had been aware of the sideways glances at the time, so eager to explain about the dress, she made a point of hurriedly returning to the washhouse, laundry basket only half full, when she knew the regulars would next be there. She was naïve enough to tell the truth, explaining she kept the dress for trips to the West End.

"Cor, you're lucky ain't yer!" came the sarcastic reply.

But the barb flew over its target's head. A couple of the natural comedians in the group then started a conversation between themselves using high-pitched approximations of middle-class voices.

"Oh, it's so nice to take the air up west at this time of year, don't you think my dear?"

"Yes, indeed my dear, I hoften pops up to Hampstead Heath for me health don't you know."

Sookey giggled at the added aitch, but immediately worried that the women may take this amiss, so hoped they would think she was self-deprecatingly laughing at the mimicry. Luckily, the women did, so the moment passed in good humour.

She now waited till she arrived in the West End and changed in a department store lavatory. She entered the store a pauper and left a lady. She wrapped her day-to-day outer clothes in some fine paper and ribbon she kept precisely for this purpose and passed it off to Nora as her latest frippery purchase. She wondered if Nora ever thought it strange that she never wore any of these purchases, just the same dress. Did she know of her friend's life in the slums?

Nora did not know; Nora did not want to know.

Chapter 11

Prostitution had been a last resort. Since cashing in her return train ticket, committing to a new life in London, Mary had tried her hand at various jobs for as long as they lasted or until a day's work was missed through illness and she found her job given to someone else. That was a common enough occurrence. The poverty in which she lived and the appalling conditions of most of the sweated labour she did, meant she was permanently suffering from one ailment or another and it was only a question of time before she became so ill that she could not get out of bed one day.

Amongst other things she had made cigarettes, magic lantern slides, ties, surgical instruments, spectacles. 8am to 7pm; 10 or 11 if she could get the overtime. Half day Saturday. Some of the best employment in terms of pay and conditions insisted upon a genteel appearance. Mary had stinted on underclothes and food to buy nice clothes to meet such a demand, but had fallen ill from near-starvation, and lost these jobs.

There was one job where a few nice clothes and no underwear was the uniform of choice. West End prostitute. But even this had not lasted long. She had soon found herself in the East End, where the steadiest work was at the Bryant & May factory in Bow. But it involved working with phosphorous. It was nasty stuff. Workers suffered from phossy jaw. Poisoned jaws decayed with pea-sized fragments of bone flaking off.

But Mary suffered from necrosis before the poison fully worked its horror. She had swollen lips and throat, closing eyes, skin that emitted pus, and a fever with accompanying delirium, nausea and vomiting. She recovered intact but vowed never to enter the factory again.

She escaped the factory by becoming a home worker in the same industry. She did the 'ins and outs`; making the trays and covers of matchboxes, pasting together thin pieces of wood by brush, forming piles of trays and lids that were made into matchboxes, tied up with string and returned to the factory. Pay – twopence-farthing a gross. She had to work sixteen hours a day to keep out of the workhouse so changed to being a canvas worker making shop blinds, hammocks, tents and coal sacks. Fifteen hours a day. Her last job before returning to prostitution was a fur-puller. A shilling and a penny for skinning five dozen rabbits. It was filthy work, with fluff everywhere, and when a friend died of consumption brought about by this job, Mary decided anything was better than this.

It was ironic that she had been too ill to last long enough in the Bryant & May factory to get phossy jaw. She still had her looks, so was able to become one of the unfortunates, the scorned, the shamed and expendable. An East End prostitute.

She swopped phossy jaw, necrosis and consumption for rheumatism, syphilis and nowadays the chance of meeting a maniac.

On the face of it, Mary and Sookey were opposites who attracted. The fiery young prostitute and the middle class slummer had little in common. Mary was intelligent, shrewd and streetwise; Sookey, though well educated, had been a poor student and had the naivety of a child.

But Sookey suspected the backgrounds of the two of them may not have been so different. Her young friend was surprisingly well spoken for someone in her situation, showed an interest in Sookey's art gallery and had the air of a well brought up young lady. It was only when she was drinking that her behaviour fitted neatly into the pigeonhole of East End whore.

They had first met when they had actually bumped into each other in the local pharmacy buying face powder. A liking for visually striking make-up and hair was something they did have in common. The collision had been Mary's fault, but she was the worse for drink and when in such condition was not the sort to apologise to anyone about anything. She rounded on the woman into whom she had drunkenly barged, ready to give as good as she got. But all she saw was a genteel smile, quickly accompanied by an apology.

"I do beg your pardon. It was entirely my fault."

Mary looked her up and down suspiciously with chin pushed forward. She wondered if the apology had been a sarcastic one. But the look of apparent genuine concern in the woman's face suddenly changed to the warmest of smiles.

"It would seem we share an interest," said Sookey,

looking at Mary's make-up and then her own.

It was the same.

The ice broken; they began the first of their conversations together. The older woman had marvelled at the younger one's striking lip rouge and asked if she could borrow some until she acquired some of her own. She wanted to rid herself of the look of her previous life.

Yes, I can see that from that cheek rouge you have plastered on yourself like some doll, thought Mary, but she kept this to herself.

"Give it a rest," she said. "This is not for the likes of you. There's only two types of women who use lip rouge, whores and actresses."

"You tread the boards, Mary?" It was honest, naïve interest.

Mary thought the question spoken in jest, so let out a snort, but there was sarcastic contempt in her voice when she answered.

"Oh yes, I do plenty of acting all right."

The two women intoxicated each other; Mary by Sookey's neediness. The only time Mary had had some responsibility in her life, it had been taken away from her. And now she was always the new young girl, in a factory, in a sweat shop, on the street. The one who needed to be shown things; the pretty one to be put in her place, to be jealous of, to resent, to be left out or belittled whenever possible. She was an only child; the still-birth of what would have been her little sister causing internal problems that ended her mother's ability to have children. The distraught woman never thought so, but she had been lucky in one way. Having only one child to feed had kept her family

112

relatively well-heeled, and she insisted her daughter stay on at school right up to the official leaving age of thirteen.

Sookey, though ten years Mary's senior, rekindled somewhat the maternal instinct of the younger woman. Sookey was someone who needed protecting; and being educated in the ways of the world. And she so lacked confidence, though Mary had enough of this commodity for the two of them. Not that she would allow her friend to stay as she was. She needed to learn. A day would not go by without Mary good naturedly mock berating her new pupil for some misdemeanour.

"For goodness' sake Sookey, look what you've done, you daft ha'p'orth." Though if she had been drinking, the same message was relayed in a robust style more in keeping with her job title and location. "Gawd help us, what you gone and done now, you daft mare."

The first time she was insulted, the older woman's flash of effrontery and embarrassment was soon overridden by warmer feelings. She saw within the sparkle in her eyes that it was Mary's way of telling Sookey that she liked and accepted her.

Sookey's medical skills had once led her to save the life of a little boy with diphtheria. And she had done so free of charge. She thought it would break down the barriers she had encountered in the slums, but although the parents had been incredibly grateful, and it led to her becoming the unofficial doctor of the neighbourhood, she was disappointed to find that people still did not award her the acceptance she desperately sought. She remained an outsider to all but her good friend Mary.

Sookey was in awe of the young woman's vivacity in

the face of the most appalling poverty. She had to sell her body, which Sookey knew she hated doing with a passion, just to keep herself fed, housed and in drink. But she fiercely refused any hint of financial assistance from her wealthier friend.

On a dark miserable afternoon when Sookey was attempting to take her friend to task for not trying a more respectable line of work, Mary had relayed her recent, though not her early, life story over a bottle of sherry.

Sookey had received the alcohol from one of her clients in lieu of payment for some writing she had done for him, when he was too financially embarrassed to hand over cash. Although pleased to see the bottle, especially as sherry was so expensive and therefore quite a luxury item, Mary had been quick to pass on the latest of her lessons.

"Get their money first Sookey. Do not do anything till they pay you. None of my lot would pay me if I let them have their way first. They would scarper, and if I were to catch up with them, they'd fetch me a facer for my trouble."

The pupil was attempting to repay her life skills tutor by providing her with more formal education. But this was easier said than done, as her young friend was already well versed in the three r's, Sookey's favoured subjects in which to give lessons at Toynbee Hall. Sookey had endured countless hours of tuition in French conversation at her finishing school for young ladies, but Mary had made it clear she had no interest in learning the language. That left just English, religious studies, history and geography, but Sookey had been a poor pupil herself in these subjects. She thought that perhaps she could combine the latter two. She assumed that, given her surname, Mary may be interested to know something of Ireland, but this proved not to be the case. Miss Kelly's Irish roots were seemingly at least a couple of generations back because she made a less than flattering comment about her ancestor's country of origin.

Xenophobia was one of the many survival techniques of the poor. Our street against the next; our neighbourhood against theirs; the East End, London, England against the rest. The country that was failing them, starving and working them to death, received a fierce allegiance from the voteless of the slums.

Mary's cultured ways when sober intrigued her middle-class friend. And her having no regional accent, save for the East End colloquialisms she had picked up along with the sizeable vocabulary of swear words she used when drunk, resulted in an inquisitive Sookey wishing to probe her on this. And she felt she now knew Mary well enough to make such an enquiry.

"Your Joe tells me you are as much Welsh as you are Irish, Mary, but I hear no evidence of it. Indeed, may I be so bold as to suggest you appear quite middling in manner. May I have the temerity to enquire how you arrived here in Whitechapel."

Sookey had come to appreciate that she needed to simplify her vocabulary whilst in the East End. But she had deliberately used the word 'temerity' to see if Mary queried its meaning. She did not.

"Well, when I first went whoring it was in the West End. Allowing gentlemen to proposition me and have me take them home to a little place I had in Covent Garden. Then this fellow picks me up and he must have put something in my drink. Next thing I know I'm waking up on a train heading for the coast. He feeds me some old Cod's wallop about servicing rich men in Paris, wearing nice clothes and being driven around in a pony and trap. Turns out he's a white slaver. I never got any further than Dieppe. Filthy hole. Mostly had grubby sailors as clients. They kept me and some other girls locked up. Looked bad for me there for a while but to keep the police happy they had to have us girls inspected regularly. I'd started pissing pins and needles at the time. I tell this inspector woman when she comes round, and she thinks I might have the pox. She insists the slavers let me go. They reckon I'm putting it on. Threaten me with all sorts. Say they're out of pocket and would come after me if they ever see me in London again. But they had to do what they were told, see. They boot me out. I've no money but I get myself back home. Got on a ship on the understanding from the skipper I was the ship's whore for the journey. Had them standing in a line waiting their turn. I get off the ship at Tower Hill walking bandy. Didn't want to risk running into the white slavers again so I turn east instead of west. Then the nuns in Providence Row night shelter here in Whitechapel help me. They had a doctor come in and sort me out. Turns out I only had something wrong with my waterworks that lots of women get."

Sookey was eager to join in the conversation to make a point, so cut in at this point.

"Cystitis, I suspect is the condition to which you refer, Mary. I wished to attend a lecture about it in Kensington last year by a chap, name of Dr Skene. Unfortunately, I was unable to gain admittance. Only gentlemen admitted, do you see. It is a bladder infection which any lady can be unfortunate enough to receive, though a prostitute is more likely to suffer from it. And there are other sexual diseases too. Can you not stop…"

"Don't start Sookey," interrupted Mary, speaking slowly with an air of cold determined menace. "I will not do sweated work again. Neither will I pass through the gates of Bryant & May. And I will not go without a roof over my head."

"But what of domestic service Mary? You would get bed & board at least."

"Yes, you're right to say 'at least`. Bed & board and not much else. I am not being a skivvy for twelve pound a year. I've seen maids looking down their noses at me because they think I'm rough, but I get neck ache from looking so far down on them for being skivvies."

Her time in Whitechapel had brought home to Sookey the amount of snobbery contained within the working classes. Everyone seemed to be looking up or down at everyone else. And Mary seemingly being from a higher class, only exaggerated such snobbery. But Sookey was not going to let her win this argument, so she continued.

"But what of this maniac roaming our streets at night? It is surely desirable to perform work during the day. Selling things perhaps? Flowers, apples, ginger beer?"

"Yes, and perhaps I can do a bit of chimney sweeping as well?" came the sarcastic reply. "Those sorts of jobs don't pay enough for me to drink. And I'm sleeping the drink off half the day so I cannot do work where you have to keep an eye on the clock. And don't worry about maniacs. I know how to look after myself."

"But surely the answer is to abstain. Could you not sign the pledge, Mary?"

Mary took a breath, smiled grimly, lowered her voice and gave her friend the eyes to warn her to back off.

"No, I bloody well could not. Drinking's the only way I have of getting away!"

The irony was that not enough of Sookey's sherry had yet been consumed to bring out Mary's drunken temper, which saved her host from a verbal assault. Mary resisted the temptation to round on her friend to tell her the home truth that it was all right for the likes of her, with her army officer widow's pension. She could bugger off to the West End whenever she wanted.

Sookey was aware that it would be advisable to change the subject. Another thing about Mary she thought both intriguing and puzzling was that, despite her lack of interest in the French language, she was thinking of changing her name to Marie Jeanette.

"I do apologise Mary. It is not for me to say such things. Let us change tack. I have of course changed from being a Susan to a Sookey, so I am intrigued by your desire to follow a similar path. Pray tell how you chose such a beautiful, dare I say exotic, new name."

"Well, when I got to France, when I told them my name was Mary Jane, they changed it to Marie Jeanette. C'est la vie, mon amie!" she said with a grim, sarcastic smile until it was replaced by a dark frown. "It was no life though. And I had no friends. I was at a low ebb. And I decided that I should not like to have the name Mary Jane any longer in any case. Jane had been a beautiful girl's name. I did not deserve it. I deserve to be a whore and have a whore's name."

Sookey noted the past tense. 'It had been a beautiful

girl's name'? Was Mary talking about a specific person? And why does she deserve to be a whore? Nobody deserves that, surely. She wondered for a moment whether Mary's reference to the past might mean she wished to discuss it. But one look at the expression on her friend's face told her not to venture there.

Instead, Sookey pondered that it had only been two short expressions, but the French pronunciation had been correct, and the translation clearly understood. The suspicion that Mary was quite well educated in her earlier life grew apace.

But Sookey thought she should say something to make it clear she understood Mary would prefer to move the conversation in another direction.

"So, you're an Irish, Welsh woman with a French name Marie Jeanette!" she said lightly.

Mary looked at Sookey seriously for a moment and then her face relaxed. She gave a faint smile before replying.

"Yes, that's right Sookey. Well, when I first met Joe, I fed him some old cock and bull story about me being born in Ireland, brought up in Wales and having a French name. Wanted to sound different I suppose. You know what it's like when you first meet a fellow. They give you a load of old flannel and you give it back. I didn't want him to know all my business. Why should he? I once met an Irish Welsh girl. She was nice and helped me start to sort myself out in a manner of speaking. So, when I first got to London, I made myself Irish Welsh. But truth be told I don't know anything about Ireland and the closest I've come to Wales was when father took me to … a train station to see the Great Western steamers on their way to Wales when I was little. Came home smothered in soot! Looked like a sweep! Could have grown turnips in my ears after that!"

Sookey spotted that Mary had stopped for a moment when she was about to name the train station. And then attempted to cover it up by switching into a joker's routine. It was clear that her roots were a very private matter. Sookey had been right not to ask the obvious questions earlier.

Mary's life story, such as it was, finished halfway through the bottle. Although not always the most tactful of people, she did not ask Sookey to reciprocate. She surmised that her odd friend had some sort of secret she must be running away from, but it was probably too painful for her to talk about. That made two of them.

Chapter 12

Social explorers, churchmen and politicians were quick to castigate the poor for what they believed to be feckless housekeeping, such as purchasing food from shops in small expensive quantities or giving trade to street vendors. But if they had insufficient to buy staples from shops in larger cheaper quantities, they bought 'tasters'; a ha'pence' of this, a 'pennyworth' of that, usually from the corner shop because they could do so on credit. Or they bought meals off the street to save precious time as well as cooking costs. Nash had been brought up in such a household, and although he was much better off than his parents because he had no family to support, old habits die hard. He still spent much of his income on things that made life easier.

He did not even own a razor. He never shaved himself, preferring, to go for a shave twice a week at a shaving parlour. Why mess about trying to get a lather over a bucket of cold water in the yard in all weathers, when you could have two shaves for a penny ha'penny at the barber?

He didn't need a shave at present but headed for one in any case, primarily to relax and think things through about the killings, and what to do next.

His closest barber shop was a squalid affair from where he had caught 'devil in the beard', a minor but irritating skin disease from the use of dirty razors. He had not used it since. There were several other places within a few minutes' walk, all of which he had tried over the years, but every one of them grossly exploited their lather lads, who worked twelve hours a day, six days a week for five shillings a week. Hardly a month went by without Nash giving some street urchin a cuff round the ear for something or another, but he had a secret regard for them.

He remembered very well his own days at that age. He had not been a lather lad but his first job as a butcher's boy has been just as tough. Four shillings a week; work till nearly midnight some Saturdays, and then back in on the Sunday morning if there was still meat to sell. And never a kind word or deed from either the butcher or his wife. The day Nash had left home to go his own way, he had resigned from the butcher's employ courtesy of piling as much meat as he could carry into a horse sack and making a run for it.

The barber shop he now used, down in St George's in the East, was run by a miserable but fair old man who treated his lads better than most. Nash walked under the haircutting and shampooing sign above the door and entered. It was his normal day for a shave but he had broken his usual pattern by visiting the barber yesterday in readiness for meeting Sookey for the first time.

"Didn't expect you in today," was the terse welcome from the proprietor. "Three shaves in a week. Got a fancy piece, have you?"

"Don't your jaw ache?" replied his client sourly.

Nash always went to the barbers at a time when he knew the shop would be busy. He liked the wait. Nobody talked to him or knew him from Adam in this part of town. He enjoyed being anonymous, just listening to the other customers. He usually stood waiting his turn, but he had a lot on his mind, so sat down on the plank next to the wall, leaned back and closed his eyes.

He considered what he had recently discussed in Sookey's gaff. He had been aware that he could not have simply started discussing with her why whores didn't bleed like other people.

Gawd, imagine her ladyship's shock if I'd have said what I wanted straight out.

"Sookey, you know doctoring don't you, so why don't whores bleed? Is it because they most likely all got syph?"

So, I go all round the houses, till she asks what I want her to ask.

"How can this monster walk through the streets with impunity?"

"Well, he ain't got no blood on him for one thing. He could walk right past a copper plain."

"Pray tell sir, how do you have knowledge of such a thing?

"Never mind all that. The fact is the wounds ain't bled much. So, I'm asking you, could a disease stop blood shedding? Pardon me for putting such an impolite question to a lady but may I be so bold as to ask, could it be syphilis what's caused it?"

"Certainly not, no illness could have such an effect. If there is little loss of blood, there can be but only one answer. The injuries were clearly inflicted post-mortem."

What the bleeding hell's 'post-mortem' when it's at home, I thinks to myself. But then she's looking at me funny.

"I repeat sir, how do you know that little blood is shed?"

I gaze at the scullery to avoid her eyes, while I think up an answer. The scullery! Christ, Rose! Crafty cow's earwigging.

I take her ladyship away to the Ten Bells, where I slips her a version of Will's story about there being no blood. But on that subject, she proves about as much use as a pocket in a shroud. She comes up with the notion the murderer must be killing them before he knifes them. And that way the heart has stopped pumping when he cuts them, and that's why there ain't much blood. There's been no mention in the papers of marks on the bodies so they couldn't have been beaten. She reckons the killer could be strangling them and then starts cutting them up when they're already dead. Post-mortem as she calls it. She says post-mortem means after death. That's why they calls the cutting up by the police surgeon a post-mortem. So I asks why would the killer waste his time doing such a thing with half of London's constabulary bearing down on him? It don't stand to reason. But she don't have no answer for that.

And she gets on my nerves. All that jawing. I were in the pub with her for hours. Talking about everything under the sun. It ain't natural. And she gets things out of you, crafty like. Bugger me if I ain't told her about my ragged schooling. It ain't right people knowing all your business. No, when her ladyship ain't about I'm a man of few words and that's how I likes it. She's more trouble than she's worth. She's got plenty of skills I could use, and it's obvious she's taken a shine to me which makes things easier, but I've got other fish to fry. I won't have nothing more to do with her if I has my way.

He was feeling uncomfortable about the whole business, when he felt a tap on his right foot, so opened his eyes to see the barber glaring down at him.

"Here, cloth ears! Woke up, have you? You want this shave, or don't you?"

It was clear that Nash had been so deep in thought that he had not heard the barber call that it was his turn. Nash would normally have grabbed the old misery by the throat and muttered something appropriately menacing. But on this occasion, he was glad of the old man's intervention. And besides, nobody knew him in this neck of the woods. He did not have any reputation to defend; no appearance to live up to. He kept silent and meekly got into the chair. He watched the barber's skill at sharpening his razor on a leather strap; not the most interesting of pursuits but it was preferable to closing his eyes again.

***

With Sookey now in the past, Nash had tried to give up thinking about why prostitutes didn't bleed much. It was not so important in the swing of things. It was more curiosity than anything that had led him to thinking about it in the first place. It was not going to help him find out who this Jack the Ripper was. Or help him decide what to do about the killer. Nevertheless, the lack of blood was an itch he could not scratch, so he had gone to the trouble of finding out where Wal Newman, the epileptic, otherwise known as Leppy, was working these days. Nash thought it would not do any harm to see if Leppy had any ideas about the blood. After all, other than a few policemen and doctors, he had more first-hand knowledge than anyone else about the body of one of the victims. If anyone could tell Nash something useful it was this fellow. But he didn't want Leppy to know he had anything but normal lurid interest in the killings.

Will had done some nosing about for him and armed with knowledge of Leppy's movements to and from work, Nash arrived on the street corner opposite the funeral parlour at the appropriate time and did not have long to wait for his man to appear. Not wishing Leppy to know he had been looking for him, the meeting had to appear happenstance.

"Leppy-ey!" shouted Nash as he crossed the street. "Good to see you out and about boy! Thought you were still inside the `house."

There was a shake of the head in reply.

"No, I been out a few weeks now Nashey. Had a bit a luck for a change."

"Oh yes, how's that? You ain't still throwing fits even when you're not throwing them proper are you?" asked Nash, referring to Leppy's previous occupation of bogus fit-thrower.

Leppy was an epileptic but did not suffer the disease as badly as some. The occasional real attack had given him the knowledge and ability to fake many others in a believable manner. He mostly worked the churches and chapels. It was important to appear a decent-looking, neat, threadbare, hollow-eyed man, collapsing in convulsions, with limbs threshing and foam spewing from the mouth. On appearing to regain his faculties, he tells the crowd, which had inevitably gathered, of his tragic circumstances.

He then produced papers, apparently signed by a clergyman (forged by a screever), describing him as a man of good character, pious, industrious but prone to seizures that had reduced him to penury and commending him to Christian charity. A resulting collection taken. It was a living. Just.

Leppy grinned.

"No, got fed up with the taste of soap."

Nash frowned.

"Used to put soap shavings under my tongue to fake the foam," explained Leppy. "Besides, I were running out of places to do it. There's only so many churches and chapels ain't there? They only looks after you the once. Second time they shies away. I tried the boozers at chucking out time but all I got was a reviver. You can't live on spirits, can you?"

"Some try," said Nash sagely. "So, what were your bit of luck then?"

"I had a real attack see. Bad one it were. Worst I've ever had. It were in that first particular, last month. Remember, it were a real thick one, couldn't see your hand in front of your face. Nobody had come near or by. Everyone just wants to get where they're going when the fog comes down, don't they? I were just coming to my senses when a couple of lads rolled me. Took me last. Gave me a good hiding an' all just for the sport." He then added with gravity, "I'll know them again though."

"Let me know if you need any help boy," offered Nash solemnly.

"No, I won't need none. Once I find out who they are I'll visit them both, one at a time. Wrong uns like them won't be so clever on their own. And I won't already be down this time, will I?"

"So that were your bit of luck, were it?" asked Nash sarcastically. "I wouldn't have a few bob each way on no nags at Hurst Park if I were you."

"Funny sod ain't you?" retorted Leppy. "Anyhow, I were in a bad way. Had nowhere to go except the `house. But I were right as ninepence soon enough. Whitechapel workhouse is worse than most, full of broken old men waiting to die. I were the only young, fit cove in there. I starts helping the nurses just for something to do. This doctor sees me and the next thing I know he's got me helping him. And then, blow me if I ain't laying out some old whore for a post-mortem as they calls it, soon after she's had her throat and private parts cut. Didn't know it at the time of course, but it turns out to be one of the Whitechapel Murderer's bits of work. The doc cut her some more to find things out."

"Post-mortem?" queried Nash. He had already had the term explained to him by Sookey but wanted Leppy to appear to be the font of all knowledge on the subject.

"That's what they calls it when they slices them up after death for the inquest. It's some sort of Italian for 'after death' I were told. Don't know what they got to start speaking eyetie for."

"I know someone who speaks it," replied Nash. "Hello is her favourite word if you please."

"Can't say I've heard of that. What's it mean?"

Nash was irritated with himself for getting off the subject.

"Never mind all that, tell us more about this laying out business. You got to see old Polly Nichols while she were still warm eh? Must have been a right old mess. Blood all over the shop I shouldn't wonder."

"How do you know it were Polly Nichols?"

Nash had to think quickly on his feet.

"You said you been out the workhouse for a while, so it weren't the last few killed, and Polly Nichols were the one sliced up right by Whitechapel workhouse so it don't take no Sherlock Holmes to work out she must have been the one you laid out."

Leppy nodded.

"Yes, never thought of that. No, she weren't that covered in blood funny enough. Loads of holes, like a ruddy pepper pot, she were, but blood just oozed out of them. You'd have had a job to fill a wine glass with the lot."

"A Rum do, that's for sure," said Nash matter-of-factly, trying not to sound too interested. "Doctor say anything about it?"

"Well, he didn't make a lot of sense, truth be told. Said as how the wounds must have been done post-mortem. What a load of old Cod's, I ask you!"

"Yes, the doctors on these murders don't know what they're on about do they?" agreed Nash disingenuously.

He thought that perhaps that Sookey were worth keeping in with after all.

Chapter 13

Shanks had gathered much useful information. Nashey had been heard preaching to all who would listen about the killings being a good thing for the East End, for poor people everywhere. Nobody else appeared to agree with this view, and Shanks thought that if it had been anyone else, they would have got a facer on the nose. And if that hadn't been enough to shut him up, a good kicking up an alleyway would have done the trick. But who would attempt such a thing on Nashey?

Shanks had found out that Nashey had been asking around about the murdered whores, and had also spent quite some time with the slummer, Soppy Sookey. One of Shanks' paid cohorts had been told by big Rose that Nashey had specifically sought her out. Rose had been only too pleased to pass on what she had overheard in her neighbour's scullery. She relayed that Nashey had wanted medical knowledge. He seemed to think that all the murdered women must have had syphilis for some reason.

"And what if they did? What's it got to do with him? Why's he interested in the murderer any more than the rest of us, eh?" Rose had enquired.

And Shanks thought the same. He was both puzzled and suspicious. He knew Nashey must be up to something.

He mulled it over in his mind. It took him a while but eventually came the flash of inspiration.

Gawd almighty! The Pickfords cove! Nashey must think he's old Jack!

But no sooner had this revelation come to him and he was putting a dampener on his own idea.

But what's that got to do with medical matters? There must be more to it than that. What if a doctor were paying Jack to kill whores who has syphilis? Perhaps Jack's collecting bits of the women's bodies for him for what them doctors call medical research or something like that?

Whatever the reasons, it was not a concept to Shanks that Nash could be choosing to let the killer go free for anything other than selfish criminal reasons. His imagination ran riot. It was clear to him that Nashey was going to blackmail the killer or whoever was paying him to do the killings. That was why he wanted him followed. Shanks could not help but be impressed by the plan.

Blackmailing Jack the Ripper himself! Only Nashey would dare such a thing!

But the only problem with the blackmail idea was that it did not explain why Nash was claiming that Jack the Ripper was good for the East End. Then came more inspiration.

Nashey was going to work the police and the newspapers somehow. Claim the reward but first get the papers to pay him for information. That was why he was stirring things up by claiming Jack was good for the poor; to help build up the frenzy in the papers. The bigger the story the more he would be able to extort from them. Play one newspaper off against the over. Blackmail the Ripper or his paymaster first, then get the newspapers to pay for snippets, work the story up even more than it already was so a big reward was offered, then turn in the killer and his mate to the police!

Shanks was convinced Nashey was taking on too much. His old nemesis would get a taste of steel or have his neck stretched for sure. He smirked slyly at the thought.

But he could not think of how he could gain from all this himself presently, so decided it would be good to keep a close eye on Nashey.

He had originally planned to use other contacts for his Aldgate post office robbery, but now he would use Nashey. Shanks had all the information he needed to break in, and the money was there every Friday night, so the job could be done in the early hours of any Saturday from now on, but he would stretch it out a bit. He wanted to see how things developed as well as have an excuse to meet up with Nashey every week. The more often the two men met, the more chance he had of winkling out scraps of information that could be useful.

***

A couple of weeks earlier, when Shanks had first arrived at her door looking to give her work, Sookey had taken an immediate dislike to him. She had kept looking nervously over his shoulder to seek reassurance from neighbour, Rose, who was only a few feet away holding court with some friends outside her place.

Sookey had taken a formal tone with her new customer.

"Very well. I am a little busy at Toynbee Hall this week

and there is rather a lot of work involved so I can have this done for you by Saturday. As to remuneration, shall we say a couple of bob Mr Shanks?"

Pronouncing 'a couple of bob' in perfect Queen's English had Shanks snorting contemptuously. He had introduced himself as Shanks when he arrived which Sookey had assumed to be his surname. He was quick to put her straight.

"It's Mr Mac Donald."

"Oh, Shanks is your first name?"

"No, my name's Niven. Shanks is just what they calls me. They say it's short for Longshanks. Because I'm tall, see."

"Might I presume you are from good Scottish stock Niven? And that you were given this name by some wag here in the East End," she asked with a barely suppressed smile curling her lips.

What the bleeding hell's a matter with the woman, he thought. She should be in Bedlam.

"Yes, I'm Scottish. Thanks to the old man. He weren't no good though. What you on about, wag?"

Sookey proceeded to give Shanks a brief history lesson on King Edward the First, known as Longshanks, hammer of the Scots.

He had made up his mind there and then that he would not pay a penny to this annoying, smirking woman.

This said, her work was of such high quality that he had used her again since. He employed her as a 'gag-maker' writing begging letters. She thought she was writing genuine letters for illiterate people in need of charity, who were using Shanks as a go-between simply because he knew someone who could write well. In reality, the recipients of such charity were just small-time con artists who paid Shanks a fee for his trouble.

And as he had no intention of paying her in any case, he had simply agreed to whatever fees she had requested.

But now he thought it was time to do something about this woman. He did not like what he was hearing about her spending time with Nashey, especially the news that they were having long talks together. It was his opinion that long talks were more personal than 'how's your father'. The only thing long talks led to was friendship. And you did not run up large unpaid bills with any friend of Nashey. No, he thought, this sort of thing had to be nipped in the bud before it went any further. He wanted Nashey concentrating on the matters at hand, namely soliciting money out of the Ripper, the papers and the police; and helping in the Aldgate post office robbery. It would also be good to get one over on the bastard, although having his fancy piece attended to was as nothing compared to how he was going to get the better of him in the long run. All he needed was time.

***

Shanks had been the one to call the meet. He had assured Nash that it was not to moan about being axed from his employment. It was about something entirely different. A pull. Nash was not enthusiastic about working with Shanks, but any source of income would be welcome given his present high outgoings.

There was a fight going on outside the pub where Nash was about to meet Shanks. It was quite a brawl. A gang of local lads were getting the better of a bunch of sailors on shore leave. The crowd were giving loud vocal support to the home team. Nash spotted Shanks. He was close to the front of the action but rather than simply watch the fight and air his opinions like everyone else, he was constantly looking round at the crowd. Someone shouted his support for the locals from the back of the throng.

"Go on lads, give them a good kicking!"

This was Shanks' cue to turn round to the flaying bodies and shout, shaking his fists for added emphasis.

"Go on, bloody kill 'em!" immediately looking round at the crowd again, beaming, like a little boy who had just done something good for his father.

Wrong un, thought Nash. You'll never be one of the crowd, so long as you've got hole in your arse. Little Sookey is more one of us than you'll ever be.

He waited for the fight to die down enough so he could shout over the din of the supporters.

"Shanks!" The recipient crooked his neck back to see who was calling him, so Nash continued. "I ain't got all bleeding night! Come on, out of it!"

Notwithstanding the noise from the street fight, which had spilled over from the neighbouring pub a few doors away, this pub was the quietest in the whole East End. It was run by a new landlord who had airs and graces. He would not allow into his establishment; prostitutes, paupers, Jews, actors, Irish, gypsies, pure collectors, cadgers and since Annie Besant had started stirring them up into a trade union, the Bryant & May factory girls, whom he considered revolutionaries. The pub had lost its soul, not to mention most of its customers. Even the Salvation Army girls no longer stood outside to tell the clientele the error of their ways. It was too long between amens.

Nash ordered a couple of pale ales and looked into the large mirror behind the bar. Other than the words on the mirror, 'Dunville's V R Old Irish Belfast`, all he could see was a foursome of old women shelling peas. The place was near deserted. Shanks arrived at his elbow.

Don't worry Shanks I've already stood the round, thought Nash caustically, as he surveyed his surroundings without enthusiasm.

"What the bleeding hell you brought me in this dead and alive hole for?"

Shanks beckoned Nash to the corner of the pub furthest from the pea-shelling community.

"I got some work for you. Thought it was the least I could do seeing as you been giving me work lately. Needed somewhere there ain't no ears flapping."

"Yes?" Nash snorted with undisguised disdain.

Shanks continued.

"With all the coppers looking for old Jack, there's never been easier pickings. I've heard tell as how snakesmen, cracksmen…"

"Yes, all right," interrupted an impatient Nash, "I know all the ways of making gelt round here. Now cut to the chase."

"Well, I know this post office what we can have over easy as anything."

"And which one are you, Pierce or Agar?" retorted Nash sarcastically.

"Who?" asked Shanks, having not understood the reference to the perpetrators of the Great Train Robbery of three decades earlier, the most notorious crime ever committed against Victorian property.

"Never mind. So where is this sitting duck?" Nash remained unimpressed.

"Don't worry about that for now, but I've been told it's got hundreds in there one Friday night every month. I don't know when the next night is yet, but I'll be getting tipped the wink soon enough, don't you worry. We could even give some old whore a good hiding and cut her about a bit in a different part of Whitechapel, and get someone to shout out, 'horrible murder!' and every copper will be over there sharp, leaving the post office area empty for us."

Nash repeated Shanks' words in his mind. Give some old whore a good hiding and cut her about a bit.

It was all he could do to stop himself from beating the sorry human specimen in front him to a pulp right there and then. He looked at Shanks as if he was a dog turd he had just found on the bottom of his boot.

"Since when were we cracksmen? I hit people for a living, and you do what you do," he said, before narrowing his eyes to change his expression from contempt to suspicion before he continued. "Where you got this from anyhow?"

"Never mind all that," said Shanks. "That's my little secret. Let's just say I got new friends in high places. And they've set me up with this pull so as to prove myself for a much bigger job in a while. Might be able a get you in on that an' all. But for now, you got the contacts for what I need for this post office pull."

So that's why he's offering me in, thought Nash. He's somehow got hold of a bit of gold dust about a post office but he ain't got a bleeding clue what to do with it. He would need a cracksman, a canary and a crow for a start off, and I know who to use.

"Yes, I got them all right. And I suppose your job's to slice up the whore eh?" asked Nash with a straight face, knowing what the reply would be.

"No, I was thinking that would be you," came the confirmation.

"I got to get all the troops and do all the dirty work have I? What you going to do for your slice?"

"I'm the only one what knows what post office and when, ain't I?"

You're going to do sod all, thought Nash. Yes, that's about right for you.

Nash listened to Shanks relay details of the robbery and had to admit it sounded like good intelligence. So, despite his misgivings about working with the wrong un, he appreciated that he could not afford to pass up the job. He needed the money, not only to carry on having the Ripper watched, but also to pay other noses to glean further information about him.

"All right I'm in," he confirmed, before cocking his wrist to flick his empty beer glass towards Shanks. "Your stand."

Shanks reached for it.

"Here, what's that?" questioned Nash, nodding at Shanks' right forearm.

"It's a tattoo. A ship's capstan. Went down Limehouse docks and had it done by some old China woman. Nobody will want to mess about with me now, will they? All the sailor boys have got them."

Typical, thought Nash. A wrong un trying to look tough.

He could not resist. "Didn't do them much bleeding good outside just now did it?"

Chapter 14

"The victims have forced innumerable people who never gave a serious thought before to the subject to realise how it is that our vast floating population, the waifs and strays of our thoroughfares, live and sleep at night and what sort of accommodation our rich and enlightened capital provides for them."

Daily Telegraph

The monthly meetings for coffee with Nora had started to become weekly ones. This was at Nora's request, with the conversations becoming distinctly different in subject matter. The whole dynamic of the meetings had changed. Rather than Nora mostly holding court, with Sookey happy to listen to all the gossip from her old world, Nora was now keen to hear everything about her friend's new life. Sookey had been both delighted and surprised by this sudden interest in the East End. A second cup of coffee was sipped, as Sookey was surprised to find Nora eager to broach the dreadful subject of the recent murders.

After they had their fill of coffee, they would continue their discussions while enjoying a stroll, and on their last walk Nora had asked if a couple of mutual acquaintances, Elizabeth and Rebecca, could join them the next time they met. Perhaps the four of them could meet for luncheon?

And it was wrong that Sookey should always have to make the journey to the West End for these gatherings. The least she and the others could do was get a taxi cab over to the East End for a change.

This had made Sookey feel decidedly uneasy. It would be awkward enough meeting Elizabeth and Rebecca again for the first time since her fall from grace, without having to worry about where and how to keep them and Nora entertained. There was also the problem of her attire. Keeping up appearances for an hour in the West End was one thing, doing it for longer in the East End was quite another. It was fortunate that she was overdue quite a sum of money from Shanks for all the work she had done for him recently. It would pay for a new dress.

Another concern was that she and these women could easily bump into local people whom she knew. She preferred to keep her past and present lives separate. But her reticence at Nora's suggestion went ignored, her friend easily brow-beating her into submission.

This threw Sookey into an immediate quandary. Where to take them? Somewhere respectable yet interestingly different from the sort of places her friends would normally frequent. Perhaps even a little down at heel to give them a flavour of the East End? There was a Spiers & Bond refreshment room in Liverpool Street Station. But she was concerned that the station was where her old and new lives converged. They might bump into Whitechapel people she knew. Nora meeting Rose, that would indeed be interesting, she thought wryly, though rather too much so for both her liking and she suspected, Nora's.

She took a stroll along Bishopsgate towards Shoreditch, through an area where the City of London and East End merged. She knew that several new catering chains had opened premises to appeal to office-workers in the vicinity. She found a Slater's luncheon and tea rooms and an Express Dairy milk and bun shop, but they were full of clerks. Hardly entertaining for ladies looking for adventure. A chop house might hit the right note, but it too would be full of men. Four ladies walking through the doors would turn the heads of the City gents, and there would surely be frowns and mutterings once the women had turned their backs to the tipped hats and false smiles. Much to her relief she eventually found an Aerated Bread Company tea shop, which was a perfectly respectable establishment, though in a rather run-down little street technically in the East End, so would be considered excitingly insalubrious by her ladies.

The four women duly met, with Elizabeth and Rebecca far friendlier than Sookey could have hoped. There was none of the awkwardness she might have expected. After the initial small talk of West End life and the mutual acquaintances the four women shared, the subject was quickly moved along to the opposite end of the city. The women were keen to know all about Henrietta Barnett and Toynbee Hall. They marvelled at Sookey's 'fascinating' life, though no doubt it was awfully hard work and not without its drawbacks. For example, what of her personal safety in such a place? This moved them neatly on to the recent murders. By this time, they were coming to the end of a long, sustaining meal, Sookey feeling not a little nauseous from the recently forgotten feeling of an over full stomach. She was also intoxicated by being the centre of attention;

having her lifestyle, which she had always assumed would appal her contemporaries, appreciated and enthused over. She was enjoying herself immensely.

With discussion of the murders in full flow, she leaned forward solicitously, lowering her voice to a whisper.

"I know something about them that has not appeared in any newspaper."

Six eyebrows headed for the globed gas brackets which hung above. She considered the next sentence which had formed in her head. She pondered whether it was wise to continue for a moment before her excitement got the better of her and she blurted it out.

"It is something to do with blood. I dare not say any more on the matter, as no doubt the authorities would not abide any loss of confidentiality."

Nora was a very effusive, confident woman. Sookey had never seen her lost for words; until now. The other two women had managed to slowly swivel their heads towards Nora, as if needing her to take the lead. Nora stuttered her way through several attempts at interrogative pronouns. Sookey got the gist and nodded with enthusiasm.

"A man sought me out to ask for medical assistance for a hand injury. We got to speaking of the murders and it transpires that he has acquired extraordinary intelligence about one of the deaths. And given my medical knowledge, he asked me for advice on the matter. But I dare not divulge any more."

She had to stop to take a breath. Her excitement was resulting in verbosity she would not have believed possible of herself, certainly not in the company of Nora, let alone Elizabeth and Rebecca. A cheeky thought came to her.

It is well I no longer wear a corset; I would faint for certainty.

But stating that she dares not say more, proved disingenuous. She continued with her gossipy monologue.

"He is certainly of roguish behaviour, but I have become friends with this gentleman, though he would chastise me for bestowing such a title upon him. We speak for hours about all manner of things. He is not well-spoken, or rich in the bank but he is not at all ill-looking."

She stopped suddenly, realising that in her enthusiasm she had become far too wanton, even brazen. But her audience were too shocked by the revelations to concern themselves with matters of female etiquette.

Sookey was enjoying her newly raised status amongst her middle-class friends. And it became apparent that she had inspired them to return to the East End in the not-too-distant future. Nora relayed that she had made once enquiries of Thomas Cook Tours as to whether there were any excursions to the area, but sadly there were not.

"It would appear it is easier to visit darkest Africa than darkest Whitechapel," she laughed. "I think we will have to entrust you to be our guide, Susan."

Sookey initially responded to the request with enthusiasm.

"Why, most certainly. I can show you my vision of a future Whitechapel Art Gallery, and there is the library, of which we are so proud. I could also introduce you to the Reverend Barnett and Henrietta, and we could time your visit to accord with a lecture or recital at Toynbee Hall."

"That would be delightful my dear," said Nora, smiling. "We could also take tea with you at your home. And we would like to see Petticoat Lane as we have heard so much of it. Our cabman today also suggested we should visit an eel and pie house for luncheon. And no tour would be complete without seeing a Cockney public house of course. But it is a serious excursion too is it not. We would also like to see the poor wretcheds who walk the streets."

Sookey's ardour had been well and truly dampened.

Chapter 15

"Under any civilised conditions it would have been impossible for these monstrous crimes to have been committed."

George R. Sims, Sunday Referee

Nash did not like the idea of the post office robbery. It meant relying on and trusting Shanks, which was out of the question. And it was also not the sort of crime in which Nash had experience. He liked to keep within the perimeters of his usual world of simple skulduggery. The prisons were full of men who had bitten off more than they could chew. And the state considered committing any crime against property, particularly an official one like a post office, a far more serious crime than offences against the person. But if he wished to continue to fund his interest in the Ripper, needs must. He would recruit a cracksman and canary, and Will could be the crow.

The prospective cracksman's lair was over in Hoxton. Nash had just been to check if Khan or young Tom Carter had any information on the killer and was now setting out to Hoxton. It was a rapidly darkening mid-evening, with the yellow-green hint of a pea-souper fog coming down.

Nash spotted Sookey as soon as she turned the corner into Commercial Street, twenty yards ahead of him. She was now walking in the same direction as him, so he slowed his pace to make sure she kept well ahead. The last thing he wanted was to get stuck passing the time of day with her.

He noticed she was not wearing anything on her head. He shook his head, imagining Rose and the rest of the neighbourhood's women tutting away at such a sight.

She'll learn, he thought.

Sookey crossed the busy main thoroughfare and headed down dark, narrow Hanbury Street. Nash thought she was probably making her way to the shops in Brick Lane. He was going to continue up the road towards Shoreditch, so was pleased to be heading away from her. He could speed up now. But rather than immediately getting on his way, he could not resist continuing to gaze at Sookey as she made her way down the street. She was heading close to the roughest, most dangerous slum in London, the Flower & Dean Street rookery.

She stopped to talk to a couple of young women. Nash would have recognised them immediately had his attention not already been drawn to someone else.

The streets were crowded and noisy with horses, carts and hordes of unwashed humanity making their way over the cobbles. It was therefore easy to follow someone up close, but equally easy to lose them if they got too far ahead. But the problem with keeping close was if the person being followed suddenly halted in their tracks.

Nash had spotted that a man had crossed Commercial Street immediately behind Sookey and started to follow her down Hanbury Street. But crossing such a busy thoroughfare there were lots of people walking in all directions, so he had not initially paid any attention to the

147

man. But when Sookey had stopped, the man halted too, bending down and taking too long tying his bootlaces. It was obvious to Nash what he was up to.

Bugger me if he ain't following her.

It was none of Nash's business, but he felt compelled to cross the road and set off after the two of them. He immediately scolded himself, muttering under his breath.

"Bleeding nose-ache you are Nash."

Seconds after Sookey had left the young women to continue her journey down the street, a small hand grabbed Nash's elbow.

"Nashey!"

It was Mary. It had been she with whom Sookey had stopped to pass the time of day. Nash had a soft spot for her and had once used her as a canary on a robbery. He could do so again. But the more Nash liked a woman the gruffer he usually tended to be towards her at the start of any meeting. He acknowledged her with the briefest of nods, and completely ignored the young woman at her side, before bending to speak confidentially in Mary's ear, barely audible over the din of hooves and wheels on cobblestone.

"Lucky, I bumped into you. Got a pull you can be in on. Should pay a tidy sum, keep you off the streets for a while I shouldn't wonder. Your fellow will be pleased. Long as you don't tell him how you got hold of the gelt that is. But I'll have to see you about it tomorrow. Ten Bells noon."

He started on his way, nodding after Sookey's pursuer, with a wag of the thumb in his direction.

"In the middle of something," he said, accompanied by a wink.

Mary assumed he was about to relieve the man of his valuables. She returned the wink and without saying a word motioned a 'let's get on our way' nod to her new friend Kitty, and the two of them turned on their brass heels and disappeared into the throng. Nash had ignored Kitty but had noticed her. The sense that he had seen her somewhere, before the recent occasion when he had dealt with her ponce, flashed into his mind again, but Sookey and her follower were on the move, so the thought was gone in an instant.

Sookey passed the shops as she crossed Brick Lane, soon disappearing into a warren of narrow, dark alleys and courts.

Where's she bleeding going at this time of night? mused Nash. There's nothing down here but trouble. And with her not wearing no hat or shawl and having that rouge on she likes to wear; this cove probably thinks she's on the game. Probably waiting for her to get somewhere quiet before asking her for business. He looks a rough sort. He'll be after a twopenny upright I shouldn't wonder. And he might not take no for an answer. Before she knows what's she's about, soppy cow's going to have his hand up her skirt. She's going to learn the hard way all right.

It was then that Nash spotted the second man following her. He also realised the location was significant. They were outside Shanks' gaff.

Intuition sent Nash's left hand into one of his overcoat pockets, and a moment later he was wearing his cap, complete with glass restored into its peak.

He was still mulling things over in his mind when the attack came. Sookey's scream was expertly muffled, as the first man grabbed her from behind, his left fist being brought back towards himself, punching her in the stomach to knock the air out of her, the right hand further stopping any sound emanating by being clamped over the mouth, and dragging her backwards into the darkest shadows. The second man dashed in and kicked her legs away from her with a boot to a calf. The first man dropped with her to the floor, manoeuvring himself to lie on top of her, his right hand still over her mouth, his left now pushing up into her throat.

The second man was just pulling out some rope from his pocket when Nash's right fist thundered into the side of his chin, and as the man spun around and down Nash pivoted and slammed his left fist into the man's testicles. The man crashed to the ground and lay still. Sookey's captor let go his grip on her to get to his feet, but he was only half up when Nash's right boot smashed into his mouth, teeth and blood splattering out. But Nash had not seen the third man.

A cosh landed on the back of Nash's head. He was badly stunned but he knew he had to stay on his feet at all costs. His legs were wilting and his vision blurring but he stumbled across the court and managed to swerve enough to hit the wall shoulder first. This both kept him on his feet and turned him enough so he could see his attacker bearing down on him out the corner of his eye. The man ran towards Nash and momentarily steadied himself a couple of feet from his prey to strike again with the cosh, but as he did so Nash delivered a straight left jab, catching the man flush on his Adam's apple. Nash hadn't had time to get any shoulder into the punch, simply extending his arm, so there was little weight behind it, but it was perfectly timed, and the man recoiled, gasping for breath.

Nash's head was still spinning badly. He knew he might pass out at any moment and had to finish this quickly. He pulled off his cap and lunged forward at the man, who had his head bowed gasping, not looking at his opponent.

"That's the last mistake you make today," muttered Nash under his breath.

The man looked up just in time to see a brown blur flash across his eyes. There was another flurry, and another. Nash had backhanded, forehanded, backhanded his cap, peak first across the man's face in three lightning-fast strikes. Beads of red started to seep out of the gashes in and around the man's eyes as screams of agony issued forth. He dropped the cosh, his hands coming up across his face, blood escaping through the gaps between his fingers. The man's screams ended abruptly as he blacked out and sunk to his knees before pitching forward onto his face. Seeing the blood flow, a flash of ironic humour as black as the night came to Nash.

"One thing's for sure, you ain't no whore, are you?"

Sookey's first attacker was now up on one knee shouting something to his mate, but his mouth was such a mess the words were indecipherable.

Nash turned towards the man and made him an ominous promise.

"You need a dentist boy. I'll save you the money."

He bent down to pick up the loose cosh, but the motion sent blood flooding to his head. He felt a wave of great heat pass through his brain, and crumpled onto the floor. He was close to passing out when a scream brought him back to his senses, at least to a degree.

The man he had been about to finish off was now grappling with Sookey, little more than a foot from Nash's face. Her attentions had managed to stop the man's advance towards the cosh for a moment. Nash dragged himself onto one knee and planted his right fist into the man's nose. There was the sound of breaking bone, a spray of blood and the man went out like a light.

"You got a nose to match your mouth now."

He looked across at the man he had hit on the chin and in the nether regions. He was conscious but making no effort to re-enter the fray.

"Yes, you stay down if you know what's good for you! Don't help your mates," sneered Nash.

He glared at Sookey.

"You 'armed!?"

Sookey had recovered from the punch in the stomach enough to answer in a frightened high-pitched voice.

"By your leave sir, I am not armed. The cosh was not mine."

Nash looked at her blankly for a moment before realising the 'soppy cow' had misunderstood him.

"No Sookey, I am asking you, have you been harmed?"

Chapter 16

"In our age of contradictions and absurdities, a fiend murderer may become a more effective reformer than all the honest propagandists in the world."

Commonweal

It was close to noon, but Nash was only just surfacing. He had not risen from his bed all morning and was only now up and about due to a need to pee. His head was throbbing from yesterday's events. The pounding headache from the coshing he had received was making it difficult for him to think, and he did not appreciate a loud thumping on his door.

"It's Will" came a shout. "You told me a give you a knock just before twelve, remember."

"All right! Shut your trap!" Nash bellowed.

He had completely forgotten. He had slept in his trousers and boots, having collapsed onto his bed on getting home. In one motion he donned his vest, shirts, and waistcoats, all of which had come off equally speedily the night before. The overcoat followed and finally his tatty old billy pot hat. He no longer had a cap. He had removed the shards of glass from it and dropped them down a drain, placing the bloodied item on to the head of an unconscious wretch lying in an alley, with his bucket of 'pure' beside him. The collection of dog mess, otherwise known as pure, for selling to tanneries, was the lowest of all low jobs, done by those who were only one short step from the workhouse.

"Here are boy, this will keep your bonce warm at least."

He grabbed a couple of weapons from his table, stuffed them into the deep pockets of his coat and marched out to join Will no more than seconds after his door had been rapped. There was the usual lack of pleasantries, Nash starting immediately on the business at hand.

"I got a crow job for you. I'm just off to see a canary in the Bells. You come an' all. I'll tell you both what it's about."

Will nodded and fell into step.

Gawd, you look rough Nashey, he thought, but wisely kept this observation to himself.

Five minutes later they were ensconced in a dark corner of the Ten Bells in Commercial Street with Mary. It was her local. She lived just over the road in Miller's Court. She felt confident in her surroundings and was in a good mood. She had just had her best night's takings, thanks to an old gent who had tried and failed to penetrate her. She had previously negotiated a five-shilling fee for penetrative sex and was not about to give the man a refund so had taken hold of his member and caressed it, speaking quietly with a mix of encouragement and foul-mouthed dirtiness until his release became apparent. The old gent's gratitude saw him donate a gratuity of a silk pocket handkerchief. Never having received a tip before, she was not sure how to react, so bobbed in appreciation.

"Thank you very much, sir."

This embarrassed him, and he had quickly scurried off into the night.

I'll be able to get three or four bob down the market for this, she had thought. That's eight or nine shillings in all, the best I've ever been paid, and just for a kneetrembler.

A fair percentage of that money had already disappeared behind the bar so she was sufficiently inebriated to be cheeky towards the old friend who had just walked in.

"Christ almighty, you look bloody rough Nashey!" she shouted in greeting, grinning broadly.

Will suddenly found something interesting to stare at on the other side of the pub, as Mary continued.

"You don't need ale by the look of you. Let me go and get you some Godfrey's you poor sod."

This was an opium and molasses syrup cordial favoured by baby-farmers to sooth starving tots.

"Don't you come it with me, you saucy little mare," retorted Nash. "I'll fetch you a facer in a minute, then you won't be so clever. Little cow."

His dark mood had immediately been lifted, firstly by the sight of Mary, with her red hair, brightly coloured clothes, and brass heels, propping up the bar when he and Will had walked through the pub doors, and then by this cheeky outburst. He had tried to keep a straight face and brought his right arm up and across his chest as if threatening to give her a backhanded slap, but he felt the upper parts of his cheeks quiver. He knew he had let slip a slight smirk.

"Well, I can't be a horse and a cow can I, make up your bloody mind," she said, having spotted the twinkle in Nash's eye and his little grin, so she knew she was on safe ground.

"I can see I'm going to have to have a word with that Joe of yours," replied Nash. "He ain't keeping you in hand enough. He needs to give you a good hiding, so you show some respect to a man."

Nash was not looking serious, despite his best efforts to do so.

He saw Mary's bosom start to heave as she drew breath to come back at him again, but he quickly jumped in, this time successfully losing his smile.

"Never mind all that, funny cuts, I got a job for you." He winked and nodded for her and Will to join him in a quieter spot away from the bar, and this done, he lowered his voice to a barely perceptible growl. "Canary work. And Will, you'll be the crow."

Mary saw it was time to behave.

"Go ahead," she nodded, "I got my lugs out."

Nash laid out the plan, as much as he knew it.

A cracksman, the skilled leader of a burglary, would have a kit which included specialist burglary equipment such as, if necessary, safe-breaking gear. If picked up and searched by the police, there was no innocent explanation for carrying such equipment; the purveyor arrested on the spot. No cracksman would ever run the risk of being caught with his tools of work on him. A canary was employed to carry them on his behalf, to and from the job. It was usually a woman, as it was far less likely that they would be stopped and questioned by the police. A crow was a look-out, but the job involved far more than simply being another set of eyes. It was skilled employment. A crow was an expert at calls and signals – whistles, bird and cat noises, coughs, sneezes, flourished handkerchiefs and striking matches in a certain way.

Will and Mary were unimpressed by what little Nash had been able to tell them about the robbery.

"I'm telling you that's all he's told me," said a conciliatory, exasperated Nash. "You know what sort of cove Shanks is. He don't trust nobody does he, so he ain't letting on about nothing till it's time, because he's worried we'll go ahead and do the job without him once we know."

"Yes, well he's right there ain't he?" snorted Will.

Mary cut in.

"But why have we got to hang about every Friday night just on the off chance that's the night? Friday night's the only time I make any money these days. Saturdays have gone right to pot since that bastard Jack's double event on a Saturday night. I got a living to make you know."

Nash wanted to get back at her with "do some other bloody trade then!" But he and Mary had had many heated exchanges about her being a prostitute over the years, and this was not the time or place for another.

"Because that's the way Shanks wants it. He's got us over a barrel, so we got to lump it. Anyhow you ain't got to hang about this Friday because I already told him I ain't got hold of the cracksmen yet, so we start meeting up next week."

The bickering continued but eventually both Mary and Will reluctantly accepted the situation.

***

Sookey had not stirred from her house all day. Hours before she had witnessed violence that she knew must exist in the slums, and she had certainly seen scraps of it in the recent past. Only last Sunday two costermongers had almost started fighting when she had agreed to buy a scarf off one man, only for a rival to try and steal the sale by undercutting the deal. All was fair in love and war until a deal was done, but once a sale had been agreed, the other coster should have conceded. He had almost got a punch on the nose for his trouble, but the word 'almost' was crucial. There had been a lot of aggressive posturing, swearing and threats, but that was all. Knowing of something and experiencing it in small ways like the quasi fight, was completely unlike seeing the real violence that lurked down dark alleyways.

She had been amazed at the brevity of the attack on her. From the moment the first man grabbed her, to the moment Nashey had sent his last victim into unconsciousness could not have been more than seconds. And there was the silence of it all. Not a word spoken. No dramatic music like such an event in the theatre. Just the sound of boots on cobbles, fists on chins and grunts of pain.

And then she had attempted to stem the flow of blood from the cuts on a man's face by applying pressure to the wounds.

Nashey, head spinning, had wanted to get away.

"Come on, let's scarper before any coppers turn up."

"But he is bleeding profusely Nashey. I must do something. Come, assist me. Your hands are so much stronger than mine, you can apply more purchase."

"I ain't touching him. Attacking a poor defenceless woman, he's a wrong un."

"Do you think these men are the Ripper Nashey? Could that be why the police's efforts have been so hamstrung? They have been looking for one man, but it is indeed three."

"They ain't the Ripper. I know who the Ripper is right enough. Gawd if I ain't seen him with my own eyes, close as you are to me now. I could have topped him there and then if I'd have had a mind. But he's useful as he is, for the time being at least."

Sookey loosened her grip on the man's face as she swivelled around at this news, staring in wide-eyed astonishment. It was only when he saw her shocked expression that Nash realised what he had said.

Christ, he thought, this knock to the head's loosened my tongue.

He needed to change the subject. Avoiding Sookey's eyes, he made his way over to the man.

"All right, let me do it," he said, knocking her bloodied hands away and applying pressure on the deepest of the man's wounds.

He felt the need to keep talking and do so for some time. He did not want to field any questions about what he had just let slip.

"Yes, it's good if he lives right enough. You can smash a man to pulp so he can't never work again and that's him off to the workhouse. Or you can bash his brains senseless so that's him off to Bedlam. But unless you kill him, nothing much happens. Some old beak sends you away for a twelve-month. But swipe a gentleman's Hunter watch and it's off to prison with you for donkey's years. My old grandfather got sent to gawd knows where on the other side of the world just for fencing a bit of jewellery, if you please. Property's worth more than a man's worth. Or a woman. I were only acting in self-defence mind, and saving a good lady's life and virtue, so it don't really matter if this fellow lives or dies, but best save him I reckon, just to keep the coppers from sniffing round."

Sookey's shocked stare had not changed so Nash continued in his verbosity.

"The blood's stopped. And he's coming round. He'll live, right enough. Look, all three of them are coming round now. Even the wrong un there." Nash winked, nodding over at the man he had punched in the testicles. "He 'll be counting them in a minute."

There was to be no argument, Sookey being pulled firmly to her feet.

"Let's scarper," he said.

"What did you say of knowing who…"

The question cut off by Nash swaying.

"Quick, grab hold, I'm passing out," he said in an urgent voice, overacting.

Sookey threw her left arm around his waist and nuzzled her head under his right arm, so her chin wedged against the side of his chest.

The two of them left the court entwined like a couple of lovers and made their way home. They were both covered in blood, but nobody took a blind bit of notice. It was a common enough occurrence for a wife to be helping her husband stagger home after he'd had a punch on the nose or drunkenly tripped and head-butted the cobbles. Sookey was in pain and had so many thoughts swirling around in her head that she didn't know what to say, so decided to wait for Nashey to speak. They walked back in silence.

Sookey had hardly slept a wink since. Her stomach ached, her calf and throat felt sore and there was bruising to her neck. But it was not her injuries that had kept her awake. It was shock, but not the physical condition. And it was not the attack she had suffered, or the sight of the violence perpetrated on her attackers, which was the cause. It was partly her lack of shock at what had occurred. She imagined what the man who had meted out the violence to save her would say to such thoughts.

"You're shocked at your lack of shock! Gawd help us girl, that's Irish and there's the truth."

Sookey had felt insecure all her life, but when she was with this man, she felt safe. She smiled at the misunderstanding she had with him after he had saved her from those ruffians. People might be armed, but they would be the ones to be 'armed.

But it was not her physical safety per se that she was thinking about, rather her general well-being. Until now the only time she ever felt fully at peace was when engrossed in making art, but that was because she was no longer in the real world. This was the first time she had felt truly safe. In what the rest of society had now come to think of as the most dangerous place in the civilised world, she felt secure for the first time in her life.

Chapter 17

"Women can't apprentice their girls to milliners or dressmakers or other trades...(they) have not the faintest chance of learning any business that will yield living wage... Whitechapel is an awful fact, for many of its women practically choose between semi starvation and harlotry."

Eliza Putnam Heath, Reno Evening Gazette

Nash, accompanied by his splitting headache, made another attempt to track down the cracksman he needed for the post office robbery. Having called at his cellar slum to find he had just missed him; he was in no mood to simply hunch his shoulders and return home. He asked around in the suspicious-minded tight-knit enclave, and it was a while before he found someone willing to tell him anything. He was eventually told that his quarry had gone to a nearby pub to watch the ratting.

Rural blood sports still flourished thanks to their enjoyment by the ruling classes, but the authorities had clamped down on all but one of the urban ones – ratting. There was far less pity for rats than any other animal, so the authorities did little to interfere. So although Nash was an unknown face in the pub, he had no problem gaining admittance to the ratting upstairs. He mounted the filthy open staircase, the banisters having long since rotted away, to arrive in what was once the upstairs parlour of the landlord, dropped his shilling into the hat of the proprietor and entered the ratting room.

The dog pit consisted of a small circus, six feet in diameter, fitted with wooden rims to chest height. Over it the branches of a gas lamp lit up the white painted floor and every part of the pit, as well as the faces of the men leaning over the rim, their features filled with the unique far away stare of the fervent gambler's excitement and anticipation. The men with the inside information; the men who knew they were going to win. At least, so they thought. Nash recognised the type. He saw them in large numbers at race meetings. He wondered where these men came from. They seemed to appear from nowhere. He never saw them on the streets, or in pubs, or anywhere else for that matter. Their country style clothing and strange accents hinted that they made their money out of town. And they spent it wildly, never buying their mates individual drinks, always getting in a bottle.

The action was about to start, and the audience who had been too late to get a pit-side view were clambering on tables and chairs. The dogs were tied to the legs of tables; the English terriers excitable, raring to go, while the bulldogs and Skye terriers were calmer. The rats then brought forward in rusty wire cages. All the dogs were now excited and ran out to the length of their leashes, barking and almost choking themselves in their eagerness to get at their prey.

The atmosphere was building. The noise climbed as shouted bets were offered and accepted, roll-ups hurriedly trodden out underfoot, hob-nailed boots hauled across the rotten wooden floor, as the last few men gathered around, pushing and shoving for the best view from the back of the throng. The big spending men from out of town, along with corduroy-trousered costermongers, soldiers enjoying the freedom of unbuttoned uniforms, coachmen still in their livery and assorted tradesmen in aprons jostled for position.

The first event was to be an eight-minute affair. More than enough rats were to be let loose; how many could Billy kill in the allotted time? Nash had spotted John the Blackguard in the crowd. He was a renowned animal catcher. If something moved on the Essex marshes, John caught and sold it. He did well with sales of songbirds to market tradesmen. Nash thought Sookey's caged bird had most likely lost its freedom courtesy of John. But his greatest ability was catching sewer and water-ditch rats.

Nash wanted to ask about for the cracksman before the first event started, after which the din would preclude any conversation. John wouldn't know his man, but others might. He turned to the fellow standing next to him, a costermonger. The coster had just placed a bet with the urgent near-panic of the gambler who had waited till the last possible moment before declaring his interest in the belief it would gain him an advantage as he weighed the odds and possibilities but nearly left it too late to get his money accepted. His bet had been based on what he believed was an astute analysis of the size of the dog.

"What rats they got for the main event?" Nash enquired, just to break the ice.

"Country barns. Dogs will be all right tonight," came the confident, curt reply, meaning that the dogs would not suffer canker from getting infected mouths from sewer rats.

Rats caught in country barns were the most esteemed. Nash nodded with apparent satisfaction.

"Good. Seen Arthur Phillips about?"

The man's demeanour changed in an instant from indifference to suspicion. He looked Nash up and down as if he were something that had just oozed from beneath the brush of a crossing-sweeper.

"What's it to you if I have?"

Nash leaned forward to within inches of the man's face, with the darkest of expressions on his face.

"Ain't you heard? Every copper's walking their plates off looking for old Jack. They ain't going to find him in here, are they? I'll find Arthur my bleeding self!" shouted Nash above the growing clamour, spraying spittle on to the man's cheek.

The coster was given a parting sneer before Nash switched his attention to the search for Arthur. He would be easy enough to spot. Nash just had to look for a dog-end wagging up and down from the corner of a grizzled old mouth. Arthur had that knack of being able to speak, shout, spit and do his full gamut of facial expressions without ever having to withdraw his thin saliva-sticky rolled-up cigarette from between his teeth.

Nash pushed his way around the outer boundary of leaning, shouting bodies and eventually saw the cracksman. Arthur was close to the front. Nash would not be able to get to him, so he grabbed an old chair that was up against a wall, tipping on to the floor a huge decrepit Old English bulldog which had been curled asleep on it. It had no ear flaps, a sure sign that it had once been a fighting dog. These vulnerable appendages would have been sliced off before its first fight. The dog gave the most perfunctory of growls in protest, but it was more meek complaint than threat. It had tasted the end of a boot often enough to know its place. Nash issued a threatening "grrh, gidoudovit" of his own at the dog and made himself comfortable. A switching ferret peered at Nash from inside the cage next to the chair. The odd ferret would be thrown in the pit to kill rats just to add a bit of variety to the bill for the paying customers.

There was not much to hold Nash's interest as he looked about the place. Along one wall were a cluster of black leather dog collars and large square glazed boxes which held the stuffed bodies of past champion fighting and ratting dogs. Pride of place was given to Bruce, a six-pounder who held the record of almost two hundred rats killed in a designated time. A row of mutoscopes lined the back wall. These were primitive 'What the Butler Saw' machines, with photographs of women undressing, showing underclothing, and sitting in highly suggestive nude postures. Each machine had a placard above it with seductive titles 'How Shocking!' 'Naughty! Naughty! Naughty!' 'Very Spicy!'

The first contest of the evening ended abruptly when the timekeeper shouted, "eight minutes up!" which was the cue for his assistant to dive into the seething mess of dead bodies to haul out the frenzied dog.

The din changed from a raucous shouting of encouragement at, or cursing of, the dog depending on what the punter's bet had been laid, to a mix of quiet murmurings of excited anticipation and loud sworn oaths and arguments, as the count was made.

"Thirty-nine!" came the shout, followed by a huge wave of abuse from the majority.

It was clear the big money had been on the dog killing at least forty rats in his eight minutes. The sweating dog, shaking with exhaustion and over-excitement, its coat caked in the fur and blood of dog and rat, was taken away by its owner. The man cursed the dog for embarrassing him by killing fewer than expected.

"You turned felon!"

But Nash noticed the man did not kick the dog as he might have expected. Nash got to his feet, lightly tapping the cage of the ferret with his boot.

"Hope you do better, boy."

The dog-owner had disappeared into a side room. Nash had to pass it as he was making his way around towards Arthur. He pulled back the curtain to see the dog owner on his knees, dressing his charge's wounds as the dog lapped up beef tea with, judging by the bottle at the man's side, a touch of brandy in it.

"You're a good un you are, Billy, I'll fetch you a warm bath when I get you home," whispered the man with affection.

Nash let the curtain fall and quietly moved back into the bestial throng.

The cracksman appeared at Nash's shoulder.

"I hear you're looking for me," he said, nodding over at the surly coster Nash had encountered on his arrival, who was looking on with a scowl.

Nash leaned to whisper in an ear.

"When you're finished here, I got work for you."

A sly smile greeted the offer with enthusiasm.

"I got money on the next one. Then I'll be with you."

The next event was the grand match of the evening. Fifty rats – could Wee Jasper kill them all in the allotted time? The proprietor of the pub owned the dog and had made a big money match with his son, who had bet him the dog would not be successful. Billy's victims were gathered by their tails and flung into a corner of the pub, some still just alive, squirming their death throes in the moving pile, as the pit's floor was swept.

Seemingly, to add a bit of showmanship to the grand match, the fifty new rats were not in rusty cages, but one big flat basket with an iron top, like those in which chickens were taken to market. The proprietor's son, daringly thrust his hand into the basket, pulling out rats from the seething black mass, and flinging them into the pit. Within a few minutes all fifty were in place, huddled together in a cowering mound. Nash thought they looked like the heap of hair sweepings in his barber's shop after a heavy Saturday's trade. They were sewer and water ditch rats. This became apparent from the sudden smell of latrine. The basket used instead of the cages to mask the smell for as long as possible. Nash suspected the proprietor's son had kept this knowledge to himself. It might take Wee Jasper just that fraction longer to subdue sewer rats. The odds had changed. Nash glanced over and sneered as he caught the eye of the sullen costermonger who had been so sure they were country barn rats.

A boy brought in a bull terrier which was in a fit of excitement.

"Lay hold closer to the head or he'll nip you," advised the dog's owner.

The boy handed Wee Jasper over to the second, who jumped into the pit with the dog. As soon as the terrier was let loose, he became calm, and in a business-like manner rushed at the rats, burying his nose in the mound till he brought one out in his mouth. In short time, dozens of rats with broken necks were lying, bleeding on the floor, the white paint of the pit, stained red. One rat was now hanging on to the terrier's nose, and he could not shift it by tossing his head, so he dashed it against the side of the arena, before a bite finished it off. The dog nosed the rat kicking on its side as it expired. Too much time wasted on one rat.

"Dead un, drop it!" shouted the second.

"Time!" shouted the timekeeper.

Wee Jasper gathered up, panting, and staring at the three rats left alive. One of the filthy wretches commenced cleaning itself, one hopped about, the other sniffed at the legs of the second. The proprietor had lost and was not a good loser.

"That dog won't do for me! He's not my sort! Here son, you can have him if you like. I won't give him house room!"

Successful punters showered ha'pennies into the pit as a reward for the second.

Nash glanced over at the costermonger again. He looked glum and was not throwing coins. Nash could not resist verbally kicking the man while he was down.

"Oi, trousers! Win on them country barn rats, did you?!"

Arthur had a new roll-up between his lips. Like the appearing and disappearing gambling set, Arthur's fags were one of life's mysteries. Nash had never seen him make a new cigarette. They just seemed to appear. And he always had a day's silver beard growth; never clean-shaven, never more than a day's growth, another mystery. The two men left and made their way to a quiet pub where their conversation could not be overheard. Arthur was not in the best of moods having lost more money than he could afford on Wee Jasper. Nash explained the job.

Arthur was an escaped convict. He had melted his pewter cocoa mug over the gas light in his prison cell and moulded it into keys cut from lock-impressions made in pieces of soap. Pewter is soft and moulded like this apt to bend or break in a lock when turned. It had taken all of Arthur's considerable expertise to get the keys to work. They had gotten him out of the cells and into the prison church. He had worked away at the floorboards in the church for weeks while knelt in prayer in the same pew. He was able to get a floorboard out and get under the chapel floor. He had crawled to a point where a narrow opening had been cut for ventilation in the prison wall. It was a tight fit but he was only a small man, so he squeezed through to freedom.

He now lived a very compact life, rarely straying far from the deepest of slums in which he lived, where policemen feared to tread, and only came out of his lair to work, and even then, only if it was truly worth his while. He rarely worked with people he didn't know. There were too many informers about for his liking. Consequently, he was less than enthusiastic about what he had been told about Shanks and his job.

"How am I supposed to know what tools to bring

if I don't know what the job is till I'm on it? And what happens if the crushers get hold of this Shanks. He sounds like he would turn us all in, soon as look at us."

Arthur was old school. 'Crushers' had been the criminal underworld's term for policemen up until a decade or so earlier. Nash had used the word himself in his youth. Now he needed to reassure the old lag, though he was far from happy with the arrangement himself.

"Bring all your tools. And don't you worry about Shanks. He don't tell me where or when the pull is, and I don't tell him who I'm using on the pull. And you don't have to turn up every Friday on the off chance. I'll only send the canary round to pick up your tools and tell you to get your aris down to the meet when the pull's going ahead. And even then, Shanks won't be there. He ain't got the arse to be in on the pull himself. He'll only see you when we split the money at the end, and then you'll just be some feller in a dark alley. He won't know you again from Adam. And me and him has had a sort of understanding since we were lads – he don't piss on me and I let him alone. He pisses on me, he only does it once. Be sure cracksman he's more scared of me than anything crushers can do to him."

Arthur's mouth had opened so wide when Nash had suggested he take all his tools, that he almost dropped his dog-end. It clung to his lower lip by the merest speck of saliva.

"Canary! If they got to take all my tools, they'll have to be a bleeding…" He tried to think of the name of a particularly large bird but couldn't think of one. "Like one of them big things they got in the zoo from one of them funny countries!"

"Vulture," proffered Nash with a chortle, but the laugh was a dry one; the situation was not funny. "I got a girl in mind who…"

"Girl!?"

Nash cut off in mid-sentence was not something that happened often, but it was understandable on this occasion. Arthur was aghast.

"Since when could some slip of a girl carry all my tools!?"

Nash thought of a certain nineteen stone rent-book sandwich-making woman he knew who could carry all Arthur's tools and Arthur as well come to that.

"What you laughing at?" asked Arthur tartly. Nash had not realised that his mental image of big Rose carrying Arthur's tools over one shoulder and Arthur over the over had shown on his face.

"Nothing," he replied sternly. "Girls makes the best canaries, you know that. You've always used girls in the past ain't you, so I don't know what you're bleeding chirping on about. This girl's doing the job and that's the end of it. Tell you what I will do, mind, I'll get you two canaries."

"Gawd help us!" replied Arthur, shaking his head.

But there was something in the exasperated cry that confirmed to Nash that despite all the shortcomings of the plan, Arthur was in.

Nash thanked God for Wee Jasper's clinging rat.

***

A second canary had been volunteered by Mary, her new young friend Kitty. Nash wanted the canaries to meet up with his cracksman to run through their duties for the robbery, so a meet had been arranged at Arthur's place.

Nash looked forward to the look on Arthur's face when he turned up with two young, slightly built, highly made-up women, who were bound to be laughing and cavorting about. He had made a little wager with himself that the roll-up would come right out of Arthur's mouth and hit the floor. He would see the cracksman without a cigarette in his gob for the first time.

But when it came to it, Nash lost his bet. Arthur's cigarette drooped precariously on his lower lip but remained in place.

A large case and a small box were at Arthur's side. He looked the two girls' bodies up and down closely, but there was no hint of lust in his eyes.

"Couldn't you get hold of one fellow at least?"

Nash was quick to explain.

"They needs to both be girls because the crushers think every cove in Whitechapel with a bag on him late at night might be old Jack carrying his knife. A man wouldn't get hundred yards carrying a case without having his collar felt. And them being done up like whores is good an' all. Crushers will likely follow them thinking old Jack might jump out on them any minute, and that leaves you free and clear."

"But why would whores looking for business be carrying something?" queried Arthur.

Nash sighed with exasperation. The old man had either been in prison or skulking in his present hole so long he had forgotten the realities of life lived on the street.

"Because, as you well know, a lot of whores is homeless,

that's why," he said caustically. "They has to carry whatever they got to their name from their last night in a doss house to the next."

"Yes, all right," conceded Arthur.

He could see that far from being a hindrance, having a couple of head-turners was ideal. He smiled at his new cohorts.

"All right ladies, here's what I got for you. Twirls, rope, rod, jack, brace & bit with blades and drills, glass cutter, chisel, jemmy, dark lantern, set of Betty's, an outsider, petter cutter, special cutter and a Jack-in-the-box. And they're all swaddled good."

He looked at Mary, the larger of the two petite women, and nodded at the large suitcase.

"You got to take that lot, if you can get it off the ground in the first place that is."

Mary opened her mouth to protest but Arthur was expecting it and quickly interjected.

"I would keep quiet if I were you. You're the lucky one, girl."

He turned to Kitty and pointed at the box.

"Now, here's a new thing. Hardly nobody's ever heard of it. Soup we calls it, but its real name is Nobel's nitro glycerine."

He paused and looked earnestly at Kitty.

"How old are you girl?"

"Old enough to be an whore," replied Kitty. She was picking up Mary's spikiness.

"So, you'd be at least nine then, would you?" retorted Arthur wearily, showing more disgust with the world than sarcasm towards Kitty.

"I'm sixteen soon enough if you must know."

"Very well, young lady, what you have there is explosive, and its quick tempered like someone else I know. It can go off at the drop of your hat. Blow you to smithereens soon as look at you if you ain't careful."

Nash was the first to react.

"Give over, Arthur! I ain't letting her carry that. We'll have to go without it and make do the best we can. Mary can't take all that clobber anyhow. Kitty will have to take some of it."

"Give the soup to Shanks," said Mary with a grim smirk on her face. "He doesn't know there's two canaries on the job, does he? Tell him a young girl's having to carry a whole case of tools because of him and his secrets, and this box of stuff's too much. Tell him it's some new special type of bib and brace or something, made of glass so you've got to be real careful with it, and he can be trusted with it more than some slip of a girl."

Nash thought it a sensible idea.

"I'll drop it round to Shanks' gaff before the first meet, and if the job don't go ahead then, he can keep hold of it till it does," he said, looking enquiringly at Arthur, who nodded in agreement.

Chapter 18

"Whitechapel is once more to the fore – a grim spectre at our shows and banquets. And there Whitechapel will remain till modern society alters and there are no more Whitechapels."

The Star

Joe Barnett was trying his hardest to make his way in the world, but it was not easy for someone who had committed the cardinal sin of not acquiring a skill. Unskilled men were ten a penny. He was in his mid-twenties and had already done numerous of jobs, many of them seasonal, some part time, dovetailed together the best he could.

This summer he had sold strawberries from a hand cart.

"Strawberries, all ripe! all ripe!" he had cried till hoarse.

He had stood next to an Italian who ran a Hokey-Pokey (ice-cream) stall in the park. Giuseppe's English was not particularly good so Joe would help him with his advertising.

"Hokey-pokey, penny a lump, that's the stuff to make you jump!" went the cry on the Italian's behalf.

In return, Joe was able to keep his wares out of the sun, under the shade Giuseppe had rigged up on his stall to keep his ice cream cool. They looked after each other's carts when calls of nature were needed and were a useful second pair of eyes against those who would steal anything from a cart that was left unwatched for a few seconds.

On days when he could not afford the outlay to buy strawberries, he might sell sherbet and water. But the freakishly awful summer weather had meant the only people to gain from it were pallbearers, chimney sweeps, gas workers and coalmen, a lot of whom had not been laid off in droves as they usually were in the warmest months. Strawberries and sherbet had proved less popular than usual, so Joe had also sold ginger cake, milk, muffins, rabbits and cheap fish. Anything he could buy without too much initial outlay, which he could sell from his little hand cart or a simple tray, or in the case of rabbits by dangling them from a couple of bars over his shoulder, walking the streets with his wares on display.

The end of the summer had coincided with the start of the Whitechapel Murders, which had led to a new job. Joe was now a newsboy. He would stand alongside several other such men (none were actually boys), each selling a different newspaper, holding an advertising board in front of him with the number of the edition at the top. There were five headlines listed below, which were usually from five completely different stories, but the murders were so dominant in the news that all the headlines now related to the killings.

Third Edition
Witnesses Saw Man With Last Victim
Police Confident Of Arrest
Sailor Clue Denied

Man With Bag Interviewed
Conan Doyle – What Does Holmes Think?

Joe was determined to make an honest living. He hated the fact that his sweetheart, Mary, was in league with local criminals, especially that menacing man Nash, and against his express wishes she continued to make ends meet by prostitution.

Her career choices were a growing source of tension between them. The couple had once lived together, and Joe wanted to return to this state of affairs. One day they would get married and become 'respectable`. But Mary was determined to retain her independence, preferring nowadays to live on her own. Joe had been told to 'bugger off' to his mother's. He knew full well why. Without him around she could more easily go out on the game.

Joe had just arrived at Mary's after twelve hours selling newspapers. His feet and back hurt, and he was in a bad mood. Mary was home, and the sort of argument that was commonplace in such a stormy relationship was quick to start.

"You only keep this shit hole on so you can entertain your men here," remonstrated Joe.

Mary was not the most sensitive soul and would rub Joe's nose in the fact that he barely earned enough to keep himself out of the workhouse, let alone her.

"At least I can get hold of some extra money when I have to, not like you. If you loved me like you say, you'd be my ponce. I could get hold of a lot more gelt if I had a ponce to look after me."

Joe was furious at such a thought.

"I ain't being no ponce! You're go the same way as them other whores you will. Bleeding good riddance to them I says. Old Jack's doing a good job."

Mary enunciated her next three words well apart from each other, slowly for emphasis. But the decibels remained high.

"You...fuck...off!" She then speeded up. "You sound like bloody Nashey you do! I wouldn't be surprised if you were that bastard Jack! No, on second thoughts you don't have the gumption, do you? Even some old whore on her last legs could put you on your aris!"

She grabbed an empty gin bottle that was to hand and hurled it. Missing its intended target, it broke the single window of the little hovel.

Joe went red in the face with rage and took a step towards her, putting one hand on his belt buckle.

"Go on then, you take your belt off to me and I'll give you a taste of my life preserver," shouted Mary, waving a cosh that Nash had given her along with a bit of advice that if any customers gave her any trouble, she 'should put this across their sneezer`.

She kept it on her at all times, along with a small knife, which gave her the confidence that she could look after herself.

Joe backed off. Mary sneered and turned for the door.

"I'm off out of it!"

She slammed the door behind her and marched off, expecting him to come running after her. He did not. So, she shrugged, sniffed, and went on her way.

***

Rose was standing on her doorstep talking to four other women, their collective entourage of thirteen children, four chickens and a dog, lined up along the side wall of her house. A couple of the smaller children were playing a game of tossing the pie man but with a stone rather than a coin, and another couple of tots were passing the time by pushing, shoving, and annoying each other. The rest sat or stood against the wall, silent, sullen, staring. The oldest child, a beanpole of a ten- or eleven-year-old girl, stared wildly into space.

Mary eyed this scene as she approached Sookey's front door, a cloud of sadness descending on her like a bank of fog coming off the river. She doubted the beanpole girl was 'all there' and pondered that death was perhaps not the worst thing that could happen to a child.

She looked away from the girl and caught her mother's eye. She nodded towards Sookey's place.

"She in?"

Rose knew Mary was a prostitute and as such beneath contempt. She did not answer, preferring to look through Mary with a scowl, before turning her back.

It did not really matter whether Rose knew if Sookey was at home or not. It would not take her a second to knock on her door and wait. But Mary had had a drink, so she was not in the mood to let Rose get away with the slight.

"Here, cloth ears!" she shouted. "Cat got your tongue, has it? No lugs and no tongue, what a palaver for a jaw-me-dead like you! "Here, I'll ask my mate Nashey if his cat's got your tongue. I'll get it for you if she has!"

She appreciated that it was not the wittiest bit of banter she had ever come up with but felt something needed to be said.

"Don't you bloody come it with me, you little whore. I'll knock that old bounce out of you…" was the start of Rose's reply.

Mary didn't hear the remainder of the sentence as she banged on Sookey's door and giggled to herself.

"Heard me that time, didn't you!" she shouted over her shoulder with a cocky, self-satisfied smirk.

Sookey opened the door and spotted her friend's smile as well as the direction it was headed.

"Hello Mary. This is indeed a fine surprise. I see you are on good terms with Rose."

"Oh yes, me and Rose are right good mates."

The sarcasm went unnoticed, so Mary kept the remainder of her cheeky thoughts so herself.

I've got my tongue in my cheek there, shame old Rose can't do the same what with the cat having it.

Sookey busied herself making both tea and conversation. And Mary was soon wearing a rather whimsical look as she was told excitedly about her friend recently making the acquaintance of a chap by the name of Nashey.

"He's an old friend of mine as it happens," said Mary. "He's one of the best. But you have to be careful to catch him right. He can fall out with the stones, that one. I heard he had his hands full with some characters before you helped your man give out facers to the lot of them. And there I was thinking you were a real Mr Brownly. You wouldn't catch him lamping old Fagin, would you?"

"Mr Brownlow is the gentleman to whom I believe you refer, Mary. As to you likening me to such a kindly sort, I thank you for the reference. I am pleased to hear you read Mr Dickens."

Sookey had said this with her usual lack of any semblance of being patronising.

"Oh yes, I never miss my trip down the library every week."

For the second time in quick succession the lowest form of wit fell upon deaf ears.

"But pray tell Mary, what do you know of all this?"

"You and Nashey gave three herberts a good hiding, is what I heard."

"Mr Nash did indeed come to my rescue when three ruffians attempted to attack me. It was he who did the 'hiding' as you put it. But I am intrigued by your use of the term 'your man'."

"Just joking with you. But there are some nasty marks on your neck, and I heard you got a punch in the belly for your trouble. How are you, Sookey?"

This was asked with genuine concern but its hitherto coy target was disappointed. She wanted the conversation to stay about Nashey.

"I am quite well now, thank you Mary. A punch knocked the wind out of my sails but had no lasting effect. My throat and leg are on the mend I am pleased to say. Here is the tea. From Ceylon. Chinese tea here tastes not a jot like a Hong Kong infusion. I have heard stories of dangerous flavourings being added here."

Mary gave an uninterested nod and thin smile.

Sookey became aware that she was boring her friend, so took the chance to return to her preferred subject.

"Have you spoken to Nashey since the attack?"

Before an answer had time to be issued, there was a loud thumping on the front door.

"My, but I am popular today," said Sookey with an enthusiastic raise of the eyebrows and a smile. "I have received so many visitors. It is my newfound infamy, I fancy."

She opened the door, and two men immediately pushed their way past her into the sitting room. One of them was Shanks, the other was a man she did not know, who was obviously in pain, head down with a dirty, red-speckled handkerchief clasped over his mouth. He had lost most of his front teeth and there was dried blood on his face, though none on his clothes. His nose was not in any better condition. Shanks spoke on the man's behalf.

"He needs help. Just been in a factory accident. Left him in a right old state. His foreman wants to know if he's fit for work, otherwise he'll find someone who is."

"I will attempt to be of assistance, but he looks like he should attend the London or at the very least seek a doctor," replied Sookey.

"Factory accident, was it?" asked Mary with unconcealed suspicion in her voice. "Looks more like he's been given a good hiding to me."

She exchanged a glance with Sookey, who herself did not believe Shanks' explanation. The injury was clearly not new. Looking at the dried blood and the colour of the bruising, it must have happened the day before. The man had clearly changed his clothes since any accident, as his original garb must have been stained with blood.

Shanks glanced at Mary for a moment and then turned to Sookey.

"Who's your monkey?"

"Oh, she is just a girl who runs errands for me," she replied.

"It is indeed fortunate she is here. I will require her to fetch some bandages, ointments, and the like from the pharmacy if I am to tend this poor chap's wounds to his satisfaction."

Inspecting the man's injuries, Sookey was now only a few inches from him. His smell was familiar to her. She found a pencil and a piece of paper and started writing furiously.

"Here you are Mary, please take this to Corton's. As always, please read the note before you take your leave."

Sookey turned, smiling at Shanks as she explained with false jocularity.

"I fear the poor chemist may not understand my hand. He commonly does not."

Turning back to Mary, she continued.

"Please check my hand is clear."

She folded the paper over and held it blank side out towards Mary, before Shanks snatched it from her.

"I'll be the judge of that."

Shanks was attempting to ape the menace Nash would radiate in such a situation. He unfolded the paper and looked down at it. Sookey's anxious stare at her told Mary that there was something incriminating on the note. Mary moved her hand slowly towards the cosh squirreled away in her skirt. The note read:

'Fetch a policeman. I believe this to be one of the men who attacked me'.

Shanks looked up and stared at Sookey for several seconds. He then looked at Mary for a similar amount of time, before turning his gaze to his injured mate.

"You read?" he enquired of him.

"Do me a favour," the man lisped.

Shanks leered as he passed the note back to Mary.

"All right Mary monkey, bugger off down to the chemists and be lively about it. I want you back here sharp or it's trouble for you and your friend here."

Mary snatched the note, read it, and pretended to have been intimidated.

"Sorry mister, I'll get back here soon enough, don't you worry."

Sookey had not recognised the injured man to begin with. It had been so dark in that alley. And no doubt that was what he had been relying on. But the injuries were exactly those which she would imagine the fellow whom Nashey had kicked in the mouth would have received. This, allied to his familiar odour, which she had smelt when he had his thumbs to her throat, convinced her he was one of the attackers. But this left her bemused.

What had Mr Shanks to do with all of this?

As soon as Mary left, Sookey busied herself rummaging around for things to help dress the man's wounds, before eventually speaking.

"I must apologise for not attending our meeting as arranged Mr Shanks. I was indisposed."

"I told you before, it's just Shanks. I got your Mr Nash to thank for the name, and I got you to thank for telling me as why he gave it me. I owes you both all right. And yes, I heard about you being *indisposed.*" There was undisguised contempt for the final word in the last sentence. "Bloody lucky Nashey happened by when he did weren't it? No telling what those men might have done to you. Bad sorts everywhere you look these days, ain't there."

Sookey's right hand came up to her throat. There was

an awkward silence while he stared at her intently with a sneering grin on his face. She thought the time would pass better if she engaged in conversation.

"Do you have the funds you were to give to me last night Mr, er I mean Shanks?"

"Nasty bruise you got there. And no, you should have got it off me last night when I had it. Had a bit of bad luck with the horses since. You'll have to wait for it now."

Yesterday he had made an arrangement with her that she should call at his gaff for the debt but had fobbed her off with a tall story that he worked quite late every night so the earliest she could come by was just after dark. She was never going to make the appointment. He had seen to that. And now he was enjoying intimidating this defenceless woman.

***

Nash was just finishing his tea. It would normally be bread and something sweet off the cart of a street vendor but on this occasion, he was enjoying a treat. A roast dinner that old Granny Hurlock had brought him just after he had got back from introducing the girls to Arthur. The old lady had included his favourite, a pennyworth of carrot & onion pieces and pot herbs. She had heard what he had done to help Sookey and wanted to show her gratitude. Sookey had saved the life of her young grandson when the poor little mite had been poorly last month. The old woman could not afford to heat the meal, but Nash was delighted by the gesture. He had still been suffering with his headache from the coshing so did not fancy it at the time, so it had sat on his table for a while. He had just been along to the local baker to pay him twopence to heat it up. He tossed the last morsel to the cat, which promptly ignored it.

"Choosey little cow! What's your name, Marie bleeding Lloyd?"

Mention of the East End's most famous daughter sent his thoughts spinning off at a tangent.

He wouldn't mind going to the local flea pit for a change. It must be a twelve-month or more since he'd seen that Marie Lloyd up the old Paragon. Of course, she's too high and mighty to perform in the Mile End Road these days. They say she earns six hundred pound a week! Funny-looking tart she were an' all, with her buck teeth and thin hair, but she could hold a bloody good tune, I'll say that for her. Good luck to her I say. At least one's escaped. I suppose I could ask Mary if she wanted to come with me. Mind you, her Joe wouldn't like it. No, best not. Them two has enough bull & cows from what I hear without me causing trouble between them. I could see if that Sookey wanted to go. It's bound to be up her street ain't it, the theatre, but I'd have to pay extra for the better seats mind, away from the rowdies. After all, she'd think it funny if I didn't come near or by after what happened. And I got to make sure she keeps her trap shut about what I said to her about me seeing the killer. Trouble is I don't want her thinking anything of it, like I want to be her fellow or something. I've seen how she looks at me. I'll just say it's because she helped me after that cove coshed me. A thank you, like standing her a gin.

There was an urgent-sounding rapping on the door.

"Christ almighty! That sodding door will be off its hinges soon enough! It's like bleeding Regent's Circus round here!"

***

Small knuckles started rapping on the door.

"It's… me… Mary… Run as fast… as I could."

She was panting from running to find help, and then running straight back to Sookey's. It had not been far, but her alcohol diet was not the regime of an athlete.

Shanks was about to open the door a crack to check Mary was alone, when he was thrown back by the door being kicked open violently. Shanks stumbled backwards, only being saved from falling to the floor by grabbing hold of Sookey's table. Nash's huge bulk took up the space in the doorway.

"Gawd help us, Shanks boy," he said grimly. "Bloody door sticks. Warped. Damp, see. Needs a good kick." He glanced in the direction of the injured man before continuing.

"You just have to give some things a good booting when they need it."

He then turned to Sookey.

"Just come across Mary here on her way to the chemist's. She said she were running errand for you, and I felt bad I ain't kept my promise to do that wallpapering you asked me about a while since. Thought I'd come round and do it now if that's all right with you. I should get it done before the light goes if I gets cracking straight away. What do you say girl?"

"That is very kind of you Nashey," replied a confused, relieved, not to say stimulated Sookey.

She was feeling shocked at her lack of shock again.

A man wrecks my door with great violence and before I know what I am about, my chest heaves with relish and I feel easier than ever before. I can make no hand of it.

Nash continued in light vein.

"Can't swing no cat in here. Some of you are going to have to bugger off sharp so I can get on."

He took off his overcoat and started to peel up his shirtsleeves. Shanks and the toothless man noticed that the coat had made quite a clank when it landed on the table. There were obviously some heavy objects in the pockets. Sookey, for her part, had noticed the huge forearms and then the bulge of biceps in the tightening shirt. Mary noticed Sookey's glance and inwardly smirked, while keeping the straightest of dead pan faces in what she appreciated was a tense moment.

Having turned to Shanks, Nash was suddenly no longer friendliness personified. His expression and voice-tone changed to dark and quietly intimidating.

"It's time you went Shanks. Better leave your boy here mind. He looks like he needs looking after."

It was not anything other than a demand with menaces. It was also a contract. Nash agreed to let the whole incident drop without retribution, without a word said. It didn't do anyone any good falling out when they were just about to work together on the biggest, most lucrative crime of their lives. The pull was still on as far as he was concerned. And in return, Shanks was to leave alone. The man with the injury was to stay. Just to make sure Shanks understood him, Nash continued.

"I been to see that friend of ours, Peter. He's ready to do that bit of business we talked about."

A peterman was another name for a safe cracker. Nash thought Shanks should understand the reference. "I got the other friends already arranged an' all."

Nash made a point of not referring to, or even looking at, Mary when he said this. Shanks did not need to know at this stage, and may never need to know, that Mary was one of his team on the job. The less Shanks knew the better. Mary understood. She kept quiet.

Shanks was furious but knew he was being let off lightly. And at least it was good news about the cracksman. He would have to deal with whatever his mate let slip another time.

"Yes, I'll be off and let you get on with it," said Shanks, carefully avoiding making eye-contact with his mate. As he made his escape he shouted back over his shoulder with false bravado. "About time you got that Peter fellow sorted out. We ain't got all day you know."

Nash smiled contemptuously and turned to the injured man.

"Couldn't leave quick enough, could he? Good mate you got there, ain't you son?"

"Dash it! I am quite done with Mr Shanks! What sort of a down-going man is he?" stormed a red-faced, hands-on hips Sookey. She was also angry with Nashey. Why had he let the man go without so much as a by-your-leave?

Nash was aware of the situation.

"Sookey, you must be thinking why I didn't pitch it in red hot with Shanks?"

"You are indeed a nut to crack sir."

"I'll tell you another time," he replied, with a wink and the tiniest of nods. But Sookey didn't understand what was meant by such gestures.

"How's that?" she queried.

Nash gave her an old-fashioned look and allowed a tinge of exasperation into his voice.

"Don't stick out!"

Sookey appreciated it was time to stop asking questions. Perhaps she could ask Nashey again when they were alone. She smiled at him and turned to the injured man, her expression immediately fading into a more serious one.

"Let me see what ails you." It was the first time Nash had heard her use the scolding, hectoring tone of the middle class.

She placed the fingers of her right hand none too gently on his chin and started to check his teeth for damage. He flinched and moved his head away from her roughly.

"Suffer me," she said in a no-nonsense nurse voice.

"Never mind suffer me. What about my suffering!?" was lisped.

"Let her have a look at your Hounslows," interjected Mary wearily. "She might save you a fortune in dentists."

"Who asked you to pipe up?" sneered the man. "What's the state of my ivories got to do with you? And who are you anyhow?"

It was a mistake.

"I'm the girl who's going to take my friend here for a little walk," replied Mary with an exaggeratedly wide, false smile. "Get your hat Sookey, let's leave his nibs here to help Nashey with the wallpapering. I wouldn't be surprised if he helped him with a few other things as well."

Sookey's "Oh, but…" was quickly quashed by Nash.

"Good thought, girl. Sookey, you were only telling me the other day you had to find somewhere to take your lady friends on their tour. Why don't you let Mary show you the Sir Paul Pindar Tavern in Bishopsgate? Might be the sort of place you could take them. It looks rough so they'll be excited right enough, but it's only full of old messengers, costers, laundresses, off duty coppers from Bishopsgate nick and the like, so it'll be colourful for them but safe."

Nash shoved his hand in his right trouser pocket and handed half a sovereign to Mary.

"I don't know if they do grub, but if they do, have a good scoff the pair of you. Mary, you look like you could do with a good nosh. When's the last time you ate something that weren't bread and scrape?" He then pointed an index finger at her. "But I want most of that back in change, mind."

Mary's cheeky grin told him silently "you'll be lucky!" as she started ushering her bemused friend towards the front door.

Sookey donned her coat and started to leave.

"Where's your hat?" queried Mary.

"I have not replaced my last one. It 'went home' as we say here in the East End."

"We in the East End," mocked Mary, "never go out without a hat or shawl on our head. It's not seemly. The only time I don't is when I'm inviting custom," she said, before changing her tone to a more cynical one and pulling a face, "so they can see my lovely red hair."

She then took off her shawl and slung it roughly over her friend's head. "Now, get this on."

As they stepped out of what was left of the door, Mary raised her voice to full decibels for the world to hear.

"Look at the state of your front step Sookey. No wonder those old fishwives over there turn their nose up at you."

The on-looking Rose et al tutted and looked away askance.

Chapter 19

"Modern society is more promptly awakened to a sense of duty by the knife of a murderer than by the pens of many earnest writers."

The Lancet

Men with similar characters and dispositions can often be the best of friends, or great rivals or sworn enemies. It is sometimes all a matter of fate; when and where they first meet, and the circumstances. George Lusk was not unlike a more respectable version of Alexander Nash. But the two men had got off on the wrong foot.

Nash believed Lusk had stolen a prospective girlfriend off him when they were young men making their first forays into the world of romance. Though the term stolen lacked a certain accuracy. More, he stole a march on Nash. The two boys had both been making their way along the Ratcliffe Highway, on the Saturday 'monkey parade', where all the young men and women of the area paraded up and down in front of each other. With the bravado, not to mention the social pressure, only a thirteen-year-old can experience at the head of a group of mates faced with members of the opposite sex, Nash was chirping cheeky remarks and offering his love and devotion disguised as insults, to the girl of his dreams, Daisy. But he had taken her first coy rejection too literally. While he was licking his wounds, young Georgie Lusk, from another group of lads, moved in and made a quick killing with Daisy. Nash had lost the girl of his dreams.

The two lads never did like each other after that. And now Nash was the sort of man Lusk used to be, but he was trying to leave his past behind. Lusk was a successful builder nowadays. But Lusk 'fancied his self' as far as Nash was concerned. Their last meeting had ended with Nash telling him so, contempt written all over his face.

"I remember you when you used to chew bread for our ducks!"

Lusk, along with the rest of the world's population, had never been employed as a duck's bread-chewer, but he understood very well what Nash was saying in his 'arse-about face' way. But the altercation had been a good while ago. Although they lived in the same square mile, their paths rarely crossed these days.

Lusk opened the door to Nash, greeting his visitor with an undisguised lack of enthusiasm.

"Yes?"

Nash made it clear he was equally displeased to see him.

"Still getting that gang of navvies in frocks together are you, George?"

Lusk was the self-appointed head of the local vigilantes, who had taken it upon themselves to do what the police could not, namely bring the Whitechapel Murderer to justice. Nash had originally agreed with their ideals, and if it had been anyone else other than George Lusk at their head, he would have joined them. Their first abortive attempt to catch and no doubt beat to death the man they believed to be the killer ended in miserable, embarrassing failure. One John Pizer, nickname Leather Apron, was their target. He was their man on what they considered was the overwhelming evidence against him; he was violent towards women, owned a big knife which he liked to flash about, was a butcher by trade so had the knife skills, and the foreign surname told you the rest. The police had managed to get to Pizer first, arresting and then questioning him only to find he had a cast iron alibi for the last murder, and relayed this to Lusk, with a warning about his future conduct.

The incident had been reported in the newspapers and Lusk's name given. Soon after the double murder and the publication of the Jack the Ripper missives, a box had been delivered to Lusk, inside which had been half a kidney and a note purporting to be from the killer. It was claimed the kidney was that removed from the body of Catherine Eddowes. The police took it seriously at first but eventually concluded it was a prank played by a medical student, though Nash suspected it was more likely that a newspaper hack was laughing up his sleeve. Lusk had become the celebrity of the day. He used his newfound notoriety to put forward the idea that small, hard men should dress up in women's clothing and walk the streets at night, ready to give the Ripper more than he bargained for. Nash thought the idea ridiculous.

Lusk cursed his sarcasm, though Nash feigned innocence.

"I was going to volunteer myself George but thought I might be too big for you. And now you're like that…"

"Damn your eyes Nash, what you after?"

Nash turned his gravest expression on like a tap.

"I want to know why I shouldn't follow you into a dark alley one night and come out the other end on my own."

Lusk was bemused, and not a little scared.

"Eh?"

"I hear tell one of your lads as had all is teeth out. He's going to have a new gas stove put in."

Nash laughed grimly at his own joke. Lusk now understood.

"Oh yes, I heard about that," he confirmed. "Case of mistaken identity, as the police would say. Lucky you were there weren't it? I heard a few of my boys thought that funny slummer woman might be the Ripper. She's got the doctoring know how they say the killer might have, and the murders started up sharp after she come to live in Whitechapel. One paper reckons the Ripper could be a woman. That's why the police ain't got a clue, see. They ain't even looking for the right sex." He laughed nervously, before adding an afterthought. "They were just going to take her down Leman Street nick. That's all. Lads, eh?"

There was another nervous chortle.

Nash had not been told anything he did not already know. He had prised this much out of the toothless man in Sookey's front room with nothing more than a punch to the testicles and an arm-lock which had threatened to have the man tickle the back of his own neck.

"Thinking Sookey, that's her name case you ain't heard, is the Ripper is even more bleeding stupid than thinking some butcher's the killer because he likes bullying women.

197

Lots of men round here knock women about when they've had a few don't they? Some when they ain't had a few neither."

Nash darkened his stare even more, leaning forward to within a few inches of his old adversary's face before carrying on.

"But your boy tells me you put him up to it. I have to hold you to account, see. And all your boys got a bloody good hiding, so what to do with you? It's only fair."

Lusk folded.

"It weren't nothing to do with me. This cove Shanks comes and sees me. He tells me this slummer woman's the Ripper and he can prove it, see. He says you saw her do the last murder but you're keeping your trap shut because you want the papers to keep going on about it to make it an even bigger case, to help the East End, so you don't want her catched."

This shook Nash. He had not expected this. His mind started to race.

Shanks must know something about my interest in the murders. He's too canny to think Sookey's got anything to do with it. But he wants to get out of paying her for the jobs she's done for him, so gives Lusk a version of what he knows to get her dealt with. But what does he know? Or at least suspect? Too much by the sound of it. Once the pull's done, I'll deal with Shanks once and for...

Lusk interrupted the promise.

"What's happened to my boy anyhow? Ain't seen hide nor hair of him since it happened."

"I told him they had dentists miles away what could sort out his Hounslows. He should disappear off and find one, and not come back if he knew what were good for him."

Much to Lusk's relief, this turned out to be a parting shot. His old adversary simply turned on his heel and left, deep in thought.

***

Questioning Lusk had not been at the top of Nash's agenda. He didn't really know why he had been to see the man when he had other more pressing, more important things to do. Sheer curiosity, he supposed, which brought on some self-cursing.

Lucky I ain't no bleeding cat. I'd have snuffed it by now.

But now Nash was at his most important venue of the day, and he was in new territory. He had never had cause to visit his local greengrocer. The closest he usually came to fruit & veg was the parsley and potato he consumed in the pie & mash shop, or pickled pears from a stall in the market. The local grocery and chandler's shop was owned and run by slum landlord John McCarthy, a businessman with a finger in many pies of the figurative variety. He rented out numerous properties in the roughest parts of Whitechapel.

McCarthy was behind his shop counter, resplendent in immaculate clean white apron down to his knees. He glanced up smiling at what he thought was to be a new customer. His expression changed in an instant when he saw who had just walked into his shop.

"Mary Kelly told me where to find you," growled Nash.

McCarthy was well aware of who Nash was and who his friends were.

"Here, I don't want no trouble. She ain't paid her rent. I told Fred to go round there and ask her for it, that's all. He didn't hit her or nothing. I got a dog in the back."

"It's as well your boy didn't hit her then, otherwise me and your dog would be falling out, wouldn't we?" said Nash with a scowl.

The man quivered as Nash's right hand came out of his pocket. The expected cosh was not there. Just a handful of coins.

"How much she owe?" asked Nash as he started sorting through his change.

"It'll be a sov by the end of next week. She won't have paid for a month or more," answered the relieved grocer, letting out a deep breath.

Nash looked up from his palm and sneered.

"I didn't ask you how much she owed next week."

"It's three weeks, four bob a week. That's …"

"I can do sums!"

Nash tossed a half-sovereign and a two-shilling piece across the counter, both coins bouncing to hit the apron before falling to the floor.

"I've seen that room you got her in," said Nash with undisguised contempt for the landlord standing in front of him. "Can't swing no cat in it. And your rent's plenty stiff for it. She has to sell herself on the streets to pay you."

McCarthy wanted to answer with "that's the going rate, take it or leave it, and if she don't pay there's plenty as will, and I ain't interested in how she gets the rent, just so long as she does," but he hated the sight of blood, particularly his own. He did not say a word as he scrambled on the floor to pick up the money and hoped the huge man in front of him would perhaps just knock over a bowl of apples and maybe steal something, just to make a point, and then walk out.

He took longer than he need have to rescue the coins, out of sight behind his counter, waiting in vain to hear Nash's heavy boots creaking out of the shop. He eventually got to his feet to face the man still standing there.

Nash had earlier asked Mary if she knew if her landlord had any places in Doveton Street. McCarthy rented out so many rooms in the vicinity, the odds were that he would have a place somewhere close to the killer's lair. Mary had relayed that he had once offered her a place somewhere in that area; she couldn't remember where exactly. She wasn't interested at the higher price; she could not afford her present hovel.

"I didn't come to pay her rent. Lucky you spoke of it. That's bunts for you. But woe-betide you if Mary tells me it ain't the case. But now to the purpose. Mary tells me you offered her a bigger room over Doveton Street way for a couple of extra bob a week, just shy of a twelve-month back. That right?"

McCarthy was relieved but wary, appalled at the thought of having Nash as a tenant. Who would collect the rent?!

"It's rented out. All my rooms is rented out."

Nash knew it would not be easy to coax information out of McCarthy, and he couldn't very well get it out of him with his usual tactics. Inflicting injuries on her landlord was a sure way to have Mary booted out on the street. But he was pleased with the original misunderstanding about the rent. McCarthy would be happy to have had the arrears paid to him and had already shown himself to be easily intimidated.

"I didn't ask if you had something to rent now," barked Nash. "I just want to know if you got a place in Doveton Street."

"Yes, I got a place there," confirmed McCarthy. "What of it?"

"Got the gaff with the red rag in the window?"

"Might have. Might not. It'll cost you to find out."

Nash looked about the shop with interest.

"Good shop you got here John. Brings in a pretty penny ever day it's open I shouldn't wonder. I see you got them funny new banana and tomato things in. I hear they make a right old mess when you knock them about a bit."

The threat was all too clear to McCarthy. He already had twelve shillings in his pocket from this man; he better not push him too far. He had heard what Nash had done to those three boys of George Lusk's. And they were nasty bits of work themselves.

"Reach us another four bob towards Mary's rent. It saves her the trouble of paying it this week. Poor girl. Must be hard for her, what with all that's going on."

Nash resisted the temptation he felt to tell McCarthy where he could stick his concern for the 'poor girl`.

Nash didn't answer. He just fished in his pockets for a couple of florins.

But before he brought out any money, he first brought out a cosh and a marlin spike, and laid them matter-of-factly on the counter, as he glared at the shop owner. He handed over the money and started to replace the weapons back in the cavernous pockets of his overcoat.

"I know the place you mean," said McCarthy. "It ain't mine. I got one a couple of doors down. Number twenty-six. The gaff you got your eyes on must be twenty-two. I know the landlord who's got that place. What do you want to know about it? I could find out for you?"

"Who lives there, what the man of the house does with his self, where he drinks, anywhere else he spends time, who he spends it with, his family, anything else you can find out about him. And you got to be crafty finding out. I don't want nobody knowing nothing about it."

"What you up to? Those places are slums. There ain't nothing worth nicking in them."

Nash touched his own nose with an index finger.

"You keep this out," he said. He then changed his tone to a more conciliatory, conspiratorial one. "Just do as I say John and I'll pass on some good bunts to you. I know it'll cost you to find that little lot out, so I won't beat about the bush. I've already given you sixteen shilling. Get me all the intelligence on the cove I want without him knowing nothing about it, keep your mouth shut, and tell anyone showing any interest in my business to bugger off, and I'll round it up to Jacks for you. No more, no less."

Jacks was five pounds. A hefty sum even for an avaricious slum landlord. Nash was making a deal he could not afford. He was more reliant on the success of Shanks' post office robbery than he would care to admit.

McCarthy guessed that Nash must be confident he could make something out of the man in Doveton Street. But he'd be damned if he could guess how. No matter.

Five pounds was a lot of money. He smiled with sly enthusiasm.

"Jacks it is."

Jack's it certainly is, thought Nash. He did not know the word 'irony' but felt it, nonetheless.

Chapter 20

"The very people who are now the most vehement in their denunciation of this ... demented murderer don't turn a hair when...thousands of women...rot to death with syphilis. Who cares too, how many young girls have their jaws eaten out of their heads by phosphorous in order that matches should be sold cheaper?"

H.M. Hyndman, Social Democratic Federation

The alcohol broke down her barriers. Sookey was aware that everyone in the vicinity must be inquisitive about their strange middling neighbour. Being a charity worker was one thing, but living in the East End full-time? Earning a living in Whitechapel? Living like everyone else? Trying to be like one of them? Sookey was ready to tell part of the story, though not all. She would give Mary a potted history of her recent problems, editing down the more painful details that had come out at the trial. She would start by telling of her nemesis, that most despicable of women.

Dinky Smith had an ingratiating but likeable manner which, it transpired, gave way to feral ferocity. She had worked for some time at fairs and circuses as a fake fortune-teller, supplementing her income with any confidence trick she could pull off. She had successfully wheedled her way into the heart of an apothecary's assistant, from whom she gained knowledge of dispensing. Armed with such information, she was quick to start making up potions and concoctions to sell at her booth.

"Probably worked the markets and race meetings. Penny gaffs as well," offered Mary.

"But it was as a trickster," replied Sookey, "what you would call a magsman I believe, where Dinky's true talent lay."

The woman used an ability to charm the gullible into trusting her while she relieved them of whatever she could. She had worked on a young, naive attorney. The plan had been to get him to invest in a non-existent cosmetics company and then she would disappear with the funds. Dinky had impressed with the ease with which she handled tricky cosmetic ingredients such as arsenic, white lead and antimony, but she had been a little too blasé with said items and had been stricken down with self-poisoning.

"Serves her bloody right, I hate magsmen," sneered Mary. "It's a shithouse crime. Bash me over the head, stick a knife in me if you will, but don't take me for a fool. You have to be a wrong un to be a magsman."

While Dinky was laid up, the attorney went ahead with renting and fitting out a little shop just off Piccadilly. The message to ladies was an enticing confectionary of the exotic and sensual. Various powders, oils and soaps stocked, and reference to their usage in a harem, a telling attraction.

"Harem?" queried Mary, with apparent innocence.

She knew the word perfectly well, but the minx in her wanted to embarrass her friend into explaining it. Sookey was duly embarrassed and wished she had not mentioned it. Ignoring the question, she continued that once recovered,

Dinky was quick to add her expertise to the venture. New York Spring Water, which it transpired was no more than an infusion of bran in hot water, sold particularly well at the outrageous price of two guineas per bottle.

"There's one born every minute," said Mary, shaking her head in disbelief.

Sookey sighed in agreement.

But those who wished to have the ultimate in ablutions could invest in a Turkish Toilet Cabinet as supplied to the sultana herself, costing twenty guineas.

"Twenty guineas! God help me, I'm in the wrong game here!"

Hearing the incredulity in Mary's voice, Sookey was quick to make a point.

"Yes, indeed. You could sell such things rather than…"

"Myself. We've had this talk, haven't we? Now, get on with your story."

Suitably chastised, Sookey relayed further revelations.

The very notion of make-up carried a hint of impropriety. The business was directed at ladies who were wealthy but not too strait-laced.

Dinky set up a house of assignation, where lovers could meet in secret. The beauty enterprise, with its treatment amenities, provided ideal cover. Business boomed precisely because its reputation was questionable. There had been an enticingly risqué quality to the enterprise.

"What's all this got to do with you living here in Whitechapel? Get on with it."

Mary clearly felt her friend was being a little verbose.

Sookey replied with a sad little sigh and endeavoured to speed up.

"Dinky then met me."

Sookey had been the widow of an army officer. She had spent much of her adult life bored in a loveless marriage in Hong Kong and was now a faded beauty. But now back home with the freedom of single status, she wished to regain her lost glamour, and a little romance would not have gone amiss. As a young debutant, her nickname had been Sookey; she had recently started calling herself by the name again. Retiring Mrs Susan Parsons was no more; enticing Sookey had returned. And though not very rich, she had owned a modest property and had £1,000 invested.

She expected Mary to issue forth with a show of shock at her friend's wealth, but the audience was well and truly captive now. It waited in silence for the next instalment.

Sookey's self-deception had made her an easy target. As well as paying large sums for cosmetics, she was plied with expensive treatments. And on a couple of occasions Sookey had encountered Lord Aylesford, a rakish bachelor. The two of them had flirted, and around this a great fantasy was woven. Sookey was given to understand that the nobleman was greatly attracted to her, but unfortunately it was crucial for family reasons to keep the connection secret for the moment. Any public recognition was impossible. Thus, the wooing was carried out by love letters through Dinky. Sookey had been robbed of every vestige of sense by the letters she received, and Dinky for her part was thrown into a frenzy of avarice. There appeared nothing she could not make her client believe. Lord Aylesford was said to be in temporary financial embarrassment due to funds being ploughed into philanthropic ventures. Sookey was happy to assist. The attorney was introduced to arrange for her capital to be disposed of through him for charitable works. In just five months, they had bled her dry.

The lover's letters had been well written and showed thought and insight. Sookey had treasured them. But their author, a clerk, had demanded ever increasing amounts from Dinky, so his services became no longer required. Lord Aylesford suddenly became barely literate, and Sookey finally became suspicious. She confessed the whole sorry business to her relatives, who were not deterred by fear of scandal. The police were summoned. Dinky duly came to appear before the Recorder of London.

In the witness box, Sookey, gaunt from remorse and shame, cut a sorry specimen. The defence counsel had a field day.

"How could such abject balderdash deceive anyone? Was it not plain that she has poured away her money buying gratification for her lewd appetites?"

The case caused a good deal of scandal, as well as entertainment. Sookey had become a figure of fun and there was loud laughter in court at her expense. Dinky was sentenced to five years at her majesty's pleasure.

There was a quiet, desultory response from the listener to the tale.

"We both know someone who will see to her when she gets out, if…"

"No, no Mary, I want it never again heard of. It was in my previous life."

This was where Sookey decided to end her story. The tale of how she made the journey from the courthouse to living in the slums would be for another time. And she could see from Mary's silence and downcast expression that she too had probably had enough for one day.

***

Nash walked into the pub which he had recommended. It was crowded but the two women had managed to ensconce themselves into a quiet corner. Mary had successfully moved the conversation on to lighter matters. Her latest outrageous, funny remark had Sookey giggling, with her left hand held over her mouth in shock, shaking her head as she laughed.

"Still here spending my gelt, I see."

It was a usual brusque Nash welcome.

"Let me stand you a drink out of your own money, you miserable sod," chortled Mary.

She got up from their table and joined Nash at the bar. She lowered her voice to a conspiratorial whisper and gave him a knowing look.

"Get him to nark on Shanks, by any chance?"

Nash returned her gaze with an appreciative nod.

"You're sharp. Mind you don't cut yourself. Yes, he narked all right."

"You didn't get any wallpapering done I'll wager."

"No. After the toothless wonder and me had our little chat I went to see a fellow about the door, and left Rose keeping an eye on the place." And then as an afterthought he added sarcastically with a grin. "She speaks highly of you."

"Oh yes, I know. Me and old Rose are right good mates. Took you an hour just to do that did it?" queried

Mary sardonically, before adding another question with an accompanying wink. "Come on, tell me, what were they up to, attacking Sookey like that?"

"Nose-ache," retorted Nash as he tapped Mary's nose gently. "You mind your own."

He picked up his beer and the two of them sidled back, smiling, to Sookey.

Seeing Nash tap Mary's nose, a wave of jealously pulsed through Sookey. She managed a tight little smile as they sat down.

"Pray, tell me plainly, the two of you, when did you first meet each other?"

She did not like the conspiratorial glance and grin the two of them then shared. Mary started to reply.

"He…"

But Nash immediately talked over her.

"I was minding my own business over by the Victoria and Albert Docks, when before I know what I'm about, this one's got her hand in my waistcoat." Nash's wide-eyed mock horror turned to a grin. "Just off the boat she were and she's thieving. It were well I catched her straight, mind. If she had got halfway down the street her days would have been numbered when I catched up with her."

"If I had got away a yard, how would a big lump like you going to catch the likes of me," she snorted back with an equally broad grin before continuing to Sookey. "He grabbed hold of me and I think he's going to knock me over at first, but he ends up telling me about Providence Row night refuge so I get myself along to it. We've been friends ever since." She followed this with a wink at Nash.

Sookey was beginning to wish she hadn't asked. She started to feel like an outsider, but then had a brainwave.

"You speaking of Victoria and Albert brings forth a recollection. I once paid a figure, it was stiff as you would say, to be received at a party to raise funds for charitable causes, attended by Queen Victoria herself. She was enquired, lest her opinion was ill, what she thought of the new museum in Kensington being named for her and Prince Albert. Her answer: 'We are not amuse-eum`."

She looked for a flicker of recognition of the joke registering in the eyes of Nash but was disappointed.

"Yes, I reckon she'd think it a right liberty if they never asked her permission," he said seriously. There was a short silence before Nash continued. "Anyhow, what with all the palaver I never got round to doing that wallpapering of yours. And I should pay you for that door. I just been to see a locksmith to sort it out; him and his carpenter mate will be round tomorrow. I've pushed the door to, so you just need to give it a bit of a yank when you gets home. Rose's keeping an eye out."

Sookey made the obvious appreciative noises and insisted she would pay for the door, and assured Nash that there was no hurry where the wallpapering was concerned. She was not sure whether she should say in a light throw away fashion that she could get someone else to do it, as there were lots of people who owed her money or a favour for services rendered but thought that Nashey might take this as a slight. She left it that she would receive him another time to do the job.

Mary then took up the conversation and soon lightened the mood again, arguing good naturedly with Nashey.

Sookey was pleased to hear that their disagreement was over a literary matter. It was a worthy, if rather colourful, argument about who was the toughest, Bill Sykes or Magwitch? It was a joy to her that Nashey, brought up with nothing but an all too brief schooling before the need to work had thrust him into premature adulthood, had read, been read, or at least heard of such stories. It was not so long ago, at the time Oliver Twist and Great Expectations were written, that there would have been a terrible irony in that few characters in similar real-life stories would have ever heard of the books, let alone be able to read, or argue over them.

But now she felt that her work at Toynbee Hall, and that of others such as the ragged schools for the poor, was making a difference. She felt a moment of peace.

She appreciated that she was completely out of place, a fish out of water, who turned disapproving heads with her middling manners and accent, yet she had never felt so at home.

She looked around. 'The Pinda' as it was called, was a squalid place. It may have had the glitz of an old gin palace once, but over the years the mirrors and bright lamps had been smashed or cracked and the former replaced with advertising boards that had got filthy with smoke. The gaiety of purple painted walls and huge drapery of a few decades ago had become a dirty, stained, pock-marked crumble, and the curtains had long since rotted with damp and disappeared. The smell and pall of stale tobacco, mildew and unwashed humanity hung in the air, and the customers were just as Nashey had described them. Her middling friends, on sticking their heads through the door, might see a den of iniquity, but these people were too weak, too broken to be part of that sort of scene. They were simply hiding from life, trying to escape, albeit temporarily.

Her concentration returned to the argument going on across the table. Nash was clearly far more impressed with Magwitch than Sykes. Anyone who could escape from the infamously horrendous prison hulks, thankfully scrapped some years since, was all right with him. But Mary was making fun of his ideas, purely, Sookey suspected, to bait him.

Sookey had come to realise that playfully criticising someone, or 'pulling your leg' as it was called, was an important aspect of human relationships in the slums. It was often a sign of close friendship, though she had found it difficult to ascertain when, and to whom, one could use such humour without giving offence, and had steered clear of it.

Nash rose to the bait.

"So how is it, contrary Mary, that a crowd of roughs followed the coppers after Sykes in Jacob's Island? Them Bermondsey coves hates coppers the same as us. They wouldn't have believed a word the police said, so he must have been a wrong un for them to chase after him. And if he were so bleeding tough, he wouldn't have let some poxy little fighting dog give him up, would he now?"

An increasingly happy, confident Sookey saw an opportunity to make her debut as a 'leg-puller'.

"I dare say Mary that is why Nashey owns a cat rather than a dog!"

She had a broad self-satisfied smirk on her face. Mary let out a large laugh, more to further belittle Nash rather than because she found the joke funny. Nash's expression darkened in an instant.

"I've told you before, ain't I? I don't own no cat. If it don't catch mice it starves," he said seriously. "It's well for you I ain't Bill Sykes. Lest you forget, just because I let her take the piss," briefly nodding sideways at Mary without taking his intimidating stare from Sookey, "don't mean nobody else can."

The blood drained from Sookey's face. She was ashen. She glanced nervously at Mary for support, but her friend was suddenly finding the floor an interesting topic for inspection as she silently reviewed the error made.

Blimey, you've gone and done it now girl. I warned you to be careful with him.

But after a second of hesitation, Mary knew she had to defend Sookey. She was not going to let Nashey upset her. She raised her head defiantly and was about to say something when Nash flicked his gaze at her and gave the tiniest, quickest of winks. Sookey was now avoiding eye-contact, staring at Nash's chest.

Nash lifted a finger and gently applied pressure to Sookey's chin, raising her head to bring her eyes up to meet his. His face collapsed into a broad grin.

"Ain't you amuse-eum?" He started to laugh heartily. "If old Queen Victoria herself heard that joke, she'd have you carted off to the Tower for sure, and she'd be right to do it an' all. I had to get my own back for the 'distress of the mind' as you would call it, you caused me there, girl!"

Sookey was wide eyed by this time, and swivelled her head slowly to look at Mary, who had much the same expression as she twisted to return the look, before bursting into laughter.

"Ever been had?! He had you there! I was just about to tell him what for, as well. He had a bloody cheek. He would have got a piece of my mind I can tell you. And a facer into the bargain I shouldn't wonder!"

"Would I now?" interjected Nash with mock aggression.

"Yes, I say!" said Mary, folding her arms across her chest in defiance.

The colour which had drained from Sookey's face moments earlier surged back, and she felt a huge blush in her cheeks. Mary saw the reddening and was tempted to make a joke of Sookey looking like she was wearing even more rouge than usual, but she felt better of it.

A memory of the people laughing at her in court came into Sookey's mind, and she felt anger course through her, but when she saw the warmth in the laughter of her two friends, and realised they were laughing with, not at, her the anger was washed away by a torrent of well-being.

"You trifle with me for sport sir. Be off with you and make haste! Be gone with you!" she said with tears streaming down her cheeks. The water had formed as sorrow but fallen as joy.

Sookey realised that the cruel joke at her expense had been an important moment. She had never felt so accepted. The conversation then flowed easily until Mary suddenly informed them that she had something to do and started to leave. This was a surprise, as she had not previously mentioned anything to this effect. Sookey enquired politely if it was anything interesting, but Mary just fobbed her off.

"No, just remembered something I got to do that's all, nose-ache."

Thinking it was most unlike Mary to be so vague, Sookey shrugged and made plans to meet her at Henrietta's coffee room the following day.

Sookey enjoyed Nashey's company in the pub for a while longer, before suggesting they retire to her house. She wanted to speak to him on a delicate matter best not discussed in public.

Having arrived there and made tea, she was not at all perturbed by being alone with this man, though she feared what Rose would say. She made small talk about the wonderfully joyful tea-pickers in China, who always seemed to have smiles on their faces despite doing a back-breaking job for long hours.

"Sounds better than the Bryant & May factory any day of the week," said Nash. "Reckon Mary would be a good tea-picker if there were such a thing here. Would keep her off the streets an' all."

Sookey agreed, but although she wanted to speak to Nashey about Mary and her line of work, there was another subject that needed to be addressed first, so she changed the subject abruptly.

"Our paths keep crossing Nashey."

They were only five words, but Nash was immediately on his guard. He simply nodded in response, so Sookey continued.

"I am glad to have this opportunity of serious discourse with you. The man Shanks…"

She left the words dangling in the air to see if he would pick them up. He was pleased to oblige.

"Rum sort of do, weren't it? He were up to no good, make no mistake, but I let him go because he would only have made up some cock and bull story. It were better to get the gen from his mate. It ain't right of course, and I'll see Shanks pays for what he's done, don't you worry."

Sookey had been over the whole episode in her mind many times but could not fathom any of it.

"Forgive me Nashey, but what has he done? I am lost on it. He asks me to visit him so he can pay the debt he owes. I am then attacked by fiends in the very court in which he lives and oblige me if he does not then visit me at my home with one of the very men who attacked me. And he possesses a threatening demeanour to boot. But for Mary, and of course you, I do not know what would have become of me."

Nash was eager to move the conversation away from the attack on Sookey, so took the mention of Mary as an opportunity to do so.

"Mary's one of the best, make no mistake," he said, with unusual affection in his voice. "Do anything for anyone she's a kinsman with, and tough as old boots she is into the bargain. She would have seen you all right. With that knife and cosh she carries if need be."

Sookey spotted the change of subject. That was twice in quick succession that Nashey had brought Mary into the conversation, and both times in a positive way.

"Are you and Mary sweethearts Nashey?" she asked, accompanied by a cheeky grin.

She knew very well that they were not, but she wanted to hear his response. She feared he might say something along the lines of 'no, mores the pity'. But his reply was far worse than she could have imagined.

"No, I don't go in for that sort of thing. I'm a confirmed bachelor." There was a brief pause before he

218

continued. "Besides, she wouldn't be on the game if I were her man. I'd knock her over before I let her do that. Young Joe Barnett's her fellow. He's a right enough young scamp, but one word from him and she does as she likes. He needs to take her in hand but he ain't the man for it, see."

"Barnett?"

But before she completed the obvious question, Nash held up his hand.

"No, he ain't related to the vicar. Queer really."

"It is not queer Nashey, it is a coincidence," said Sookey, pronouncing the last word deliberately, with an enthusiastic smile to ensure she did not sound condescending.

It worked. Nash was impressed, just as he had been when they first met, by her ability to educate without sounding like the old harridans who used to teach him in his ragged school.

"Queer word for a queer thing," said Nash lightly.

Sookey smiled again and continued.

"Mary is book-read from schooling and as you know is well spoken when she's not in drink. So, when Henrietta is back from a visit to her sister in the north, I will enquire of her if there could be a paid position for Mary as my assistant at Toynbee Hall. All Hall workers have, to date, offered their services without regard for remuneration, but only middling people are in such a situation, and they do not always offer the fittest of things. We need a girl like Mary. And it is not just the moral question. She needs to get off the streets with this fiend still undetected. Can you not chastise her Nashey?"

"Chastise? What's that when it's at home?"

"Give her a good talking to. Tell her off."

"Tell off Mary? Easier said than done girl. I've been on at her about her whoring ever since I first known her. More since these murders started up. She don't listen to nobody. She says she needs the gelt from whoring to pay her rent. I says to her, if you didn't drink like a fish, you could earn enough money charring or something to pay your rent without whoring. But she comes back with she drinks herself stupid so she can do the whoring in the first place. I tells her that's arse about face."

Sookey could only guess at what the last sentence meant but she understood.

"Indeed Nashey, but what can one do?" she asked.

"Tell you what I will do," he said conspiratorially. "I know a copper who likes a bit of dropsy. I'll drop him a few bob to see if he can get hold of a police picture of one of the murdered women for me. I hear tell they takes pictures of them in the place where they do that post-mortem thing you told me about. See if I can scare Mary by showing her. But you should try her an' all. She might listen to a cleverer, much older lady like you."

Sookey knew very well that she was someway less intelligent than Mary and she was not sure she liked Nashey saying that she was 'much' older. She was only ten years Mary's senior after all.

"I have already tried and failed on the subject," she said. "I think your suggestion of a police photograph is the fittest. But allow me to also correspond with my acquaintance Walter in France. The painter in the gallery whose work you did not regard? In a recent letter he told of seeing such a photograph of a victim in a local newspaper if you please! There has been no such thing here. It would seem their stomachs are stronger in France. I will request he dispatches a copy post haste."

She was surprised at her own candour and apparent casual immorality. She was shocked, at her lack of shock; again! She glanced across at Nash, who was blinking back at her with a mix of surprise and something else which she could not quite put her finger on. Was it what she hoped? They shared a hesitant, embarrassed chuckle, and then there was a brief pause as they looked at each other. It was he who broke the spell.

"We'll see what we can come up with. But let's hope you get her that job in the Hall, and then she'll be off the streets anyhow."

"Yes, indeed," replied Sookey.

But that is all she said and there was another pause. Nash thought he should say something.

"Don't think I've forgotten to do that wallpapering of yours."

"Perhaps you could come to the Hall and give a lecture on the art of wallpapering!" came a light throw away reply. But Sookey realised as soon as she had said it that this was not the time for such frivolity.

She had become side-tracked from her original concerns over Shanks' behaviour. She continued, changing voice and expression to great seriousness.

"Did Shanks have me attacked? For what purpose? Why did he bring that man to my house? He must surely have known the game would be up soon enough?"

"I shouldn't put much mind to it girl," assured Nash. "Coves like Shanks don't look further than their nose. The prisons are full of them. He just wanted to get out of paying you what he owed. Got hold of some roughs and paid them to give you a good hiding so you'd bugger off out of Whitechapel. Probably told them you were well-heeled and likely to have some finery on you worth half inching into the bargain. It all happened in the pitch dark so you wouldn't have got a good look at the bastards, so when one of them started up about his mouth, Shanks goes to you to sort him out. Thinks that's funny, cove like him, and not having to pay you like a proper doctor were just bunts. You said yourself he told you he weren't going to pay you nothing, and his threatening you were his way of telling you not to ask him for money again."

He saw from her frown that Sookey was finding it difficult to believe Shanks could be so stupid, so he continued.

"Criminals ain't like they are in some book, see. Sherlock Holmes wouldn't take no time to catch Shanks would he? So books has to have clever sods as the criminals, don't they, so as they're hard to collar." Sookey still had a slightly quizzical look on her face, but he could see he was wearing her down. "Tell you what, give us a famous criminal case. Not the Ripper. Some other one. Go on."

Sookey enjoyed these sorts of conversations with Nashey. She remembered the long chat they had about the costers' rhyming slang.

"Very well."

She pondered for a minute, pursing her lips and narrowing her eyes in concentration.

"The Fanny Adams case. There sir, pray enlighten me."

"Blimey girl, sweet Fanny Adams, that must be a score and more year ago. I don't even remember it myself, only what stories I've heard tell. What made you think of that?"

"It was precisely a score and ten years ago. I was a small child. Three years younger than Fanny. It was such a shock to my parents. I remember not being allowed out to play in the park, even with my governess, for a year thereafter."

Before answering, Nash did a calculation.

Little Fanny were eight if I remember right, so you're five and thirty are you Sookey? You look good for your age, mind.

"Now, the cowson who did for her, took her away in front of her two sisters, so they told the coppers who he was, and then when they poked around at his work, they found his diary with 'I killed a little girl today' written in it. Didn't need no Sherlock Holmes to work that one out did they?"

Sookey shook her head ruefully.

"I see your point. The whole business does not command itself to reason, but you have convinced me Nashey, I will forget about Shanks."

Yes, but I won't, thought Nash solemnly.

Chapter 21

"At length, our masters are aroused and behold! A Royal Commission is enquiring into the particulars of the housing of the poor."

H. Davis, Commonweal

Khan had been given new duties. He was to follow Shanks. There was a chance Shanks might meet up with his Post Office contact, and any snippet of information gleaned about the robbery might prove useful. It was also imperative to keep an eye on Shanks because he appeared to be too close for comfort to the truth regarding Nash's interest in the killings.

Khan was also to be kept in reserve for the post office job, in case he was needed for something at the last minute. At the very least he could keep an eye on the wrong un throughout the night of the robbery.

Tom Carter, a reliable but dim young lad Nash used for assistance with simple skulduggery on occasion, had been alternating shifts with Khan selling matches across the street from the Ripper's bolthole. They had kept watch on the Doveton Street gaff fourteen hours a day. The only time the killer was not kept under observation was between four in the morning and two in the afternoon. He was followed to Pickfords, where he would work at least a ten-hour shift. Nash had come to appreciate that there was little point in following him while he went about his duties. But by the time he left work, a man was waiting outside the Pickfords depot. But with Khan now deployed elsewhere, Tom had been joined on the surveillance team by his brother Jem. Like his sibling, he was not the sharpest tool in the box. He would not think too deeply about what they were doing or ask any questions.

With both the robbery and surveillance organised, Nash was pleased to be back at the more pressing task at hand. Eager to receive his 'jacks' fee, John McCarthy had passed on plenty of useful information. Nash now knew that a man named Charles Lechmere lived in the Doveton Street gaff. He was in his thirties.

Drank at weekends in The Lion in Bethnal Green and was also known to down a few sherbets on his way home from work at any of the pubs in Commercial Street. He liked the ladies; was known to pick up prostitutes in the Flower & Dean Street rookery. He sometimes went by the surname of Cross, his stepfather's name. The stepfather and Lechmere's mother lived near Nash in Cable Street. Lechmere had his own family too, but they were not living with him at present. McCarthy hadn't been able to find out where they were. Lechmere was a bit of a rum cove by all accounts. Didn't mix with his workmates. Kept himself to himself.

"And of course, his claim to fame," added McCarthy, "is that he were the fellow who found the body of the Ripper's first victim over in Buck's Row. It were him and some other cove who turned up, who went off and found a copper. He's been in all the papers."

Nash tried to keep his face straight while his mind raced.

So, this Lechmere were nearly caught over Polly Nichol's body by some fellow, but he brazens it out by pretending he's just found her and gets away Scot free. He must have a way of talking to people, even coppers, so they believe him. He ain't the mad maniac everyone thinks. Well, he is mad all right but not so as nobody can notice.

Not for the first time, Nash pondered that this adversary was not someone to be taken lightly. It was a chilling thought. But before he could think any more on the subject, he had McCarthy to deal with.

The landlord had relayed the information about Lechmere finding a Ripper victim's body with a knowing twinkle in his eye. And there was no point in Nash denying that this had something to do with the reason he was interested in the cove. He knew McCarthy would assume he was up to something regarding the murders.

"We all got to make a few bob out of these here murders ain't we John," he said with a conspiratorial wink. "But you don't need to know any more. That's why I'm paying you such good money, to keep your and every other cove's sneezers out."

McCarthy simply nodded. He just wished he could work out what Nash was up to, so he could do something similar himself.

***

Between now and the Post Office pull, Nash would himself spend as much time as possible keeping an eye on

226

Lechmere. As a result, he arrived at Doveton Street at three in the morning to tell Tom he would take over. Half an hour later there was the sight and sound of the killer's front door opening. Lechmere appeared.

It was the first morning for weeks that had not been foggy. A clear moonlit night was coming to its end. It made it easier to follow someone. But equally, a target, particularly one with good reason to have their wits about them, was more likely to spot any pursuer. So, knowing his man was heading for Pickfords, Nash could afford to follow from some distance.

The two men were making their way through the Flower & Dean Street rookery when Lechmere spotted a gaudily dressed young woman loitering on the next corner. As he approached, the woman sidled over to him and said something. He stopped and looked interested in her for a moment but suddenly shied away and carried on walking. The prostitute did not react. She simply went back to standing on the corner as if the interaction had not taken place, returning to the trance-like first of the three acts of the prostitution play. The second, which was turned on and off like a tap, was the cheery smile and query as to whether a man wanted her services; the third was the thousand-yard stare over a shoulder while she performed them.

The woman spotted Nash as he hove into view and immediately switched to act two.

"You're a big boy, ain't you darling," she said knowingly while putting her hand playfully on his chest.

Blimey, you're young, thought Nash.

Little Kitty! That's where I seen her before! It were

Kitty who offered herself to the killer just before he went on to murder Kate Eddowes!

Nash now realised that it must have been her youth that had saved her from being attacked. Lechmere clearly preferred to kill older women.

He untangled himself from the attempted embrace and reached into his trousers. The young woman was surprised to find a piece of silver rather than a piece of anatomy issuing forth.

"Here, take this," said Nash. "Now, get yourself off to a lodging house for some kip and then go down Toynbee for some soup in the morning."

The prostitute, mystified by both the generosity and advice, looked at him blankly, so he continued.

"And woe betide you if I see about again tonight. You hear me girl?!"

"Yes, mister," she said, like the pathetic little waif she was, before scurrying off.

Chapter 22

"The exclusive culture of those whose sensibilities are so shocked by the brutality, the responsibility for which their greed and cowardice evades... when the dark side of this inglorious inequality is thrust on their notice, they are shocked and read moving articles in the newspapers."

William Morris

Sookey had seen a lot of Mary and Nash since the fateful joke in the Pindar, but she was not going to see either of them today. She was busying herself in Toynbee Hall and her art gallery, preparing for the guided tour of the slums for her new fair-weather friends. The itinerary was to begin by taking the group for mid-morning coffee at Toynbee Hall, where they would see the poor wretches who availed themselves of the facilities. She was then going to show them a Dr Barnardo Free Day school, where six hundred hot breakfasts and four hundred hot dinners were offered four times a week.

There was certainly no denying that Thomas Barnardo was doing a fine job, but on the one occasion Sookey had met him she had not taken to the smooth Irishman. She did not like the way he called his boys 'cases' and she had heard rumours of financial improprieties and cruelty in his homes, and of faked photographs of desperate children.

Given that Nashey had clearly benefitted from schooling, Sookey had once asked him if he would be willing to try to influence boys to go along and learn a trade at a Barnardo school. She had been surprised at his reticence.

"What's the use of teaching little lads skills when they'll just be thrown on the scrap heap with every other cove? They got to sort out men not having no work first, but charities don't try and do nothing about that do they? It ain't no good giving people linctus against cancer, is it? You got a find a cure for it in the first place."

She had not really understood what he meant at the time, but she was beginning to. There was certainly something wrong with the economics of the country. Unemployment was certain, due to a surfeit labour market. Charities were treating the symptoms rather than effecting a cure. She wished she understood politics and economics better, but both had always proved beyond her.

A decision was made not to ask Barnardo to receive her guests at the London Hospital. Apart from her aversion to him, there was a rumour that all the doctors at the hospital were Ripper suspects. The supposition that the killer must have anatomical knowledge, which was put forward after the second victim, Annie Chapman, had been found eviscerated, was now accepted to the point where theory had become fact. It was rumoured that as well as Barnardo, even the hospital's most eminent surgeon, Dr Treves, the saviour of the poor wretch Joseph Merryck, the Elephant Man, was being shadowed by detectives.

Sookey did like Frederick Charrington, who had done marvellous philanthropic work against drink and vice. He had given up his family fortune from a brewery to work in the East End. It made Sookey feel guilty that it had taken a fall from grace in her old world to send her to the slums to do her bit. It would have been so much better if she had come to Whitechapel with her wealth intact. Think of all the good she could have put that money to. But there was a rumour that Frederick had hired the killer in his fight against prostitution. This was surely not so, but she felt it best, on balance, not to introduce her friends to him.

She remembered the shock on her friends' faces when she told them she had intelligence on the murders. Nashey had since told her that she should forget everything she had heard about the case. For example, he now doubted the credentials of what he had been told about the lack of blood found. He suspected it was just a rumour, and like all the other rumours had no basis in fact. What a silly goose she had been to spread such gossip. So much had happened in so short a time since she last met Nora et al. She felt that thanks to Nashey and Mary she had learned more about the human condition recently than the rest of her life put together.

While at Toynbee Hall, as well as seeing her embryonic art gallery, her group would attend a talk she was to give on calligraphy, to the Association for Befriending Young Servants. They were then to enjoy luncheon in a public house.

She had previously asked Mary to show her around the quietest, safest, least boisterous establishments in the vicinity, but in certain ways, they were more shocking than the rough ones. They had been full of broken people, one step from the workhouse, who just sat there staring into the solitary drink they could afford, coughing and wheezing with their latest illness.

She had decided that the Sir Paul Pindar tavern in Bishopsgate, where she and Mary had got a little tipsy that evening when they were spending Nashey's money, would have to suffice. With a bit of fortune it would have the same mix of characters, including some worn out prostitutes whom her friends would be sure to be both shocked and pleased to see, and some off duty policemen glad to hide somewhere, away from the taunts and insults of all and sundry due to their failure to catch 'Jack'.

Her friends had insisted that they should spend the afternoon on a walking tour of Whitechapel, including seeing some of the sites of the murders, an idea which Sookey found most distasteful. They were then to finish with tea at her humble abode.

She was dreading the afternoon. It was far more into the unknown, and who knew what sights and sounds they might see and hear. And then there was the, not insignificant, matter of her home. Nashey had completed all but one strip of wallpapering. He had deliberately left a strip for her to do because he felt she needed to practice the skill herself. Rose had shown her how to clean the front step and helped her wash everything that was washable at the baths. Mary had helped her distemper the scullery and clean as well as tidy inside the house, including scrubbing the ground-in filth on the windows so the glass glistened in the sunlight for the first time in a decade. She had bought the best cakes from the Aerated Bread Shop, and the most expensive Ceylon tea from the British Tea Table shop in the City. But her home still smelt of the slums. There was no escaping that.

***

Sookey's lady friends piled off a growler cab, but she was surprised to find a man alighting with them.

"This gentleman is Mr Lloyd George," said Nora. "He is a friend of mine who, when I told him of the work you are doing here in Whitechapel, expressed a keen interest. So, I felt it incumbent to invite him along on our little jaunt. I do hope this is acceptable my dear."

She then took Sookey by the arm, guiding her away a few feet before whispering conspiratorially.

"He's Welsh but terribly bright. My husband says he will go far. Politics and all that. Needs to keep him on side, you know the sort of thing."

Sookey did mind. She minded a great deal. She was nervous enough as it was, without dragging a 'terribly bright' young man, who no doubt had an agenda, around the slums of Whitechapel.

Her right hand went up to pat the top of her blouse and check the top button was in place. The bruising from her attack had disappeared but the stress she was feeling led her fingers to seek some reassurance.

"Pas de tout, pas de tout!" she cried with a cheery wave of the same hand.

It was a spontaneous attempt to avenge herself on Nora. She knew her friend had been bottom of the class in French back in her finishing school days and professed to have not retained any of the language. Nora looked at her with a slight tilt of the head and an expression that said, "what are you talking about, please do not embarrass me in front of this man by misbehaving," but she said

233

nothing. She held her expression and waited. Sookey simply smiled.

Lloyd-George came to Nora's rescue.

"Que je suis contents de vous voire!"

Sookey would normally have returned the attempt at "how pleased I am to see you" with something appreciative, but she was no longer the shrinking violet Nora no doubt still believed her to be. She feigned being a little disconcerted at the temerity of the man. After all, he should have waited until it was appropriate to engage her in conversation. At the sight of Sookey's raised eyebrows, Nora was quick to enter the conversation in a rather strained voice.

"Why, I need to take the two of you to task," she said with friendly mock admonishment. "I have not yet made the introductions yet the two of you are off in foreign climes together."

Having won this little skirmish, Sookey felt good about herself as she went through the social formalities which followed. Lloyd-George's Welsh accented English proved to be far more impressive than his French. And the other two women, who had not said a word since they stepped out of the cab, now threw in the expected small talk. Normal service resumed. Everyone charming to one another.

The first half of the tour went to plan. Either side of the visits to Toynbee Hall and her art gallery, Sookey had chosen routes which avoided the most overcrowded courts that teemed with the most pathetic of the poverty-stricken. There were two reasons for this; she did not want to shock her friends even more than was inevitable; and she spent some of her time in these places administering medical care or doing clerical work for some rather rough diamonds, so being recognised and approached for help was quite possible. It could be awkward. She would prefer to be inconspicuous.

She began to relax a little as she led her entourage away from the slums and reached the busy main road on the edge of the City where they were to stop for their mid-day meal. Though technically they were still in the East End.

"In front of you is the Sir Paul Pindar Tavern in Bishopsgate Without," she said, motioning with an outstretched arm, before continuing in a light self-effacing manner. "I admit to being a dash poor guide, as I know not who this knight of the realm was or how this great thoroughfare is considered to be without the City."

Her audience smiled but Lloyd-George introduced a note of seriousness.

"It's accompanying streets are clearly not without the worst poverty I have ever seen."

The astute use of language had the group mumbling sad agreements at the sentiment conveyed.

"I fear you have not seen the worst of it, sir," replied Sookey solemnly.

The group stood in silence; nodding heads bowed.

The spell was broken by a terrible clatter of hooves on cobbles as a crowded bus was brought to a sudden halt by a traffic jam in front of the group. The ten customers on the top floor of the vehicle were sitting in two lines of five, back-to-back 'knifeboard' style, all looking out to the side. The five facing in their direction swapped gazes with Sookey and her entourage, until the bus driver, also sitting on the top floor, wedged in a gap between advertising boards, accompanied the use of his whip with some oaths to impart on his horses that they could now move on.

As the bus headed off, Sookey's eyes were drawn to the sea of Nestlé's Milk advertising placards festooning almost every square inch of the vehicle. She craned her neck to see her group's attention had followed a similar course.

"I am afraid you will be unable to partake of milk where we are about to go, ladies and gentlemen," she said with a wry smile.

Her audience was relieved at the change of dynamic and laughed a little too heartily.

Sookey returned to being a tour guide.

"Look about you. On the second and third stories of the public house there are fine two-hundred-year-old bow windows. I believe the front of the tavern to be originally part of Sir Paul Pindar's mansion."

The 'fine' windows were caked in soot and a large banner reading Barclay Perkins Stout fluttered across them in the stiffening breeze.

"What are those men doing?" asked Nora.

Next door to the pub, two men, one struggling with a large awkward-to-carry camera, the other grasping the accoutrements that came with it, ran hurriedly under the pull-down shade of Louis Harwitz' picture frame manufacture shop. They were hoping it would hide them.

"They are a newspaper reporter and his photographist," said Sookey. "You can scarce look about you without seeing one of these teams making haste to create photograph work and report on this area since the murders started."

As she was saying this it became apparent to her what was about to happen, and she was keen to avoid it.

"I believe them to be just sheltering from this accursed wind. The photograph equipment is a difficult beast to control, methinks. Allow us to adjourn for luncheon inside," she said, motioning for them to walk across the busy street to the pub as soon as a gap in the traffic allowed.

The women started to follow her, but Lloyd-George stayed put, still looking at the men.

"Are they welcome here?" he asked.

"Indeed, they are not sir," replied Sookey. "It is believed that local people are shown to be morose in photographs because the reporter asks them to be straight-faced, so the image is not blurred. This is indeed so, but if you look at the faces, there is no welcome in the people's eyes. There is a difference between straight-facedness and sullenness is there not? Come we must adjourn; the ladies are waiting sir."

But the astute Welshman was looking down the street.

"Local leaders create and mould opinion here?" he asked. "They are the assessors and makers of the common conscience? The church abandoned? Leaders' beliefs and prejudices seep through the slums and condition minds? But lower orders bring forth a common emotional upsurge with illegal deeds their leaders allow, but which propriety forbids them to perform themselves? I have heard of attacks on foreigners, Ripper suspects, and now perhaps..."

Sookey had already seen what Lloyd-George was watching. A small gang of young men were walking determinedly up the street. They were closing in on the cowering newspaper men, their shouted obscenities within earshot. She looked round at her guests. Lloyd-George was rubbing his chin in deep thought. The women had just spotted the gang too and Sookey noted the panic in their eyes. She smiled reassuringly and said lightly,

"I do believe Mr Lloyd-George is not hungry. More's the pity, for they have fine fare here. He seems keen to view the progress of our local football team. They are a little boisterous at times, I fear. But such is the way with young men in Whitechapel. Let us make haste to the 'Pindar' as we call it here in the East End."

Sookey had said 'Pindar' in a flat Cockney accent. She had hoped it would amuse her friends, but it was ignored. They were too busy looking to scurry dangerously through the traffic towards the safety of the pub. She had been dreading taking them into the place but was now only too relieved to get them through the doors.

***

Nash was at home, and had just been interviewed by the police for the second time since the murders had started. Every able-bodied man who lived in the area had been interviewed at least once. There was growing police belief that the murderer lived somewhere locally.

Nash lived close to all the murder sites including almost next door to one of them; and was known to the police as a violent, nasty bit of work who was often out on the streets late at night. If he had been a foreigner or known to have any medical knowledge or knife skills, he would have been of further interest to the authorities.

But it was well known that Nash did not like knives. He considered using one beneath contempt. Before the murders started, he carried a knife as a last means of defence, but had never had cause to use it, and ceased carrying it recently for fear of being stopped and searched by the police. He did not miss it. If you needed a knife to get the better of someone, you were not much of a man as far as Nash was concerned. It had always made him smile with contempt that some thought themselves tough because they carried a blade and were not afraid to use it.

Nash had true alibis for the nights of the first two murders. He had been in public places such as assorted gambling dens. It was ironic that such a night owl had more alibis than men who simply slept in their beds each night. But Will Roud remained his weak alibi for the night of the double killing.

The police's first visit had been easy. Sir Charles Warren, the man with overall responsibility for the Ripper investigation, had flooded Whitechapel with West End police. They had no knowledge of, or contacts in, the East End. The wool was pulled over their eyes at every turn. But having come to know more about the murders and who was perpetrating them, Nash had found the second interview more difficult. There was a lot more to lie about, to leave out; more he could get tripped up on. And this last pair of East End detectives had been spry enough.

Nash was sitting at his table thinking about the encounter when there was an official sounding thump, thump on the door. He jumped up, cursing to himself.

They're back! Shit! I must have let something slip and they've picked up on it.

"It's Will!"

Nash blew out a large breath and flung open the door.

"What the bleeding hell do you want!?" was the less than enthusiastic welcome, but it was water off a duck's back to Will. He had known Nash a long time.

"You told me to tell you if I ever hear of any trouble with them newspaper wallahs. Gawd knows why. They got a bleeding cheek if you ask me…"

"Nobody has asked you, have they? What's happened?"

"A couple of newspapermen are just about to get a good hiding from young Briggsy and his mates."

"Are they now," said Nash solemnly, quickly donning his coat before filling its pockets. "We'll see about that."

Will pondered about Nash's behaviour.

Ever since you've been knocking about with that slummer woman, you've been acting right queer. What's it got to do with you if Briggsy wants to give a couple of fellers from the papers a good hiding? Bastards deserve what they get. Should keep their noses out of it.

But he had known Nash long enough to know this was best left unsaid.

Nash arrived just as Reg Briggs was holding the camera above his head, about to smash it to the ground. Nash was impressed the young lad could lift such a heavy, awkward thing so high.

"Put that bleeding thing down!" bellowed Nash at the top of his voice. "And do it gentle an' all. And the rest of you, leave them two go."

Reg was the leader of Whitechapel's toughest street gang. It had a different name from Nash's teenage days, but it was a similar affair. Nash accepted that young Reg should not lose face, so was prepared to let him shout the odds, even give some lip, but he could not afford to let newspaper staff be fearful of entering the slums. They were his mouthpiece.

He did not want to hurt anyone but would if forced to, so had brought a selection of weapons. He eased out of one of his deep pockets, a monkey's fist. It was the least dangerous implement he owned. A pathetic weapon by his standards, which he hoped would have the desired effect of telling Reg that he did not want any trouble. The weapon was an idea he had got from a lascar off the boats. It was a length of rope that fed into a mushroom ball of very tightly woven rope, the ball covered in several coats of thick red lead paint which gave it a top-heavy feel. He could swing it fast, but it was only rope so he could use it to hit someone hard without doing any real damage. It would stun rather than seriously injure. He could also throw the implement some distance with a quick underarm whip if necessary and it would land noiselessly, not giving his position away.

"Clear off Nashey, this ain't got nothing to do with you. They got it coming, keep gawping at us through these camera things like we were beasts in the zoo. Writing in their papers. Telling the world and his wife all about us."

Nash noted that Reg had not told him to 'fuck off' as he would have anyone else. Reg was wary. And for all his bluster, he had lowered the camera, and the rest of the gang had stopped their attack on the two newspaper men. They'd had the reporter and his colleague pinned to the wall of the shop and were raining blows at them but fortunately had barely made contact with anything soft and painful yet, the men's arms, elbows and knees having taken the brunt of what was, without the gang's leader, a largely posturing attack. It was lucky that vicious young Reg had busied himself with the camera rather than the men. Nash had arrived just in time. Once the men had gone down, the boots would have been in. The wrong uns in the gang, having been at the back when they were facing someone who could fight back, would have waded forth.

Nash was hoping Reg was astute enough to realise the situation. It was, he thought, one of those Italian sayings Sookey had taught him, a quid pro quo. When both parties did all right out of a deal. Reg saves face with his mates and the area at large by standing up to a known hard man, who for his part keeps the reporters safe.

"On your way son," said Nash quietly, with the shortest of winks that only Reg could have seen. He left the "bugger off while you're ahead" unspoken but trusted Reg would hear it, nonetheless. While Nash's left hand dangled the monkey's fist, his right slipped on his glinting cap before being stuffed back deep in his pocket, fingering something heavy and lethal. He was ready to replace the rope weapon if necessary.

Reg was not the leader by chance. He knew the score. If he rushed at Nash with a shout for his mates to join him, his trusted lieutenant Bill would be at his shoulder quickly enough, but others would hesitate and there would always be some who waited for their mates to do the dirty work. The gang would get the better of him in the end by sheer weight of numbers, but Nash would wreak severe damage on those who attempted the first blows. Reg spat down at Nash's feet before speaking.

"What you protecting them for?"

Nash looked down at the oyster of spittle, and then back up at Reg, with the grimmest of smiles.

"Because they keep coming round here gawping at us, taking pictures with their cameras and writing about us in their papers. Telling the world and his wife about the East End. Now you're as wise as ever, ain't you boy?"

Reg shook his head in disbelief at what he was hearing. As he turned to leave, he fired a passing shot.

"You're off your bleeding head you are Nashey. It's that fancy slummer tart of yours that's done it. She 'll have you in Colney Hatch loony bin before long, you see if she don't."

Nobody treated Nash like this, least of all in public, in front of the baying congregation that had gathered. But Nash didn't react and kept his thoughts to himself.

I'm going to have to have a word with you boy. And I don't like Sookey being talking about like that neither.

But it would have to be another time. For now, he took the insults. It was a small price to pay. Reg turned round to his gang.

"Come on lads, let's leave this old Mary Ann to look after his little mates here."

The gang moved off and Nash wandered over to the journalists.

"Sorry about that, fellers. Always a few young scamps shouting the odds ain't there? It was all kid stakes really. They wouldn't have hurt you. Ain't hurt you, have they? Gear all right, is it?"

Nash went on a charm offensive and explained to the men that they would be completely safe from now on, and so would all their colleagues in the press. He would see to it.

He was what you might call an unofficial neighbourhood leader.

Lloyd-George joined them, introducing himself. Nash would normally have been aloof and surly towards any stranger, especially one who spoke with a strange accent, but the man interested him. He was dressed and sounded like a gent but there was also a working man's stamp about the fellow. And there was a sparkle in his eyes which implied that he might be genuinely interested in why Nash had just behaved as he did.

"Alexander Nash, Lloyd."

Nash thrust his huge hard hand into the one proffered him. The two newspapermen were eager to get away from the scene of their near mishap. They left Lloyd-George and Nash to discuss the newspaper coverage of the murders and the effect they were having in introducing the troubles of the East End to the world.

The pub was now full of an excited crowd, discussing what they had just seen. The tour group had been alone in the pub save the staff for a while. Everyone else had left to view the rumpus outside. The exodus had been a relief to Sookey. Up until then the air had been blue, courtesy of an off-duty soldier with a loud voice entertaining a small knot of drink-buyers with a tall tale of derring-do in far off climes in the name of Queen and country. He appeared to believe the eff word was compulsory at least once in every sentence.

The women had originally expressed an interest in visiting an eel, pie and mash shop, but having had Mary take her into one the previous week, Sookey had decided that a public house would be a safer option for a meal. Sookey had dealt with most things the slums had thrown at her, but the sight of the live eels writhing in tubs on the shop's counter, had made her feel quite queasy. The cold public lavatory-like tiling and the hard wooden stalls, facing each other railway carriage-style, which were always full enough with customers to ensure the group would not be able to sit together, was another drawback. The final straw had been the disgusting looking green liquor, complete with dubious bits in it, which Mary had recommended she have on her pie. Sookey suspected the recommendation to be an attempt at a practical joke, knowing Mary, though she feigned innocence as she giggled at Sookey's horrified face. The decision was an easy one; they would eat in a public house.

Thus, the whole group were now eating a popular working-class delicacy. The pub, which did not cook food, had imported the meals from a nearby fish 'n' chip shop. The group were delighted with the newspaper crockery and human cutlery. It was just the sort of local colour they had been hoping to experience. But Sookey had indigestion, primarily due to her attempt to speak throughout the meal to try to drown out the soldier's swearing.

None of the group had wanted to bring up the subject of what was happening in the street outside. They had all guessed it was something unpleasant. An awkward silence having settled on the group courtesy of their tour guide having finally run out of things to say, it was a relief when their Welsh associate rejoined them. Sookey was quick to engage him.

"Mr Lloyd-George, pray tell us plainly sir, what was that commotion about? It is well you stayed, lest we should not receive report."

Lloyd–George was surprised by such candour.

"Madame, I am without relish to do so."

Sookey continued to prompt him.

"The crowd around us seem in high spirits from the event. I believe the young scoundrels were ill-favoured towards the chaps from the newspapers?"

Lloyd–George was warming to this woman. She was not the sort of sycophant that he usually had to waste his time charming. She was nothing like her friends and, if truth be told, he was somewhat pleased to report on what he had seen.

"Well madam, the ruffians were attacking the poor men in most villainous way, and the camera was about to be smashed beyond repair, when before I knew what I was about, a man hove into view from out of the ken. He stuck out with the leader of the ruffians. I can make no hand of it, for he was no policeman and was a solitary man against many so they could have sent him to his account, but it was clear as a transparency that for all their bluster, the gang were wary. He was a huge man. He did not pitch it in hot. He issued forth threat by mere presence. That and strange villainous weaponry! The newspaper men saved from further attack and the gang left readily enough."

Sookey had to ask, but she already knew the answer.

"Did you hear of this man's name sir?"

"Yes indeed, I introduced myself to him. Man by the name of Nash. Called me Lloyd. Thought it my Christian name do you see? I did not correct him. He did not appear to be the sort of chap one contradicted."

A warm glow of pride coursed through Sookey.

"You state it was over readily sir. But you were some minutes after us?" enquired Nora.

As she was asking this, Rebecca was whispering in Sookey's ear.

"You appear to have a flush my dear. What ails you?"

Sookey waved her away dismissively.

"Oh, such events give me distress of the mind. It is well they occur rare. It is a trifle. There, it is gone I fancy."

This caused her to miss the beginning of Lloyd-George's reply to Nora.

"… when I relayed to him that I had recently joined the Liberal Party and become an alderman on Caernarvon County Council, he called for 'coves like me to lift the shadow of the workhouse from the homes of the poor'. Quite eloquent for such a chap, what? He even suggested we tax those who had more than enough to pay for those who did not."

"Good gracious, socialism!" and other similar utterances came forth from Nora et al.

"You do not seem as shocked by Mr Nash as others sir," opined Sookey.

Lloyd-George looked seriously at her.

"Madam, there was a time I would have joined the good ladies in their gasps, but my eyes are opening. I must hold you to account for this Hogarthian picture of appalling degradation seared into my mind. I am not a man for Mr Hyndman and his socialists I fancy, but though a proud radical liberal," he leaned forward and continued in little more than a conspiratorial whisper, "I hold at least some small respect for the idea that some form of taxation, though not income related of course, may be

required to reduce the hardship of the deserving poor."
Aware that this was not the time, nor place for such serious
discussion, he brightened and turned to Nora. "My fellow
Welshman, Sir Alfred Danes, I believe is to become the
new Superintendent of the Metropolitan Police. He has
promised me an expedition here. I suspect he will not be
as charming or informative a host as your Mrs Parsons."

"You do me an honour sir," responded Sookey formally
before changing to a knowing smile.

"I trust you did not convey your association to Mr
Nash. He is not well disposed towards the police force. I
fear he would have given you short shrift."

There was a nod of fearful agreement.

"That, I should not like to witness madam. He is also
a salesman, I fancy. He has asked, well, insisted, that I give
a lecture at your Toynbee Hall. I told him that I spoke at
Temperance Society meetings in Wales, do you see. And
that I had a rather, how shall I put it, fiery delivery."

"You know this man Nash, Susan?" asked Nora
incredulously.

"He is the roguish man of my acquaintance whom
I spoke of on a previous occasion Nora," said Sookey as
matter-of-factly as she could manage. "But I can assure
you, for all his intimidatory demeanour, he is a fine chap.
If Mr Danes' predecessor and his cohorts were so fine, the
Whitechapel maniac would have been brought to book
and women would be safe to walk the streets at night." She
turned her head from Nora to Lloyd-George and without
taking breath continued. "Monday November the 12th
would suit us very well at Toynbee Hall. Shall we say three
o'clock sir?"

She had no idea if the Hall was free on the twelfth. She had a poor memory for such things and needed help to keep abreast of what was happening at the Hall, and when. It was one of the jobs she had in mind for Mary. It was also rude of her to assume that Lloyd-George could make himself available at whatever time suited her. But she had been determined to end her little speech on a suitably proud, business-like note. The other women shared nervous glances at each other before turning their gaze to Lloyd-George.

"I believe the 12th at three o'clock may be acceptable," confirmed Lloyd-George, smiling. "I hope to see Mr Nash there."

He, for his part, had no idea if he had a prior engagement. He had so many these days he would need to check with his diary, back in his hotel room, but he would endeavour to be at the Hall as agreed. He was only in his mid-twenties but already a politician who knew the importance of doing what he promised.

Chapter 23

"Local street walkers are fleeing to the workhouses to escape the terror. If all the unemployed and other unfortunates could be induced to follow their example, a complete breakdown of the present poor law system would ensue."

Justice

Henrietta Barnett had initially refused Sookey's request for an employed assistant. The sixteen 'settlers' who worked and, Sookey apart, lived in Toynbee Hall, were not only unpaid, but contributed to the Hall's coffers to be there. The Hall expected its workers to be young members of the social elite, there to receive one form of education, while they themselves provided another to the less fortunate. It was a symbiotic relationship. The hope was that these future politicians, lawyers, and captains of industry would enlighten others in the ruling classes about the need to improve the living conditions, health and education of the poor. Whitechapel residents would in turn be expected to use the education they received at the Hall to improve their lives through self-help. The Barnetts were not there to provide employment for them.

Sookey's timing had, however, been exemplary. Henrietta had been about to ask her to take on a greater workload next month. Henrietta had arranged with Charles

Ashbee, a leading designer and entrepreneur, to set up a Guild of Handicraft. It was to teach primarily metalwork – jewellery, enamels, hand-wrought copper, and ironwork. Such an enterprise needed far more space than could be assigned to it within the confines of Toynbee Hall, but the art gallery was still in an embryonic stage and had plenty of room. This said, it was very much Sookey's project. She had found the building in which it was housed, around the corner from the Hall, and most of her army widow's pension was being spent on its conversion, upkeep and rent.

Consequently, Henrietta was feeling a little uneasy about asking Sookey to donate much of her space to the new guild as well as oversee the project. But when Sookey responded to her rejection of the waged position by offering to fund it herself, Henrietta saw a quid pro quo. She agreed that Sookey could pay a local woman out of her own pocket to be her assistant, on the understanding that she herself took over the running of the Guild of Handicraft, which was to be housed temporarily at least, within her art gallery space. And this assistant would work only in the gallery and was not to set foot in Toynbee Hall itself or liaise with any of the settlers.

These terms were agreed, and it was confirmed that the position would be offered to a local woman, a Miss Marie Jeanette. Henrietta had seen the young woman often enough accompanying Sookey in her coffee room and had been surprised at how well-spoken she appeared. A little white lie was told about Marie's present occupation. Her penchant for loud clothing and even louder make-up explained by the fact that she presently worked at a stage costumier in the City, where staff were expected to dress in a suitably theatrical way. The worldly-wise Henrietta did not believe the tall tale for a second, but she knew a bargain when she saw it. The exotically named, respectable City shop girl was acceptable.

Sookey had a lot more money coming in these days so could afford the deal. She thought it strange how suddenly everyone for whom she did some work, whether it be as doctor, writer or private tutor, paid up immediately and never haggled about the price. Until recently most people had fobbed her off with excuses and promised to settle the following week but never did, and even those who did pay had always negotiated her original price down to the smallest of fees. Even the repellent Shanks had got someone to drop off on his behalf the considerable sum he owed her. She was relieved he had not brought it in person.

When offered the job, Mary was immediately suspicious.

"Who's paying me?" she asked, narrow eyed, chin raised, arms folded across her chest.

Sookey answered with an enthusiasm that she hoped would support a plausible falsehood.

"Oh, there is a fund at the Hall, out of whose coffers you will be remunerated. I believe it is money Mr Toynbee himself left in his will for precisely such purpose."

But her friend saw straight through her as always. All Sookey's attempts at 'leg pulling' in response to all the jokes Mary so successfully played on her, always ended in failure. Mary always knew when Sookey was lying. Her eyes would flutter.

"Oh, yes?" came back with unhidden scepticism. "You're paying if I'm not mistaken."

The eyes started fluttering again.

"I assure you…"

"Don't worry," Mary interrupted, "I'll take your money. I know you can afford it these days. So long as there's a full day's work to be done. You know I will not take charity."

"Oh, very well," conceded Sookey, dropping the pretence, "you see through me like glass as always. I do not know how you achieve it. I will be your employer. And I can assure you, as to the work, you need to roll your sleeves up, as you would say."

"Very well," said Mary smiling, "I will take the job. When do I start?"

Sookey clapped her hands in joy.

"Wonderful! At the start of next month. I am afraid Henrietta would not allow any earlier, as she must tell her board members first about how the Guild is being organised." A frown then surfaced on her features. "You state you know I can afford it. Do you have any idea why people pay me these days when they scarce used to?"

Mary felt the urge to grin but managed to keep a straight face.

"Oh yes, I know a good reason why," she said knowingly.

Sookey's friendship with Nashey was becoming well known in the neighbourhood, and it was not advisable to effectively steal money from friends of such a man. Hence Sookey's debtors now paid up sooner rather than later.

Mary continued via a little embroidery of the truth. "It's because you have been accepted by everyone. You're one of us now."

Sookey was not sure what delighted her most; Mary's acceptance of the position, or her own acceptance by the

253

neighbourhood, though when she considered what Mary did for a living at present, she knew there was only one answer.

But she appreciated that she needed to curb her joy. It was time to assert her authority. She adopted her best teacher's voice.

"Very well Mary. I will see you at nine o'clock sharp on your first morning and be sure to be on time. I will not abide tardiness. And of course…" she hesitated at this point, knowing something else needed to be addressed, "you must not be suffering the effects of drink or smell of it."

She had feared a scowl might be coming her way so was relieved to see a smile, albeit a sad one, issue forth from her new employee.

"I've done enough drinking for one life. Time for a new one. I might have a few on a Saturday night and sleep it off on Sunday, that's only natural after all, to keep the demons away, but that will be my lot."

Sookey knew not to ask about the demons.

"Excellent," she said. "Your first job is to help me prepare for Mr Lloyd-George's visit, and then we must get to work on Mr Ashbee's Guild of Handicraft. They are both very important men. There is plenty to do, my girl."

The last two words added a note of grating pomposity. But for all Sookey's funny little ways, Mary respected her enormously. Consequently, she managed to keep a straight face despite having an overwhelming desire to snigger at the little speech. She thought about doing a little bob to her new employer but thought even Sookey would realise that she was being disrespectful.

"Yes," she said seriously. "You can rely on me Sookey. I will not let you down." "Or myself," she added silently.

A boundary had been set.

***

Sookey had never been to the home of either Nashey or Mary. Nothing had ever been said but it was clear that they would feel awkward receiving her into such basic surroundings. They always met up in a public place or occasionally at her home. But she could not wait to tell Nashey the good news of Mary starting work at Toynbee Hall. It was time to pay him a visit.

The recent clear day appeared to have been a one-off. The fog had returned. But it was not a thick pea souper, so she felt able to venture out. She almost got hopelessly lost at one point but eventually found her way to his tenement.

She knocked on his door.

"Who's there!?" came a less than friendly bellow.

"It is Sookey, Nashey."

The fog meant that there was not the usual noise of horse's hooves on cobbles to hide sounds, so she would have heard any reply that issued forth but there was none. She had to wait a full minute before the door opened with Nash in the middle of donning his coat.

"I were just getting ready to go out girl," he said in greeting. "You were lucky to catch me. I'll walk with you. You should not be out in this, you know."

And with that he quickly closed the door behind him and joined her. As they set off, he tried to remember what others said in this situation. He didn't want to say what he usually bestowed on anyone who arrived at his door unannounced. Then it came to him.

"To what do I have the pleasure?"

Sookey smiled wistfully and with a slight nod was the embodiment of formality.

"Good morning, Mr Nash. I trust you are well this fine day?"

This threw Nash for a moment.

Fine day? It's cold, miserable and foggy. She being a funny cuts? Yes, of course, she's codding with me.

He went with the joke.

"Indeed madam, it is glorious out. Where might we be off, to make most of it?"

Still in her most formal, middle-class voice she replied.

"Thought we would go down the boozer for a tightener me old cock."

He looked at her in astonishment and they both burst out laughing. He then apologised for not letting her in to his gaff but explained that he only had one chair, so it was not suitable for entertaining a lady. In the event they did not go to a pub. They agreed to go to her place, though not before she scolded him for not letting her see Doris.

"Who?" he enquired innocently, which was met with a suitably old-fashioned look.

Once safely out of the pall, Nash was delighted to be told over a cup of tea the good news about Mary.

"I am so relieved to be getting her off the streets," said Sookey. "Especially with so much fog about. No doubt the fiend will be using its cloak to lurk in wait to strike again."

This gave Nash something to consider. He had not really thought about the weather in relation to the killings, but now he came to consider it, he realised that all the murders to date had been on wet miserable nights. Nights when the streets would have been quieter than usual. The killer was much less likely to be seen on such nights. Clever. Not for the first time, Nash realised the man he had allowed to escape was not to be taken lightly. But he thought the women of Whitechapel were safe for the time being.

"No, his nibs won't strike in no fog," he said with confidence. "When you a commit a crime, you need to be able to leg it after, sharp. You can't do that in no pea souper. You could find yourself feeling your way along the railings to get home, and bump straight into a member of the constabulary. He asks you to empty out your pockets and before you know what you're about he's got one hand on your blood covered knife and the other on your collar."

Nash felt that he now knew Sookey well enough to share his view with her, that the killings were a necessary evil which would help poor people in the long run. But when he did this, Sookey made it clear that she was horrified by his revelation.

"Use your head Nashey," she implored. "Nothing can justify such means, not even the great poverty of the East End."

Nash looked at Sookey and thought what he thought fifty times a day, every day since the night of the double murder. He was quite aware that his was the costliest advertising campaign ever devised.

Picking up on the tension now in the air, care of Sookey's bristling expression and body language, he realised his mistake in broaching the subject.

"Yes, you're right of course," he said head down, nodding thoughtfully. A couple of seconds passed before he chose to alter the course of the conversation by picking up on Sookey's last sentence. He looked up and issued forth a cheeky smile with accompanying wink.

"You know, instead of 'use your head' you should have said 'use your loaf'. Loaf of bread – head."

Sookey was relieved at Nashey's obvious desire to change the subject. She relaxed and brightened. The last time they had chatted about cockney rhyming slang she had been set a poser.

"I am afraid that I never managed to complete the homework you set regarding my favourite rhyming word," she said. "I fear I am unable to calculate how taters translates from cold. I confess I did try to cheat by asking Mary, but she simply said I should read my Mrs Beeton. This conundrum did not assist me."

Nash laughed and told his pupil about 'potatoes in the mould' rhyming with cold.

This saw the conversation drift on to Mrs Beeton and her untimely death, as rumour had it from syphilis passed on by her husband, who had used prostitutes before they were married. Not the most pleasant subject by any means, but better than the one dominating many conversations in Whitechapel these days, and from there, other subjects kept the discussion flowing.

Nash talked about himself in more detail than during earlier chats. Sookey heard about his fondness for history when he was at the ragged school; mock censure and shared laughter ensued when Sookey admitted she had let the cat out of the bag to Shanks about the origin of his nickname.

Nash told her about the fight with his father; working for a kidsman; becoming the leader of a boy's gang; he scaled down his occupation of violent crime to one of working in the docks and doing a bit of ducking and diving with the odd bit of petty pilferage thrown in, just to make ends meet, when things were tight because there was no work about. He felt that she did not need to know any different; ignorance was bliss.

Sookey felt a real bond with this man, and when he asked her what brought her to live in Whitechapel, she told him. But some of the details she had relayed to Mary would have been too embarrassing to tell a man, so she abbreviated the story. Like Mary, Nash interjected comments at various stages. He did not like magsmen either, not that he had ever had one of them try anything on him.

"No, I dare say they have not Nashey," she said knowingly.

When she had reached the same point at which she had stopped with Mary, he asked the obvious question.

"But how did you get from the court to here?"

She hesitated before continuing, explaining that she had lost everything; financially and emotionally. Both her own family and that of her in-laws were furious with her. They had endured a great deal of shame and embarrassment by association, and thanks to the cost of the court case were considerably out of pocket too. They felt it incumbent that Susan should become financially independent. They were cutting her off. She must start a new life. Take gainful employment. Reclaim self-respect. It would be nice to see her at Christmas time.

But employment opportunities for middle class women were rare. One position that she briefly considered was that of governess. But it was a lonely life, living apart from and mistrusted by the servants, and a social outcast from the middle classes who scorned those of their sisterhood who had to lower themselves to work for a living. Such women were casteless. But there were a huge number in need of such employment, so there were many applicants for each position, and the law of supply and demand ensured it was lowly paid. A teacher could have been an alternative, though it was more an upper working-class role. Women were popular with primary school governors because they could be employed at lower rates than men, but they did not teach older age groups due to a perceived inability to keep order amongst the bigger boys. She had been interested in entering such employment but something else then came to mind.

After the trial, she had struggled to come to terms with the emotions she was feeling. Not the obvious ones of great sorrow and the like, which were terrible but understandable, but another imperceptible feeling that she could not quite put her finger on for some time. Part of her felt …what? Unlike the other feelings, it was positive. Then in a moment of epiphany, it came to her. She felt free! It was a sort of intoxication. Her mind had a clarity that she had never experienced before. She had always felt dull and unfulfilled, striving for something without ever knowing what it was, and certainly never finding it. She could have the most enjoyable day, the most pleasant experience, yet never feel completely content. There was always something missing.

But for the first time in her adult life, she knew exactly what she would do next, and it was not what someone else or society deemed appropriate.

Her life in Hong Kong had been a cosseted one, but she alone among the officer's wives had dared venture into the town with just a lone servant for guidance and protection. She had seen at first hand the harsh realities of extreme poverty.

Now she would live in London's East End full-time, though not as a slummer. She had worked in slums before with her middle-class friends. Part time; very part time; the latest thing to do. Let us do our bit. No, this time she would be *of* the slums; one of us, not one of them. Accepted for what she did; what she was. And now, with little to her name, she was not 'slumming it'.

She appreciated that she was not terribly bright, but she had been well educated, so people who were less fortunate now came to her for help and advice on numerous matters. She had finally found her niche in life. She felt a different, better, livelier person, as if part of her brain had revived courtesy of a wonderful new drug. The worst events of her life had, in a terrible way, been the best thing that had ever happened to her. She was reborn.

"What happens in the long run makes up for what happens along the way," said Nash. "In a queer sort of way that little cow of a magsman's done you a favour, girl. If I met her, I would not shake her hand, rather I'd give a facer to be chomping on, but you can be thankful to her so to speak."

The end justified the means as far as Nash was concerned, or at least that was what he kept telling himself.

Chapter 24

"The gentleman who occupies his spare time in mutilating and murdering in the neighbourhood of Whitechapel, has quite unintentionally done Society a service."

Commonweal

Charles Lechmere wished he had never been born. He had, however, found a way to alleviate his low self-esteem. But the sexual gratification and feeling of joy that the attacking of a woman's womb afforded him, was only temporary. It was not long before he felt terrible again and the desire to kill returned.

He had killed four times now, though he did not really count the first of the two on the same night. He had not had time to attack the sexual areas before he was almost caught by the man with the horse and had to make his escape. And in his desire to get away he had nearly bumped into that big fellow coming out of a tenement at the end of the street. He had been concerned the man had seen him, but there had been no mention of the encounter in the press.

It was the second time he had been lucky. When he had attacked his first victim, he had been crouching over her body, starting the act of disembowelment, when another man had happened along. He had had two choices; run or brazen it out. He had chosen the latter. With a flick of the wrist his slaughterman's knife was slipped quietly up his coat sleeve as he played the role of shocked bystander.

"Here, look, I think someone's attacked this woman!" he had proclaimed looking down at his victim, wide eyed. The other man knelt to feel her pulse, his back to the killer, giving Lechmere the chance to turn away while he surreptitiously dropped the knife back down his sleeve before folding the jack-knife blade in on itself and slipping it into his pocket.

Polly Nichols had still been alive at that point. The other man had insisted the two of them go off together and find a constable. By the time they had done this, and a doctor had duly arrived on the scene, she was dead. Lechmere gave the police a witness statement and was never questioned again. He was in the clear.

But he was not fully getting the satisfaction from the murders and mutilation that he craved. The problem was that he had so little time to do what he wanted with the bodies, for fear of the arrival of a policeman or a bystander.

Thus, he was now waiting for the chance to pick up a whore who had her own place so he could kill and mutilate her indoors at his leisure.

But with all the police roaming the streets, and there being far fewer whores about at night, not to mention London being fogbound for the past month, such an opportunity had not arisen. The one time the weather had cleared, the only whore he had come across was too young. He needed his victims to be mother substitutes.

He also had the feeling that he could be under watch. He had spotted different men hanging about outside his gaff, and on one occasion thought he might have been followed. Could they be plain-clothes police? Or was he just being overly anxious? No doubt the latter, but he could not take any chances. He had already moved his scant belongings back in with his family a few miles away in Poplar, where he was starting a new job on Monday, using his knife skills professionally for once, slaughtering animals for the cat's meat trade. He had one more shift to do at Pickfords, after which he would head straight for Poplar.

It would seem his murder spree in Whitechapel had ended and he would have to take up the cudgels again in another part of the East End. There would be plenty of whores to choose from in Poplar no doubt. And it would have the added benefit of not being full of policemen. To begin with, at least.

***

Sookey had treated Mary to new clothing, more suitable for working at Toynbee Hall. She was soon to look the epitome of respectability in her new dull green ensemble, of cloak buttoned to the neck with just a hint of white blouse showing above, and a matching green ankle-length skirt. The brass heels were gone too. Mary thought it too uniform-like for her liking, but she looked forward to seeing Nash's face when he saw her. She did not look unlike a Salvation Army girl. She had her 'amen' ready for him and guessed what his colourful reply would be.

But Mary was wearing her prostitute's garb and make-up one final time. She could not very well back out of the post office robbery now, just because she was starting work at Toynbee Hall next week.

Nash suspected plain-clothes police were attempting to follow prostitutes, hoping the Ripper would tackle one and get himself apprehended. But no doubt many uniformed officers would believe any woman on the streets at night, even a prostitute, should be warned of the danger and be encouraged to get herself home to safety. Thus, a woman canary was not such a good option after all. The whole point of a canary being a woman was that the police were less likely to stop her in the early hours. The last thing Nash could afford was for a member of the constabulary to stop a woman to have an advisory word, only to find she had every cracksman's tool imaginable about her person.

Mary had, therefore, changed jobs from canary to crow, though she would not signal a warning in the usual manner because she did not have the whistling skills. She needed to keep an eye out for the police and be a decoy if and when necessary. As soon as any policeman showed up, she was to ensure he saw her and, it was hoped, follow her. She would lead him away from the robbery area. Nash had also employed Khan to stand by. If the copper did not show signs of following Mary, Khan was to approach her as if he was a customer and they were to start off together in the hope the officer would now follow them. If he didn't, Khan was to pretend to start to get rough with her. That should certainly do it. If the worst came to the worse, Khan would make himself scarce before Mary cried out 'murder!'. Any policeman should respond to that. Mary would then provide her rescuer with false information which would lead him away from both the robbery and Khan.

Will was to take his chance as the canary. If stopped by a copper, Will would cosh him and make a run for it. Young Kitty needed to shadow Will, and if he had to scarper, she was to grab as many of the tools as she could manage and get rid of them as quickly and quietly as possible. She would immediately lighten the load by dropping all the small stuff into the nearest horsetrough. Nash had not told Arthur this part of the plan.

Mary was at home waiting till it was time to make the rendezvous with Nashey and the others. A young neighbour at the end of her tether, Lizzie Albrook, had drifted in for a shoulder to cry on. Lizzie was a part-time prostitute but had stopped over a month ago after the last murders. Without the extra income streetwalking afforded her, she was destitute and starving. Not for the first time, Mary had sympathised with the poor wretch.

After Lizzie had left, Mary thought back to the shouting match she had with Nashey last week. It was as well Sookey had not been there; some ripe language having been tossed back and forth as voices got louder and louder, even before Nashey had gone too far.

"People in high places is starting to take notice I'm telling you!" he said. "Council and government coves are going on about it in the papers. Children in common lodging houses, the homeless, abandoned nippers, the housing of the poor, getting rid of the rookeries, rebuilding. They didn't want to know till old Jack got to work, did they? Didn't hear nothing, didn't see nothing."

He was immediately annoyed with himself for calling the maniac 'old Jack'. Mary was red in the face. She glared at Nash with disgust.

"Four women lay dead and buried, and horribly murdered at that! And you're saying that's all right are you!? Are you!!? And there's the likes of my little mate Lizzie, and there's loads of them like her. She's in a terrible state because she's too scared to work the streets now. They're lying in the gutters like dogs! They have to whore, otherwise it's the workhouse or starving and we both know the answer to that one, don't we? The only money they get is off men with their cocks out. Nobody else is going to give them anything, are they!?"

Nash had known he was losing the argument. He had lost it with himself often enough this past month. But he continued regardless, becoming abusive and raising his voice to a shout as a last line of defence.

"What do you know of it anyhow, you stupid little whore?! The murders is doing good I tell you! Showing thems in charge they got to do something! They ain't been listening for many a year, but they are now all right!"

Mary was incandescent. She had never been so furious and was getting more and more angered with every word that spewed out of Nashey's mouth. She started to speak quietly, slowly, grinding out the words in the clear enunciation of cold, determined rage.

"Some of us have tried doing the work they give us. Like working down the Bryant & May match factory. Phossy jaw. Seen that have you? Your jaw falls to bits. I walk the streets knowing every time I pick up some disgusting, sweating pig, he could have a knife waiting for me." Her voice had cracked and become shrill on the word 'knife'. "You have no idea what that's like have you, cunt?!"

She hit him with a right cross, her little fist smashing into his teeth. He must have seen it coming. In her fury she had brought her arm back too far. But he stood there and let her fist hit him. She waited for the retaliatory blow. She wanted him to hit her. She wanted the bruise, the cut, the badge of honour staring at him the next time they met. She would have won. One more man exacting violence on a defenceless woman. But it did not come. He just walked off, blood oozing out of his lower lip from where her ring had hit home, the rage in his face seemingly not levelled at her.

She flexed her hand at the memory. One of her knuckles still hurt. In her rage she had forgotten to hit him in the calculated, controlled way he had trained her. She had hit him as hard as she could. But the memory hurt more than the hand.

That had been after last Friday night's abortive meet. The third without the pull going ahead. Both had spent time with Sookey in the week since, but they had managed to avoid each other. Mary had told their mutual friend about the falling out, even telling her what the parting comment and action had been. Sookey was not at all shocked at the swearing or violence but was visibly upset by Nash's views.

"I have had similar conversation with him," she said. "He is a nut to crack is he not? I sometimes wonder what sort of a man he is. He is a rum cove when it comes to these horrible murders. And he claims to know the identity of the killer. He says he has seen the man, plain as day. He let this slip when suffering from a blow to the head when he rescued me from those ruffians. I have since tried to broach the subject with him, but he insists he was not of right mind. But I tell you Mary, I am not so convinced."

Mary was astonished.

"I'll have it out with him when I see him, you see if I don't."

Sookey grimaced and told Mary she did not think that was a good idea.

It was time to change the subject.

"I believe you see Nashey every Friday night Mary. Am I not to receive invite?"

"It's business Sookey, but don't worry, not my usual business. We're just helping out a friend with something that's all. Private matter. But I told Nashey when we last met, before we had the bull & cow, that with me starting work for you I will no longer have time to meet up with him after this Friday."

Mary had never wanted to commit crime. Prostitution was not illegal though soliciting was, but she had always considered this to be more a crime against herself for past shortcomings than a criminal offence. Though she had always kept this to herself. And agreeing to be involved in the post office robbery came purely out of a desperation to pay the rent. But now she was starting work for Sookey, it was time to end the criminality; to end the self-harm.

Though what she had relayed to Nash as her succinct verbal letter of resignation from criminality was that 'after Friday Shanks can stick his job up his arse'.

Mary now lay on her bed singing loudly, a typically sentimental Victorian ballad. She was sober and bored as well as hungry and weak, not having earned enough to eat properly for days. It would be easy to fall asleep.

Chapter 25

"The current unemployment meetings in Hyde Park...
and the Whitechapel murders...are both effects of the same
cause."

Justice

The men who had hired Shanks to do the robbery would
not wait any longer. It had to go ahead this week. And
Shanks was perfectly amenable to this. He had not been able
to acquire much more information about Nash's interest in
the Doveton Street man. Nash himself had been guarded
whenever the subject of the killings had been broached.
And whenever one of Shanks' noses had tried to extract
information from anyone who might know something,
they had been met with a surly, suspicious 'what's it to do
with you?'. All mouths were well and truly clamped shut
on the matter. It was clear to Shanks that for the time being
at least, Nash was content to let the newspapers carry on
building up the case. Perhaps he was waiting for the killer
to strike again before he did anything more?

"It's on!" Shanks delivered the news to Nash with
excitement and enthusiasm. "And the fog's cleared an' all,
which should make things easier."

He went on to relay the location of the post office and
the additional information Nash needed to commit the

robbery including the type of safe that was to be cracked. Nash knew nothing about safes but nodded sagely.

"I reckon you need to bring that special bib & brace for a safe like that. Me and Peter will get down to the post office with the others." Nash had taken the precaution of not calling Arthur by his true name whenever speaking of him to Shanks. "You make your own way. If you see us collared by the coppers, make yourself scarce down some empty alley. Make sure there ain't nobody else about, and then smash the stuff to smithereens on the ground. Then scatter off."

Nash gave a sly, wicked smile at Shanks, who mistook it for grim determination.

"Right, Nashey."

Nash got hold of Will to tell him that the pull was on and that he needed to make his way to Arthur's to let him know and pick up the gear. Nash, Khan and Kitty converged on the meeting point, and were soon joined by Arthur. Minutes later Will arrived carrying the gear. All bar one member of the gang were now in situ.

"Where's Mary?" queried Nash.

"Don't know Mr Nash," mumbled Kitty sheepishly.

Nash was furious.

"Sod her," he said. "The pull's on but we ain't waiting around for her ladyship to turn up when she feels like it."

Mary had already been late twice. The first time when a client had only paid her for a twopenny upright, but once pinned against a wall in an alley she was forced to give the man a kneetrembler, only for him to renege on his promise of paying the extra funds when they had finished. The ensuing altercation had ended with Mary receiving a cuff to the cheek from an elbow before the man sped off into the night. Her second lapse into tardiness had been caused by her falling asleep drunk which had resulted in her being awoken by Nash thumping on her door.

"Just as well it ain't bleeding on ain't it," was the opening line of a deluge of abuse delivered from no more than a few inches from her down-turned face.

She had made no mistake in being on time the following week.

Nash now passed on intelligence given him by Shanks about elements of the job before rearranging the workload.

"Kitty, get down there and do what Mary were going to do. Khan, you'll have to keep an eye on her and Will as best you can. You all know what to do. Go on, scarper."

As the gang headed off, Nash relayed to Arthur what type of safe he was to tackle.

"Know anything about it, cracksman?" asked Nash.

"Enough. Won't need no nitro."

"Shanks will have to keep hold of the nasty stuff," said Nash sardonically.

Arthur snorted and gave his cohort the grimmest of knowing looks.

Shanks' information had been surprisingly good. Nash and Arthur were to break into a warehouse in Duke Street, just around the corner from Aldgate post office, then make their way on to the roof. This was adjacent to the roof of the post office, which had a trap-door big enough for a man to get through.

Will delivered the gear without any trouble. When Shanks arrived, he was informed that he need not have brought his gear. He grudgingly agreed to return it to his place for the night (Arthur could pick it up in the morning), but emphasised he was not willing to wait to receive his share of the loot. He would be back later to meet up as previously agreed to take his cut.

Nash and Arthur duly made their way to the trapdoor. Nash had a jemmy ready, but it was not locked. Being such a big man, he took his time climbing through the small opening.

"Just bleeding well get in there will you, leaving me standing here in the rain like two of eels," said the old cracksman, now taking on the role of leader for the first time.

Arthur had a cigarette between his lips as usual, but it was unlit. Even the smallest red glow could give away their presence to a nosey policeman. He and Nash made their way gingerly down some steep steps in the pitch dark before Nash felt they were sufficiently distant from any windows to light a match. He spotted the door into the office that Shanks had told them would contain money and forced it open. More matches allowed them to find £3 in a quickly jemmied open drawer, which was actually the postmaster's own money he had left there. There was no sign of any other cash.

"Three bleeding sovs! That bastard Shanks! Where's the safe?"

It was clear from Arthur's tone that Nash was going to have to stand in a queue if he wanted to give Shanks a good hiding when they got back.

"Down here!" urged Nash from the foot of a stairwell, in the loudest whisper he dare.

He forced the door, and they were into the cellar. Arthur's safe stood behind a barred entrance. Arthur got to work on the bars while Nash was match-man. Arthur took a length of rope and a strong metal rod, passed a double loop around two bars, inserted the rod between strands and turned it end over end, twisting up the rope and drawing the bars together. The bars became bent enough for him to slip between them, but Nash was too big to get through the small gap. He passed the matches to Arthur, who struck one and a second later threw a horrified glance at Nash.

"It ain't the safe Shanks said! It's a Bramah-locked plate. We need the bloody nitro!"

"I'll do for him!" replied Nash solemnly as he turned to go back.

"Just codding with you," said Arthur, beaming at his joke. "It's the right one. I'll have it open in no time."

"It's as well you're the other side of them bars cracksman," came through gritted teeth.

Nash handed Arthur his dark lantern and petter-cutter drill. Nash held a lit match while Arthur lit the lantern. It threw a spot of light the size of a shilling from an oil-fed wick, and Arthur used it while he clamped his drill to the keyhole of the safe, allowing powerful leverage on the cutter, which was made of hardened steel. It bit a small opening over the lock through which the wards could be manipulated. It was highly skilled work to use the tools effectively and quietly. Arthur was earning his share. As good as his word, the safe was open in double quick time. Nash passed him a jemmy and a chisel, and he got to work on a locked compartment within the safe. But despite some tips proffered by Nash, he could not budge it.

A heavily sweating Arthur got back through the bars and took hold of a small jack worked with a ratchet and pinion. It opened a larger gap in the bars which Nash was just able to struggle through. Arthur sat down, exhausted. Nash had not forgiven the old man for his inappropriate joke.

"Should have used that in the first bleeding place shouldn't you, old man!"

Nash got to work on the metal of the compartment and his greater brute force did the trick. He wrenched it open and hauled out a huge wad of something. When the light hit it, they saw it was stamps. Nash grimaced at Arthur and threw them on the floor with disgust.

"Give over!" exclaimed an exasperated Arthur. "What you expect in a bleeding post office, stupid sod. Strike us a match and be quick about it."

He bent down and licked his filthy fingers for grip. Under match-light he rifled through the pages and then started counting on his fingers before giving up and asking Nash.

"Here, what's a thousand fivepences?"

Nash had to think for a while. He eventually provided an answer.

"Bit more than a score. Don't ask me how much more, mind."

Arthur proceeded to quiz Nash on ever increasing amounts and numbers and asked him to keep count. He reached the last sheet of stamps.

"What's all that lot come to then?"

"About two hundred and seventy pound."

The two men nodded at each other, and Nash scrambled with enthusiasm to pick up the loot and stuff it into his extra-cavernous overcoat pockets. Arthur then said out loud what Nash was thinking.

"No need for Shanks to know about these stamps. He's only interested in the money ain't he?"

Nash smiled approval at the old rascal, before turning to try another larger compartment which was rather easier to get open. It contained sovereigns, half-sovereigns and a large assortment of smaller value silver coinage. There was more counting by match light.

"About fifty pound," muttered Arthur as he looked uncertainly at Nash. At least it was money this time, but they had expected more. It joined the stamps in Nash's coffers. There was a locked drawer which, despite all Nash's most violent efforts, proved difficult to budge. The sound of weaponry on buckling metal was echoing around the empty post office.

Will had taken over as crow. And having had no success at attracting attention with his repertoire of whistles and animal calls, his urgent whispered cry tried to make itself heard above the din.

"Nashey! Arthur!"

Arthur thought he heard something, tapped Nashey and put his right index finger to his lips.

"Nashey! Arthur!"

The two men froze on the spot. The voice continued.

"It's Will."

The two of them dashed up the stairs two at a time to find a head dangling through the trap door.

"Pack it in, I can hear you from the street. There's a copper having a crafty drag on his pipe in Heneage Lane. He'll be coming this way sharp enough."

Arthur quickly packed up his gear and handed it to Nash. The three men retraced their steps over the roof. Will offered to go back and pick up Arthur's spare tools, which he had left in the warehouse while he went to fetch his confederates.

"Leave them," ordered the old man with resignation.

Arthur was sad at leaving his tools but knew the chances were too high that Will would get stopped. He could no longer ask Will to do something he was not prepared to do himself. The constable would have finished his quick drag by now and might be on his way into Duke Street at any moment. He may be about to spot the signs of a break-in. Or be looking towards the warehouse at the very moment when three heads popped out.

These heads were steeling themselves to leave the premises. Nash would normally have held coshes in both hands and led the three of them out of the warehouse, dealing with whatever came at them, but he was weighed down by the bounty as well as the tools. If it came to a straight running race between them and the police, he was handicapped by carrying the top weight of a gold cup winner, and the going was getting decidedly heavy. The coinage also jangled noisily as it slid around in his pockets with every step he took.

"You making enough bleeding racket are you?" said Arthur sarcastically. "Didn't you bring nothing to wrap it in?"

He was starting to realise he was working with amateurs.

"Didn't think," said Nash, furious with himself.

Will saw the glum expression. He knew this state of mind. There was nothing more dangerous than Nashey when annoyed with himself. He thought he had better stop Arthur from saying anything more.

"Both of you shut up! I'm the crow. I lead. Any trouble, I scarper and the copper chases after me. You go second Arthur. Nashey, you bring up the rear. Wait for my signal."

With this Will emerged into Duke Street. The stench from the open slaughterhouse next door assaulted his nostrils. It was not the sort of street you walked down unless you had to, and Will was pleased to see that policemen obviously had sensitive noses. The street was empty save a wretch lying in the gutter.

He made his catcall. The others emerged and they started to walk quietly towards their agreed meeting point with Shanks. During the planning of the night's events, Shanks had tried to insist they split the takings up in the alley where they were due to meet, so he could see that he was not being fleeced, but Nash had shouted him down, insisting the money be split behind closed doors in the post office. If he wanted to be in on the split, he could make his way over the roof with them. But Shanks had turned down the invitation and accepted he would take whatever he was given as his share. The annoying frustration now was that due to the necessarily speedy evacuation of the post office, they would have to do exactly what Shanks had wanted all along.

Will was passing the wretch in the gutter, when the man's left hand came out and grabbed him round the ankle.

Copper! Nash dropped Arthur's gear to stuff both hands in his postage stamp-filled pockets trying to lay hold of a cosh. He thought the man might have a beat-policeman's whistle on him; he had to get to him before a high-pitched sound pierced the night air. The man issued forth a panic-stricken whisper.

"You took your bleeding time!"

It was Shanks. Had Nash not been delayed, he would have been removed of his consciousness, possibly for good, but ignorant of this fact, Shanks had the temerity to complain.

"I've had to lie here getting soaked to the skin. Couldn't hang about waiting for you all night, could I? Coppers everywhere. Look at the state of me!"

He was not supposed to meet them so close to the post office in case any police spotted him loitering. All three of his fellow gang members were furious. Nash wished he had been quicker to wrap his fingers around a weapon.

"That's nothing to the state you'd be in if I'd just coshed your lights out!"

Nash carried on with his critique of his co-conspirator while Arthur turned his back, seemingly to keep an eye out. He discreetly cast away his dog-end, tugged his cap down and brought his muffler up to his chin before turning back to speak to Shanks for the first time.

"It took a while because we had a lot of work to do getting things opened," he explained.

Shanks understood this to mean that they had been successful. He immediately forgot his bedraggled circumstances to display the excitement of a small boy about to receive a present.

"How much you get?"

"Fifty pound or thereabouts."

Shanks' expression changed from excited to crestfallen to undisguised suspicion, in a moment.

"Fifty!? I were told four hundred."

Nash and Arthur looked at each other grimly. Nash took one step towards Shanks before Arthur stepped in between them.

"Tell a lie, it were fifty-three weren't it Nashey?" He laughed, trying to defuse the tension. "We forgot them three sovs we got out of one of them drawers. There were a bit of the safe we couldn't get open in time because we had to scarper sharp. Must have had your other gelt in there."

Arthur realised he was being rather defensive, when he felt quite the opposite towards Shanks. His expression and tone of voice changed.

"It were your idea to do a pull with half of London's constabulary on the doorstep weren't it? And now we're going to get our poxy collars felt while we're standing here like cods in a trance!"

The four men shared sheepish glances before nodding agreement and scurrying off around the back of the slaughterhouse. Then it was Nashey's turn to vent his frustration at proceedings. The splitting up of the money was taking too long for his liking as he and Will stood guard while Shanks and Arthur counted every shilling under a gas light.

"Christ almighty, don't count every mortal thing. We ain't got all night. Will here's got all your gear to get home for you, case you've forgotten cracksman. Just chuck me all the small stuff and I'll pay Will and the rest their share from that. We can sort out the rest when the dust settles. You keep hold of it for now Shanks." Nash then glared at Arthur. "Don't worry, he won't be able to get one over on us, we know near enough how much it all is."

This was code for "I got £270 pound worth of stamps in my pocket, so don't get us nabbed by the coppers worrying about the odd sov here or there." Arthur understood and nodded silently.

Shanks was also in full agreement, his devious mind immediately thinking about how he could make more than his share out of the arrangement.

For their part Kitty and Khan had long since left the scene. During the recent Friday meetings, Shanks had briefed Nash as to the regular habits and foibles of the policemen on the relevant beat. PC Harvey passed by the post office every twenty minutes and would stop in a dark spot nearby for a quick draw on his pipe. Aldgate Post Office was just off Mitre Square, where Kate Eddowes had been killed by the Ripper, so there was a plain-clothes officer on patrol in the vicinity too. Armed with this information, Kitty and Khan, though untrained in such work, proved to be good decoys. When PC Harvey had got too close to the post office for comfort, the two novice actors rather overplayed a negotiation, with Khan, probably the gentlest man in the whole of Whitechapel, pretending none too convincingly to threaten Kitty. But it worked a treat. Both the uniformed and plain-clothes officers were successfully led away from the post office.

Kitty and Khan quickly escaped their pursuers and went their separate ways. Kitty lived down a particularly narrow dark alley near the Ten Bells. It was not an alley a woman should be walking down at four o'clock in the morning. She looked around to reassure herself. There did not appear to be anyone about. The tension of the night's work suddenly left her. She sucked in a huge breath like the neediest of cigarette smokers, then blew out her cheeks in relief and shook her head; this life was not for her.

Some while later Nash passed by the same spot on his way home. But for the time lost arguing and counting the money, he might have seen a man he knew also start to make his way home after a night's work.

***

Nash was trying to get some sleep only for his mind to be racing, flitting between thoughts of the robbery, Mary and Sookey. He would have expected the robbery to still be in his head, and angry though he was with Mary he was eager to clear the air with her, but thoughts of Sookey also kept forcing their way into his mind. And they were just random. One moment he was remembering the events of the night, and the next he was thinking about Sookey's previous life.

Poor little cow's had it hard right enough. Not hard like me, but no better for all that. I never thought of people like her. That turd of an husband. There's worse things than knocking your old lady about. Taking her somewhere worse than here. On purpose, if you please. Then he don't hardly speak to her, and she ain't got no other bugger to talk to neither. No wonder she talks so much now! Then that magsman cow sees her coming, she loses everything, everyone takes the rise out of her, and she ain't got a soul in the world to help her. Then she comes here on her own and puts up with the likes of Rose and her mates looking down their noses at her, and she helps everyone, with never a bad word.

As the gang had been about to split up and go their separate ways after the robbery, Shanks had asked why the canary who had not turned up should be paid. Nash had been about to reply when Arthur replied for him.

"Because you've sodded her about the past month that's why you little shithouse!"

An affronted, "here!" was all Shanks could muster in reply.

Nash looked at the old man with renewed respect.

"You were a right handful when you were younger, I'll wager."

That should have been the end of the conversation but Shanks did not have the common sense to leave it. He continued to Nash.

"Who were she anyhow? Whoever she were, you should at least give her a good hiding when you see her. That'll teach her not to turn up."

A glowering Nash made it clear he would not be answering the question or following the advice.

"Mind yourself! We still ain't talked about that little matter of Sookey and your mates, have we?"

Shanks shrank into his filthy wet overcoat as he professed his innocence.

"They ain't no mates of mine. That cove just knocked on my door because he knew me see, and it happened right where I live. I put him up for the night then took him to Sookey's because where else were I going to take him?"

Shanks had darted a glance at Arthur looking for a sympathetic nod, but all he got was a look of contempt.

Every friendship of any kind that Nash had ever been

in, had ended with violence, occasionally physical, more often verbal. His relationship with Mary would not go the same way. He was going to see her the next morning and would break the ice by handing over her share.

His thoughts continued to meander from one crime to another; one woman to another.

Gawd knows what would have happened if that cowson had got to me with that cosh. Fancy Sookey holding on to him. And she'd already been half strangled and had a punch in the belly for her trouble. Or a punch in the Derby Kelly as she now tells it. She likes her coster rhyming that one. She's a funny cuts. Not like Mary's funny, but she makes you laugh right enough. 'We are not amuse-eum'. I ask you! And she takes my codding with her an' all.

He then considered the deep pockets of sixpences, shillings, florins and half-crowns now in his possession.

Least none of us will be caught trying to pass off notes. We could have done with Sookey reckoning them stamps up. And she knows more about over things than them teachers they got in schools. She's clever and soppy as a box o' lights at the same time. Never known anybody like her.

He would let Will, Mary, Kitty and Khan have their shares of the cash when he next saw each of them. The cash and stamps were in a little hide-away under his floor. His heavy coat had protected the latter from the rain, so they were in pristine order. He would fence them and give half the proceeds to Arthur and share his half with the others.

He would tell Mary he was keeping some of her share back to make a point to her about not turning up for the pull but would let her have it as a surprise present at Christmas. She would have probably spent the rest by then.

She had plans to move to a bigger, less squalid, higher rent gaff. And despite what she claimed, he doubted she would give up her drinking just because she was starting work at the art gallery. She would probably invest in more expensive drink like that Polish muck that was less discernible on the breath. It all cost.

Chapter 26

"All this hysterical cant will die down, and men, women and children will be left in precisely the same conditions of life as those which render these murders possible."

H.M.Hyndman, Social Democratic Federation

It seemed to Nash that the killer was an opportunist. The man's walk to work in the early hours, particularly if it was raining, usually being his best opportunity of finding a victim undetected. And now the fog had cleared, it might only be a question of time before he would attempt to strike again.

But Nash wanted his cake and eat it. He needed the Ripper case to continue to dominate the newspaper headlines yet had come to appreciate that he could no longer risk any more women being attacked, so had decided that once the post office robbery was out of the way, he would lie in wait for Lechmere. But not to kill him. The best way to gain the most newspaper column inches was to wait for him to start to attack a woman and then apprehend the wretch and hand him over to the authorities. The belief was that the ensuing court case followed by the man's hanging would provide publicity over a good length of time.

But while Nash had been waiting for the robbery to go ahead, and London had been fogbound in any case, so women were likely to be safe, he had continued to have Jem and Tom help him simply keep an eye on the killer.

Tom was on duty and had done his usual following job. The target had been well on his way towards Pickfords when he had gone to the aid of a young woman who was been harassed by a man near the Ten Bells pub. Tom wondered whether he should follow the orders Nashey had given him, namely that he was to blunder in on any meeting the man had with a woman. But the two of them shared a joke and it was obvious they knew each other, so he thought it best to keep in the shadows. They had set off together with Tom in pursuit and had then taken him by surprise by quickly darting down a tiny alleyway and disappearing into a little slum. Tom didn't know what to do, so simply waited outside. The man was in there some time but eventually came out on his own. Tom followed him, but instead of continuing to Pickfords, he headed back home to Doveton Street. Having seen the man disappear indoors, Tom thought he had better report to Nashey.

***

Mary's thoughts had drifted to Nashey. The last civil conversation they had enjoyed was a brief spell of welcoming banter last Friday, before the blazing row, when he arrived to tell them the job was again not happening. She was just finishing telling Will, Khan and Kitty her terrible rice pudding joke. She was using a cockney accent for what she believed was added comic effect.

"You got any cold rice pudding guvnor? No, he says, come back tomorrow it's hot today."

Kitty thought it amusing. The others did not.

"That's not the all of it," Mary continued. "She goes back the next day. You got any rice pudding left? What if I have, says he. She says, serves you right for making so much!"

Again, only her youngest friend found the joke funny.

Nash made a typically grumpy entrance.

"Don't think Marie Lloyd's got too much to worry about, do you? And for someone who ain't got enough to eat half the time, you spend enough bleeding time talking about nosh."

"Well, look what the cat, Doris I believe, dragged in," retorted Mary, remembering that Sookey had recently told her that Nash's cat now had a name.

She guessed, correctly, that it would be a source of embarrassment to him.

Mary was smiling at the memory of Nash's colourful reply when Christ Church struck the hour. She was due to meet the others in another hour. But she knew that time was going to drag. And she was feeling rough. With her change of career imminent, she had given up drinking. And had done so with a flourish, emptying her gin bottle down a drain in front of a delighted Sookey. But having climbed aboard the wagon, she was now finding it hard to maintain her balance on it. Her body craved alcohol. But lack of funds meant her willpower could not be put to the test. She had no gin at home and had no means of replenishing her stock of it.

She took out her knife to look at her reflection. A whore's cheery make-up could only hide so much. Her skin was grey. There were lines. Bags. It was the worst, the oldest she had ever looked. The workhouse sprang into her mind, the most unwelcome of arriving guests.

She got up from her bed and peered through her sole, tiny broken window, to end the spell. It had the desired effect, her thoughts turning to how she would spend her cut from the robbery.

I'll pay a windows man to come and mend that break. I'll ask old Khan if he knows somebody. He used to be in that game.

She could see into her court and spotted someone she knew passing by. The rain was easing so she grabbed her key, locked her door and ventured out. Having a chat would pass the time.

George Hutchinson was a regular customer of Mary's. Nash had met him once and immediately labelled him a wrong un. Mary had educated him to the reality of her situation.

"Beggars can't be choosers Nashey."

She quickly slipped into the darkness of Miller's Court and hurried along a narrow passage to catch up with Hutchinson as he entered Dorset Street. But it soon became apparent that Hutchinson was roaring drunk, had no money on him and was after a quick kneetrembler on credit. He would not take no for an answer and an increasingly irritated Mary now wished she had stayed in her room.

"I just told you; I've given up the game."

"Yes, it bleeding looks like it." George was looking at what was for the world to see her prostitute uniform of brightly coloured dress, lace up boots and caked on make-up. "I'll pay you. Tomorrow. I always pay you, don't I?"

"I told you, no!"

Mary put her head down and quickened her gait to get away from him.

"The favours I done you in the past."

Hutchinson had the temerity to instil incredulous disappointment into his voice. The only 'favours' he had done her was pay a pittance for pounding away at her up against a wall most Saturday nights. And since the Ripper had started, he'd had the bare faced cheek to demand a regular, and therefore safe, client's discount.

Thank Christ I don't have to put up with this any longer, mused Mary.

"Sod off George! I'll have Nashey on you!"

That threat brought the required response. He stopped in his tracks, gave her a look of contempt, and turned away, lifting a leg and letting rip a huge raspberry of a fart as he did so.

"Don't tear it I'll take the piece," said another man, who had suddenly appeared out of the shadows.

Mary looked around. She recognised the man. She did not know him by name but had serviced him for fourpence on several previous occasions.

"Twist!" she chortled, as Hutchinson disappeared.

The man started laughing at the crude toilet humour.

"Was that fellow trying to rob you?" he asked, putting a hand around Mary's shoulder in protective mode.

"In a manner of speaking," she replied, shrugging his arm off. "But don't get any funny ideas. I'm not working tonight. I have something urgent to do."

She started to move away.

"I'm in hurry myself, truth be told," said the man.

"Even if you had been working I ain't got the time. Got to be in work on the hour. And no more alleys for me. Got to get off the streets to have your fun these days, what with all the coppers about. All takes time, don't it? Shame, I just come into a bit of money an' all. Had a good day at the races. Would have paid extra to someone with their own gaff, like you."

Mary wanted to get rid of this man and be on her way. She would make him a ridiculous offer, and when it was inevitably declined the two of them could go their different ways.

"Yes, a right crying shame. Still, even if you had time, it would have to be two bob, and that just for a kneetrembler. I've no time for anything more, and you need to make it worth my while, given it might make me late for my important meeting. I'm not doing it for any less."

This was six times her usual fourpenny kneetrembler fee. The man flashed what could have been a silver coin. He had used his cousin's workshop lathe to shine up a ha'penny to make it look like something far more valuable. It would certainly not fool anyone in daylight, but in the darkness of Dorset Street in the early hours, it might do the job.

He peered up at the clock of Christ Church. It was purely for effect. It was too dark to see the time. He winked at her.

"I have got a few minutes."

Mary looked him over. Well, he is a regular. He's not mad or foreign and he's not carrying a bag. So, he's safe enough. And that bastard Shanks is just pissing us about every Friday. And that nasty bit of work of McCarthy's,

Fred, will be round first thing tomorrow morning to threaten me for the rent again. It's probably only because they know I'm friends with Nashey I haven't already been given a fat lip and thrown out on my ear. And I won't be getting any wages from Sookey till the end of next week. Two bob would come in handy. One last kneetrembler? Why not?

She nodded her agreement.

"All right my dear come along, you will be comfortable."

She took his arm and led him quickly through an arch and along the passage leading into Miller's Court. She unlocked her door, lit a candle, and threw her hat on the bed.

"I wasn't codding about having somewhere to get to you know. Ten minutes, that's all you've got."

"That's longer than I normally get," came the honest reply.

Chapter 27

"Surely the awful revelations consequent upon the recent tragedies should stir the whole community up to action and to resolve to deliver the children of today, who will be the men and women of tomorrow, from so evil an environment."

Dr Thomas Barnardo

Sookey was desperate to busy herself. She had spent the early morning giving her home a thorough sorting out. Coal collected from the scuttle and put in the fireplace; wood joined it. Having dangled sticky foul-smelling paper traps to kill bugs, she then got out her lime and whitewash brushes and carbolic soap to lime-wash her bedroom with the aid of Klenzit Kleener. Next, boot blackening was on the agenda, followed by washing. She didn't want to go to the washhouse; others would be there. Every bit of clothing, bar what she stood up in, plus her spare bed sheet, was hand-washed in cold water, then hand-wrung till her wrists ached.

She turned her attention to her front step. It was still in reasonable condition from when she and Rose had cleaned it for the visit of her friends, but she cleaned it again. Rose stepped outside to bash a filthy mat against a wall but as soon as she heard her neighbour's door creaking open, Sookey darted back inside.

It was still early enough for her to be sure nobody from Toynbee Hall would make an appearance at her art gallery to discuss the Guild of Handicrafts. She took a roundabout route there to avoid the crowds that were gathering in the area, before completely rearranging her whole art exhibition. She had originally liked the new piece that Walter had sent her from France. It was interesting, full of thought-provoking power. It had pride of place in the gallery. But there was something distasteful about the prone female form which grabbed her eye. She took the picture down and relegated it to the floor of the back room, facing the wall. She had neglected her own work of late, so attempted some drawing, but could not stop her mind wandering to other things. She thought about going round the corner to the Hall, but people would be arriving there to get the place ready for the Sunday service. She could not face meeting anyone at the moment and had turned her back on God.

Returning home, she retrieved the wallpapering materials from where Nash had left them, and made a paste that was hopeless, but carried on with grim determination. She measured and cut with the precision of an artist, but her control of the paper was as poor as her paste. After several abortive attempts to put the paper up she conceded defeat and left the house to go sit in the Spiers & Bond café in Liverpool Street station. Perhaps leaving the East End for a while would help.

***

Tom was illiterate so had simply used his finger to scrawl a letter T. The gutter had been his stationer, a bit of squashed fruit his ink, a fragment of packing box his paper. He had asked Nash's tenement superintendant to wedge the missive under Nash's front door.

Nash had found the piece of wood under his door on his return from the robbery. It had probably been left there a fair bit earlier and Tom would be asleep now. And besides, Nash needed to be safely off the streets. The police could be finding signs of the break-in any time soon, and would flood into the area with numbers. He would get some kip and go round to see what Tom wanted at noon, when the lad would be surfacing.

A few hours of fitful sleep later, Nash wanted to call on Mary to read the riot act for her not showing up but felt that she should come to him to apologise. He should not have to run around after her. But although she was in his bad books, he was sorry about their falling out over his beliefs about the murders. When the time was right, he would joke with her.

"Here, you wait till I tell your new employer what you called me. She'll be giving you the boot all right." And she would be sure to pay him back with interest. She would say something like, "I've already told her, don't you worry, and if you keep on about the murders I'll call you more than that next time and give you another facer into the bargain."

He decided to pop round to visit Sookey en route to see Tom. There was a fair chance Mary would be there in any case. It might be best if they met on neutral ground. Sookey could act as peacemaker.

There was no answer to his knock. Big Rose was cleaning her step. She got to her feet with some difficulty, knees cracking and walked over to him.

"She's not in Nashey," she said in what sounded to him like a rather tired voice. "Left first thing for her gallery. She left me a note. Pushed it under my door. Want to come in? Stan's indoors. Have a nice cuppa tea with us?"

Nash was taken aback by the friendliness. She had made it clear on the increasingly frequent occasions when their paths crossed that she did not like him, disapproved of Sookey's friendship with him and did not care for the influence he had over her easily led neighbour, for whom she had come to have a grudging respect. Nash was puzzled, because it was not just that she was being friendly and speaking gently. There was a certain tone to her voice, a certain expression in her face.

She's talking to me like I'm some little nipper she's trying to keep easy. Rum.

He decided to simply give a brief nod.

"No, that's all right, girl. I got to get down that way to see someone myself. I'll knock into her there."

As he started to turn away, Rose called after him.

"Yes, you will most likely. Gawd bless you boy."

Nash walked away perplexed. *Gawd bless you boy?*

He was halfway to Sookey's when he got a shout from across the street.

"Nashey-ey!"

It was old Bert Walker, who went by the nickname Lace Curtains because he sported a long silver-grey beard. He ran over to Nash, making himself breathless.

"It's your Sookey, Nashey!" he puffed.

"Here, she ain't my Sook..."

"She's just collapsed down the Lane."

Nash feigned indifference.

"Daft mare's been working too hard by the sound of it Lace. Forgot to eat I suppose, then she puts her stays on too tight and before she knows what she's about she's tasting the cobbles."

Bert blinked.

"Ain't you going to see to her boy?"

Nash pulled a face.

"They would have picked her up by now, wouldn't they? She's probably made a bob or two an' all, people thinking she's some old leppy!"

Bert's stern expression made it clear he did not appreciate Nash's attempt at humour.

"All right Lace, keep your hair on!" said Nash. "I'm going that way anyhow. I'll see she's up and about."

Bert nodded his satisfaction and put a hand up as a gesture of leaving.

"Gawd bless you, lad."

Nash made his way towards Petticoat Lane market, marching quicker than he would have liked to admit.

Everyone's blessing me today. What's a matter with them all? They been to church? Old Rev Barnett bribed them with a jumble sale or something to get them to listen to one of his bleeding sermons?

***

It was easy to spot her. Some of the sightseers who had just arrived in the area had gathered round. But they were beginning to drift away as she started to show signs of recovery. She had just been helped to her feet when Nash arrived. He was about to launch into a typically robust

297

greeting given he had an audience to entertain but one look at her face told him such humour was out of the question. It was not the embarrassed, flushed face of someone who had simply worn her corset too tight. She looked terrible and was trembling. It looked like she had not slept for a week, her normally beautiful black glistening hair was dull, matted and twisted, and there was no trace of her doll-like make-up. She was staring at the people around her wildly.

"Sookey?" said Nash enquiringly.

Sookey swivelled her head and looked at him, blankly for a moment before focussing.

"Nashey," she stumbled into him, her face plummeting into his chest, his arms automatically enfolding her.

"Come on, let's get you home and get some grub inside you, girl."

She pulled away from him a couple of inches and gazed into his eyes. There was no pain there at all. Where had he been? He did not know.

"Yes Nashey, get me home."

They walked entwined, staggering like partners in a three-legged race. It was not unlike another walk they had once shared, but neither of them was thinking of that now.

As they appeared at Sookey's doorstep, Rose gave them the shortest, saddest of smiles before retreating into her home. They stepped through the door and into the living room. Nash looked around in shock. The place was a shambles, crammed with all sorts, and smelt much damper than usual. He found it difficult to manoeuvre her through the sea of washing and peeling wallpaper, so picked her up in his arms and carried her through to the bedroom. It was empty save an incongruously expensive looking brass bedstead and mattress. Evidence of a carbolic spring-clean was in the air. Nash laid her gently on the bed. He took his huge coat off and put it over her.

"I'll pop out and get you some grub," he said, to reassure.

As he started to lean back up and away from her, she grabbed his shirt collar and stared up at him with tears welling up in her eyes. She had not cried when that man McCarthy had been kind enough to knock on her door to tell her the news, but she was going to now.

"Suffer me to tell you. It is well it is me. It does not command itself to reason. Our dearest friend Mary. She is murdered! By the Whitechapel fiend!"

She only just got the final sentence out before starting to sob uncontrollably. Nash lowered himself onto the bed, staring incredulously at her before looking away. The trembling fingers of his right hand roamed aimlessly across his face. Sookey regarded him. The effect of her words had been even greater than she could have imagined. He was staring into space like a madman. She sat up, placed her head over his right shoulder and held him. He felt the convulsions, the liquid from her eyes and nose dripping on to the back of his shirt, as she heaved for breath between the sobs. It was the natural reaction to great loss. He just stared, the natural reaction to a different, equally powerful emotion.

***

The two of them laid together, heads sideways on the mattress, facing each other, a few inches apart. She had just finished telling him everything she had heard, the facts, the conjecture, the rumours. Nash had gone into denial. It must have been the boyfriend. He would go round there and kill the little bastard. Sookey shook her head sadly. No, it was the fiend. She could not bring herself to say the name that everyone called him by these days. It had been confirmed by the police. The wounds were rumoured to be horrific.

Sookey started to reminisce about her dear friend, talking of things they had shared together. She was just coming to the end of another bout of sniffling when she looked into Nash's eyes with the deepest of stares and leaned across and took him in her arms. Nash hugged back. They stayed in that position for some time before she brought her head back in front of his, gave the kindest of serene smiles and gazed at every little nook and cranny of his distraught face before lowering her lips to his.

His coarse beard growth rubbed painfully into her chin. A mental image of her husband's regime flashed into her head. He would always shave beforehand. Not for her benefit, but for his. He did not want the servants sniggering at her flaky chin. But the present was not for thinking about others; this was just two people helping each other along the path. She felt a heady mix of embarrassment and nervousness. Her heart was pounding out of her chest. Was she about to faint again? She did not care.

They kissed uncertainly, flinching slightly as they butted noses whilst attempting a minor change of position. She had her right palm resting on his huge torso. Her thumb brushed against a button and without thinking she slipped it open, tucking her hand beneath his shirt. She felt thick coarse chest hair. A pang of shock at her own brazenness flashed through her, so she freed herself from the embrace. She stared up at the big face and saw he felt as awkward as she did, which was strangely reassuring.

Nash could not hold her stare for more than a second, looking to the side for a moment before returning to her. He repeated the gesture. She reached up and held his chin firmly, so he had to hold his gaze at her. Her fingers drifted away as she stretched her neck up and their mouths came back together a little too hard. There was a clink of teeth, and they pulled away from each for a moment in shock, sharing a chuckle of embarrassment before returning hesitantly to the matter at hand.

He suddenly felt intimidated for the first time in his life. Sookey had achieved something nobody, not the toughest of men, had ever managed, and this with the gentlest of weapons. This was not as he had heard about such things, when in his youth it had been the most popular topic of conversation among the boys in the gang. And it was not the impression he had got when nodding sagely at men in the pub, talking about 'how's your father'.

Nash's only previous sexual experience, with anyone else at least, had been back on his sixteenth birthday, with a dollymop, a quasi-prostitute who had expensive entertainment and gifts lavished on her, on the understanding that the benefactor would have sex with her at the end of the evening. This had been funded by a kidsman, in a moment of rare generosity in appreciation of his young charge's pickpocketing prowess. The dollymop experience had been an empty one young Nash had chosen not to repeat. He had been popular enough with the local girls and had embarked upon the fumbling of a testosterone-driven male adolescent, but it had not gone well. And he had become only too aware of the hardships unwanted pregnancies and venereal disease caused in the slums. He came to decide that it would be safer not to pursue the opposite sex in future.

He had only once been tempted to change his mind, but had hesitated to make his feelings known, losing the young woman to another, and it was against his code of behaviour to try and woo her away from this rival, though he was confident he could have. But it was too late now.

Nash and Sookey now nestled on a bare mattress beneath his coat, both fully clothed, right down to his huge boots. They kissed, caressed, hugged. They stayed like that for some time before Sookey motioned with a tug of his shirt, for him to remove his clothes. She nodded at him and started to unbutton herself. Not a word spoken.

Nash got to his feet and felt a mix of panic and embarrassment as he hobbled around the room trying to unburden himself of his boots, which were imprisoning his trousers. He needn't have been so self-conscious, as Sookey had her head buried beneath the coat. He had to cede to the strength of the laces, his fingers scrambling dementedly at the things to let him free. He finally managed it and ducked quickly under cover to join her.

All Sookey's sexual experiences had taken place in the dark, under bed covers, within bed clothes. A short burst of staccato movements and it had been over. The man had achieved his release; the purpose achieved. Her mother had never told her a thing. There had been the giggling conversations with girls at school, but no real, accurate information had been gleaned, and the subject had certainly never been broached in the polite circles of her adulthood. Her disastrous, painful wedding night had been a voyage into the complete unknown. Eight years married; Sookey knew little of love making.

There had been a much more recent conversation about sex with someone who had experienced a lot of it, but Sookey forced this memory from her mind, kissing Nash reassuringly.

Their union was essentially that of two teenage virgins. A lack of expertise compensated for by desire, longing and a fondness for investigation. When they had finished, she still awaited her first orgasm, but she was far from disappointed. She had not reached the mountain peak but had at least made the foothills, rather than the sea-level of her marriage. It had been splendid.

***

After leaving the note for Nash the previous night, Tom had assumed the target would have made his way to work in the interim, so had left his brother to pick up the surveillance outside the removals company later in the day, as usual. But Jem had waited in vain outside the place for the man to appear at the end of the shift. Lechmere must have stayed at home after Tom had seen him return there.

Now aware of all this, it was obvious to Nash that there was every chance Tom may have been spotted by some bystander hanging about outside Mary's gaff. The police could be knocking on Tom's door soon enough.

Nash made the decision to come clean with the

brothers about who they had been following these past weeks. Jem and Tom accepted the trouble Nash had got them into with remarkable grace, offering their unstinting loyalty. But Nash repeated what he had told them when they had first been given the job. Should they have their collar felt by the police concerning this work, they were to nark on him. Both men were quick to complain about such orders, but Nash insisted so vehemently that they had grudgingly agreed.

The brothers were told to immediately head 'over the water' to Rotherhithe in South London. He would meet them in the Spread Eagle & Crown pub in the middle of the village. Nash then donned his light shoes and went for a training run over to his sister, whom he had kept in touch with over the years. She now lived with a Surrey Docks stevedore and their five children, all under the age of six, in Rotherhithe. He knew the family were struggling financially and would welcome a couple of paying guests into the garret in the eaves of their slum. Arrangements were made for Tom & Jem to disappear for a while.

With his associates safely hidden away, Nash made his way back to the East End, his mind in turmoil about how exactly to deal with the killer. His once held view that he would apprehend and hand over Lechmere to the authorities to be hanged, was now a thing of the past. He now wanted to bludgeon his quarry to a pulp.

He could mutilate the body, so Lechmere looked something like his victims, before dumping him, along with his knife, on the steps of Leman Street police station with a sign pinned to him stating 'I am Jack the Ripper'.

Another part of him thought that if the death of poor

Mary, and those other women, was to be of any meaning, it was important that the Jack the Ripper legend remained. If the world came to know the identity of the Ripper, he would just be another murderer in a long line of them. Cotton, Muller, Wainwright. They had all been famous cases at their time, but who remembered them now? And look at all the fuss there had been over the persecution of that little fellow, Lipski, a twelve-month back. He was innocent if Nash was any judge. But they still hanged the wretch, and everyone quickly forgot about him.

No, if Lechmere was brought to book and hanged like those others, the people who had been forced to face up to the problems of the poor these past few months would suck in a large breath of relief and Whitechapel would be left to return to how it had been before the murders began. Whereas, killing the Ripper in a different way, quietly, would mean he would never be apprehended. And if he was never caught, he would live on in the minds of the ruling classes. The publicity, guilt, social investigation and improvements would continue. Nash was thus considering killing the man dispassionately, without fuss, quickly and quietly, making sure there was no evidence left on the body to suggest the murdered man was the Ripper. Any items of value would be taken to make it look like a robbery. The man will have simply been the victim of some dastardly East End villain.

The problem was that Nash's code of correct behaviour believed the right thing to do to avenge Mary would be to kill the man in such a way that everyone came to know who had killed her, and that justice had been served. But he also knew the right thing to have done was to have killed the man when he had the original opportunity back on the night of the double murder. Nash accepted that he had sold his soul that night, and there was no going back on that now. He would kill the man quietly. The legend of Jack the Ripper would live on.

He would wait outside Lechmere's gaff for him to leave for work, follow him till he was in some dark spot in the infamously crime ridden Flower & Dean rookery, and despatch him to hell.

At three in the morning Nash was standing outside 22 Doveton Street. But an hour went by without any sign of Lechmere. Nash started to wonder what was going on. He should have been out by now. Was he going to miss another day's work today? Had Mary managed to injure the cowson, so he was indoors licking his wounds? People would soon be stirring and the streets teaming with life. What to do?

An increasingly impatient Nash decided. Having looked about him to make sure the coast was clear, he kicked in the killer's door, which gave way surprisingly easily, suggesting it was unlocked. Nash hurtled at a rate of knots into the living space, marlin spike in hand. But his great boots immediately skidded to a halt. There were no signs of life. No food or tobacco on the packing case that had clearly once served as a table. No coal in the grate. No bedding on the poor excuse for a bedstead. No candles. It was clear. Lechmere had done a moonlight flit. The bastard had escaped.

Chapter 28

"The circulation of the Star… (the day after the murder) reached the enormous total of 298,840 copies. This number exceeds the total ever circulated in one day by this or any other evening paper."

The Star

Emotions had run high. It had been the most emotional day of her life. Nashey's too, she suspected. But it was another day and Sookey was not sure what their relationship now was.

She was desperate to see him; to laugh and cry with him; tell him more things about herself; hear more about his life. Lay with him again. But they had not made finite arrangements to meet. They had both hesitated at their moment of parting and left things unsaid. They would no doubt bump into each other again soon enough. It had been easier that way at the time, emotionally drained as they were. A moment of awkwardness was easier to deal with than any moment of revelation. This left Sookey in a quandary.

Should I wait for him to visit me? There were the funeral arrangements?

This brought instant self-criticism.

I want an excuse to visit Nashey and immediately think of poor Mary's funeral as a tool by which to do it. What sort of a woman am I?

307

Mary had always paid the first threepence she had earned every week into her funeral club. If it was a choice between the funeral club and threepence worth of food to keep herself fed, she went hungry. She had even paid it ahead of her rent when under threat of eviction.

This had seemed a little bizarre to Sookey. Surely food and rent were more important than insurance. She remembered the one time she had broached the subject. Mary's reply had been one of cold, angry certainty.

"There's only one thing worse than living in the workhouse as a pauper, and that's dying as one, having a pauper's funeral and an unmarked grave. There will be no pauper's funeral for this Mary Jane."

It was the only time Sookey heard Mary refer to herself in the third person. She had thought it rather intriguing, but Mary's angry expression had quickly given way to a sad faraway look which told Sookey not to pursue the matter.

Sookey had liaised with the necessary authorities and overseen the funeral arrangements. Mary's boyfriend Joe Barnett had suggested Mary be buried under her preferred French name. Sookey had allowed this because not a soul had come forward from Mary's previous life before she had arrived in the East End, to offer their condolences, which given the high profile her death had been given in the newspapers, seemed odd. And given Mary's secrecy about her earlier years, her penchant for telling tall tales, and things such as her middling accent being a puzzle, Sookey was far from convinced that Mary Jane Kelly had been her friend's real name in any case.

The polished elm and oak coffin had metal mounts and a brass plate:

Marie Jeanette Kelly, died 9th Nov. 1888, aged 25 years

There would be four pallbearers. Sookey hoped Nashey would not mind being omitted from the task. She felt it would be disrespectful to Joe. The coffin was to be carried in an open carriage drawn by two horses with two coaches to follow from Shoreditch mortuary. Sookey had never discussed religion with Mary but given her supposed Irish roots, Leytonstone Roman Catholic cemetery was selected as her final resting place. Given that there was every chance Mary was not Irish, this was done with some trepidation, but Sookey did not know what else she could do.

She needed to walk round to see Nashey, amongst others, to let him know what was happening, but decided she would visit others first, and leave him till last.

***

Nash's travails continued. He had just got back from Bloomsbury, where he had fenced the stamps. Nobody in the East End could manage such high value, high profile goods. The robbery would normally have made the local newspaper; maybe even a small column in one of the nationals. But taking place as it did on the same night as another Ripper murder, and just off the very square where the previous killing had occurred, it was national news.

The police were now an even greater laughing stock than ever. How could a gang have ransacked a post office not much more than a stone's throw from where yet another horrible murder was taking place, and the hordes of police in the area had not seen a thing? PC Crisp had seen an Indian man acting suspiciously with a young prostitute, though not the one killed. The newspapers propounded that perhaps the killer was not Jewish after all. An Indian was an obvious alternative; another 'alien'. An inaccurate description of Khan was added to a long list of possible Ripper suspects. Along with another man who had been seen hanging about outside Mary's abode during the night.

Nash knew he had to be very careful because all known receivers of stolen goods would be under heavy scrutiny from the police, who did not take kindly to being made to look even greater fools than they already appeared. If they could not catch the Ripper, they would at least nab the post office robbers.

There were receivers such as certain shopkeepers, kidsmen, pub-landlords and lodging house superintendents whom Nash had used in the past to fence things he had stolen, but he suspected that they tended to hunt with the hounds and run with the hare. He thought they might be informers when it suited them. And turning in the post office gang to a very grateful police force would certainly suit them. Such men dealt with dangerous men like Nash on a regular basis so were careful not to openly help the law, but the police menaced them as well, so they had to play one off against the other the best they could. Nash knew he could not trust any of them. And the reward being offered was another reason for a normally trustworthy type to turn informer. The only receiver he fully trusted was his old mate Taff Hughes. He had been a kidsman in Whitechapel but the high number of police in the area these days had sent him off to a new lair in Bloomsbury.

Nash had once saved Taff's life when they were young, toshing for anything of value they could find in and around the sewers that fed into the Thames at Limehouse. Taff had been overcome by gas, an occupational hazard, which was the reason toshing was always done with a mate. He had been lying head down in watery human detritus with a gang of huge rats starting to nibble at him. He might have drowned if he had been lucky. Nash had hauled him out and back to the safety of the river. Choking from the fumes and stench, exhausted from the monumental task of dragging someone almost as big as himself by their coat collar through ankle deep muck and water, Nash had collapsed with his load into the shallows of the river, ensuring he kept his friend's face up, out of the water. On his knees and gasping for air himself, he had slapped and splashed his mate until he had come round.

Taff had fallen awkwardly when he had passed out, and the wound sustained had got infected, no doubt from the filth and rats' nibbling. Taff had eventually had a leg off in the London Hospital. This was the second most feared building in the vicinity. Only the workhouse brought more anguish. Taff had entered the hospital not expecting to come out, so it was with relative relief that he escaped its dreaded walls with no more than a leg lost. Taff had always been suitably grateful. He would never turn in his old friend.

Nash had arrived at the kidsman's new abode to find Taff's disability did not stop him from still being a nasty bit of work. A couple of his young thieves had just returned home empty-handed, so their employer had removed the strap that held on his wooden leg and, despite a precarious balance, was managing to flog them mercilessly with the strip of leather. Taff was very pleased to see Nash, though not half as much as the young lads. They quickly made themselves scarce as the two old partners talked about times old and new.

Back in his own lair now, Nash was thinking of Sookey. He was confused. He had always avoided this sort of thing for precisely this reason. It made strong men weak, decisive men dither. People could get to him though her. Imagine if Shanks found out; being more than just friends with her was just the sort of thing the wrong un might try to exploit. But Nash could not help but give an ironic snort. Had it not been Shanks who had first thrust them together? Nash found it difficult to believe that any of this could have happened but for that attack on Sookey.

Who would have thought it; him and a woman like Sookey of all people. He wanted to see her again; but what could a woman like her really think of a man like him? They had both been so upset and one thing had led to another. But that was then. The moment had passed. She would probably be ashamed of him now, not to mention herself. What was he supposed to do?

He had a full wash down in the yard and then started to tidy up his room. He remembered his mother, hands on hips in astonishment, once seeing him wash behind his ears for the first time, when he was about to go on his first monkey parade in search of girls.

"Gawd help us," she said. "I thought you were growing cabbages in them lugholes of yours. I suppose there's a first time for everything!"

Nash did not own any cleaning implements save an ash-pan and brush for the fire. He was making do with this for the jobs at hand when he saw Doris peering at him with the look of superiority and inscrutability that only cats can summon.

"What you looking at? Christ almighty, let's go and see her and get it over with."

Nash grabbed the cat by its scruff and went on his way.

Nash arrived at Sookey's to find there was no answer. He thought he would knock at Rose's to ask her if she knew where she was, but before he did so, decided to shove the cat out of sight into one of his coat pockets.

A minute later Rose was informing him that her neighbour was doing the rounds about the funeral and was probably on her way to see him at his place, when a little white head popped out of a pocket and miaowed.

The two of them bumped into each other en route. Neither had the confidence to say they were just on their way to seek out the other. Nash thrust the cat forward as an icebreaker. It had the desired effect, and after some small talk, mostly about animal husbandry, they had fallen into step, heading for Nash's tenement.

They spent the rest of the day together, with the two of them finishing Nash's cleaning job, before they went to Sookey's to rescue her attempt at wallpapering. By the end of the day, it was clear to them both that they were 'walking out' together. The confection of sobs and reminiscences were still there, but they now realised that they were an understandable, natural part of their relationship, not the foundations of it.

***

Nash could not tell Sookey the truth. The expression on Mary's face, the last time he ever saw her, haunted him.

The look of contempt and disgust when she had been told why the Ripper's killings were a good thing for the common cause. He could not face that expression being etched across Sookey's features, as it surely would if he ever told her the truth. He remembered the criticism she had imparted on the previous occasion his theory had been put to her. So, he had invented a concoction of half-truths and lies, some little and white, others as big and black as Newgate's knocker.

Nash relayed that he had been making his way through the City when a man passed him coming out of Mitre Square as he himself entered the square. Seconds later Nash had found the body of poor Kate Eddowes and fled for his life into the East End, fearful of being collared as the killer by a City policeman. He quickly found himself following the very same man he had just seen leaving the square. Imagine his shock when he sees the man stop to wipe a huge knife clean and fold it away into his pocket. It was obvious Nash was following the killer! He followed him for a while longer but eventually lost him in a maze of dark alleys.

Sookey had listened in shocked silence until now, but she could not wait any longer to ask the obvious question.

"But Nashey, why did you not inform the police of your findings?"

Nash shook his head with the certainty of someone well-rehearsed.

"What did I have to tell them? Fellow were about 5 foot 4, stout, dark haired, whiskers, ruddy chops, shabby dressed, deerstalker hat. That's half the coves in Whitechapel. No, they'd have been thinking I were making it up in case some nose ache had seen me in the square. They'd have been calling me Jack sooner enough, you mark my words."

The explanation would not have fooled any but the most gullible. Fortunately for Nash, the audience was precisely that.

"So, what is to be done now?" asked Sookey.

He wished he knew.

Chapter 29

"Since the recent calamity in the east of London, several benevolent persons have come forwards to provide night shelters for the outcast men and women."

Dr Taylor to the Sanitary Committee of the Mile End district

In the weeks following the murder, Nash suffered from depression. He would wake up in the early hours. There was none of the usual grogginess of awakening. As soon as consciousness returned, he was wide awake. His sleep-starved mind collapsed into unconsciousness readily enough every evening, but his demons woke him as soon as they could.

Nash's mind started to try to heal itself by transference of blame. He could not stop thinking about Mary, and the part Shanks had played in her death. His messing them all about regarding the robbery had gone on for weeks. Mary had been behind in her rent again and couldn't feed herself thanks to Shanks' shenanigans. She had obviously decided she needed to make a few bob selling herself that Friday night rather than rely on Shanks' robbery finally taking place.

As far as Nash was concerned, she would be alive today if Shanks had been straight with everyone. Nash became obsessed with thoughts of Shanks' guilt rather than his own.

He remembered an incident from their youth. There had been a fight on the Isle of Dogs with some Deptford lads who had got the Greenwich ferry across the Thames looking for trouble. Nash had not been there, having been otherwise engaged in some pickpocket work for a kidsman. But many of his gang had and been given a beating due to being badly outnumbered. A bloodied and bruised Will had told Nash of the taunts they had endured as they 'scarpered with our tails between our legs'.

Nash had returned to the scene of the crime with numbers and serious weaponry. The Deptford boys were nowhere to be seen. He decided that if they were going to invade his side of the river, he would do likewise. His gang took the ferry before stumbling through Greenwich and eventually finding their way to Deptford, and got plenty of looks from surly young individuals, but their gang prey was nowhere to be seen.

They decided to try to set fire to a woodyard just off Deptford's Douglas Street market. That would warn South London boys not to set foot north of the river. Shanks was the one member of the gang not there; Nash having made a point of not taking him along. Although the police had been quick to descend upon them, all bar the none-too-fleet of foot Nash and little Harry had escaped. Fortunately for the two held in custody they had been caught before having a chance to inflict any real damage, otherwise it would have been off to prison for committing the cardinal sin of harming property. They were up before 'the beak', successfully pleading for mercy thanks to a masterful performance by Harry, the big-eyed little innocent of the gang, when in walked Shanks. He told the magistrate that he was a member of the gang and had been at the market but had been lucky enough to escape. He admitted to a crime he did not commit to gain what he thought would be greater respect from gang members. It had the opposite effect. As soon as they were back on home soil, he was told in no uncertain terms that he was no longer a member of the gang.

And if he could admit to something he did not even do, what might he say if the police felt his collar now? A wrong un like him would crack in an instant; tell them everything about the post office robbery. And then there was the attack on Sookey. She could be lying in the next grave to Mary. He was going to have to do something about Shanks.

***

Kitty was to receive Mary's share from the robbery. The girl's original share was to have been quite small, but she had stepped up to do Mary's work, so it seemed only fair. The expression on Nash's face when he had asked Shanks if he was happy with the arrangement was such that no objection was raised.

There had also been an agreement between all participants in the robbery that they would lie low till after Christmas, and this included not spending any more money than usual. The police would be looking for unusual spending behaviour.

But Nash was concerned about Kitty. She was only young, had no previous professional criminal experience, and it was said that she was now in a state of shock following

Mary's death. And he knew he should have done more for Mary. He must not make the same mistake again. So, when he visited Kitty in her little slum to hand over her share, he made some small talk, enquiring about what she was going to do with herself in the coming months.

"Can you hang on to my share Mr Nash?" she asked. "Mary had been on at me to give up being on the game." She stopped for a moment looking upset before continuing. "She thought I should try the Providence. As you know, they helped her out when she first come back from France. They won't help me if they know I got money. You can give me what's owing when I gets myself straight."

The Providence Row Night Refuge & Home for Deserving Men, Women & Children was only open in winter. It had recently opened its doors for the season. It was a Catholic Church-run charity which offered free board and lodging, as well as domestic service training for girls, and provided stock money for those who wished to set up in business such as selling fruit or flowers.

Nash approved of the place. It appreciated that there was a surplus labour market and as a result there were people down on their luck through no fault of their own who needed another chance. And most important of all, it kept people out of the clutches of the workhouse. Nash was also pleased that Kitty's share was not simply going to be paid into the burgeoning coffers of John McCarthy and the local pub landlords.

"Yes, I can do that for you," he said. "You'll have to get up there early, mind. They open the doors at five and by then there's always more lining up than they can take. And you'll have to give account of yourself."

"Yes, I know. I was wondering if I could give you as my witness."

"Me! Dear o' lore! I ain't so sure my name will get you a place in there, girl. Why don't you give McCarthy as your witness? He's a leech of a slum landlord right enough, but he's the sort of fellow what thems in charge think are upright citizens. And he can tell them you've always paid your rent on time but can't afford it no more because there's no work about. That's the sort of thing they like, see."

"Well, Mary…" she stopped. Nash assumed she was choking up again, but there was another reason for the hesitancy. "Mary told me as how the people in there like to save girls from vice. But if you're already given to vice, you're what they call undeserving. You have to hint that you haven't gone that way yet but could if you're not saved. Me giving someone like you as my witness, it looks like…" She stopped again, this time looking suitably sheepish. "It looks like I'm in with a bad lot. So, I need to be saved, see."

"You conniving little mare!" said Nash, pretending to be offended when in fact he was most impressed. "Sure you don't want to go the whole hog and give Shanks as your witness!"

Kitty felt ashamed. She had obviously gone too far.

"I am sorry Mr Nash. I…"

"Just codding with you girl," reassured Nash, letting a chuckle escape. It was the first time he had laughed since he had heard of Mary's death, and he was aware of the fact. A moment of guilt coursed through him, but he quickly recovered his composure. "Yes, alright, I'll be your witness. Don't worry, you will be saved! You going to train to be a skivvy or hawk stuff?"

320

"Hawk stuff," she said confidently. "Wood in the winter, don't know about next summer yet. See what comes up as making a few bob."

Nash nodded. He thought Kitty obviously had a head on her shoulders. The small talk was over as far as he was concerned. It was time to change the subject.

"Remember I said I knew you from somewhere?"

"Yes, Mr Nash."

"I saw you the night of the double event."

Kitty frowned, bemused, but didn't say anything so he continued.

"Backchurch Lane. You were sitting on a bench blowing bubbles. You asked a man for business, but he weren't interested."

The silent frown remained so again Nash went on.

"I were following him. Followed him into the City. Had an idea to give him a tap and swipe what I could. Then he kills Kate Eddowes."

It had never occurred to Kitty that the man who had rejected her that night might have been the Whitechapel Murderer. Her eyebrows headed north. Her mouth gaped. She started to moan. Then came the tears. Not just for herself but for Mary.

Nash realised that he should have led up to this rather more carefully. He sat Kitty down on the slum's solitary chair and not without some awkwardness bent down to attempt a reassuring hand on a shoulder. He then offered an overcoat sleeve on which she could wipe her weeping nose.

"Here are, Spindle, cuff it," he advised.

He hoped that bestowing a new nickname on the petite young girl might raise a smile from her. A snotty chortle did issue forth, but it was still ten minutes before he was able to have the conversation with her that he wanted. And even then, she was not able to provide any useful information.

No, she hadn't seen the man before or since. No, she doubted she would recognise him again. She barely looked at the man. But yes, she would let Nashey know if she ever did spot him. And yes, she would of course keep her trap shut to all and sundry about what he had just told her.

***

Kitty left her lodgings, dropped off the key with McCarthy, and arrived at the refuge several hours before the doors were due to open. But there was already a long line of people ahead of her. She engaged the woman in front of her in conversation.

"Do you think we'll get in?"

"Should do," came the reply. "Look, it's mostly men ahead of us. Still some room in the women's section I fancy."

A little after five o'clock the woman's confidence proved to be well founded, when she and Kitty were admitted as some of the men in front of them were turned away.

A kindly, black-robed sister asked Kitty for her details, which included one Mr Alexander Nash's name & address being given as someone who could speak for her worthiness. She was given a ticket which entitled her to an initial five nights' board & lodging. It was explained that her account of herself would be checked and if any information she had declared was found to be false, her ticket would not be renewed. But if all was well, she would be allowed to stay up to six weeks.

She was taken into a brightly lit, lofty room where there was a long table with chairs either side, sat down and given a bowl of cocoa with a small loaf. A line of worn, white haired faces which were, like the slums they had just left, devoid of their fine original features, sat opposite and beside her, all too tired and weak to make any conversation. She noticed how the tables and floors had been scrubbed to within an inch of their lives. She had never seen anywhere so clean. But it was extremely basic too. The place provided no more comfort than the orphan's workhouse in which she had once lived. But she felt safe and cared for here. That was the most important thing to her. She soaked in a shiny tin bath, and then it was time for bed. In her dormitory she had a wooden bunk raised eighteen inches above the floor, a mattress, a pillow covered with American cloth and a sheet covered by a hide of leather.

The following morning the cocoa and bread meal were repeated, before a nun explained that efforts could be made to find her work, or she could enrol in a domestic service training course. Kitty conveyed that she preferred to receive help with buying some stock. She explained her plan to sell wood, and Mrs Gilbert, the wife of the manager, arranged for her to receive a loan.

Kitty Johnson, wood seller by day, off the streets at night, had been saved.

Chapter 30

"Now all is changed. Private enterprise has succeeded where Socialism failed…some independent genius has taken the matter in hand, and by simply murdering and disembowelling…women, converted the proprietary press to an inept sort of communism."

George Bernard Shaw, Blood Money to Whitechapel, 1888

Nash was surprised to receive a visit from Shanks. It transpired that he had another pull. This one made the Aldgate post office job look small in comparison. It was easy work too. No great skill was involved, there was very little security to overcome and no risk of capture. Nash snorted.

"There's always risk!"

But Shanks continued undeterred. It was such a delicate matter that nobody else could be in on it, and the utmost secrecy needed to be maintained. It was going to be just the two of them. It was a job way out in the sticks.

Nash had no intention of ever again working with the wrong un sitting in front of him. It was all he could do to stop himself ploughing a huge fist into the man's face where he sat. No, on second thoughts, it would have to wait till Shanks stood up; punching someone when they were sitting down was the sort of thing a wrong un would do. But Nash held himself in check and let the man talk. Curiosity had gotten the better of him. And besides, he might find out something to his advantage.

Shanks told him it was to be arson. Set fire to something big in such a way that the whole lot went up. But his employers were powerful, important men. They stood to gain a great deal, but they could not afford any mistakes, and the men who did the job had to be able to disappear into the night and never heard of again. That's why they were paying such big money for such a simple job. On being told how much he would be paid, Nash could not help but show startled enthusiasm. He knew Shanks would be keeping a high percentage of the money for himself, so the large amount being offered to Nash showed what a big job it was.

"Warehouse, is it?

Shanks gave a snivelling smile.

"In a manner of speaking."

"Insurance? Got to be a warehouse to be worth the sort of money you're talking about. What's it got in it anyhow?"

"Never you mind."

"When and where?"

"I can tell you when this time, but I ain't telling you where till we get there on the night."

"Again! After last time!"

Nash reached forward, grabbed Shanks by the throat and began to squeeze. Shanks started to gurgle, before he managed to blurt out four barely decipherable words.

"Crystal Palace! Debt trouble!"

Nash released Shanks, allowing the half-strangled man to drop to his knees, wheezing and coughing. Nash stomped to the door, flung it open, grabbed the coughing man up by his coat collar and flung him out on to the tenement's landing.

"Go on, fuck off out of it! Come round here again, I'll top you!"

When he had calmed down sufficiently to think straight, Nash thought about Shanks' proposal. He sifted through in his mind the information Khan had given him after he had followed Shanks in the lead up to the post office robbery. When he had given Khan the job, it had been primarily with the intention of him digging up a clue as to the identity of the inside man in the post office who must have fed Shanks the information. Nash had told Khan that if Shanks met up with anyone who looked a bit different in any way from the usual low ranks Shanks fraternised with; a clerk, a gentleman, anyone like that, he should follow him rather than Shanks after they go their separate ways.

Khan had followed such a man. A gent. After meeting Shanks in the City, the gent walked to London Bridge station before getting a train followed by a cab.

Khan had stuck close to his quarry, taking the same forms of transportation, eventually to a fine house miles away, south of the river. Khan had used up the last of the money Nash had given him by then, so had to walk for hours to get home to the East End. But he was not shown any concern by his employer, who had been annoyed at the time. It had cost Nash a lot of money and all he had to show for it was some gent's address in the 'back of beyond'. Catford.

Nash had taken the information to a private enquiry agent, who had managed to find out some details of the man who lived at the address. There could have been a legitimate reason why Shanks and a south London gent had met, but Catford was only a stone's throw from Sydenham, where the Crystal Palace was located. Coincidence? Nash did not think so.

***

All the words whose spelling he was not sure about had been written down on a piece of paper in random order. Nash thought he knew how to spell most of his own words accurately enough, but he was also borrowing some from Sookey's vocabulary, so asked her to check them. He was pleased to find that he had spelt 'intelligence' and 'forsake' correctly. 'Skeem', 'Sinseerly' and 'blaggard' had been wrong. He could understand the first two being spelt as they were, but blackguard?

Sookey was curious as to what he was up to.

"Is the letter to someone of your acquaintance?" she asked.

He tapped her gently on the nose.

"Nose-ache."

She remembered when Nashey had tapped Mary in a similar fashion. Sookey lowered her head sadly. Nash mistook this for her being a little 'vexed' as she would put it, at not being told what he was up to.

He looked at his handiwork.

Dear Mr Burgess

I am writing to tell you of our mutual friend, Mr Niven MacDonald, what you might or might not no as

Shanks. He told me of your little plot to burn down the Crystal Palace. He is telling it all over the shop. All that money. He is giddy with it. I followed him and that led me to you. To the purpose, I trust you will make haste to sort out this situation by ending your interest in this scheme and this blackguard, lest I be forced to tell my good friend P.C. William Thick. I am sure he would be most vexed and his intelligence grow apace. It is well you restrain Shanks or your days will be numbered. I tell you plainly sir, your secret is safe with me if you forsake Shanks. I only tell you this because I am no friend of Mr Shanks. You have met him. I am sure you understand why.

Yours Sincerely

Mr Alexander Esq.

Nash did not like what he had done. It was a conniving sort of thing to do. Writing a letter just to get one over on someone was the sort of thing Shanks would do if he could write. Nash doubted the letter would ever be read by anyone other than a manservant in any case, and he would throw it away thinking it to be a hoax, not wishing to burden his master with it.

Nash was sending the letter primarily because writing it had made him feel better, just as he had to admit to himself the near strangulation of Shanks had too. There was also the promise he had made Sookey. After he told her of the violence he used on Shanks, he had never seen her so angry.

"Have you not seen enough!" she shrieked.

In her anger she had tried to insist he should not use violence, but he reminded of her of the time he had saved her from three villains.

Nash duly posted the letter. He considered it simply a piece of non-violent mischief, and if it did manage to find its way to its intended receiver, Shanks would be furious when he found out from his employers that he was no longer required for the Crystal Palace job. And the best of it was that he would guess who was responsible for doing him down, but not have the gumption to do anything about it. Though Nash hoped otherwise. It would give him the excuse to deal with Shanks once and for all. Either way, he had promised himself that the wrong un was to be put out of everyone's misery when the time was right. He had not forgotten Shanks' part in Mary's death. But he had promised Sookey he would not use violence against him, so it would have to wait for the time being.

The following day Shanks was found dead; his throat cut in a court off Little Somerset Street.

Nash felt almost nothing. No shock, pleasure or remorse, just a pang of concern. Could Shanks have told his employers who he was planning to do the job with? Nash doubted it. They would not have wanted to know. The less they knew the better. And Nash had rejected the job. No, he could not see Shanks confirming who his accomplice would be, at the very least until it was certain. But might they have got it out of him before they killed him?

Nash made enquiries about the death. Shanks had left the Hoop and Grapes pub in Aldgate High Street just minutes before he was found lying dead in a dark court. With the number of police around these days, killers on the street had to be quick. There would not have been time for any torturer to glean information. Nash felt he was safe, but as a temporary precaution took to always wearing his glass shard cap and carrying his most lethal weapons whilst out at night. If any paid assassins followed him into a dark alley, any survivors would have earned their money.

But as concern for his safety receded with time, it was replaced by a darker malaise. With the death of Shanks, came the end of Nash's subconscious transference; there was nobody else he could now blame for Mary's death other than the killer and himself.

***

Nash buried himself in the hunt for his prey. Every policeman known to accept bribes paid for information; every witness questioned. He used his robbery proceeds to fund the fixation. News of Nash's interest in the Ripper filtered down to the ears of the authorities, who knew him to be a friend of the last victim, so he was interviewed, but it was a perfunctory affair. The police were so overworked that one man showing even greater interest in the murders than everyone else was not considered particularly worthy of attention.

He was working legitimately for the first time in his life, having got work in a couple of pubs in the area, Monday to Thursday. The amount of rebuilding work going on had brought a lot of tough men into the area looking for work, and when they found it, they had plenty of wages to spend in pubs. Someone had to keep the drunks in check, so Nash had got work in the Princess Alice next to Toynbee Hall, and just along the street from there in the Commercial Tavern. In between them was the Ten Bells. He had turned down work there. Too many memories.

He could have worked Friday and Saturdays too but preferred to leave these days exclusively for his search.

Nash no longer saw much of Will and Khan as they now had legitimate full-time work with plenty of overtime. Khan worked long hours for the Whitechapel and St. Georges Board of Works. He was part of a gang of men working within a huge budget, putting in more and more gas lamps with double the illuminating power of the few previous ones. They were also being trained to start work on the installation of electric light. Will had got a job with George Lusk, of all people. Lusk had never had it so good. Well-to-do slum landlords, who had done very nicely thank you for decades from the rents of the poverty stricken in Whitechapel, had been keen to dispose of their property, tainted now as it was by the murders. Lusk was one of the builders charged with the job of demolishing these properties and then building Stafford House, which was to be new, decent housing for the poor. When he was finished there, he had work on the demolition of part of the Flower & Dean Street rookery. Reverend Barnett's Four Per Cent Industrial Dwellings Company had bought the north side of this site and was going to employ Lusk, amongst many others, to erect the Nathaniel Dwellings, which was an enormous undertaking that would eventually house 800 poor in 170 new flats.

His promise to Sookey that he would cease to use violence, meant Nash no longer committed any crime, though he had one scare, when Francis Horarti, who was working for Taff, was arrested in possession of a hundred and twenty 5d stamps. But young Frankie must have been more afraid of Taff than he was the police. He took his sentence and kept quiet.

Chapter 31

"Everyone should duly note that only a homicidal maniac could induce these poor wretcheds to prefer the 'bastilles of starvation' to the less dubious horrors of selling their bodies."

Justice

Kitty had been in touch to ask for her share of the robbery proceeds. She was now living over in Shoreditch. Just to be on the safe side, Nash would pay her in small value coins. The sort of cash that a wood seller would get hold of. Thus, he arrived at the address she had given him, with pockets laden.

A resplendent looking Kitty answered the door and bid him to enter. The living room of the little slum reminded him of Sookey's place. It was surprisingly homely. There was wallpaper without any bugs in it on the walls; a wooden table cluttered with clean crockery and cutlery; there were a couple of wooden chairs in good condition; coal neatly stacked in a bucket with accompanying irons; a cleaned-out grate; and a caged songbird chirruped away in the corner.

"Looks like you've landed on your feet, Spindle. Place is spotless. Good to see you're doing all right," was Nash's attempt at small talk.

"Well, not having no ponce taking my last, helps. And when I started hawking the wood over here in Shoreditch, where no cove knows me from whoring, I soon spotted as how it were mostly men who were buying off me. So, I started looking after myself, dinning my hair out, new hat and shawl and the like, and business took off. Like bees round honeypot, they are. I play the game. Dozen times a week I gets asked to walk out, but I always says no of course. But I don't dash their hopes. I keeps them dangling all the time there's wood to hawk to them. And they don't knock the price down neither, so I makes good money."

Nash was impressed, not just with how well and pretty Kitty looked but by her business acumen too. But he thought it would not do to let her know this. He was his usual terse self.

"Good. Now, here's your gelt."

He reached into his pockets and pulled out the cash she was due. A couple of old socks full of sixpences and shillings, were dropped onto the only bit of table that didn't have plates, knives and forks covering it.

It was none of Nash's business what she was going to do with the money, but he asked anyway. Kitty did not consider the question intrusive. Quite the opposite. She was keen to tell him of her plans.

"I had a mind to get myself a stall down the market, but I put some feelers out and you know what them costers are like. I got warned off. They made it crystal they didn't want no slip of a girl swiping their trade."

This immediately brought out the protector in Nash.

"We'll see about that! You get yourself a stall and if there's any trouble, I'll…"

"No need Mr Nash. I got a better idea. You've seen all the building going on round here? Well, the LCC are clearing the area above Club Row. The Old Nickel's being knocked down and they're going to build something called the Boundary Estate. So, the Club Row animal market has been pushed into only a few streets. It's terrible crowded and rougher than ever. And all men."

Nash thought he could see where this was going. It was time to offer some advice.

"You be careful. The costers down the Lane might be nasty bits of work but at least they ain't got no dog they can set on you if you fall out with them, like them lot in the Row do. And what do you know about selling animals? It ain't like selling wood. You won't be able to make eyes at fellows while you're selling them some dog that's tearing at the leash and yapping away."

"Ain't going to sell dogs. Ain't going to sell to men neither," said Kitty with a self-satisfied grin on her face. "Going to sell birds. Women like to buy birds, but they've been put off going to the market lately because it's so crowded with roughs who look like they'd swipe your purse or worse as soon as look at you. And somebody called Booth's been stirring it by all accounts. Reckons Shoreditch is full of vicious, semi-criminals as he calls them. Women from outside the East End won't go near the place."

"That Sally Army bastard should keep his sneezer out…"

Nash was about to vent his spleen on his favourite subject, but Kitty had heard it all before and was keen to stop him in his tracks.

"No, he ain't the Sally Army wallah. It's some other Booth this time. This fellow's Charles Booth. He's had people shown round the whole of London by coppers and they've reported what they've seen."

Nash had seen several policemen showing well-to-do looking men about over the past months. He had assumed they were politicians, councillors, newspaper editors and such. He was disappointed to find this was not the case.

"Christ almighty!" he exclaimed, "We've got more Booths than Wilton's Theatre."

Kitty chuckled at what she thought was quite a funny joke but when she saw the accompanying expression on Nash's face, she realised it was no laughing matter. A speedy return to the matter at hand was advisable.

"So anyhow, with this money you've just given me I'll be getting a stall in Bacon Street. It's part of the market but not as crowded or rough as Club Row or Sclater Street. And ladies can buy off another woman, see. Should pay well."

Nash was not so confident about her prospects.

"Birds is hard. You got to know what you're doing with birds. You'd be better off trying to sell guinea pigs, rabbits, fowl, squirrels and the like. I've even seen a goat or two for sale down there. You might be able to make a few bob doing that."

"You're right, birds is hard," agreed Kitty. "That's why it's where the money is. But I got a partner. She knows all about birds. She's from one of them funny countries. They must have lots of birds there. Different ones to what we've got here I shouldn't wonder, but if you know birds you know birds, see."

"Who's this then?" asked Nash.

"Her name's Brinoo. Queer old name. It's Mohammedan, whatever that means. I just calls her Brin.

What with that and her funny way of speaking some people thinks she's Welsh."

The mention of someone being mistaken for Welsh, who clearly wasn't, had Nash think of Mary. Kitty read his thoughts.

"Mary's why I've changed my ways," said Kitty with an air of hard, determined defiance in her voice. She wanted to say that she didn't want to end up like her but didn't think it was right to say so out loud. She left it unsaid but Nash understood.

"It's good you have, Spindle. Them lot in charge won't help you so you help yourself, and you can't do that from the bottom of no glass or with your hand down some fellow's trousers."

Nash saw Kitty was looking down at her feet and realised this was not the time or place for his soapbox, so he changed the subject back to Brinoo and injected some humour into his tone.

"Anyhow, tell me more about this Mohammedan Welsh bird expert of yours."

Kitty, relieved at the change of subject, brightened.

"Well, she's been buying birds for a while, off some fellow called John the Blackguard. He catches the birds in Essex by all accounts. He lives up to his name an' all. Been robbing her blind for ages he has. Charging her well over the odds. She barely made enough to keep herself out the workhouse. I told him I'm in charge now and if he wants to carry on selling to us it'll be for a lot less. And we'll want a lot more birds an' all if the price is right. He soon got the picture."

"Yes, I know the fellow. You need to be spry to get the better of him. But you're a match for him all right," affirmed Nash with a knowing, appreciative nod. "So how d'you get to know this woman then?"

"She wanted some wood off me. She didn't have no money but offered me a bird as a swap. We got to talking. Turned out she lived right over in St George's, but she heard about me hawking wood and walked all the way over here. Plenty of wood hawkers over her way of course, but all men. She didn't want to try and do a swap with any of them. They might want to swap for something she didn't want to give, if you get my meaning."

Nash was intrigued. He looked round the room and noticed that there was two of everything in the house. Kitty read his thoughts again.

"She lives here with me now. She's a bit older than me but not much. She's a bit hard to understand, what with her only being off the boat a few years, but we've taken to each other. She's skulking in the yard. Too shy to meet you. Don't really take to men, see."

Nash gave Kitty a wink and moved to the back door. He opened it and saw a young Indian woman looking back at him. She looked familiar.

Chapter 32

"The actual murders…may seem to be altogether disconnected from the manner of life prevailing in the neighbourhood, but…the ultimate cause of it all may be traced to the miserable state of existence of the overcrowded population."

Fife Herald

Lil Brewer was on the autistic spectrum. She was considered an imbecile but had hitherto managed to avoid being locked away. Plenty with less severe mental health problems than Lil had been carted off to South London's 'Bedlam' or one of the other mental hospitals hidden away in the countryside so society could turn their backs and forget about them. But in Whitechapel, such was the level of atrophy in the human specimens that roamed the streets that it was difficult to ascertain whether someone's appalling condition lay in physical or mental problems. Many broken men and women in workhouses showed classic signs of mental illness only to be written off as the undeserving poor.

Lil got free accommodation in the lowest of common lodging houses in return for cleaning out its disgusting toilets. She slept in her single set of rags in a box room next to her stinking workplace. She fed herself by prostitution, but her autism meant she was barely able to let her body be entered, her neck craning away in disgust. She was also unable to make eye-contact or make conversation with her clients. She made them feel exactly how every man should feel each time they use a woman's body. Thus, Lil was not a whore to whom customers returned a second time.

She was wandering aimlessly along Poplar High Street, when she was approached. Her usual customers were the lowest of debased men, either off a boat or out of a dosshouse. This man, though shabbily dressed, was a grade up from her usual clientele.

"Working tonight?" asked Charles Lechmere.

"Pooka Sullivan had no sense, he bought a fiddle for eighteen pence," came the unexpected reply, followed by Lil wrenching a breast out of her blouse.

Ignoring this strange behaviour, Lechmere engaged in conversation.

"Eighteen pence. One and six. I have that," he said, flashing what could have been a silver coin at her before beckoning her into a dark spot. "Over here."

He moved to guide her arm at the elbow, but she shrank away from him, to walk unguided into the closed-end alley proffered. No sooner had she arrived in the gloom, and his hands were around Lil's throat, thumbs together pushing hard into her larynx. She immediately went limp, her tongue flopped out of her mouth, and she stared the stare of the already dead. It was like strangling a rag doll.

As Lechmere strangled his victims and they started to pass out, he usually became sexually aroused. It was their eyes rolling back, their moment of expiration he enjoyed rather than the sadistic pleasure of inflicting pain per se. He wanted the last sight on this earth his mother substitute saw, was his face enjoying killing them. And then it was time to take a knife from his pocket.

But Lil would not make eye-contact; would not put up a fight for life. There was no life to gain pleasure from extinguishing. Lechmere took both hands off her throat and grabbed her at the sides of her head in a vice-like grip.

"Take your hands off her."

It was a steady controlled voice. Lechmere spun round with the staring eyes of a cornered animal, allowing the rag doll to drop to the floor. He saw a big tough-looking man loom out of the shadows. The man, now standing still just a few feet away in the darkness, both hands in deep overcoat pockets, cut an intimidating figure, yet Lechmere breathed a sigh of relief. No uniform, no truncheon, no whistle. So, no policeman.

Lechmere's problem was that whilst the East End had lots of closed-end alleys and courts which were ideal for his purposes, affording him optimum privacy, it meant he always had to leave by the same route by which he arrived. And now this big man blocked that route.

Lil broke the silence with a series of coughs and rasping intakes of breath as she regained consciousness. The noise moved Lechmere to action. He slowly, carefully felt in a pocket and withdrew a second shined up ha'penny, before tossing two coins onto the ground, next to the alley wall, a few feet to the side of the man. It was hoped the fellow would immediately move to retrieve them, giving Lechmere a chance to flee past him. It was too dark to see the value of the coinage.

"Half sovereigns," claimed Lechmere quietly.

The man could just as easily attack Lechmere first and pick up the coins afterwards. Or perhaps he had no interest in money. It was a move borne out of desperation.

But the killer's luck held. The man moved for the coins and Lechmere pumped his knees. He was past his would-be nemesis in a second and sprinted into the street. Being a poor human specimen in every sense of the word, he was soon gasping for breath. Starting to slow, he craned his neck to find nobody was in pursuit.

A lascar, just off a ship at Limehouse docks, had been out looking to give a prostitute some business. He had seen Lil earlier and remembered her from a previous encounter. He had not wanted to repeat it, but there was not another woman to be seen on the streets at this time of night, so had retraced his steps looking for Lil. Anything was better than strapping a skate to a mast.

When the offer of the half sovereigns had been made, the lascar was drawn to the coins like a moth to a flame. When he picked up the ha'pennies and cursed his bad luck, he looked down at Lil in his exasperation as if he expected some sort of recompense from her. She lay on the cobbles, face up, coughing and gasping for breath. She looked through him as if she was blind. Which temporarily she was, the whites of her eyes now the darkest of red, having filled with blood.

Not for the first time, a man preoccupied with other thoughts had chosen to allow Jack the Ripper to escape.

***

The desire to kill had first come upon Lechmere quite suddenly back in the summer, and now equally as sharply it had receded.

He had not had time to fully complete his attacks until the killing of the woman indoors had meant he had all night to do with her what he pleased. But she had been younger than he would have liked. He preferred his victims to be middle-aged hags. And while he had enjoyed a great sexual high from the destruction of her body, he had soon come back down to earth and felt sorry for himself once again. He was not gaining the long term benefits he desired from these murders.

And the attack on the imbecile woman had been foolhardy. Just because it was in Poplar, well away from Whitechapel, he had thought he could revert to killing on the streets with impunity. But he had not become sexually aroused when he was throttling the woman.

He wanted to stop. He would not kill again.

Chapter 33

"The riots of 1886 brought in £78,000 and a People's Palace; it remains to be seen how much these murders may prove worth to the East End."

George Bernard Shaw

Nash was like a bear with a sore head, first thing in the morning, whilst Sookey could be irritable when she first got home after a long day at Toynbee Hall. And the two of them were from such contrasting walks of life that they did so many things very differently. Nash had a disgusting way of clearing his throat first thing in the morning, which had Sookey covering her ears. He smothered all his food with 'gear oil' as he called it, but Sookey thought the strong brown relish horrible. His housewifery skills were almost non-existent, and he did not see the point of cleanliness in the home. He saw the number of women in the slums whose lives were dominated by the need to stay clean. They seemingly spent every spare minute scrubbing something or another, but these drudges still died young.

As for Sookey, she could not complete the simplest task that involved the use of any reasonable level of common sense.

"Trouble with common sense is it ain't so ruddy common is it girl?" philosophised Nash, as he put his arm round a distraught Sookey after she had made a terrible mess trying to cook a concoction involving a cod's head and 'parings' from the tripe shop. Nash had been relieved to see it go on the floor, if the truth be told. He had seen it going. Could he have reached out and caught it as it toppled? If it had been one of his favourites, he would have dived to catch it, and if he had been too late, he would have thought nothing of picking it up off the floor and tucking in.

Nash's use of the word 'ruddy' had been quite deliberate. He would let the odd 'bleeding', 'bloody' and 'sodding' slip, and blasphemies were commonplace, but Sookey was aware that he would use much more colourful language when she was not around. She felt this was just part of the wider problem of him never feeling able to be completely himself with her. She would protest to him that he should be with her as he was with others, but this was met with a shrug.

"Men needs two lives girl: three or four sometimes. Some are salt of the earth at work, then go home and knock their old lady about. Miserable so-and-sos six days a week, then Sundays keep the nippers happy like a comedian on the boards. Others, like foremen, can be different. Cowsons to their men, then good as gold at home."

The two of them were fortunate enough to be able to retain two homes. They would have found living together impossible, just as so many couples in the slums did, who had the sorrow, loathing and bruises to show for it.

They spent most of Sunday and the early evenings of Monday to Thursday, together. Their relationship had grown closer, mentally, and physically. Sookey now enjoyed sexual fulfilment for the first time in her life. On one occasion as her breasts slowed their heaving and her blood slowed, a post-coital clarity of thought took her back to Mary. She remembered the only time they had discussed sexual ecstasy. Mary had hitherto assumed it would be a taboo subject with her upright middle-class friend, and Sookey had thought the last thing a woman who had to prostitute herself would ever want to do, was talk shop.

"No, there's no such thing," said Mary with the confidence of an expert. "It's an old wives' tale. I've had more men inside me than I've had hot dinners," and with a sad laughing sigh added, "well I haven't had so many hot dinners lately. But I would have had a rapture by now surely to God."

Sookey had smiled as Mary continued.

"I did enjoy a good apple though, while I had some piece of filth poking away at me the other night. God it was tasty. It's the closest I've come to one I can tell you!"

The two women had then swapped tall or perhaps not so tall tales of what they had heard being done by various women to pass the time, while men did what men did. Sookey told of how Rose claimed to knit. Mary burst out laughing.

"You wait till I see her!"

"No Mary! That is told in confidence!"

Sookey's face was a picture. Mary stared mock innocently at her crestfallen friend, before the two of them collapsed into laughter.

Back in the present, Sookey's reminiscing smile faded.

"It is no laughing matter; none of it."

***

Sundays were the one day of the week when Sookey had something of a regular routine these days. She would head for the market to buy fresh produce for lunch and then buy a newspaper. Being such a poor cook, she felt that the freshest possible ingredients were required just to make a meal edible, let alone appetising.

There had been cooking lessons with Rose, but the tutor herself displayed limited culinary skills. On the occasions when there was enough money in her family purse to afford more than the scraps that led to the rent-book sandwich incident, Rose spent it on something from the pie-man for her husband and the odd treat for the rest of her family's sweet tooth.

Sookey would cook a Sunday lunch the best she could in time for Nash's return. She would not see him from Thursday evening to late Sunday morning. Having caught a few hours' sleep back at his place, he would always be quiet when he arrived. Not morose, but subdued and distant, exhausted from lack of sleep, frustrated and disappointed that despite the weekend's efforts his prey had yet again escaped capture. Sookey thought it was time to give up the quest. It was obvious the monster was no longer at his work. Gone to his account in hell, or put away in a mental institution.

At least, the meal would cheer him up. Not the food so much as the leg-pulling about her cooking. But Sookey did not have the savage ripostes of Mary and was sensitive about her shortcomings, so Nash tried to stop short of being cruel with his humour at his lover's expense.

They would spend Sunday afternoons doing as little as possible, recuperating from the rigours of the week. Sookey had once entertained the thought of the two of them going for an afternoon ride on one of the new velocipedes. They were quite the fashion. Everyone was trying them, and her friend Walter had brought back the latest Peugeot model from Dieppe. But Nash was less than enthusiastic about the proposal.

"You ain't getting me on one of them things. Bleeding death traps they are."

Sookey thought it most amusing that a man who usually feared nothing, was afraid of a couple of wheels and a few spokes.

Nash thought a quiet read was a much better idea. Rose had educated Sookey to the fact that it was a man's right to have first read of the newspaper on a Sunday. The usual routine was that Nash would buy a national Sunday paper on his way over to Sookey's, and she would have already bought the local rag for him. Nash preferred to read the local news first so would start reading it as soon as he arrived home and would read out sections for them to chat about together while she put the finishing touches to their meal.

***

Nash had summoned Khan for a meeting at Kitty's place.

On his most recent visit to Kitty, Nash had taken Sookey along, and with a woman by his side had managed to speak with Brinoo for the first time. He had asked which birds she and Kitty would be selling.

"Linnet, goldfinch, bullfinch, greenfinch, sir," she said.

"Yes, they like a songbird here in the East End. You two might do well."

That would normally have seen the end of Nash's attempt at light conversation with a stranger, but the girl's familiar looking appearance intrigued him, so he continued.

"Whereabouts you from Brinoo?"

"Delhi, India, sir."

"Blimey, you're a long way from home girl. What brought you all the way over here? Work I shouldn't wonder?"

The girl answered this and several more questions before Nash nodded, seemingly to himself, as if self-satisfied. Afterwards he had asked Sookey if she may have met Brinoo once before, a while back. Perhaps written a letter for her? And after this discussion, he had made some calculations involving a couple of twos and was now about to ascertain whether this sum totalled four.

There was a knock. Nash had already tipped Kitty the wink. Brinoo was told to answer the door. She opened it and Nash's arithmetic proved correct. The father and daughter collapsed into each other's arms. Nash nodded to Kitty and the two of them made themselves scarce by leaving via the back door and yard.

***

There was a chill winter's wind, so Sookey was huddled up. She had filled her gardening trug, a relic from her previous life which had been pressed into service as a shopping basket, with the ingredients for her next culinary attempt, and now headed for a local newspaper. She walked towards the newsboy head down against the elements and it was only when she scrambled in her pockets for the change to pay for the newspaper that her head came up to focus on the man proffering a paper towards her. She saw that it was Mary's old sweetheart, Joe Barnett.

The last time she had seen him was at the funeral. The enormous tearful crowd that had gathered to pay their respects, and the mass of carts, vans and tramcars, had completely blocked the streets. The strength of feeling for a young woman few of the crowd would have known, but whom they knew lived on her own in poverty, with few friends, and was forced to walk the streets to keep herself out of the workhouse, had taken the authorities completely by surprise.

They had to quickly mobilise large numbers of police to keep order. Bowed heads with hats and caps in hand, lined the six miles to Leytonstone, but the police had ordered the carriage driver to whip the horses, so they almost galloped most of the route, much to the disgust of the throng. The authorities failed Mary to the last, not affording her any dignity or respect, even in death.

Joe was one of the few allowed to attend the grave, while hundreds were locked outside the cemetery gates. She had exchanged a few words with him after the ceremony, before leaving him alone at the grave.

And now his head was down against the cold wind, not looking her in the face, so it was with relief she realised he probably hadn't recognised her. Or if he had, he clearly did not want to engage in conversation. Which was all right by her. Any conversation would have been uncomfortable for them both. Abandoning her usual 'hello,' she made sure the correct money was given, took a newspaper without a thank you and quickly darted away, folding the paper neatly, precisely into quarters to make it more manageable.

She positioned the newspaper carefully in the trug so as not to get it dirty from the vegetables or bloody from the meat. On getting home she extracted it and opened it up with a view to pushing out the wrinkles caused by her tight folding into quarters. Her eyes caught a word which, being so unusual, stood out like a sore thumb.

Later she was preparing the meal when she heard Nash coming through the door, so stopped what she was doing, and faced him. Nash started to nod a greeting but was immediately taken by the strange expression on Sookey's face. He had not seen this stony look before. Without her eyes leaving his, she picked up the local newspaper and handed it to him in such a way that the births and deaths section was staring up at him. Nash looked quizzically at her but did not say anything. He peered down and within seconds she saw his expression change to the same as her own. It was an announcement that, Charles Lechmere, of Doveton Street Stepney, had died of mental illness at Guildford Union workhouse, Warren Road, Guildford, Surrey.

No wonder I couldn't find him. The cowson were miles away, out in the sticks.

***

With his hunt for the Ripper at an end, Nash could no longer deflect his mind away from guilt. Scholarly articles, written by wise men, could always be found, upholding the view that the Whitechapel Murders had led to social reform. Nash sought them out. He tried to gain solace from such prose in his darkest hours. But would any of these men have written such things if they had been partly responsible for one of those deaths? He knew the answer, and he knew that he would have to live with that answer to his grave.

***

The bird business was a success. Brinoo and her father worked all the hours in their respective trades, living on scraps to ensure as much of the money they earned was put towards the cost of their fare home. But once they had bought their tickets, Khan carried on working. He needed a little more money before he left Britain's shores. And he needed advice. He sought out Will Roud. Their paths had not crossed since they worked together on the post office robbery, but Khan knew the man could be trusted, and explained to him what he wanted to do. Will was only too pleased to assist.

Will advised that newspapers charged by the word so death notices were usually kept very short; a name and where the deceased had died. But this notice needed to also include where the dead person was from so Nashey would believe it was his man. And the death needed to be explained and to have occurred somewhere far enough away for him not to be able to investigate further.

Will wrote the death notice and took it to the office of a newspaper Nashey was known to read. And if Nash were to initially miss it, Will would be sure to bring it to his attention.

Khan paid for the insertion. It was the least he could do. A thank you to his friend for finding his daughter. He knew how difficult it was to search for something that could not be found.

Author's Notes:

My first novel, *Whitechapel*, set during the murders of 1888, was written is response to my exasperation at the poorly researched true crime books and jokey Jack the Ripper tours that have proliferated over the past few decades. I wanted my novel to tell it how it really was. But in retrospect I overdid the accuracy. Too much 19th century cockney dialogue using apostrophes to spell out the accent, not only slowed the narrative but was an inelegant way to write dialogue.

So in this novel I have endeavoured to effectively rewrite my original novel, not only making it more readable, but also introducing and fleshing out more female characters, whilst also reducing the killer to the merest of bit players. It really is not about him. The bare bones of the original plot have been retained but most of it has been altered.

The novel is historically accurate. The only change to history is that for dramatic purposes I changed the timing of the post office robbery to being on the same night as the final murder, when in fact it took place on the same weekend as the two murders on one night.

Mary Kelly, Catherine Eddowes and Elizabeth Stride were real women, and this novel attempts to bring them to life and to respect their memory.